OLD WOUNDS

Other works by Dianne Palovcik:

In Trouble – 2019
0-978-1-77354-169-3 Paperback
0-978-1-77354-185-3 eBook

Not All Widows Wear Black – 2021
978-1-77354-374-1 Paperback
978-1-77354-375-8 eBook

OLD WOUNDS

DIANNE PALOVCIK

To: Marg
Enjoy the read & thanks
for the support.
Dianne

OLD WOUNDS

Published by Dianne Palovcik, Edmonton, Canada

Author photo by Carlyle Art

ISBN:

Softcover 978-1-77354-538-7
ebook 978-1-77354-539-4

Disclaimer
This is a work of fiction based on historical facts. Names, characters, businesses, events and incidents are either the products of the author's imagination or used in a ficticious manner. Any resemblance to actual persons, living or dead, or actual events is purely coincidental.

Publication assistance and digital printing in Canada by

PageMaster.ca

ACKNOWLEDGEMENTS

Writing a novel is inherently a solitary undertaking. However, I believe it is not mastered alone. Family, friends and on occasion, a complete stranger becomes part of the writer's journey. And so, I offer my deep appreciation to those who have helped me along the way.

To family. I want to acknowledge the support of my husband, Rudy. Thank you for your ongoing encouragement and patience.

Friends. A heartfelt "Thank you" to my many good friends, near and far who have offered words of support. Thank you for asking about my writing and being patient with my rambling responses.

My readers. Thank you for reading *Old Wounds*. I hope you enjoy the story and the characters you meet in the pages of my work.

To my first readers. Barbara Baker, Carol Rachul, Maria Roach and Kathie Sutherland have made a very valuable contribution toward the final edition of *Old Wounds*. You have wielded your red pens and made notes with great care and thought. Your time and talent is very much appreciated.

CHAPTER ONE

Sunday, October 14, 1917

Murdoch Ramsay is a risk-taker at heart. The thrill of danger has always appealed to him. Even as a child, he was the first of his friends to take a dare, bet on a game of marbles, smoke a cigarette or make a challenge out of any trivial matter. Anything to feel the tingle of risk and bolster his view of himself.

Today, Murdoch is sitting on a bench overlooking the Halifax harbour pondering his future instead of the usual Sunday lunch with his parents, Charles and Ella and younger sister, Rose. Gazing across the water gives him time to be free from his father's biting remarks about his future plans and relief from his own self-doubt.

Doctor Charles Ramsay expects his son to follow in his footsteps and become a successful surgeon. When the national conscription debate was settled in late August, Murdoch felt it unjust that he be exempt from active war service because he wore glasses. He was certain his father had spoken with the recruiter to ensure eyeglasses came under the 'unfit for service' category.

The Halifax harbour, one of the deepest, ice-free harbours in North America was an active place. Murdoch counted six ships at anchor, both naval and merchant. Dock workers moved medical supplies, food, blankets, clothing and horses from nearby rail cars to the supply ships being loaded for the war effort in Europe. Troop ships were loading men for war service and disgorging personnel from the battlegrounds in Europe. Murdoch spotted the uniforms of the Royal Canadian Navy and the British Royal Navy.

Three years on with no end in sight, World War 1 had brought prosperity to the bustling port city of fifty thousand inhabitants. But that wealth was counterbalanced by an increased demand for bootleg liquor, gambling and prostitution. The city's residents also had a front row seat to the human devastation the war created. Multiple thousands of troops passed through the port. Too many never returned.

Directly in Murdoch's line of sight he saw a hospital ship release hundreds of maimed soldiers who managed to make it home. Many of their comrades were left behind, their bodies hanging on barbed wire fences or lying in fields of mud. Some survivors were on stretchers, others helped by medical people, fellow soldiers, dock workers and local volunteers. A lucky few managed the walk to waiting vehicles from the military barracks at Citadel Hill or a hospital. To a man, they all bore the vacant stare of horror, a living nightmare they would endure for the rest of their days.

The harbour wind carried a shout in Murdoch's direction. In the midst of the god-forsaken scene before him, two soldiers embraced. They'd found comfort in each other, a bond created by the hell of war. Beside them, a sailor dropped his crutches, fell to the ground and kissed his homeland. Murdoch's eyes filled with tears for them, for himself.

Without forethought, Murdoch rose from the bench and began a brisk walk toward Point Pleasant Park. As a child, he'd spent many hours there with his mother, Ella. Today, he trusted it would offer a respite from his own unhappiness.

***

The following morning, Ella Ramsay lingered over her second cup of tea, tears in her eyes. If her older sister Adele had lived, she would be forty-seven today.

Ella and Adele Kennedy shared their outward appearance. They were tall, fine-boned, curly-haired brunettes with dark eyes. But the sameness ended there.

Five years older than Ella, Adele was unafraid of life, possessed both a ready wit and strong will until pneumonia took her life at age nineteen. In contrast, Ella was the insecure one, comfortable in Adele's shadow, enjoying the fun her older sister offered. Without Adele, Ella slipped deeper into her shell, becoming a quiet young woman frightened to trust her own judgment and take risks, even small ones.

When the doorbell rang, Ella quickly wiped her eyes and pushed thoughts of Adele from her mind. Reaching the front door she inhaled deeply and opened it, expecting her daily maid. Instead, she came face to face with a young man offering her a yellowed envelope.

She frowned. "May I help you?"

"This letter's for you." The tall, fair haired man inched toward her, his blue eyes locked on Ella's face, his muscular frame stiffened. "Don't you recognize me, Mrs. Ramsay?"

Ella studied the person before her but couldn't recall the face. She accepted the envelope and glanced at the return name and address. Both were intimately familiar. She winced.

"I'm an old neighbour, Mrs. Ramsay. Alexander. My friends call me Alex."

"Old neighbour?" Ella struggled to maintain her composure. "You must be mistaken. I've always lived in Halifax."

"That's true but you visited your grandfather across the street from me when I was eight, thirteen years ago. May I come in?"

Truro. Ella grasped the door to steady herself. *Rose's blue eyes.* "You better come in for a moment."

Alex stepped inside and looked around. The rich colours and textures in the sitting room on his right caught his eye as did the elegant dining room on the left. The long hallway was decorated with family portraits and pastoral paintings. A large vase of dried flowers sat on a hall table. Alex crossed his arms and pinched his lips together in apparent disapproval.

So shaken, Ella whispered, "You have something to tell me?"

Alex leaned toward Ella. His posture signalled a promise of impending trouble. "Yes, I do. My father died two months ago and this envelope was found in his safe, attached to his will. By the way, you were not mentioned in the will but this letter is supposed to be yours."

Ella muttered her thanks and commented about travelling all this way simply to deliver an old letter.

"It was no trouble at all. My intention is to make things right. Finding you is what I needed to do."

Alex's unsettling fervour convinced Ella to change the topic. "And your mother? Your father mentioned she was ill the last time I saw him."

"She left us."

Ella did not miss the accusatory tone in Alex's voice. "I'm very sorry to hear that." She presumed Dora Wallace had died and she had no desire to continue the conversation. She moved her hand toward the door knob. "Thank you again for making the journey from Truro."

Alex smiled. "Actually, I moved to Halifax earlier this month so my visit was no trouble at all. Perhaps we'll meet again, very soon. Good-day, Mrs. Ramsay."

Ella leaned against the closed door, her breath coming in short spurts. Alex bore a truly remarkable resemblance to her twelve-year-old daughter Rose. Clasping the letter against her chest, she returned to the kitchen, thankful her husband and children were gone for the day. Charles at the city hospital, Murdoch at work and Rose in school. She thought back to her time spent in Truro.

In the spring of 1904 Alexander and his father, Henry Wallace, lived across the street from Ella's grandfather, Philip Watson, in Truro, a train ride from Halifax. Philip Watson was a widower in poor health during that year. Ella and her mother, Georgie, took turns staying two weeks at a time with him during the last months of his life. Their visits allowed his nurse to take two days off each week.

Philip Watson and Henry Wallace developed a close friendship over the years in Truro. Grandpa Watson explained that Henry's wife, Dora preferred not to have visitors and certainly didn't visit her neighbours much at all and only with Henry. She cared about her young son Alexander, was a good cook and pleasant but often awkward in public.

Ella looked at the envelope. No matter its' content, she blamed herself for what happened with Henry. If Alex contacted her again, how would she face what she had done? Her old insecurities rose like bile in her throat. She opened the wax-sealed envelope.

January 12, 1909
My Dear Ella,
This letter will become part of my last will and testament. It has been five years since your grandfather passed away and I last saw you. Again, I apologize for my behaviour during our last evening together. I hope you have found a way to forgive my betrayal of your trust. I know you admitted to being a willing partner but that does not excuse me. You were in a vulnerable position because of your grandfather's illness and a matter relating to Charles. Dora's depression continues. She remains under the care of a doctor in a Halifax

asylum, a place and word I deplore. The Executor will instruct Alexander to deliver it to you after my death. With deepest fondness, Henry

Seeing Dora's name sent Ella back in time to the last time she saw Henry's wife. Henry and Dora came to visit her Grandpa Watson, bringing with them two of his favourites, clam chowder and apple pie.

Dora was waif-like, a thin woman with hazel eyes and narrow nose. Her curly, greying hair was tamed into a severe bun at the nape of her neck, revealing a long scar behind her left ear. She sat on the edge of her chair, fidgeted with her hands and the buttons on her cardigan, poised to spring off her chair without a moment's notice. She was significantly more agitated than Ella noticed during previous visits.

As usual, Henry carried the conversation with the occasional reassuring smile in Dora's direction. She smiled toward him in return until she suddenly jumped up from her chair. Henry quietly suggested she and Ella have a walk in the orchard while he finished his conversation with Philip.

Dora said very little in the orchard, except to express her love for her son Alexander and how worried she was for his future. In mid sentence she abruptly stopped walking and stared at Ella. "Alexander is a very delicate boy." quickly followed by, "You know I will die soon, don't you?"

"Good heavens, Dora that can't possibly be true. You're a healthy young woman."

"I don't feel right, never have. I worry about everything, all the time. I don't see any way to make things better. Dear Henry, bless him. He tries so hard to make everything right but it won't happen." She looked toward the sky and whispered, "Best it's finished."

Before Ella could respond, Dora rushed through the open orchard gate and across the road to her home.

It was shortly after that visit when Dora was placed in a secure facility for the mentally ill. Henry was left a broken man and Alex was sent to live with his aunt. Without close family, Henry relied on Ella's visits to her grandfather for conversation and kindness. With one impulsive act in May 1904, their visits and friendship ended forever.

Alex had implied that his mother was gone. Presuming Dora had passed away, Ella put Dora out of her mind. Alex however, was very much on her mind. She placed the envelope in her sweater pocket, intending to put it in the cedar chest later, then went into the backyard. Thankful for the high fence that prevented neighbours and passers-by from seeing her, she cried until she could cry no more then glanced at her watch. Her half-day maid was late. Jenny must not see her looking like this. She raced up the stairs, dropped her sweater on top of the locked cedar chest in the bedroom, washed her face then powdered her red nose and puffy eyes. She needed to hurry. The key to the chest was hidden downstairs.

As Ella left the bathroom, Jenny came out of the bedroom holding the envelope.

"Hung up your sweater. Who's Henry Wallace?"

"An old friend." Ella took the letter from Jenny's hand, hoping Henry's name would never be mentioned again. "I didn't hear you come in."

"Knocked twice. We got rain comin'. Sorry I'm late. Sister needed help. New baby."

"I understand, Jenny. Family comes first."

Initially, Ella found Jenny's clipped sentences disconcerting then found herself using the same habit in response. At home it didn't matter but socially speaking, such poor diction would be a faux pas. She must take care. Charles was very particular about how his wife presented herself in Halifax society.

Ella wondered if Jenny's other habit could help her solve her problem with Alex. Jenny was a pleasant young woman but she carried stories from the homes of her employers then gossiped with her friends. Ella's neighbour, Mable Cameron warned her to be careful as she had firsthand experience with Jenny's gossip. Mable described Jenny as the neighbourhood newspaper.

"Finished rooms upstairs, Mrs. Ramsay. Dusting here?" Jenny pointed to the sitting room.

"Come sit with me and have a cup of tea. I haven't asked about your mother recently. How is she?"

"Bad cold now. Thanks for the blankets." Jenny paused. "No Murdoch lately. Move away?" She picked up her cup and stared over the rim at Ella. Several strands of her unruly hair had sprung loose from her maid's cap but Jenny didn't seem to notice.

Ella disliked lying about Murdoch or anything else for that matter but lately she had taken to rumpling Murdoch's bed linen in case Jenny suspected he didn't come home at all.

"No, he's living at home. He's keeping busy at his office position at the shoe factory."

"Ta for tea. I'll dust."

Ella continued to sit at the table with her hands wrapped around the tea cup. Murdoch's recent ways were troublesome. She was frightened for him. Ordinarily easy-going, he'd become secretive, coming home in the wee hours of the morning and making vague excuses for his overnight whereabouts. She'd detected the smell of alcohol on his breath a few times. He was headed for trouble, if not already in it.

The Halifax city police did not hesitate to place drunkards in Rockhead Prison overnight. Ella needed to keep Charles in the dark as long as possible. He would not abide Murdoch blemishing the family name if he spent a night in jail. She drummed her fingers on the side of the tea cup, glanced out the window then leaned back into her chair. She couldn't protect Murdoch herself. She needed discreet help. It was then she remembered working beside Edward Quinn at a church supper and auction for the less fortunate in the community. He was a guard at Rockhead and spoke kindly of those in trouble. Could he help? She needed a better understanding of the man so she needed to get Jenny talking about the Quinn family.

Minutes later, Jenny was at the kitchen door. "Going now, Mrs. Ramsay."

"Can you spare me a few minutes?"

"Yes, Mrs. Ramsay."

"Rose seems happy with school. She often speaks of her friend, Nellie Quinn."

"Nellie draws faces. Drew Angus Martin in his store." She nodded. "Spittin' image of 'im it was. Draws people from memory. Has a brother and sister..."

Ella nudged her in a new direction. "And Nellie's father, Edward?"

"He's called Ed. At Rockhead. Likes puzzles."

"Puzzles?"

Jenny shook her head. "Not games. People puzzles. Tryin' to help 'em, Pa says." She paused to take a breath. "Want more?" Jenny loved finding out things about people. She waited, a hopeful look on her face.

"No, that won't be necessary, Jenny. Thank you."

"McNeil house now. Four boys. Always a shambles." She rushed down the hall, put on her coat and shouted 'Bye' from the front door.

Ella remained seated, unsure how Ed Quinn could help Murdoch. She'd let the idea percolate in her brain while shopping. Then there was Alexander Wallace. Perhaps she had overreacted to his manner. She'd wait to see if he interfered in her life again.

She put on a warm coat, boots and hat for the short walk to the street car to visit the downtown shops. The milliner would be first on her list. The new winter hats for Rose and herself should be ready. Then it would be on to the tobacco shop for Charles' special blend pipe tobacco. His birthday was coming up and since he seemed to have everything he wanted, she'd buy the usual appreciated gift.

"Good afternoon, Mrs. Ramsay. Your hats are ready. And thank you again for bringing the extra lining fabric from the wool coats. The matching hat bands will complete the ensemble beautifully. May I suggest the leather gloves with darling little buttons? I also have a most lovely beaded reticule, a perfect compliment to your hat. Try it on your wrist. I'm sure you'll adore it."

"No thank you, Ina. Nothing for me today but gloves for Rose, please."

"Absolutely. She's getting quite grown up, isn't she. Twelve now?"

"Yes, hard to believe."

"Last Sunday after church I remarked to my husband how bright Rose's blue eyes were and how fair her hair is. You, Charles and Murdoch have much darker hair and brown eyes. She must have inherited her looks from a grandparent, probably your husband's side as I know your parents very well."

Ella knew there was a question in the statement but she did not acknowledge it. Instead, she smiled without comment.

Ina carried on. "There's such a difference in your children's ages, too." She paused. "I had my two children close together. It's such a blessing when that happens. And how is Murdoch? I hear he's working at the shoe factory."

"Lots to learn in a business office. It will take time." She passed the cash to Ina, put on her gloves and stepped toward the door.

"Mrs. Ramsay, I feel I must tell you this before you leave. I saw Murdoch a few nights ago near the harbour with some unsavoury looking young men. I mean dock workers, of course. Or maybe they were men from the supply ships. Too bad, if you ask me. But I suppose he has to associate with that sort for the sake of the business. Everyone wears shoes." The tilt of her head suggested she expected a response.

Ella nodded. "Have a lovely afternoon, Ina." *You and Jenny could start your own newspaper.*

Ina's comments confirmed Ella's concerns. Murdoch didn't deserve anything less than her best effort. She must take a risk and arrange to meet Ed Quinn. Uncertainty niggled on the edge of her thoughts, ready to pounce on her good intentions. She took a deep breath and committed herself to action.

Later, inside the tobacco shop, she breathed in the sweet, spicy scent. Hugh Andrews came to mind. Her old regret.

The following morning Rose skipped into the kitchen, her braids bouncing against her back. "Aren't my new bows pretty, Mama? Miss Jenny says they match my dress perfectly."

"They certainly are pretty. Are you ready for breakfast?"

"Yes, Mama. Can I go to Nellie's after school today? We're planning something secret. It's so secret, I can't even tell you!"

Ella cradled her daughter in her arms. "It certainly must be a big secret and yes, my darling, you can play with Nellie after school. Remind Mrs. Quinn you need to leave by five o'clock."

Rose's face turned very serious. "Oh, it isn't playing. We are making something very important but I can't tell you any more about it."

Ella turned toward the stove and filled Rose's cereal bowl with porridge.

"Where's Papa? He's usually here to kiss me good-bye before school."

"He had to go to the hospital early today. Don't worry, he'll be home for dinner this evening." Ella returned to the table with Rose's milk and porridge and her own second cup of tea.

"Will Murdoch be home tonight? I'd like him to read a story at bedtime. He's always so funny. He makes me laugh."

Ella wished she knew the answer to that question herself. Telling the truth was important even though she struggled with it herself from time to time. The truth about Murdoch would be unkind for a twelve-year-old who adored her big brother.

"I don't know, darling. He's all grown up, has friends and things to do with them."

"The last time he was here, I heard Papa yell at him and Murdoch yelled back. It made me sad. Are they angry with each other?"

"Sometimes grown-ups get angry with each other but that doesn't mean they don't care for each other or they'll never speak to each other again." She smiled a Rose. "Don't worry, darling. Finish your milk. It's almost time for you to leave."

After Rose kissed her mother good-bye and went out the front door, Ella returned to the kitchen table. She rested her chin in her palm, exhaled deeply and thought about her nineteen year-old self.

In 1895, Doctor Charles Ramsay was a prominent surgeon in Halifax and known socially by Ella's parents. As they were distressed by the thought of her marrying Hugh Andrews, they introduced Charles to Ella following a church service.

Ella was charmed by the good-looking, likeable doctor. Charles viewed Ella Kennedy as the perfect wife. She was attractive and socially connected, the ideal partner for his personal aspirations. He proposed marriage within weeks of meeting her. For her part, Ella anticipated married life with Charles would be filled with new experiences and an enviable social life. Relying on him would be a good choice for a husband.

The first year of marriage was new and exciting. When Murdoch was born in 1896, the Ramsay home was filled with joy. Family, Charles' fellow physicians along with their wives and immediate neighbours attended a grand celebration.

After the marriage, Charles settled into a hospital routine which quickly demanded most of his waking hours, leaving Ella to create her own way of life. Not unlike other wives of husbands unable or unwilling to detach from work, she found herself doing good works and the occasional luncheon with women from church.

In the late summer of 1904, Ella realized she was pregnant. Both she and Charles were surprised but happy. Rose Ellen Ramsay was born in February 1905, a little sister for nine year-old Murdoch.

Charles' air of entitlement came naturally. That and his tall, lanky frame suited his style, allowed him to tower over people, command their attention. As a surgeon, he was impatient with others, expecting them to defer to his superior intelligence and skills. His own father, now retired, was also a surgeon. He'd failed miserably on the political stage in Halifax and Charles intended to prove he was the better man. Charles had a secret or so he thought. A past indiscretion with a nurse was known by a few people, including Ella.

While Ella cared for her husband and loved her children beyond measure, she was unkind to herself. She harshly criticized herself for being weak under pressure. Murdoch's troubles and Alex's visit now forced her to confront her old insecurities.

CHAPTER TWO

FRIDAY, OCTOBER 19

By Friday afternoon, Murdoch had been late for work two mornings in a row and now back late from lunch. He tip-toed through the front door hoping his boss, Corbin Davis was in his office behind a closed door.

Marie LeBlanc, the company secretary lifted her head, smiled and waved at the late arrival. Once again her curly, unmanageable brown hair sprung loose from her already messy bun. She glanced at Murdoch and smiled.

Murdoch nodded toward the owner's office door. "Mr. Davis in there?"

"Uh-huh." Marie nodded toward Murdoch then returned to her work.

"That's good."

Marie leaned out of her chair, her head toward Murdoch. "Why are you whispering?"

"He might hear me."

Marie rolled her dark blue eyes then straightened up in her chair. "Don't be so daft. The door's closed and he's meeting with a red-haired man named Bill. He was friendly, needs a haircut and a new suit though. You know him?"

Murdoch shook his head. "No. Probably a new buyer." He paused. "I'm impressed. You sized him up pretty quick. Remind me to ask for your help if I need a private watchman."

"You'd have to speak with my father about that."

"Your father?"

"He's a watchman for the city. Sort of a policeman, you might say. And why would you need a watchman?"

Murdoch shrugged. "I have no idea but who knows. The city is full of all sorts of new people now." He was quick to add, "And what other things don't I know about you, Miss LeBlanc?"

"That's for me to know and you to find out, Murdoch Ramsay." Marie dropped her head and began typing.

Murdoch walked toward his office area, a desk and chair behind a large metal room divider. The soothing scent of Marie's lavender lingered in the front office, reminding him of his mother and his guilt for deceiving her about his troubles.

Marie liked Murdoch but was certain he didn't take much notice of her. She let him settle at his desk then rose from her chair and went to see him. "I've sorted the noon mail. Here are the sales orders, arranged by required delivery date."

"What would I do without you, Miss LeBlanc?"

"Survive, but barely!"

Corbin Davis was surprised to see Bill Turner, an old friend from the farming community near Truro. He rose from his chair and shook Bill's hand, vigorously. "Good to see you, Bill. In town on police business?"

"Yup. Nasty business. I'm looking for a fella that needs to explain himself to the law." He looked around the office. "Thought it was time we caught up with each other. What's it been? Two years?"

"About that." Corbin pointed to the chair in front of his desk. "Have a seat."

"Looks like you're doing well for a farm boy."

Corbin laughed. "I'll not complain."

"And the social life?"

Corbin ran his hand through his thick salt and pepper hair. "Not as good as the shoe business, I'm afraid."

"You better change that or you'll be an old bachelor with pots of money and nothing else."

"You've got a good point there." He sat back in his chair. "So tell me about you and Ruby."

"We're happy but no children. Got a cat though." He smiled. "He runs the household."

"Can you stay a while?"

"Sure can."

"Then you can tell me what's new in Truro. I'll get the tea. Still take milk, no sugar?"

Bill nodded. "Well, your memory seems to be holding up, even if your hair isn't."

Bill left an hour later.

After Corbin bid farewell to Bill he went to Murdoch's desk. "My office please and bring the new orders." He waited for Murdoch to walk though the doorway. "Have a seat." Corbin then closed the door and sat on the corner of his desk. "Murdoch, I'm going to come right to the point. You have me puzzled."

"How's that, sir? Is there a problem?"

"There very well could be, if you continue being late in the mornings. Also, you missed a potential buyer earlier in the week by being late back from lunch. Can you explain why you have this problem with time?"

"I'm sort of a sleepyhead, sir." Murdoch smiled disarmingly.

Corbin tilted his head. "If you're going to get anywhere in this world then you better get yourself a good alarm clock, young man. Now let's talk about the new orders. Pull your chair up to the desk."

When Murdoch left, Corbin wandered to the window, hands in his pockets. He liked Murdoch but after two months he was not convinced Murdoch was going to be successful in his job. He had a natural charm to connect with buyers and possessed the ability to understand selling a product but the drive to sell was missing. He walked toward the window. His view from the third floor was a busy one. He watched people scurrying back and forth seemingly unaware of the world around them. The fall leaves were changing colour. 'A sight to behold', his mother used to say.

Corbin was raised on a farm and learned early on that hard work and lots of it was the only way he'd get ahead in the business world. After years of working on the dock in Halifax and saving money, he opened a shoe factory. He was successful but alone. Maybe young Murdoch had the right idea. Enjoy yourself. A saying crossed his mind. 'We're dead a long time'.

When Detective Will Henderson returned to the police station from his afternoon meeting, the desk constable handed him a note.

Hello, Will
Wanted to let you know, I'm in your town tracking a suspect in a Truro murder case. The suspect is a smart, cagey bugger with a nasty streak who likes to beat up prostitutes. I'll check-in with you Monday morning or sooner if I get him. Bill

***

Shortly after four o'clock Corbin Davis stepped into Murdoch's office. "Don't forget that alarm clock young man."

After removing his hat from the coat stand, he turned toward Marie. "I won't be back, Marie. Lock up at five, please."

"Yes, Mr. Davis."

Murdoch waited until the front door clicked shut then went to Marie's desk. "That a usual routine?"

"Not at all. I leave at five and he's usually still here or I meet him on the sidewalk coming back."

"Something's bothering him."

Marie shrugged. "He works hard, just needed to leave a bit early today."

"Maybe." Then Murdoch returned to his desk.

A few minutes after five, Marie stepped into Murdoch's office. "I'm leaving."

"Guess I should go too."

Outside, Marie wished Murdoch a pleasant evening.

Murdoch replied, "You too." And turned to walk home. Moments later he muttered, "You fool. You missed your chance."

Thanks to Corbin's warning about lateness and his mindless response to Marie, Murdoch had a battered ego and no evening plans. The smart money would have been to go home but Murdoch decided to go for a drink.

***

Close to ten-thirty that evening, Murdoch's clumsy run from the police constable was over. He stumbled over the sidewalk and abruptly landed on the street, too tipsy to get back on his feet. The steady pounding of the constable's footfall drew closer. When it stopped, the odour of turpentine wafted toward Murdoch's nose. Strangely, he found the smell comforting. His grandfather used to waterproof his boots with turpentine before they went fishing. He wanted those days back.

"Ya think a drunk could outrun the police?" Constable Ivan Buckle snorted then chuckled. "Stand up, Murdoch. I'm arresting you for being intoxicated in a public place. Overnight in Rockhead, again. Your pa won't like this."

"Gimme time, I'm dizzy."

"Come on, Murdoch. Get movin'. Your money can't help 'ya here. Here comes the paddy wagon. Get up." Buckle pushed his boot into Murdoch's back.

Taking a ride in the paddy wagon to Rockhead and the potential for embarrassing his family were high stakes. Yet, Murdoch couldn't help himself. Drinking made him feel powerful, if only for a few hours.

The ride to Rockhead was uneventful. Murdoch was thankful he didn't throw up on himself. Standing outside the prison door, he knew full well the stench on the inside. He took a deep breath and stepped forward.

"Evening, Constable Bucklehead." Prison Guard Alfie Johnson smirked then pulled Murdoch closer to the desk and booked him in for the overnight stay.

Constable Ivan Buckle clenched his fists but remained quiet while Johnson turned to escort Murdoch toward the cells.

Ivan Buckle had been 'Bucklehead' since first grade when Frank Murphy bestowed the nasty name on him. Over the years he built up considerable anger toward all sorts of people who called him Bucklehead but Frank remained the primary target of his revenge. When the opportunity presented itself, he intended to take care of Frank Murphy for good. He smiled then left the prison to hitch a ride in the paddy wagon back downtown.

Prison guard Johnson gagged as stale body odour wafted from Murdoch's overnight accommodation.

This was Murdoch's third arrest for public drunkenness since mid August. He knew from previous incarcerations, the mattress was to blame for the nasty air. He hesitated outside the cell door.

Johnson placed his hand on Murdoch's back and pushed. "Way 'ya go." *Rich toff.*

Murdoch pitched forward into the windowless room containing a bucket and stained mattress. The door clanged shut, adding to his already buzzing headache.

Johnson twisted the key in the lock and turned to leave. "Sleep it off, Murdoch." He didn't get far before he heard Murdoch gag then heave.

The rising swell of discomfort in Murdoch's stomach quickly turned to nausea. He spewed a pulpy mash of fish chunks, potato, beer and rum in the general direction of the bucket. Most missed the target and it flowed in a wave across the uneven floor toward the door.

Johnson covered his nose. "Ah, damn it, Murdoch. Sit down before you fall down. I'll get the shovel."

Murdoch curled into a ball but the stinking mattress and his buzzing head denied him sleep. He decided to pace and sit on the floor to kill time until morning.

Shortly after midnight, Ed Quinn began the first of his several overnight rounds in the men's wing of the building. Seeing Murdoch in a cell again, he decided to stop. He covered his nose with his handkerchief and stepped forward. Johnson had emptied the bucket but failed to rinse it thoroughly. *I swear he does it on purpose. Vengeful little bugger.*

Ed winked at Murdoch. "I'm Ed. I'll take your bucket and bring back a clean one, just in case."

"Suit yourself." Murdoch kept his head down. His stomach was empty but he was dizzy, his head pounding something fierce. He hoped this Ed fella got sidetracked and wouldn't return. No such luck.

Ed unlocked the door and stepped inside the cell with a clean bucket. "Didn't I see you in here a few weeks ago? Mr. Ramsay, isn't it? Murdoch Ramsay. What's goin' on young fella?"

"Life."

Ed stepped into the hall and locked the cell. "That you or the drink still talkin'?"

"Both."

"Pretty quiet here tonight. I'm havin' a mug of tea with milk. Care for one?"

"If you're buying."

"Deal. Sugar?"

"Please."

A few minutes later Ed passed the mug through the bars, sat on a stool he'd pulled from the office and began in a quiet voice. "So Murdoch, you're a well-dressed young fella with a bright future. What brought you here tonight?"

"I like to drink but I don't have a problem with it." The testy reply included an angry glare.

Ed moved on. "If you say so. If you want to talk, give me a shout."

"Nah, think I'll have a sleep."

Early the following morning, Murdoch shook the cell door. "Hey, anybody there? I need out."

Ed's shift was over but he answered Murdoch's call. "Hold on a minute."

Murdoch was pacing when Ed arrived at the cell. "My time's up."

"Close enough. Want a bun and tea? I'm leaving in a few minutes. We could walk into town together."

"No, thanks. I need to leave right away." He walked through the door, not wanting to stay and get a lecture from a prison guard. An hour later he cautiously opened the front door of the family home, hoping his father had already gone to the hospital.

Rose danced down the stairs, her blonds braids swinging back and forth. “Good Morning, Murdoch, want to dance with me?”

Murdoch bowed, picked her up and twirled down the hall to the kitchen. His head felt worse but his love for Rose outweighed everything else.

“Good morning, Mother. What’s for breakfast?” His cheerful tone was at odds with his pounding head.

“You look dreadful and you smell fishy. Where have you been overnight?”

“Stayed with a friend. I’ll clean-up before eating.”

“Good morning, Papa.”

Charles nodded. “Murdoch.”

Murdoch wasted no time heading for the stairwell leading to the upstairs bedrooms and bath.

Charles Ramsay normally spent a great deal of his time at the hospital so it was with keen interest Ella studied his face over the breakfast table on Saturday morning. He was clearly lingering over his own meal and pretending a show of interest in both his children. He nodded and smiled as Rose related her school activities and games with her friends. Murdoch kept his head down, hoping his father would ignore him. That worked until Rose stopped talking and dipped her spoon into her bowl of porridge. Charles turned his head towards Murdoch.

Murdoch stood up and took his dishes to the sink then rushed from the room. “I’m going to the harbour.”

Later, when Rose skipped out of the kitchen and Charles made no effort to leave, Ella knew there was a difficult matter to discuss. *It’s Alexander Wallace. He’s already spoken to Charles.*

Charles put his cup down and stared at Ella. “A terrible accusation was made towards me last evening. I’ve been threatened with violence by the father of a young child who died. He vowed to get even with me because I killed his little girl.”

While Ella was relieved for her own sake, she was frightened by the violence Charles was facing. “This is dreadful news. What happened? Are you in immediate danger? What are the police doing?”

“The child’s appendix had already ruptured. Bacteria was coursing through her body. There was nothing I could do in time.” Charles shook his head. “People must accept my judgment. I’m a doctor for God’s sake.”

Ella reached for his hand. “Surely you can’t be blamed.”

“You can’t stop people from thinking they know best. This man’s hate is alarming.”

“You’re frightening me.”

“I’m going to the police station this morning to speak with Detective Henderson. Then I’ll check on my patients.” As an afterthought, “I hope Henderson is as sharp as Detective Gilfoy.”

“And who is Detective Gilfoy?”

“He was a detective in ninety-five. My father knew him, spoke highly of him. Gilfoy retired a few years ago. Will Henderson was a senior sergeant at the time.”

Ed Quinn’s children anxiously waited his arrival for breakfast. Nellie and her younger siblings, Lewis and Jane were staring out the kitchen window. When Ed opened the door, he immediately had an armful of children.

“Papa, Mama’s going to make pancakes. It’s like Christmas.” Lewis then danced around the kitchen, a huge grin on his face.

“Good morning, everyone. What’s the special occasion, Clara? Did I forget something?” He was pretty sure it wasn’t their wedding anniversary, or was it?

“No occasion.” She greeted Ed with a hug. “I had a visit with Mary MacKinnon yesterday. She’s finding it hard since Morris’ death at Vimy. With no children, her days are long. Earlier in the week, she was tidying up her pantry and found a bag of pancake flour. She decided we needed it more than she did so here we are, having a treat. We’ll have my homemade strawberry jam and save the precious maple syrup for Christmas.”

Clara then turned toward Nellie. “Take this plate of pancakes and jam across the street to Mrs. MacKinnon, please. Breakfast is almost ready so don’t stay to chat more than a few minutes. Put on your coat, dear. It’s going to rain.”

“Yes, Mama.”

Ed poured himself a mug of tea. “I’ll go over tomorrow afternoon. She’ll likely need some things done around the house before the cold weather sets in.”

With breakfast over, Ed went for a nap. It refreshed him and allowed time for chores and errands before a good sleep late in the day. Murdoch came to mind the minute his head hit the pillow. *That young fella’s heading for trouble.*

The police station was quiet when Charles stepped up to the desk. “Is Detective Henderson here?”

“He’s in his office. Your name, sir?”

“Doctor Charles Ramsay.”

“Have a seat, sir.”

Henderson followed the constable out of his office. “Come in, Doctor Ramsay. How can I help you?”

“I don’t know if you can but I’m here to find out something.”

Henderson nodded. “Go ahead.”

When Charles finished his story, Henderson took a deep breath, leaned back in his chair and stared at the ceiling.

Charles waited patiently, not his usual response to being detained. He'd heard about Henderson's quiet confidence and commitment to his work. He'd also heard Henderson sometimes looks like he slept in his clothes and perhaps he did. Today was not one of those days.

"Oliver White, you say."

Charles nodded.

"I don't know that name, which is a good thing. Here's what I'm prepared to do. I'll have a look at the files myself. I don't want the man's name bandied about for nothing. Where can I reach you?"

"I'm going to the hospital now. I should be home by five. If you have a piece of paper, I'll jot down the telephone numbers. Thank you, Detective."

***

As Charles entered the hospital, Oliver White lunged for his throat, knocking him to the floor. "So, you're back to kill somebody else, you bloody bastard. You killed my Mattie."

Charles protected his head and tried to roll away as White pounded his body, yelling 'murderer' and 'my little Mattie'.

The assault was over quickly as the hospital attendant yelled, "Oliver, stop" and with a visitor's help, White was subdued. His rage ended quickly.

Charles looked up and nodded in the direction of the attendant and visitor. "Thank you."

Charles pulled his body up from the floor and found his broken glasses under a chair near the reception desk. He looked at the attendant and nodded toward Oliver White. "You know him?"

"He's one of our janitors, Dr. Ramsay."

For everyone's safety, the attendant tied White into a chair with strips of cloth bandages to await the arrival of the paddy wagon.

"Nurse Petersen, I am going home after I check on the two surgery patients from late yesterday. Ask Doctor LaPointe to cover for me the rest of the day."

***

Seeing Murdoch's wretched appearance at breakfast forced Ella to act. She needed to speak with Ed Quinn. Today. Showing up at his home was simply not done but Murdoch was in trouble, deep trouble.

Shortly after lunch when Murdoch left the house and Rose went to a birthday party, Ella rushed upstairs and changed into a more suitable day dress. She telephoned for a taxi before she could change her mind. When it arrived she settled into the back seat with absolutely no plan other than she intended to save Murdoch from himself.

Ed Quinn opened his front door, expecting to see a neighbour. "Mrs. Ramsay, come in."

"Thank you and it's Ella."

"Is there something I can help you with?"

"I hope so. Do you know my son, Murdoch?"

Ed hesitated long enough for Ella to confirm her suspicions. "So you have seen him inside Rockhead?"

"Mrs. Ramsay. Ella, it's not my place to talk about my work at the prison, including people who I may see there." He paused. "But, come to the sitting room. We can speak privately." He closed the door behind him and ran his hand through his greying sandy hair.

"Thanks, Ed. My reason for being here is to ask your support in finding help for Murdoch. He's drinking, out overnight and coming home in terrible shape. How can I make him see how all of this will end badly. I'm at my wits' end. Where can I turn for help? And you should know, I'm desperately trying to keep this from Charles."

"To be honest, I have spoken with Murdoch but he wasn't willing to talk at that time. I'm happy to try again but this shouldn't be at the prison. Someplace neutral when he's sober would be ideal."

"He often goes to the harbour after dinner to watch the troop ships coming and going." Ella hesitated. "He tried to enlist in the fall of '14 at eighteen but he was deemed medically unfit. The recruiting officer told him he couldn't serve because he wore glasses." She paused again. "I think he believes his father spoke with the recruitment office before he ever arrived to ensure Murdoch would be rejected. But that is irrelevant now. He has a good work position but I'm afraid he'll lose that." Her eyes filled. "Sorry, I'm rambling."

"I understand. I'll accidentally meet him as soon as I can. It might take several days."

Ed knew from experience that a conversation with a prisoner could go badly. He wasn't certain Murdoch would appreciate being approached even if it was outside the prison walls.

"Charles, you're home!"

Charles stared at her angrily. "I was assaulted by that mad man at the hospital. He's a janitor, for heaven's sake. I'm a doctor.

We should be held in high regard. And where were you?" His eyes were dark.

Ella had to think quickly. "I decided to take a long walk around the neighbourhood." She scolded herself for lying with such ease, but it was for a good cause.

CHAPTER THREE

SUNDAY, OCTOBER 21

Charles Ramsay was a stickler for punctuality. Attendance at church was no exception. He could not understand why Ella, Murdoch and Rose always took so long to get ready for any event. In frustration, he paced around his 1914 McKay Touring car.

The McKay was Charles' prized possession. Built in Kentville, Nova Scotia, the car was a status symbol of his success. But Charles craved more recognition. The idea of standing for public office had been running through his mind for some time but he'd kept the desire to himself. Since politics was often a topic of discussion among his well-connected friends, today seemed the perfect day to speak of his political aspirations with the church crowd, after the service of course.

When Ella, Murdoch and Rose gathered around the car, Charles was all smiles. Dressed for church, his family looked perfect for a successful politician's campaign.

Ella was relieved that Charles was feeling better after his assault at the hospital but her own worries constantly lingered around the edges of her thoughts. She buttoned up her duster coat and stepped into the car.

***

Following the church service, Murdoch made his excuses for skipping the usual family lunch and walked away from the church. His destination was the wharf where he could be distracted from his worries by the comings and goings of other people, especially the uniforms.

Ed Quinn took notice of Murdoch's hasty retreat and saw his opportunity. He turned to Clara. "I have something to attend to before I have lunch. I should be home in less than two hours. I'll eat then." He kissed Clara's cheek and strolled toward the sidewalk.

As Ed sauntered off, the congregation mingled in pairs and small groups, sharing news and views. Laughter carried across the front lawn as young children ran about in a frenzied game of tag, complete with shrieks and squeals.

Unlike the other members of his family, Charles hesitated at the bottom of the church steps and assessed the crowd before him. Three well-heeled men were engaged in what appeared to be a serious conversation. He casually walked toward them, hoping to hear a few words before he interrupted them. When one uttered a disparaging remark about a sitting member of the provincial government, Charles smiled. Today would be the first day of his campaign.

As Ella walked toward a group of women, she caught sight of Alex Wallace standing among the deep stand of fir trees along the church property line. Her heart dropped. Without even a nod of recognition, he held his stare and moved back between the trees and out of sight. A shiver rolled down her back.

Alex was aroused by the fear he knew Ella felt. He needed physical satisfaction but he'd wait for the sun to set, then go hunting.

***

Ed spotted Murdoch sitting alone on a bench near the Sailors Hotel. He had already planned his approach and maintained a brisk pace until he was almost in front of Murdoch. He made a sudden stop.

"Good afternoon, Murdoch. Mind if I sit for a few minutes to catch my breath?"

"Suit yourself." Murdoch kept his head down.

"Lovely fall day for a walk. I often come here for a walk before my night shift at Rockhead. I'm early today. You come here often?"

Murdoch glanced sideways. "I do. It's a busy place. Lots to see. People to watch."

"You work near here?"

Murdoch straightened up and turned toward Ed. "At the shoe factory. It's not far from here."

"I know it. Good place to work?"

"It's all right. Not very exciting."

Ed chuckled. "Exciting is not something I want where I work. It usually means trouble."

Murdoch laughed quietly. "I can see that. I'm in sales. I meet the buyers, that sort of thing."

"But you like exciting?"

"I do. Always have, even as a kid. Take a dare, bet on a game of marbles." He kept his occasional sip of his father's whisky to himself. "I like taking risks to see if I win. If I win, I feel successful."

"I had a boring childhood compared with yours. And now, what do you do for excitement?" He didn't really want to force an answer from Murdoch, so he continued. "I bet you drive your father's car? It's pretty fancy."

"You'd lose that bet. He rarely lets me near the steering wheel. He's always been stern, needs to be in control of everyone and everything."

Ed nodded. "Lots of responsibility being a doctor. Guess it spills over at home."

Murdoch nodded. "I'm not a child anymore but he makes me feel like one."

"I gotta go but have you ever thought about your work in shoe sales as taking a risk? The excitement and success when the buyer decides to purchase from you? It's like betting on yourself." He shook Murdoch's hand. "Thanks for the conversation."

Ed walked away hoping he'd left Murdoch with something new to consider.

Church on Sunday meant nothing to Frank Murphy. His parents nagged but he ignored their preachy argument, figuring that paying room and board was all he owed them. At twenty-six, he was his own boss and had made up his mind about church and certain people. He leaned against the brick front of a factory in the wharf area, a half-smoked cigarette hanging out the side of his mouth.

Germany was Canada's wartime enemy and Frank was convinced any German-speaking man landing in the city off the supply ships intended to spy on Canada's military. His hostility toward German men came from his father, Jimmy. For years, Jimmy Murphy blamed his business misfortune on a business partner from Europe who spoke both English and German. There was nary a mention of Jimmy's own lack of business acumen as a possible cause of the failure.

While Frank was deemed ineligible for war service due to his flat feet, he meant to protect his homeland somehow and catching a spy was the least he could do for King and country. Despite the absence of any proof that spies were afoot in Halifax, Frank maintained his belief. So, during his smoke breaks he studied every man stepping off a supply ship from Europe. He couldn't understand the German language but he sure knew when it was spoken. During the week his work interfered with his obsession. Sundays however, were ideal. He had all day and night to catch a spy.

Just before sunset Frank heard a man call out 'Guten Tag' toward a local. He pulled his cap over his brow and followed the German-speaker. So far so good, the fella wasn't interested in women or liquor. Frank fantasized about this. He'd catch the bugger doing something shady like taking a note from a fella in a pub. He'd step between them, grab the spy and march him to the police station.

Frank's imaginary idea failed suddenly when his spy walked the uphill streets leading toward Citadel Hill, the fortified military stronghold housing both men and weapons. He reconsidered. This promised to be a better catch. He'd be a big hero, saving the Citadel from the Germans. His picture would be in the newspaper, maybe a reward.

Growing up, Frank didn't pay much attention to the Citadel. It was there before he was born, on top of the big hill, protecting the city. He'd never bothered to walk up and look around the place so when his spy began to climb the winding dirt trail, Frank was unnerved. The tall grass offered him little cover and the sun had not fully dropped below the horizon. Stopping for a few minutes, was the safe thing to do. He counted to sixty five times, then started walking again.

The spy's body was sprawled on a patch of grass, his chest wound oozing blood, lots of blood. Frank took a deep breath to settle himself as best he could and smelled lavender. Spooked, he rushed straight down the hill not stopping until he came to the first cross street.

Constable Ivan Buckle was on motorcycle patrol and had stopped for a smoke at the base of Citadel Hill. When Frank Murphy raced across the last open stretch of grass, Ivan jumped on his bike and roared up the hill in the direction Frank had come from. When he found the body, he smiled from ear to ear. *Gotcha, Frank.*

Too frightened to go to the police, Frank rushed into the closest drinking hole and got stinkin' drunk.

It was almost eight o'clock, well past home time for a Sunday, when Detective Will Henderson pulled on his overcoat and grabbed his hat from the top of the coat stand.

"Have a quiet evening, Fields."

"Thank you, Sir. I hope it is. That botched bank robbery was enough excitement for today. Any word on Constable Smith?"

"He'll be all right. The leg's not broken but he'll be black and blue for a while."

"Thank you, Sir."

As Henderson stepped out the door, the front desk phone rang. He waited on the sidewalk, just in case. A cold wind was blowing up from the wharf. He pulled on his gloves and slowly moved onto the sidewalk.

Fields was soon at the door calling out, "Buckle called from a call box, Sir. A body. On the trail at the Citadel. Sergeant Bailey is already there. I'll call a taxi for you."

In the wee hours of Monday the body had been transported to the morgue and the scene secured for evidence gathering.

Sergeant Jim Bailey would be looking for the killer of a fellow copper and Detective Henderson's red-haired friend, Detective Bill Turner.

The guard at the Citadel's open draw-bridge reported no military personnel or civilians had entered or exited the facility since late afternoon. The overnight chain gate to prevent German subs entering the Halifax harbour would be lifted at shortly after seven o'clock so Bailey's constables were checking for missing personnel on all military and supply ships before they left the docks at sunrise.

Detective Henderson stood quietly in the darkness, his eyes scanning the city of Halifax at his feet. He pulled his wool coat tighter but it could not create the kind of comfort he needed.

Steps away from Henderson, Sergeant Bailey was pacing, his six foot wiry frame wound tight.

"Well done, Sergeant. Go home for a rest. I'll speak with you later today. Constable Buckle should come too."

Bailey moved to his detective's side, patted Henderson on the back. "I appreciate your support tonight, Sir and I'm very sorry you lost your friend. Constables Renault and Stevens are heading up the search teams until noon. We will get him, Sir."

"Thank you, Sergeant." Henderson turned his eyes toward the harbour. "I always appreciated Detective Gilfoy's support when I was a sergeant so I wanted to pass on the favour."

Bailey tried to lighten the mood, if only for a moment. "How is Gilfoy these days, Sir?"

Henderson nodded. "Good, good. He's growing roses in his old age!"

CHAPTER FOUR

MONDAY, OCTOBER 22

Dead Spy at the Citadel, Monday morning's sensational newspaper headline was far from the truth. The body was found on the trail outside the Citadel and the word 'spy' was pure fiction. But it sold newspapers.

The spy story was all the talk at Frank Murphy's place of work Monday morning. Frank had a splitting headache so kept his mouth shut. Nobody seemed to notice his silence, especially about the spy part. He'd been there, seen the dead man and hoped to God nobody saw him running away. He wouldn't be following spies for a long while. He didn't intend to be the next body.

Frank's foggy brain began to clear by noon. He knew for sure he'd not met anyone on his walk up the path and never saw anybody at the bottom when he raced down. He saw no reason to go to the coppers. When he stepped outside to eat his lunch at the picnic table, he took a good look around. Seeing no strangers, he sat down with his back up close to the side of the building. *Maybe somebody did see me. Maybe I should shave off my moustache?*

Frank's young girlfriend, Billie Stewart was tired of hearing about spies but she was in love with Frank and did her best to turn his obsession away from the Germans. However, Billie had her own obsession. A wedding proposal from Frank would allow her to escape her demanding parents. When she heard about the body near the Citadel, she raced to Frank's work site.

"Oh my God, Frank." She ran to give him a hug. "Were you following Germans yesterday? Are you alright?"

"Keep yer voice down."

"Why? It's in the paper."

"My name isn't. Now keep quiet. I don't wanna talk about it."

Billie whispered, "What did you see?"

"A dead fella. It's gone from my mind."

"It may be gone for you but the killer hasn't forgotten. How do you know he didn't see you?"

"Cause I didn't see him."

Billie let that one slide. "Where do you think the killer went? Back to the Citadel or down the hill?"

"How the hell would I know? Who cares?"

"The police care. You could be a witness."

"To what? I saw the body. That's all. I'm keepin' my mouth shut and you should too."

"And you believe nobody else saw you?"

"The police sure as hell didn't."

"So that leaves the killer."

"Why the hell are you bringin' that up again?"

"Because you and the dead fella weren't the only ones on that trail."

"But I didn't see him!"

"Keep telling yourself that, Frank. But you're wrong. He could be looking for you."

"Stop sayin' that." He took a deep breath. "I'll stay away from the wharf after work and on Sundays for a while."

"A while? How about forever."

"You better get back to work or you'll get sacked."

"No, Mr. Martin won't fire me. He likes me and besides, he couldn't run the store without me." Billie turned on her best smile. "If you're afraid, we could leave town together for a while. Take a train ride. That would be fun."

When Frank didn't respond, Billie walked away and Frank rolled his eyes. *Bossy*

***

"You barely touched your lunch, Ivan. Usually, I can't get a word in edgewise. What's the matter with you?"

"Nothing, Ma."

Alice Buckle tried to keep the conversation going. "How 'ya like that bicycle you're ridin?"

"It's a motorcycle and it's fine, Ma."

Her patience ended, Alice came straight to the point. "Whether you say so or not, somethin's bothering you. Take a walk before you go to work this afternoon, clear your head. At least sit in the backyard."

Ivan Buckle's dream came true when he became a police constable. At last, he had the power to put certain people in their place. Toffs and hoity-toity women wouldn't get away with doing anything they wanted. Best of all, he'd have a chance to get even with Frank Murphy.

By afternoon the heavy grey clouds had become a steady downpour. Despite the disagreeable weather Ella intended to take the short walk to visit her neighbour, Mable Cameron. She needed relief from her own worries and to know more about a recent blackmail story in the newspaper. Mable fit the bill and seemed unbothered by her occasional impromptu visits.

Mable was quite an accomplished gossip who gleaned her particulars from her many shopping outings. Ella did not pass on Mable's entertaining stories and the tittle-tattle. Today however, she needed to glean some special gossip from Mable for her own purpose.

Before dressing for her visit with Mable, Ella removed the long black key from the china cabinet and went upstairs to the bedroom. She sat on the end of the bed, turning the key over and over.

While living with her parents, the key had red wool tied to it and hung from the lock of her cedar chest. When she married, the wool was removed and the key hidden in the silver sugar bowl inside the china cabinet.

Ella rarely opened the hope chest given to her on her eighteenth birthday but today she would. Her wedding certificate, the children's birth certificates and now Henry's letter were in a large envelope on top of her wedding dress. The second envelope, buried beneath Rose's christening dress might be the answer to her Alex problem.

When Ella received considerable funds upon the death of her Aunt Betty, she did not tell Charles about her windfall. At the time, she could not explain her reasoning, even to herself. She checked the balance in her bank book and looked through the investment certificates. Maybe Alex could be bribed.

Ella popped her umbrella then stepped into the Scotch mist, as her mother called it. The walk to the Cameron home would be uncomfortable. Her button boots were pretty but not warm on a cool, rainy day. She moved quickly.

Ella liked the new clothing for women the war helped create. Women were working in factories and businesses, replacing men who went off to fight in Europe. The disappearance of high collars and absence of heavy veils and overbearing plumes from hats was a godsend. Looser waistlines were more comfortable and shorter hemlines made puddles easier to navigate. Her mother however, maintained her reservations regarding the display of ones' ankles. 'It is most unlady-like' was her usual complaint.

***

Mable Cameron employed a full-time maid, something Ella had no desire to do. Given Murdoch was an adult and Rose at school, it seemed extravagant and pretentious. She let the door-knocker drop and waited to be greeted by Mable's maid, Esther.

"Good afternoon, Mrs. Ramsay. Mrs. Cameron is at home. Please come in."

Mable rose from her brocade armchair to embrace Ella. Her hair was piled high on her head, adorned by several decorative hair pins. "Welcome, my dear. You look radiant."

Ella knew this was bullocks but smiled pleasantly. "And you as well, Mable." *Bullocks, again. Both of us are well past the radiant stage.*

"Esther, bring the tea service and dainties." Mable paused until Esther left the room and closed the door. "So Ella, what is all the news in your household?"

"All of us are quite busy with work, school and charities."

"Yes, I heard about your recent work with the church. Those poor souls who have very little truly need our thoughts and prayers. What is it exactly that you do?"

"I have joined a few ladies once a week to knit socks. It's a small part of the war effort to support our sailors and soldiers. They're here in droves coming from and going to Europe. By the way, we are always looking for knitters. As they say 'many hands make light work'. Would you like to help?"

"I cannot knit. What could I possibly do?"

"Perhaps find new people to knit or buy wool."

Esther's knock and entrance were unfortunate timing for Ella. She sat patiently until Esther left then immediately picked up where she left off, before Mable could change the topic.

"We are seeking someone for the committee who is well connected with important families in the city. I cannot think of anyone more suitable than you to head-up that part of the committee. You know all the influential people, Mable. Your contribution would be invaluable and your efforts would not go unnoticed by society at large."

"If you think I can do this work, I will try."

"I certainly do, Mable. I will pass your name on to the committee. Thank you."

"Lemon square?"

"Thank you." Ella took a quick breath. "Mable, you are so well informed about the city's news, I wonder if you know anything about the dreadful bribery trial in the newspaper a few weeks ago. The outcome was never mentioned. I hope it did not involve anyone we know."

"In fact, I do know something. Indeed, it was a sensational story about infidelity in a dreary marriage." Mable's face displayed a balance of sadness and glee. "Following a lover's tiff, the wife tried to bribe her amour to keep quiet about the affair but he refused. She was charged with violating some law and spent a few days in jail. We don't know them personally of course, but I'm told they are well-known in certain circles. Pots of money, that sort of thing. The moral is don't try to buy your way out of trouble. By the way, you're the quiet one about your own family affairs."

She knows about Alex! So thunderstruck, Ella didn't respond.

Mable carried on. "Alfred is already planning for the election campaign. I know Charles wants to keep the news quiet until a proper announcement." She smiled. "I don't know how I can help but Alfred has several connections within the party and socially, of course. You must be terribly excited."

Ella was not in the least bit excited but she could not possibly allow Mable to see her surprise nor guess her outrage. "It's certainly going to be a new adventure."

Shortly after, Ella glanced at her watch and made her excuses to leave. "I have a roast to prepare for the evening meal. Thank you for the lovely chat."

Bugger, twice. One for Alex Wallace and one for Charles.

***

Constable Buckle hesitated a moment outside the door of the police station, shifted his compact frame inside his uniform and grinned. What he saw on the Hill was proof of Frank's role in the murder of Bill Turner. There could be no other conclusion.

"Good afternoon, Constable Buckle. I'll see if Detective Henderson is ready for you."

Ivan Buckle did not expect both Detective Henderson and Sergeant Bailey to be in the room for what he thought would be his information about Frank Murphy's guilt. He sat down, a little less confident than when he left home.

Detective Henderson spoke first. "Good afternoon, Constable Buckle. Thank you for coming. Sergeant Bailey will be taking notes. Have a seat and tell us what you saw on Citadel Hill late Sunday evening."

"I saw Frank Murphy run away from the Hill. I drove the motorcycle up the hill and found the body. I contacted Sergeant Bailey and the police station. Frank Murphy was the only person there and he ran away. He killed Bill Turner, I'm sure of it." He smile confidently.

"Do you think another person might have been there and run off in a different direction?"

"No, Sir. I would have seen someone else. There was nobody else there."

"Have you considered the killer might have gone into the Citadel barracks?"

"No, Sir." Buckle took a deep breath. "Frank hates Germans. He thinks they are spies. He was there."

"And you know this because Frank has told you he hates Germans?"

"He wouldn't tell me that, Sir. But other people told me. We need to arrest him, Sir."

Both Henderson and Bailey stood. "Thank you for your information, Constable."

Buckle was boiling inside but managed to find his way to the sidewalk in front of the station. He'd have to prove Murphy's guilt another way.

***

Following Buckle's departure, Henderson spoke first. "Well, there's a constable with an opinion and not afraid to speak it."

"You're right there, Sir. Opinion is the correct word. I'm concerned."

"So am I."

"I'll caution Buckle to keep his conclusions to himself, Sir."

"Do you know Frank Murphy?"

"No Sir, I don't. I haven't met him as a policeman nor as a city resident. I'll check him out."

"Now then, your findings on Bill's murder, so far. But first, when's the autopsy expected?"

"It'll be a day or two, Sir."

"Anything on the ships?"

"No military or supply ship personnel were reported missing. We need a motive, Sir."

"Bill was a policeman. Revenge is certainly one motive. Have you called the Truro station?"

"About an hour ago. They'll get back to us with a list of possible names, Sir."

"Excellent. Let's have a look at the evidence box."

***

Corbin Davis lingered over his evening meal long after he finished eating. His friend Bill's comments swirled around in his mind. Bill was right. He needed to do something or end up old and alone. He carried his plate and cutlery into the kitchen.

"A lovely dinner as usual, Mrs. Williams."

"Thank you, Mr. Davis. Coffee and whisky in the study?"

"No, thanks. I'm going to the theatre this evening. I need a new direction in my life."

Daisy Williams waited until she heard her employer go up the stairs. She shook her head. "That man has everything he needs, except a wife. These young people and their newfangled ideas! What in heaven's name does a new direction mean?"

Across the city in a cheap boarding house, Alex Wallace had a clear direction for his life. He was well pleased by settling one recent score in Truro and could now return to the ruination of Ella Ramsay's life.

Unlike most young men, Alex had a diary and kept track of his grievances, including the time lines to settle all of them. So far he had been on time for every one. He spent many evenings recounting the past treatment each of his victims had inflicted on him. He made sure each of them paid for their sins with his personalized kind of justice. He reread his diary stories, never wanting to lose his anger about the people who ruined his life. Those stories and his retributions began with his father, continued with his aunt Agnes, his mother's quack doctor and Albert Evans, his former employer in Truro. He'd wait a few days before writing his Halifax accomplishments.

Ella Ramsay had been on Alex's revenge list for some time. She'd stolen his father. It was also her fault his mother became ill and he was sent to live with mean aunt Agnes. He'd come to Halifax to unearth her weaknesses but the damn woman appeared to be perfect. She was getting on his nerves. He needed someone to release his frustration.

As the evening grew darker, so did Alex's frustration. He desired the usual physical release for his pent up feelings. Forgoing a bath, he splashed cologne on his shirt and went in search of a willing partner on the seedier streets of the city.

Corbin Davis hadn't been to the theatre in recent years. Initially, he had good reason to stay away. The theatre had broken his heart. Work became a diversion, then a way of life. He found it easier to blame the theatre for breaking his heart rather than the woman who really did the damage. He convinced himself the parting had been mutual but the truth was, he'd let Margo escape without a fight. He loved her and could not bring himself to stand in her way. When the bright lights of a bigger city beckoned, like a fool, he let her go.

Corbin entered the theatre cautiously, carefully avoiding a glance toward his usual space, row twelve, middle seat. Instead, he stopped at the back row and sat in an aisle seat. He soon realized his decision to attend the performance had been made hastily.

Finding himself in the very building of his loss, he regretted the decision and stood, prepared to leave.

As Corbin moved into the aisle, he bumped into a tall blonde wearing an eye-catching red wool dress. *He caught a trace of lavender.*

"Oh my goodness." She pressed her right hand to her chest. "I'm so sorry, sir."

The British accent caught Corbin's attention. "No harm done. I'm sure you weren't expecting someone to be leaving before the performance began."

"Well, that is certainly true." She smiled as she folded her black shawl over her arm. "Do you know something I don't?"

"No. I simply changed my mind."

"Well, we're all free to do that." She paused. "By the way, I've been told this performance is quite good so I'm staying put." She laughed. "You could change your mind again. I won't tell anyone."

"Then I will and I'll hold you to that promise."

"Agreed. I'm Josephine Robinson." She held out her hand. "Jo to my friends."

Corbin took her hand. "Corbin Davis. My friends call me Corbin."

Their laughter was spontaneous and genial.

Alex Wallace hunched over the wash basin in his dreary room. He frantically scrubbed his hands then the cuffs of his coat. A gold broach and an earring fell into the basin. When the rusty smell of blood turned his stomach, he gave up and threw the coat over the back of the only chair in the room. Tomorrow he'd toss the coat into the harbour and buy a new one.

Alex convinced himself that what happened on the wharf wasn't really his fault. He'd pushed good money down the front of her dress and she should not have fought back. Stupid cow. Her gold broach would be worth something. He kept it but wasn't so sure about the earring but he kept it anyway. He pulled his diary from under the thin mattress and sat on the bed. Reading it usually settled his mind but not tonight. He pulled the chair to the locked wardrobe, took the key from his pants pocket and reached into the top shelf. Among his few personal items was a monogrammed whisky decanter and crystal glasses.

Alex hadn't wanted much from his father's estate, except the decanter, the money from the bank and the sale of the house. He didn't care about the fine furniture and fancy dishes so loved by his mother. He sold it all.

Alex's select memories of his mother were all he needed to honour her life and fuel his revenge for her mistreatment. He sipped the whisky, freed himself from all thoughts of the battered body he'd left on the wharf and fixed his mind on Ella Ramsay.

CHAPTER FIVE

TUESDAY, OCTOBER 23

Early Tuesday morning, Detective Henderson was informed a young woman had been left for dead at the wharf.

Sergeant Bailey shook his head, his eyes downcast. "Her life's hanging by a thread, Sir."

"Any identification?"

"No, but the constable who found her thinks she might be a working girl."

"Oh, dear." Henderson exhaled heavily. "Well, somebody knows who she is, cares about her. What's your plan?"

"I'll talk to the constable. He has a good description, her approximate age, hair colour, height, what she was wearing. I'll send him out to the area to talk to other women."

"Late evening will be the best time to find someone but send him earlier if you think it will help. Remind your constable to be considerate of their circumstances."

"Consider it done, Sir."

***

Detective Will Henderson knew the wharf area well, as a child then a constable. He came to Halifax from a small fishing village on the south shore of the province after his father was lost at sea. His mother found house work and began a slow climb out of poverty.

Growing up, Will could relate to people who lived around the wharf. He knew the alienation, the fight to survive, the shadier side of life and the oft-found suspicion of the police.

Over the years Will and his mother were able to afford better housing and eventually were living on the same street as a policeman who took an interest in Will's well-being. In short order, Will knew he wanted to be a policeman but never forgot where he came from. When he became a constable, his mother often sent cakes to Detective John Gilfoy as a 'thank you' for giving her son such a good start in life.

Bailey's constables had completed the rounds of the city hotels on Monday looking for a man who made a hasty departure late Sunday. The results were disappointing. Today, they were canvassing boarding houses.

Bailey knocked on Henderson's open door.

"Any news so far, Sergeant?"

"Nothing from the boarding houses, Sir. On the better side of the news, I'm expecting a phone call from the Truro station telling me who Detective Turner was following or at least a few names for us to work with." He paused. "The young woman on the wharf died earlier today. There'll be a full autopsy. I was told the beating was vicious, primarily to her head."

Henderson shook his head, rubbed his forehead. "She didn't deserve that." He paused a moment. "Have you spoken with Constable Buckle?"

"Yes. He seemed more than surprised that his observations weren't evidence of guilt. He's only been on the job for a few months so maybe he's a bit naive; however, there was a whiff of revenge in his tone."

"We'll have to keep an eye on him. And Frank Murphy?"

"No arrests, Sir. Likes the drink though. Quick with his fists. Lives at home. One constable told me he heard Frank hates Germans. That's hearsay and hate is a pretty strong word. The constable has been with us for five years, does thorough work."

"Why would Frank kill Bill Turner? Bill's not even German."

Alex Wallace left his boarding house well before the sun came up Tuesday morning. He had a job to do before the light of day could expose his wrongdoing. On his way to the wharf he picked up a few hefty stones and placed them in the pockets of his bloodied coat before dropping it into the harbour.

While walking back to his boarding house, he bought a warm coat, picked up the morning newspaper and stepped into a bakery. Planning for a lengthy stay to warm up and read the paper, he ordered a pot of tea and a bun.

Lady of the Night Dies The newspaper's headline caught Alex's interest. He shrugged, thought it was probably another working girl, not his. She was breathing when he left her. The news story continued by chastising the police for their woeful response to two killings in two days. Alex smiled, read the details, confident he had once again "stumped the coppers". Then came the last sentence. 'There is considerable speculation the out-of-town policeman's death was committed by a man who came to Halifax to do the job'. The words set Alex's senses tingling. He rushed to his boarding house. Afraid the landlady would give his name to the police, he left two-nights worth of money on his account. Fearing the taxi driver would remember him, he carried his belongings to North Station through the drizzle. He intended to take the first train leaving Halifax, no matter where it was going.

***

Marie LeBlanc arrived early for work, as usual. She expected Mr. Davis within half an hour and wanted his morning tea and newspaper ready. Surprised but pleased, she heard Murdoch call out her name as she dropped the morning paper on Mr. Davis' desk.

"You're early!"

"Well, a fella's got to show some initiative now and then."

Murdoch was at his desk when Corbin arrived.

"Good morning, Marie, Murdoch. Another busy day ahead. Murdoch, get the daily sales report ready. After a look at the paper I'll come see you."

"Right you are, sir."

Within minutes, Corbin was at Marie's desk.

"I'll call you later."

After speaking to Marie, Corbin went directly to the police station where his worst fears were confirmed. Bill was dead. He telephoned Marie.

"Lock up at five and tell Murdoch he's in charge. I'm going to Truro on the train. I won't be in for the rest of the week. Thank you and I'm sure the two of you will manage just fine."

Marie raised her voice. "Murdoch, Mr. Davis is going to Truro. You're in charge for the rest of the week."

Murdoch sauntered toward her desk.

"Very funny but you can't fool me."

"Seriously, he's going to Truro but don't ask me why."

Murdoch turned and walked toward Corbin's office door.

"Where are you going?"

"Into his office. He wasn't using the telephone so whatever is on his desk is the problem."

"Are you playing Holmes or Watson?"

Murdoch turned to stare at Marie. "Who?"

"Never mind. I'll explain later."

Murdoch returned with the newspaper, tapping his finger on the headline. "It's about this."

"Don't be daft. Mr. Davis is a respectable citizen."

Murdoch shook his head. "Not that part. The policeman's murder part of the story. Wanna bet he's going to Truro because of the dead policeman?"

"Betting is a sure way to lose money."

"It's fun. You should try it sometime."

"I can think of better ways to have fun. Now, why would Mr. Davis go to Truro?"

"Because the story says the dead policeman is from Truro."

"You're right." She paused. "This time."

Murdoch hesitated with a reply. "Someone told me as I like to bet, I should bet on myself. Guess this is my big chance." He smiled. "I could talk to you for a while but I better look at the orders and check the inventory then have a walk around the factory. Someone might have a question, not that I would know the answer."

"Don't doubt yourself. You might just know the answer."

Marie found Murdoch most confusing. He was smart, quick with figures but never showed any desire to impress Mr. Davis. He had loads of charm but didn't seem interested in using it to make friends as he never mentioned any. Most importantly, she hadn't figured out how to convince him to notice her. *I may be just what he needs.* She had three days to get his attention.

Marie enjoyed her work meeting the people who came to the office and was a quick typist which pleased Corbin. Her family however, offered her a few challenges.

Marie thought her father was a bit crusty, especially when it came to her social life. He often told stories about the rough lads he saw during his work as a night watchman. 'You need to be careful, young lady. Too many of those innocent-looking lads are trouble.'

Marie's mother was a different challenge. A deeply religious woman, she wanted her daughter to see the young men of their parish as ideal husbands. She already had the perfect candidate and was planning a scheme to bring them together.

***

The morning paper regarding two unsolved murders gave rise to lots of anger at the police station.

Sergeant Bailey was fuming. "What in damnation are they doing, Sir? Saying the killer could be from out of town is irresponsible."

Henderson had grown immune to newspaper reporting. "I understand your annoyance. In the past I said the same thing but we can't control what they say, only what we do."

"But there could be some policeman who's angry or vengeful enough to talk to them, Sir."

"Or it could be two reporters talking about possible motives for killing a policeman. One of them could use the idea for a story. Don't waste your energy on the newspaper. You won't win. Unless you have proof of someone tipping off the reporters, we have two murders to solve so we better get on with it. Agreed?"

"Yes, Sir."

Henderson put on his glasses. “Let’s have a look at Detective Turner’s autopsy. It says here Bill was stabbed from the front by a single, well-placed lunge. He had no other injuries. The coroner suggested the murderer could be in the medical field, maybe a surgeon.” Then he looked at Bailey and shrugged. “Or the killer delivered a lucky blow.”

Bailey responded. “He faced Bill, Sir. Wanted him to know who was killing him.”

Henderson shifted his eyes from the report to the evidence box sitting on his desk. ”Bill’s money is there so it wasn’t robbery. Your lads found the knife?”

“No, Sir. Searched in the dark and again after the sun rose. I’m convinced Bill was targeted. Revenge or maybe a paid killer. After all, his connections and work are in Truro.” He stood. “I hope Truro can help.” As he opened Henderson’s door to leave the desk constable was about to knock.

“Sergeant Bailey, Sir. Truro is on the line for you.”

Henderson paced in front of his desk until Bailey returned.

“Sir, we have three possibles. All were arrested by Detective Turner in the recent past. All are considered dangerous. Michael Freeman, served time for robbery. Alexander Wallace, served time for vicious assault and Joseph Young also served time for vicious assault. Their whereabouts are unknown. As far as Truro knows, none have family in Halifax. Wallace and Young play no favourites. They assault men and women.”

“Got descriptions?”

“I have, Sir.”

“Let’s hear them.”

“Freeman has brown hair and dark eyes, five feet ten, round face, looks innocent but is cunning. No record of violence. Wallace has light coloured hair, blue eyes, sharp features, six feet, smart, speaks well, arrogant with a mean streak. Violent. Young has a prominent cleft chin, brown hair, dark eyes, also six feet, walks with a swagger and violent."

CHAPTER SIX

Tuesday, October 23

Will Henderson's growing years were filled to overflowing with his mother's many Scottish phrases, stemming from her youth in Edinburgh. She had a saying to cover every life circumstance and numberless stories to accompany them. Just this morning she reminded Will not to open his umbrella inside the house for fear it would bring on bad luck. 'It's bad luck, don't ye ken. Ye might ruin your best chance of finding your friend's killer.'

Will studied the descriptions of the three potential suspects. He desperately wanted to look Bill's killer in the eye and soon. He was terribly impatient as Sergeant Bailey and his constables were unable to find a break in Bill's murder. As a diversion, he reviewed his preparation for a pending court appearance. It would fill a half-hour or so. With a mug of sweet tea at the ready, he picked up the folder to re-read his written recollection of the incident.

Will witnessed a traffic accident near the Public Gardens in July. A motor car hit a pedestrian. The car, travelling five miles per hour, caused a bruise on the man's leg. The gentleman decided to sue.

Motor cars were gaining popularity with the citizenry. Horses pulling wagons and carriages were often skittish, their drivers frequently annoyed. Pedestrians regularly got up in arms about the smell of gasoline. But despite the occasional uproar, Henderson knew it was the way of the future.

Sergeant Bailey knocked on the door. "Sorry to interrupt, Sir. We have a lead."

"Go ahead."

"One of the constables was puzzled by what he heard from a boarding house."

"Continue."

"I believe we have a runner, Sir. A fella left early this morning and the cleaning woman found a spot of blood on the handle of the water pitcher. She described the man. It could fit Wallace or Young. I'm off to North Station."

"Or he cut himself shaving."

Bailey shrugged. "I'm just going where there's a trail, Sir. I'll fill you in on the details when I get back."

"Carry on. Oh, and don't put your umbrella up inside the train station."

Bailey turned away from the open door, a confused look on his face. "What?" Then he hastily added, "Sorry, Sir. What did you say?"

"Never mind. I'll tell you later."

Henderson sipped the tea and continued with the review of his accident statement. Once satisfied, he reflected on the old days when horses were the only mode of police transport. Now, Constable Buckle and a two others had motorcycles and the station had four motor cars counting the paddy wagon.

Alex Wallace did not lack intelligence nor cunning. Upon arrival at North Station, he willed himself to focus on survival. He studied the departure board. Two trains were preparing for departure, their times mere minutes apart. One was headed north, the other south. He approached the ticket booth and bought passage on both trains then slowly wandered his way outside to lean against the side of a small shed closest to both tracks. The narrow roof overhang provided a bit of relief from the continuing rainfall.

When the police rushed onto the property, Alex casually pulled his cap down over his forehead and stared at the day old newspaper he'd found on a bench inside the station.

Sergeants Bailey and Surrette with two constables stepped inside North Station in time to watch the passengers slowly getting ready to board one of two trains idling just beyond the exit door. All passengers stopped at the exit door, reluctant to step out into the steady rain until the last possible minute. No one resembled Young or Wallace. The four policeman moved outdoors.

In the beginning, the rain worked in Alex's favour. He was partially hidden but the minutes were ticking by and the trains would leave soon. He kept an eye on the coppers and the few hardy passengers slowly gathering outside.

Minutes later, Alex realized most passengers were still inside the station and likely planning to rush outside at the last minute. If the police had noticed him and concluded he wasn't moving, he would attract their attention. He had to make a move soon or miss both trains.

The police scrutinized the outdoor group huddled under the station overhang, clearly looking for someone in particular. Their lingering presence heightened Alex's uneasiness. His heart began to thump. He took short breaths. His sweat soaked underwear clung to his body. He was rooted to the spot. *Do it, just do it or you'll be stranded in Halifax.*

After a furtive glance at the big outdoor clock on the station tower he held the folded newspaper over his head, picked up his bag, walked behind the shed and came out from the back side. Giving the police and passengers a wide birth, he strolled toward the station door.

Once inside, he threw the soggy paper into a bin and edged himself into the middle of the large group waiting inside the exit door. Keeping his head down, he exhaled a long, but quiet stuttering breath. So far, so good.

The conductor's voice carried into the ladies' private waiting room and across the general waiting area. "Ladies and gents, last call for Truro, north track and Yarmouth, south track."

Alex kept his head down and shuffled along, his shaky legs carrying him toward the south-bound track. As he reached the top step to board the car, the conductor held out his hand.

"Your Yarmouth ticket, sir."

The ten minute wait to get all the passengers seated felt like a lifetime for Alex. He feigned interest in his ticket stub, praying the coppers would not board the train nor recognize him as they passed by while the rain tapped on his window.

When the whistle blew, Alex felt a slight jolt as the car moved from a standstill to forward motion. In a few hours he would be twice the distance away from Halifax than Truro and in the opposite direction. He almost wept with relief.

***

As Alex was planning his escape, Corbin Davis stood outside North Station in the downpour, his mind barely able to comprehend the death of his childhood friend, Bill. His visit with Bill's wife Ruby would be awkward. He was open to an honest conversation but wasn't so sure about Ruby.

Finally relieved to be out of the miserable weather, Corbin hung his dripping wet overcoat on a nearby hook and settled in his seat. He had the next two and a half hours to think carefully about the meeting with Ruby in Truro. Their last time together in the same room was the marriage of mutual friends, five years ago. Ruby had given him a wide berth, allowing he and Bill to have a rambling conversation at the reception. He closed his eyes, visualized the scene at the Turner front door. Ruby might slam the door in his face.

***

The car ride back to the station was silent until Bailey muttered, “Maybe we should have searched both trains.”

Surrette shook his head. “I don’t think so. The train conductors are serious about being on time.”

“You’re right about that. We’re not even sure he got on a train. Let’s get dried off, have some tea. There’s apple cake in the lunch room. Detective Henderson’s mother sent it in with him this morning.”

Leaving the other three in the lunch room, Bailey took his tea and cake into Henderson’s office.

Henderson’s face looked hopeful. “Get a result?”

“No, Sir. The rain didn’t help. Everybody kept their collars up and hats down.”

“Don’t get discouraged. Who knows, Frank Murphy might have something worthwhile to say on Bill’s death this evening. Perhaps one of the constables will turn up something on the wharf about our young lady.”

***

“Well, aren’t I the lucky woman. I have a handsome man to share my train ride with to Truro. Gertrude Matthews is my name. Everyone calls me Gussie. And you are?”

"Corbin Davis." Corbin nodded then dropped his head and focused intently on the newspaper, hoping Gussie would take the hint.

"Did you see the police roaming around outside the station in the pouring rain?"

"They were?"

"My goodness, yes. Four of them looking at all of us. I bet they were after the murderer of that police fella from Truro. So terrible. His poor family. I'm on my way to meet my first granddaughter. And you, Corbin?"

"Visiting a friend." *I hope.*

"Well isn't that lovely. You know, we need to do more of that. Visiting friends and what with the war on so many families are worrying or already got the bad news letters from overseas. Death is not pleasant at any time but these young lads who're dying haven't even had a life yet. War is a terrible thing but we can't let those fellas from Germany take over the world. You're not over there?"

"No. I own a business in Halifax."

"Well, aren't you the smart fella. It's a busy place what with all the usual military there and boats comin' and goin. Do you know Truro?"

"Very well. I grew up on a farm in Colchester County."

"Well then, you'll be right at home visiting friends."

And so it went. Gussie talked, Corbin mostly listened while watching the trees and occasional home fly by as the clickety-clack of the train made its' way to Truro.

In the end, Corbin was thankful for Gussie's distraction but now he had to concentrate as he had no idea what his reception at the Turner front door would be. The sights and sounds of a bustling factory town and hub of rail transportation was somehow comforting. His home town was doing well.

After finding his rented room, Corbin chose to walk the few blocks to the Turner home. The house was modest and welcoming when compared with the large two-story homes built for the well-to-do mercantile families. He strolled up the path, past the vibrant fall colours. The brass knocker seemed an intrusive start to the visit. Instead, he tapped on the door. A familiar woman dressed in a plain navy-blue dress with white collar and cuffs opened the door. Her severe bun matched the look on her face.

"Ruby thought you would come today." Then she whispered, "How dare you?"

Years of history flashed through Corbin's mind. From the age of thirteen, Ruby and her older sister, Mary spent several summers with their grandparents on the farm outside Truro. Corbin briefly vied for Ruby's attention but she chose to marry Bill.

"Come in. Thankfully, the neighbours aren't outside to see you."

Corbin ignored the inference and stepped over the threshold. "Thank you, Mary."

"Give me your coat. Ruby's in the sitting room."

Corbin paused for a deep breath.

"Go on then. The door's open." Mary turned on her heel and returned to the kitchen.

Corbin entered the sitting room and quietly closed the door.

"Hello, Ruby."

Ruby stood with her back to him, framed by a large window overlooking a back garden of fruit trees, shrubs and flower beds, the blooms now withered, drooping and faded. The sun streamed in, leaving its' warmth and a tapestry of shadows across the hardwood floor. "I knew you would come. Thank you."

"How could I not?"

A lengthy silence brought their brief interaction to an end.

Corbin stepped forward and put his hand on Ruby's shoulder. "I'm so sorry about what happened to Bill."

Ruby turned and walked away from him to settle into a chair near the fireplace. "The funeral is Friday." The tone of her words gave the impression she was offering information more than conversation.

Corbin was struggling with a response when the door opened.

Just as Ruby pointed to a chair for Corbin, a large ginger cat raced across the room and jumped onto her lap. Seemingly aware of Ruby's need for comfort from her wretched circumstances, the cat curled up and began purring, loudly.

"This is Marmalade. He's a big talker when he's not purring."

"Then he's good company, just what you need."

"And he doesn't tell me what I should do."

Corbin guessed the reference was to Mary. He said nothing.

"I see you haven't lost your tactfulness."

Corbin smiled and was about to reply when a sharp knock on the open door also briefly interrupted Marmalade's purring.

Mary walked into the room carrying a tray with tea and sugar cookies which she placed on the small side table nearest Ruby. "You should eat something, Ruby." She walked out, leaving the door wide open.

"I'm a bit preoccupied, Corbin. Could you close the door?"

As Ruby and Corbin smiled, Marmalade purred on.

Corbin did not expect Ruby to be fully at ease with one visit, especially not under the circumstances. Following a brief discussion about Marmalade, the funeral, her garden and how long and where he was staying in Truro, Corbin finished his tea and stood. "I'd like to visit tomorrow afternoon around two. Would that be acceptable? If you need assistance with something, I'd be here to offer a suggestion or two."

"That would be helpful. Thank you."

"Stay seated. Marmalade is having a sound sleep. I can show myself out."

On the way to the front door, he looked toward the kitchen. "See you tomorrow, Mary."

***

Frank Murphy fought off the hankering for a stiff drink all afternoon. The thought of his upcoming police interview never left his mind, not for one minute.

"What the hell's the matter with you Frank? The rest of us are keepin' up and you're holdin' up the work. Quit or get movin'."

"Yeah, well you haven't got my worries."

His workmate snorted. "Likely woman worries. That Billie woman's got you wrapped around her little finger. You better marry her or get rid of her. She ain't goin' away on her own."

"What I do is my business."

"Maybe it's the murder that's got your attention. I hear you were around the Hill that night."

Frank clenched his fists, took a step forward. "Who told 'ya that?"

"Ease off Frank. I ain't the one spreadin' the word. I heard it's comin' from a copper. Maybe somebody's tryin' to stitch 'ya up." Then he laughed.

After quitting time, Frank walked to the police station where he leaned against an outside wall and finished the third cigarette he'd smoked in the last hour. His thoughts rambled. It was the worst day of his life. He was being stitched up for a murder. The minute he stepped into the damn place, they'd lock him up. This was his last day of freedom. *Maybe I should hightail it for the train now.* After grinding the butt under his boot, he had second thoughts about the train. He'd never been on a train. He muttered to himself, “Hell, I’ve never even been on the ferry across the harbour to Dartmouth.” He rounded the corner and stepped up to the police station door knowing he was innocent and hoping the police would think so too.

“Good evening, sir. How may I help you?”

“Sergeant Bailey around? Frank Murphy’s the name. He wants to see me.”

“Have a seat. I’ll find him for you.”

Bailey emerged from his office. “Evening, Frank. Come in, have a seat.”

After the first few minutes Frank figured everything was going well. He told Bailey about the evening of the murder. The man spoke German, he followed him through the streets toward the Hill. “I stopped when I was out in the open.”

“How long did you wait before continuing to follow the path to the Citadel?”

Frank shrugged. “A few minutes, for sure.”

“You hear any voices?”

“No.”

“Then what happened?”

“I started walkin’ again and found the man on the ground. He was bleedin’, bad.”

“Lyin’ on his front?”

“No, back.”

“What happened next?”

“I ran straight down the hill.”

“Did you see anything or hear anything?”

“No.”

“Close your eyes, imagine yourself on that hill. Think hard, Frank. You’re on the hill, then going down the hill. At the bottom of the hill you ran across the street.” Bailey sat quietly.

“The dead fella had red hair. I stumbled over a rock near the bottom.”

"Anything else?" Bailey kept quiet. People found silence awkward and talked to fill the void. He hoped Frank was one of those people. He leaned back in his chair and waited.

In due course, Frank leaned across the desk, a look of surprise on his face. "I heard an engine after I crossed the street."

Bailey nodded. "And where was this sound coming from?"

"Behind me, somewhere."

"And what sort of engine sound was it?"

Frank frowned, stared at the window.

Bailey waited.

"A motorcycle startin' up." The penny dropped. Frank leaned back in his chair, his eyes wide with astonishment. "Who told 'ya I was at the Hill that night?"

"A tip."

Frank stared at Bailey. He didn't need the name. *Bucklehead.*

Bailey moved on to deeper questions. "What do you think of Germans?"

"Don't like 'em."

"Because?"

"I just don't."

"Come on, Frank. You must have a reason. Did you kill that man on the Hill because you don't like Germans?"

Frank squirmed under Bailey's stare. "My pa. He hates them. I didn't kill nobody. You gotta believe me."

"That's all for now, Frank. Don't leave town."

Frank bolted outside. In need of a beer, he stepped into a drinking establishment frequented by his older brother Joe.

"How'd it go?"

"They think I did it, Joe. Told me not to leave town. I'm certain it was Bucklehead on the Hill."

"Pay no attention. Bucklehead's just gum flappin'."

"Easy for you to say."

"Go on, get a drink and settle down."

When Frank returned with his beer, Joe leaned across the table.

"So why do 'ya spend time worryin' about German spies when we have ammunition in the harbour that could accidentally blow us all up! Now that's a real worry. You should be spendin' your spare time with Billie Stewart instead of hunting down Germans."

"Nah, she's too serious for me."

CHAPTER SEVEN

Wednesday, October 24

Detective Henderson was eager to find out what happened during Frank Murphy's evening interview so he rushed to the station early and knocked on Bailey's open door. "Good morning, Sergeant. How was the interview?"

"Have a seat, Sir. The poor bugger is probably still shaking. He first told me he came upon the body when he was out for a walk. But when I pushed him about Germans, he confessed he'd followed Bill to the Hill."

Henderson furrowed his brow. "But why?"

"Apparently Bill spoke a few words of German near the wharf and Frank thought he had a spy in his sights, doin' his bit for the war effort."

"Did he ask how we found out he was at the Hill?"

"No, but I've a feeling he was holding back something about that part. He did remember hearing a motorcycle so he probably put two and two together and figured it was one of us."

"How'd you end it?"

"I told him not to leave town. He was pretty rattled when he walked out."

Henderson shook his head. "This case has the makings of a novel. The bad guy hunts down and kills a police detective who speaks German and sets up a spy chaser to take the fall. What's next?"

"You think the killer and the spy chaser are two different people?"

Henderson blew out his cheeks, tilted his head. "Could be one theory."

"If you want to start writing in your free time Sir, my full report is on your desk."

"Don't get cheeky, Sergeant." Then he sighed. "I might just do that in retirement."

Billie Stewart stared into the mirror and cursed under her breath. Fighting with fine, straight hair every morning was absolutely the worst part of the day. After the struggle with multiple hair pins, she figured she looked at least presentable. She smoothed the skirt of her yellow work dress and smiled.

Yellow was Billie's favourite colour. Yellow flowers, wallpaper, anything with the colour yellow. At sixteen, she spied a scarf with yellow flowers in Angus Martin's dry goods store and she had to have it. She convinced Angus to put it aside for her until she had the money to buy it. The scarf was the beginning of their friendship. Two years later, Billie became Angus' first store assistant.

Now nineteen, she'd been working in Angus' store for a year. She enjoyed her work and meeting people but most of all, she delighted in the independence she felt as a young woman in the world of business. Opinionated and outspoken, Billie often caused a stir inside and outside the store. Angus admired Billie's spunk and agreed with her progressive ideas, such as women having the vote and the ability to hold public office.

Billie's family and Angus had a strong negative opinion about Billie's take on one part of her life. She was infatuated with Frank

Murphy. Billie didn't agree with any of them, simply because she wouldn't. Period. She believed everyone was mistaken about Frank. She intended to prove them wrong and marry him. However, Billie had a bit of a problem. Frank didn't appear interested in marrying her or anyone else.

Without children of his own, Angus considered Billie the daughter he never had. He was protective of her despite the frustration she occasionally brought into his life.

Having only Sundays off never seemed enough time for Angus to enjoy life. In his quieter moments, he thought Billie would eventually be perfectly capable of running the store herself. In a few months he would see how she could manage on her own one day per week.

Thinking about Billie naturally lead Angus to thoughts of Frank Murphy. From what he'd heard around town, Frank was not a good catch for anybody. Now, there was idle chatter he might be involved in the murder on the Hill. He frowned, ran his hand over his receding hair line and put on his reading glasses just as Billie arrived for work. He'd keep his uneasy thoughts to himself for the time being.

Marie LeBlanc woke to a sunny, warm Wednesday morning. With no wind to create a chill, it was time to ride her new bike to work. When she entered the kitchen wearing a split skirt, her mother's lips pinched and a deep frown appeared on her forehead.

Marie struck the first blow. "I'm riding my bicycle to work."

"But you're going to an office. What on earth will people think?"

"Nothing, Mama. They'll think nothing. Women have had bicycles for years. Besides, I can use it for work. It's faster than the tram. I can leave work when I'm ready and I have no tram tickets to buy. You always encouraged me to save my money so now I am."

"The streets are filled with cars. You'll not be safe."

Marie shook her head. "Hardly. And why are your arms crossed?"

"That split skirt. What respectable young man would be interested in a young woman riding a bike in a split skirt?"

"Frankly, I don't care, Mama. I'm not interested in any man right now. And by the way, I plan to learn how to drive a car!"

With that, Marie picked up her lunch tin, marched to the front door and went to work, without breakfast.

Murdoch was already in the office when Marie arrived.

"Good morning, Miss LeBlanc. Your face is awfully red. Did you miss the tram?"

Marie pulled off her sweater, plunked her lunch tin on the desk and sat in her chair, her back to Murdoch. "Don't be so daft. I rode my bike."

"Excuse me for asking, but did you get out on the wrong side of the bed this morning?"

Marie squared her shoulders, straightened her back and turned around. "What do you mean by that?"

"I mean you're cranky."

"Cranky is for cats. And besides, I am not cranky."

"If you say so." Murdoch walked toward his desk behind the screen. "When you're ready, I'll have a look at the new orders before going to the factory floor."

Marie snorted. "Very well." She began opening the envelopes and tore one, badly. "Damn."

"Everything alright out there, Miss LeBlanc?"

"Perfectly fine, Mr. Ramsay."

Murdoch smiled. *She's feisty. I like it.*

***

Inside the Ramsay home, Ella's early morning nightmare was as vivid as a real experience. Alex was everywhere inside her home, haunting her every move. He muttered unspeakable threats in her ear, promised to push her down the stairs, hold her hands on the hot stove and smother her in her own bed.

She woke with a start, kicking Charles who opened his eyes and groaned.

"What happened?"

"A dream. Go back to sleep."

Ella was wide awake, worried about Alex's next move and angry with Charles and his secret political campaign plans. Unable to fall asleep, she put on her dressing gown and went downstairs to read. When she heard Charles coming down the stairs, she stood up and met him at the bottom step.

"You're very pale. Are you unwell, my dear?"

"No, simply a bad dream. It will pass. I'll get dressed and start breakfast."

At the breakfast table, Ella noticed Rose staring into space. "What's the smile about?"

"I'm thinking about my secret."

"The one you and Nellie are making?"

"Yes, it's so pretty."

"I'm sure it will be a lovely surprise. Please finish your breakfast and I'll do your braids."

When Rose left the table to get her ribbons, Charles looked at Ella across the kitchen table. "Are you sure you're well?"

"Absolutely."

"If you say so. I'll call you between noon and one o'clock. By the way, where is Murdoch? I didn't see him at breakfast."

“He left early for work. Mr. Davis is out of town for a few days and he and Miss LeBlanc are in charge.”

“That’s a good sign. I hope he can keep it up. He’s so unpredictable. Well, I’m off then.” He kissed Ella’s forehead then hugged Rose as she came into the kitchen with her hair ribbons.

“What is unpredictable, Mama?”

Ella took a moment to make sure Charles’ word was not a condemnation of Murdoch. “When people do things that are not expected.”

***

By mid morning, Henderson and Bailey had completed their review of the young woman’s autopsy report and examined the scant contents of the evidence box. The report noted the victim had lost a lot of blood from head wounds and she was missing an earring.

“Not much to go on, Sir.”

“You’re right. The autopsy shows one earring was ripped off. I’m guessing it was caught by the killer’s clothing. Anyone in the wharf area hear or see anything?”

“No, but I expected that, Sir. Folks around there keep themselves to themselves. Coppers aren’t exactly considered their friends.”

Henderson nodded knowingly. He decided an evening walk around his old neighbourhood was in order. He’d wait a few days to see if the constables had any success in finding the young woman’s name.

***

Following the conversation about new orders with Marie, Murdoch completed his walk about in the factory and returned to the office before noon.

Marie was hungry, thanks to her morning tiff with her mother and missing breakfast. She'd already made the pot of tea and opened the cookie tin holding her lunch, knowing Murdoch usually went to the bakery to have his lunch.

"I'm going to the bakery. Can I bring you something?"

"No, thanks. I have buttered biscuits, a piece of cheese and an apple." *He certainly has more money than I do.*

Marie was surprised when Murdoch returned within minutes, carrying food for himself and two slices of apple cake. She chuckled. "You must like apple cake."

"I do but the second one is for you."

"Thank you." She took a deep breath. "I apologize for my snippy words this morning. That's not the way to behave in a place of business."

"We all have bad days now and then. I know I do."

"Do you think women should ride bicycles, wear split skirts and drive motor cars?"

Murdoch frowned. "Where did that question come from?"

"Well, to answer your question first, before you answer mine, it came from a heated conversation with my mother this morning."

Murdoch nodded. "Ahh. That explains a couple of things."

He expected Marie to challenge his comment. When she didn't, he continued. "The answer to your question about bicycles, split skirts and motor cars is 'yes'.

"Do you know how to drive a motor car?"

Murdoch replied cautiously. "Yes."

"Can you teach me how to drive one?"

Murdoch laughed. “Probably not. First, I’d have to convince my father to let me drive the family motor car more than I do now.”

“So your father is difficult too. Mine’s strict and my mother thinks I should marry some fellow from church.” Marie abruptly stopped talking, her face turned beet red.

“That must have been a humdinger of a conversation this morning.” Murdoch paused. “I’ve had those talks with my father. He has my future planned for me. Be successful, have the right friends.”

“Don’t you want those things?”

“Yes, but his idea of success isn’t mine. I like having fun too.”

“What kind of fun?”

Murdoch dropped his head. “You won’t like my answer.”

“Does this fun make you late for work?” She could hardly believe her boldness. She barely knew Murdoch.

“I like to gamble. Sometimes I drink too much. So, yes that’s why I’m late for work.”

Amazed that Murdoch would tell such a thing, Marie couldn’t think of a suitable response.

Murdoch feared he’d lost his chance for a friendship by admitting to such behaviour.

Both were grateful when the telephone rang,

“Davis Footwear. Miss LeBlanc speaking. How may I help you?”

“Hello, Marie. Corbin Davis here.”

“Hello, Mr. Davis.”

“I need to explain myself. But first, is everything in order at the office and in the factory and is Murdoch there?”

“He is and we’ve had no problems so far with billing, orders or on the factory floor.”

“Excellent. Can you share the hand set with Murdoch?”

Marie waved for Murdoch to stand close to her. “Mr. Corbin wants to speak with the both of us.”

“I’m still in Truro. I want to express my thanks to both of you for a job well done.” The line went silent. ”My friend Bill will be buried later this week.” He took a deep breath which was clearly heard by Marie and Murdoch. “I’ll be back Monday afternoon. I will call early Monday morning in case either of you need help.”

“Thank you, Mr. Davis. We are so sorry about your friend and we will see you Monday. Goodbye.”

“Goodbye, Marie.”

Marie looked at Murdoch, tears in her eyes. “Poor Mr. Davis.” She dropped her head into her hands.

Murdoch patted her shoulder. “May I take you to lunch at the bakery tomorrow, Miss LeBlanc?”

“Certainly, Mr. Ramsay.”

“It’ll be a little celebration for our good work.”

“That sounds lovely.”

“Even better, we’ll get to know each other.”

True to his word, Charles called Ella shortly after twelve-thirty to check on her health.

In the background Ella could hear a female voice.

“Hurry up, Charles. My lunch break is almost over.”

She’s here again. Just the sound of Lois’ voice brought back all the lies, horrible memories, feelings of betrayal. This time, she would not put up with any of it.

***

Corbin's second visit with Ruby was more lengthy than he anticipated. They spoke of Bill's recent visit in Halifax, the funeral arrangements for Friday morning and the paperwork Ruby could expect in the coming days.

During their conversation, Ruby revealed Mary's stifling protection. "She told my longtime friends and neighbours their visits were limited to half an hour."

Corbin excused himself and went into the kitchen.

"Mary, we will not speak of this conversation again. Beginning this minute, when Ruby's friends and neighbours want to be with her, they will be for as long as they and Ruby wish. Do I make myself clear?"

"If you insist. I was only looking after her best interests."

Corbin ignored her defence. "Ruby must not feel abandoned now or in the future. She is quite capable of understanding her own best interests at this time. Long after you return to Montreal, she will need these people in her life."

When he returned to the sitting room, he nodded toward Ruby. "You should have no more difficulties with Mary. And speaking of difficulties, I don't wish to upset you but I need to speak of our personal trouble before I return to Halifax. Would now be acceptable?"

Ruby nodded. "Please allow me to speak first. Bill is dead through no fault of yours. He loved his work, even though it was dangerous at times." Tears welled up in her eyes and rolled down her cheeks.

Marmalade was sitting on the window ledge, keeping an eye out for intruders in the backyard when he sensed something amiss. He was soon on Ruby's lap.

Ruby buried her face in her handkerchief and wept. Spent, she leaned back in the chair and continued. "Your strong support of Bill's career choice so long ago angered me and I took that out on you. It wasn't fair and I apologize." She wiped her eyes. "There never seemed to be a chance for the two of us to have that talk together, until now. Regret is such a sorrowful burden. I hope you are able to think of me as a friend."

"Absolutely, I do and always did." Corbin smiled warmly. "About your future. Do you have friends here and in Halifax?"

"I do. I have a friend who moved to Halifax but I haven't seen her in many months. She did send me a sympathy card, suggesting I visit when I was up to it."

"When you're ready, contact your friend and let me know. If your friend doesn't have the space for a guest, you can stay in my home." He quickly added, "I have a live-in housekeeper. Your good name will not be besmirched. Bring Marmalade."

CHAPTER EIGHT

Thursday, October 25

During breakfast Ella was unusually quiet. It was not the time nor place to discuss private things. A time of reckoning would come soon enough.

Charles was confident Ella did not know about his political plans but he acknowledged to himself she likely overheard a female voice call his name while he was on the phone with her the day before. Afraid to ask her if there was a problem, he ate quickly and left for the hospital.

In the car, Charles smiled to himself. Given a bit of time, he knew he could create a believable story to tell Ella about his desire to enter politics. He'd target her empathetic nature and she would be supportive by the end of the evening meal.

Lois Fillmore was unpredictable, a trait Charles found exciting during their earlier affair. Now, that same trait could very well dash his political ambitions and cause the demise of his marriage. He had to get rid of her. Safe inside the stillness of his hospital office, Charles pushed his lab coat sleeves back from his wrist and picked up a patient file for review. He'd deal with Lois later.

"Excuse me, Doctor Ramsay. Nurse Fillmore would like you to check on your post surgery patient in Room 115."

"Thank you. I'll be right there."

Charles knocked on door 115 and stepped into the room. The patient was asleep. As he turned to leave Lois wrapped her arms around him and pulled him behind the partially open door.

"I couldn't stay away any longer." Lois took his hands in hers. "Are you happy I'm back?"

Charles tried to pull away but she managed to hold onto his hands until he forcibly pulled himself free.

"I've missed you, Charlie." She touched his cheek, Charles winced. "I've never stopped thinking about you."

Charles whispered. "You can't be here, Nurse Fillmore."

"Stop calling me that. You can call me darling, again. We belong together."

"You're wrong. We ended this years ago."

Lois moved to embrace him. "You did. I didn't."

Charles stepped back, glanced toward his sleeping patient. "Get away from me. I have a family."

Lois countered. "You did then too but that didn't stop you."

Charles leaned in close to her face. "We'll see about that. I know people."

As Lois opened her mouth to reply, Charles bolted from the room.

Hugh Andrews fancied himself a crime writer. When not covering the usual births, weddings, deaths and business stories for the Truro newspaper, he dug into unsolved crimes around Nova Scotia. He made it his business to chat up all the older folks in town, hoping he would happen upon a juicy lead for a big crime story. He supported every social event and promoted every business with good content and was a fixture at sporting events where he cheered on the local teams while smoking his pipe.

Hugh grew his hair a bit too long for the times, stroked his bushy moustache when mulling over things and favoured cozy, wool sweaters over business suit jackets. He was well liked in his adopted home town where his friendly laugh and good nature opened every door. At times there was a sadness about him but in all the years he'd been in town, no one had been able to wheedle a hint about it from him.

When Bill Turner was killed in Halifax, Hugh's grief ran deep. He and Bill were close in age and solved many of the world's problems over a beer. They were best friends.

After Bill's death, Hugh became tenacious about seeking out the circumstances surrounding the death. He visited the police station daily. But by day four, every sergeant and detective was too busy to take an interview. Hugh understood. They needed to focus on the murder and he honoured their grief over losing a comrade.

Bill always encouraged Hugh to keep searching for the ultimate crime story to write; but, when Bill was brutally murdered, Hugh re-thought his old crime story. He had the perfect opportunity to be a real time crime writer and maybe find justice for his friend. He decided to attend Bill's funeral then leave town.

Halifax was not a city Hugh wished to spend much time in but for Bill, he was driven. He set aside his old pain and arranged for two reporters to cover his responsibilities, then packed his clothes for the Friday afternoon train to Halifax, right after Bill's funeral.

Davis Footwear was a busy office and bustling factory on Thursday morning. Multiple new orders for fall footwear and the military requests plus a problem on the factory floor demanded

Murdoch to perform quickly. By eleven o'clock, he was convinced both he and Marie would be working through lunch, not enjoying each others' company at the bakery.

"Murdoch, there's a telephone call for you. Can you take it in Mr. Davis' office?"

"Yes. Put it through." Murdoch picked up the receiver. "Murdoch Ramsay. How may I help you?"

"You don't know me but I have information for you."

Murdoch curiosity peaked. "May I have your name, sir."

"It doesn't matter who I am."

Now irked, Murdoch asked again, "May I have your name, sir. Then you can give me your information."

"Watch for a letter addressed to you at Davis Footwear."

"Who are..."

When the telephone line went silent, Murdoch went to Marie's desk.

"Did that caller identify himself to you?"

Marie frowned. "No. Why?"

"He wouldn't tell me who he is but he's going to mail information to me."

"Information about what?"

Murdoch shrugged.

After a few moments, Marie said, "Do you think we will make it to the bakery for lunch? I didn't bring anything to eat."

"I'll bring lunch back for us."

"Let's go tomorrow." Then she realized she sounded very forward. "Excuse me. I assumed too much."

"No, you didn't. Tomorrow should be slower." He crossed his fingers on both hands.

***

Ella was clearing her lunch dishes when the doorbell rang. She couldn't imagine who would be visiting without telephoning. Her parents were in Ottawa visiting her mother's cousin, Norma. Norma's husband had been killed during the months long bloody and muddy Battle of Passchendale. Then she also remembered her impromptu visit with Mable. Times are changing. It could be Mable.

Their smiling postman held out an envelope. His familiar face, uniform suit and hat both with red trim and a brown leather mailbag was not what she'd expected but very welcome.

"Good afternoon, Mrs. Ramsay. We haven't spoken for weeks. How is Rose? Phoebe is in her room this year."

Ella took the envelope. "She's growing like a weed, as they say. And full of energy. And Phoebe?"

"All excited about some hush hush art project we are not supposed to know about."

Ella nodded. "We too are in the dark about this secret."

"Have a lovely day, Mrs. Ramsay."

"You as well, Mr. Fletcher."

The envelope had a Yarmouth postmark. She carried the puzzling envelope into the kitchen, trying hard to remember who she knew in Yarmouth. She gave up, opened the envelope and glanced at the first word. 'Bitch'. Ah, yes, she thought. Some men are now using this word to disgrace women as the suffragette movement is gaining notice.

Bitch I hope you miss me but never fear, my intent to expose your misdeeds of adultery and falsehoods will soon be realized. In the meantime, I look forward to destroying your personal and family life. AW.

***

Ivan Buckle thought in absolutes. Things were black or white, right or wrong and Frank was guilty. After Bill Turner's murder, he replayed the evening on the Hill, his time at the Citadel gate, then riding down the hill and seeing Frank bolt from the scene. He rehearsed the anticipated interview questions to keep his own presence at the gate out of his answers. It paid off and he walked away from Henderson and Bailey feeling very proud of himself. Confident he was in the clear, he then attempted to craft a story to ensure Frank's guilt. Despite his efforts, Ivan's imagination failed him, as it often did when he was faced with solving problems. He decided planting evidence was the only solution and moved on to thoughts of stealing something from Frank.

***

Angus Martin stuck his head into the storage room. "Almost time to close up for the day, Billie. Finish up whatever you're unpacking. I'll start to count the cash."

"Will do, Mr. Martin. I'll lock the back door and be finished in a few minutes."

When Billie returned to the front of the store, the sun had already set.

"The days are shorter now. Be careful walking home. Stick to the main streets with street lights, no back alleys, missy."

Billie rolled her eyes. "Yes, papa."

Once outside, Angus and Billie bid each other a good evening, then Angus entered the alley off Barrington Street, a shortcut to his own home several blocks away. A few steps in, he heard a shouting match taking place about halfway along the long, dark alley. He leaned against a nearby building. Both men sounded drunk. He figured the melee would be over quickly.

Two men were standing toe to toe as a few others began to back away from a punch up in the making.

"Can 'ya not shut your fat gob for one frickin' second?" Frank Murphy lurched toward his adversary, swaying side to side.

"You should talk, 'ya stupid fool. What would you know about a war ship. You never seen inside one in yer life."

"And how would you know that, huh? When did 'ya get on shore?" Frank answered his own question. "Today, you self important arse. Just cuz yer in a sailor suit don't make you smart. You need a lesson in manners." Frank put up his fists and made a jab in the air.

"Whoa there, Frank." An onlooker stepped forward. "There's no call for that. Have you forgotten we're at war? That fella's defendin' us."

A friend of Frank's spoke up. "That fella's right, Frank. Come with Joe and meself. We'll have a walk to the wharf and get 'ya sobered up."

The onlooker then spoke to the sailor. "Have a good evenin' and thank you for your service to Canada."

Joe Murphy grabbed his brother's arm. "What are 'ya thinking! The coppers could be watchin' 'ya making a fool of yerself."

Seeing and hearing Frank in action, convinced Angus he really had to do something to convince Billie to forget the man.

Ella and Charles had little to say during the evening meal as Rose and Murdoch both had a story to tell.

Rose glanced toward her parents and brother. "I have a story. Can I go first? Please, please."

Ella chuckled. "Of course. I'm afraid you might burst if you don't!"

"Mrs. Quinn helped us make cookies after school today."

Ella asked patiently, "And who is us?"

"Nellie, of course and Phoebe was there, too. The best part was using cookie cutters. I used the heart one." She sat back in her chair, a big smile on her face. "We are going to have a surprise for dessert."

Murdoch looked at Rose. "I can't make cookies and I'm glad you know how. Now I know we'll never be without dessert."

"Murdoch, you are so silly. Mama can make cookies."

"But she might be away some time and then what would happen? We could be cookieless."

Rose rolled her eyes at him. "Not now, silly. I'd make them. So, do you have a story?"

"I do. Mine's a mystery."

Rose leaned across the table toward him. "Does it have ghosts?"

"No. It's about a mystery man. He called me today and said he would send me a letter with information that I should know."

Ella put her fork down. "He asked for you!"

Charles muttered, "Hmm. Refused his name, did he?"

"More than once. I expect the letter will be a complaint about an order or maybe a pair of shoes or boots he doesn't like. By the time it arrives, Mr. Davis will be back from Truro."

Rose quickly lost interest in the story. "Can we have dessert now?"

After dinner, Charles asked Ella to join him in the sitting room. Once there, he paused and appeared to be weighing what he would say first. Content that he had the right words, he said, "First of all, I need to apologize to you, my dear. I have made an important decision and not let you know about it immediately. To be blunt, I have decided to run in the next provincial election."

Ella keep her face unreadable as best she could.

Oblivious to her stone face, Charles rambled on with the details of his plan, already in place. A select number of well heeled men have been meeting for several weeks. The nomination meeting is next week. Some several minutes later, he stopped.

Ella tilted her head toward Charles. "And with whom did you discuss this idea to run for political office?"

Charles smiled with complete confidence. "Only my supporters. They would know whom and what to consider."

"Clearly not." Her soft voice dripped with sarcasm. "Your medical career. What will become of that?"

"I plan to leave the hospital when I'm elected. Maybe work a few hours a week, just to keep my hand in, not lose my touch."

"You sound very confident. I'm sure others will run for this position. Is that not true?"

"I expect so but my supporters are confident of a win."

"Hmm. And about our family finances. What will happen to them?"

"Don't worry. I've considered everything."

Ella thought about her own secret cash of money. *And you're not getting one penny of it.*

Charles stood and went to the liquor cabinet. "Let's drink to my success."

Ella enjoyed the sherry but not for the reason Charles had in mind. While she had Charles' attention she decided to mentioned the female she heard while they were on the telephone.

"On the telephone with you yesterday, I overheard a female call out your name. I found it very unprofessional behaviour for a nurse."

"I've already spoken with her."

Charles went to bed with a clear conscience, thinking he'd easily resolved two matters with Ella. Actually getting rid of Lois wouldn't be so simple.

Ella went to bed fully aware she was now facing two very large problems: Alex's threat and a woman coveting her husband. Exposing both problems would result in the same outcome. She would be without Charles. She fell asleep thinking about a life without him.

CHAPTER NINE

FRIDAY, OCTOBER 26

The city of Halifax hanged murderers in 1917 and Alex Wallace knew it. If unearthed, his fate would be to swing from the gallows tree at the end of George Street. But, in the meantime, Yarmouth would be his safe haven. The discarded Halifax newspapers at the train station would keep him abreast of the city's news.

Alex cautiously stepped off the train and walked down the main street. The town appeared to be prosperous, active and big enough to ensure his anonymity. He purchased new clothing, found lodging in the Grand Hotel, then took a walk along the port, hunting for an activity to keep his mind off his unfinished business in Halifax. Killing off the Ramsay bitch would have to wait awhile.

Alex determined the busy port area was likely his best chance to find the female kind of excitement he occasionally craved. Standing on the wharf, he begrudgingly admitted his father's money was making all this possible. He quickly dismissed that charitable thought. *The man ruined my life. He deserved to die the way he did.*

With an idea in mind, Alex engaged a well-dressed gentleman also watching the fishing boats come in with their catch.

"Good day, sir. A lovely day to enjoy the view across the Atlantic."

"Indeed. Are you new in town, sir?"

"Yes, I am." Alex extended his hand. "May I introduce myself. I'm Alexander Ward and I'm looking for a new business opportunity. My friends call me Alex."

"Walter Simmons is my name. Pleased to meet you, Alex."

"Tell me a little about your fair town."

"Originally wood shipbuilding made the place wealthy. When that declined, business men invested in factories, iron-hulled ships and the railways. That's what you see today."

Alex nodded. "I noticed several large homes earlier today. Wealthy families then?"

"Many and the social life is bustling."

And so the exchange continued with Alex quickly adding that he was looking forward to the fine lodging and food at the Grand. It never hurt to impress people when the chance arose.

In the finish, Alex wrangled an invitation to dinner the following evening at the home of Walter Simmons.

Immediately after leaving the wharf Alex went in search of the Simmons home. It was what he hoped. The house was a large white Victorian home with a widow walk on the roof, providing a vantage point for women to watch the sea for their husband's ship. He surmised that Simmons was likely the owner of many ships and the widow's walk certainly added a sense of wealth to the already impressive house. Alex was delighted. An available daughter would be a stroke of good fortune.

Bill Turner's funeral in Truro was large by any measure. Businesses closed for the morning and many fellow police officers including those from other parts of the province, lined the street leading to the church. The church parking lot was filled to overflowing and people were walking from every side street.

Corbin left the boarding house early and joined a lengthy line of mourners inching their way into the church. His parents' deaths and years in Halifax had removed him from the day to day experiences of small town life and the people who kept Truro vibrant. They worked for and supported businesses, the railway and factories. Glancing about, he recognized many faces and recalled most of the names. Several people nodded in his direction. He nodded in return.

Without warning an unexpected rush of melancholy overcame his thoughts. Happy memories of skating on the pond, birthday celebrations and dances tumbled together with heartbreaking recollections of family illnesses and deaths of young and old in the community. Relief came when he was seated and the comforting sound of the church organ filled the air with familiar hymns. Only the sadness of Bill's death remained.

When Ruby, Mary and Bill's much older brother followed the casket into the sanctuary, Corbin stood with the other mourners. Unable to accept what was happening, he lowered his head. Lost in his own thoughts, he sat and stood as prompted by the actions of those around him until the final words of the celebrant captured his attention.

"We know life is a fleeting experience. When death ends a life on earth it also leaves behind a legacy. Bill's legacy of dedication to his family, friends and community will endure through each of you."

Outside, Corbin spoke briefly with many fellow mourners. As he left the church grounds with the sole intention of walking to the cemetery alone, he heard his name being called.

"Corbin, wait."

He turned and saw Jo Robinson walking in his direction beside a tall man wearing a well-worn black suit.

"Hello, Jo. You know Bill?"

"Ruby and Bill." She opened her mouth to say more, then changed her mind.

"Corbin, this is Hugh Andrews, Bill's dear friend."

Corbin extended his hand to the black haired man with intense, dark eyes. "Good to meet you, Hugh. How do the two of you know each other?"

Jo spoke first. "It's complicated."

Then Hugh interrupted. "It's simple. You make it complicated because you're complicated."

"I do not and I am not."

Cobin joined in. "I can tell this could go on longer than we have time. What is the short version?" He made the mistake of looking toward Jo, not Hugh.

"I'm a writer. But you don't know that as we spoke briefly at the theatre the evening you bumped into me. You were leaving the aisle and I was entering it. Because the curtain was about to open, we didn't get a chance to..."

Hugh interrupted. "See why it's complicated, Corbin? She writes novels. I write for a newspaper, few words and to the point. I'll finish her rambling part. We both met at Bill and Ruby's quite often and last year I worked with Jo when she had a short story published in the Truro newspaper."

Corbin nodded his understanding. "We probably should go to the cemetery."

Hugh made a final comment. "We can finish this on the train, that is if you're returning to Halifax today."

***

Murdoch's prediction came to fruition. Friday morning's office work was orderly and the factory was operating smoothly. At eleven-thirty he took off his glasses and went to Marie's desk.

"I think we are going to be free to have lunch at the bakery. I'll take a walk around the factory floor and be back by noon."

"Why are you whispering?"

"I don't want to spoil our lunch out."

Marie shook her head. "Sometimes I don't understand you, Murdoch."

"You'll have to meet my grandmother."

"Pardon?"

"She's Scottish. That explains everything."

The bakery was busy with local people picking up food but nobody stayed to eat.

Murdoch expected Marie would ask about the mystery caller. He was prepared.

When he brought dessert to the table, Marie decided to satisfy her curiosity. "Any ideas about your mystery caller yesterday?"

"None. I didn't recognize the voice. He said nothing about the information nor who it was about. It must involve my family. If it were otherwise, why would he call me? I wonder how he knows I work at Davis Footwear. It can't be about Mama but my father could be up to something."

Marie ignored the obvious question about his father. "You care a great deal about your mother, don't you?"

"Yes and my little sister, Rose."

"My little brother Leo is nosy, always asking questions about what I'm doing with my friends."

"Rose is twelve. How old is Leo?"

"Nine."

"Maybe by twelve, he'll have so many friends he won't care about what you do."

"I hope you're right."

They continued eating quietly until Murdoch asked about interests and hobbies.

"I like bike riding, being in the park, skating in the winter and reading anytime. You?"

"All those things but I skate badly. Rose skates better than I do!"

"This has been a lovely lunch time. I'm glad we know each other a little better."

"So, let's go out for a real lunch at a restaurant near the Public Gardens."

"When?"

"No better time than tomorrow, unless you have plans."

She nodded. "I'd loved to." *Now, I need a plan to outwit my family.*

"Then let's meet at the entrance to the Gardens at noon."

Marie muttered, "Sounds lovely."

***

Corbin said his goodbye to Ruby at the cemetery. For better or worse, she would have Mary for a few more days, then time alone to begin her life without Bill. He made a mental note to call her in a few days.

Jo and Hugh decided to spend an hour or so at a local restaurant before boarding the train. They'd invited Corbin to join them but he declined.

Bill's sudden death reminded him of how short life can be. He chose to wander around town thinking about his future. He'd proven he was good at business but his personal life needed attention. He thought about selling the business, then moved on to the idea of a business partner. But who? Seeing the park, he sauntered in and sat on the nearest bench. *You're working on business again. Business is not your problem. Connecting with people and enjoying their company is your problem. Do better.* His thoughts turned to the train ride home. He'd hoped to consider his future plans during the ride. Now he would spend the time with Jo and Hugh. Jo seemed an interesting travel companion. He looked forward to a conversation with her. He didn't know Hugh. Believing he was a pretty good judge of people, he saw Hugh as a typical newspaper reporter, always after a story and looking for an edge to get it. The missteps and misdeeds of others were his bread and butter. He would listen more and talk less with Hugh present.

By the time the train reached Halifax, Corbin had a very different opinion of Hugh Andrews. Hugh had a close friendship with Bill and intended to help solve Bill's murder. The latter was a bit of a stretch in Corbin's mind but he supposed anything was possible. He exchanged telephone numbers with Jo and received a dinner invitation for the following evening.

It had been a few years since Hugh Andrews spent any length of time in Halifax. However, he was not in the least bit surprised by his first impressions coming off the train. North Station and its' surroundings were always busy but in the midst of war it had taken on an unmistakable sense of urgency. The excitement of travel no longer dominated the atmosphere. Certainly, there were still those travelling for business and pleasure but the uniformed men and their reason for being in the city was clearly evident on their intent faces and quick march walking.

Hugh immediately saw a war story. But that was not the story he was hunting down. He was after the murderer of his friend and nothing and nobody would knock him off the scent. He kissed

Jo's cheek, promised to visit her in a few days then shook Corbin's hand and headed for his hotel.

Hugh had no formal police training but he knew how to sniff out details of a story. He'd already decided the police station would not be his first stop. First off, he didn't want the police to know he was in town plus he figured the locals might offer a lead or two that he could unearth. Freshened up, he chose an eatery near the wharf and settled in for a leisurely evening meal. By Monday, after a third meal there, he could casually engage the locals in general discussion. Tomorrow he would get the lay of the land by walking the trail up to the Hill and find out what the fellas in the Citadel had to say.

Angus finished his brandy after dinner but was no smarter about ridding Billie of Frank. He must say something to Frank or find a better match for Billie, who had a good mind for that sort of thing?

Will Henderson's mother sat at the kitchen table, a cup of tea in one hand and a biscuit in the other.

"Just don't let a black cat cross your path and you'll have good fortune."

Despite his mother's prediction, Will's expectation of success at the wharf was low. It had been six days since the young woman's battered body had been found on the wharf. Her name still eluded the police.

Will dropped a flashlight into his coat pocket and stepped into a city engulfed in blackness, except where the streetlights fought to keep darkness at bay. He was convinced the victim didn't live in Halifax and so it was little wonder nobody was missing her. He thought long and hard about how to pry what little information might be available out of the locals. Everything considered, he decided the best plan would to be observant and engage people in conversation, as he did as a young copper on the wharf.

The first hour was fruitless despite Will being dressed in well worn clothing and easily looking the part of a local. Residents and outsiders seeking entertainment or companionship were intent on a destination, be it brothel or gambling. He kept his slow walk constant, eyes alert for any opportunity to make casual conversation. He wasn't a pipe smoker but he used the pipe as an excuse to sit while remaining vigilant.

Well into the second hour, the pace and number of people slowed. Those still out and about were now more likely to engage in casual conversation. As he perched on the edge of a park bench near the waterfront, an elderly man moved slowly toward him.

"Evenin'. Mind some company?"

Given the man's elderly appearance, Will was surprised by the strength of the man's voice. Will looked into a pair of sharp blue eyes and replied. "Not at all. Have a seat, sir."

"A fine fall evening."

"It is indeed. You come here often in the evening?"

"Sure do, young fella. I spent many a year on the water. A fisher all my life. No place like it. I walk every evening to keep the old legs workin'."

"I imagine you know most folks around here." Will realized the error of disclosing his objective 'way too soon.

"I do. Who 'ya lookin' for?"

As his mother would say, in for a penny, in for a pound. "My name is Will and I'm a policeman."

"Pleased to meet 'ya Will the policeman. My name's Sandy." Then he shook his head. "I don't know why my parents gave me such a high falutin' name as Alistair. It never stuck. My sandy coloured hair gave me my name by the time I was two." He chuckled. "Bet your name's William."

Will laughed. "It is."

"Now what about your person. Maybe I can help."

"Monday night last week a young woman was killed on the wharf. Did you know her?"

Sandy shook his head. "No, but I heard she wasn't from around here. My neighbours say she was from Truro. Poor little thing. She meant no harm, just tryin' to get by as best she could."

"Do you think your neighbours would talk to me?"

"I do. Want to go there now?"

Will stood up. "I'm ready, if you are."

A few blocks from the wharf, Will entered the small, tidy home of Sandy's friends.

"Cookie and Maisie, I'd like you to meet Will Henderson. He's a policeman. He has a few questions about your young friend, Mollie Brown."

Cookie put on her glasses, stepped forward and clasped Will's hand in both of hers. "Constable Will Henderson?"

"Yes, ma'am. Now Detective Henderson."

Cookie smiled. "Well, I'll be darned. My dear boy. I remember you and Detective Gilfoy from that dreadful time in ninety-five with that horrible man, Thomas Bishop. I was Mrs. Bishop's housekeeper."

Cookie's smile was as warm as Will remembered. "Yes, of course. I'm so pleased to see you again. You're keeping well?"

"Very well, for an old girl."

"I believe Mrs. Bishop remarried."

"She did. A very fine man by the name of Robert Fraser. They have two children. William is twenty-one and Katherine is eighteen. But you're here on business. How can we help you?"

When Maisie made a pot of tea and served ginger cookies they all settled into a conversation about Mollie Brown and what the neighbourhood knew of her life and death.

An hour later Will was on his way home, knowing Mollie Brown was from Truro and had been befriended by sisters, Cookie and Maisie. He reflected on Cookie's firm conviction that Mollie's death had been a planned, viscous murder. Her words rang in his ears.

'Mollie was not a prostitute. She had a fine little job looking after two young children for a well-to-do family near the Hill. Wasn't there a man killed at the Hill around that time? Maybe Mollie saw something on her walk home. She could have been killed on purpose. Why else would she be dead?'

CHAPTER TEN

SATURDAY, OCTOBER 27

Marie's sleep was so fitful she finally got up and paced around her bed. Her impetuous decision to accept Murdoch's lunch invitation was wrong-headed. She couldn't wear her good dress on Saturday without drawing attention from her parents and a little brother who seemed to stick his nose into everybody's business. Beside all that, what possible reason could she use to leave the house just before the noon meal, dressed for church. It was hopeless. Lunch with Murdoch was truly out of the question.

After a few deep breaths, she decided to tell Murdoch she wouldn't be able to meet him. She was sure the Ramsay's would have a telephone. She'd tell her parents she was going for a walk and call Murdoch from Mr. Martin's store. But who might answer? What if they asked for my name and why was I calling? Murdoch might not be home. She collapsed onto the bed. The day was ruined and it was only seven o'clock in the morning!

Resigned to her fate and feeling terribly sorry for herself, Marie joined the family for breakfast. She pushed her food around the plate so often it caught her mother's attention.

"Is something the matter, dear?"

"No, Mama. Just a poor sleep."

Gizele LeBlanc sipped her tea then looked at Marie.

"Do you remember Adolphus Dupont from church?"

"No." She feigned interest, a concerned look on her face. "Should I?"

"Probably not. He was eighty-nine and ill for some time. His funeral is later this morning. Since you don't remember him, I see no reason why you need to attend the mass. I've arranged for Leo to play with one of his school friends."

Marie dropped her hands onto her lap, crossed her fingers and casually asked. "When is the mass?"

"Eleven-thirty followed by the burial and a light lunch in the church rectory. Could you bring Leo home by two-o'clock?"

Marie answered offhandedly, "I can." But her heart was flying. Suddenly breakfast tasted much better.

Marie had never eaten lunch at the fancy restaurant near the Public Gardens or any fancy restaurant for that matter. She was positive none of her friends had either, so she had no fear of being tattled on by green eyed young women from church. She'd have to rely on the basic table manners her parents taught her at their kitchen table. Straight away, she imagined herself dropping food in her lap and being the centre of a grand faux pas. Perhaps she should stay home and make her excuse to Murdoch on Monday morning. You're not a coward, she said to herself then plucked up her courage and continued to get ready.

So used to wearing a long dark skirt with a white blouse for work, Marie was quite excited to wear her new day dress. Well, it was really her only decent day dress.

Fashionable women were showing their ankles. Marie had convinced Mama to make her just such a dress for special occasions. Her mother called it the 'too short' dress but reluctantly complied.

Marie considered lunch with Murdoch a special occasion. She was thrilled with the turquoise cotton day dress with lace collar and cuffs. The three quarter length sleeves were perfect to display her silver bracelet from Aunt Emma. The fear of dropping food flashed through her mind, again. “Stop it”, she said aloud. “Stop it. Right now”.

Younger women were wearing smaller hats with dresses or none at all. Before leaving the upstairs, Marie borrowed a hair comb from her mother’s dresser. It wasn’t fancy but would replace her church hat.

Ready to leave the house, Marie had a last minute moment of weakness. *What if someone from church sees me*? Then she remembered most of them would be attending the funeral. She glanced at herself in the small mirror near the front door then stepped outside, headed toward the Public Gardens.

By the time Marie reached the Gardens her face was flushed with excitement. She wished she’d put a fan in her reticule. Seeing Murdoch across the street, she waved excitedly and almost stepped in front of a passing motor car.

“Well aren’t you all dressed up, Miss LeBlanc.”

Marie frowned. “Did you think I’d wear my office clothes?” She knew instantly she’d sounded snippy and reminded herself to not be so sharp with her tongue.

“I just meant you look lovely in that blue dress. I like it. And no hat with feathers all over it. How modern of you.”

Marie smiled. If he only knew I didn’t have a good enough hat to wear.

“Take my arm, Miss LeBlanc. The restaurant is mere minutes away. I like their desserts.”

“So you have a sweet tooth?”

“I do, especially for jam roly-poly. And you?”

“I like roly-poly but love Plum Pudding at Christmas.”

Murdoch curled up his nose as if a bad smell had passed under it. "Not for me."

"Why?" She remembered to respond in an agreeable tone.

"All those dried out pieces of fruit boiled in a cloth bag. Dreadful. And it leaves a bad taste in my mouth."

"You haven't tasted my mother's pudding. It would change your mind."

"Then we have at least one special event during the Christmas season. I'll try your mother's pudding."

He'd gotten the better of her. Marie was tongue tied. But worse, he'd just invited himself to her home for Christmas pudding!

"Here we are." Murdoch opened the door for Marie.

Marie's feet moved but her mind was locked on a vision of Murdoch in her modest family home, eating Christmas dinner in their kitchen.

***

As Marie and Murdoch were being seated for lunch, Nellie Quinn and Rose Ramsay were shopping at Martin's Dry Goods Store. Each of the girls had a small allowance. Rose had a penchant for hair ribbons and Nellie, drawing paper and pencils.

Nellie's drawing talent was exceptional and her ability to remember details was astonishing. On her last visit to the store she brought Martin his picture. The likeness was remarkable. He framed her work and hung it on the wall behind the counter where everyone could see Nellie's remarkable talent.

Knowing Nellie's gift, Angus always had a good supply of quality drawing paper and pencils on hand. He suspected she couldn't always afford art supplies so he made sure he was the one tallying up her bill and reducing it by fifty percent.

“Thank you, Mr. Martin. You have the best prices in town.” Then she spun around to look out the front door.

“Rose’s mother is treating us to a fancy lunch today.” Then she spun back to face Angus. “After lunch we are going to Rose’s house to draw.”

“That sounds like a perfect day for two young ladies. Where are your fancy hats for this fancy restaurant?”

Both girls giggled then Rose looked at Angus.

“Big fancy hats at lunch are going out of style. Besides, we are at war. This isn’t the time for showing off.” She seriously studied Angus’s face. “I heard my mother say that this morning.”

Angus smiled. “And she’s correct.”

Marie had been so wrapped up in her manoeuvres to keep her lunch a secret from her family, she’d totally forgotten to consider what to talk about with Murdoch. If she prattled on like some ninny, their first lunch would be their last. Even the plum pudding would be out of the question, which for a moment certainly sounded like a good idea. Murdoch wore expensive clothes and his father had a car so they were probably wealthy. She’d never seen the Ramsay family in her church. Now that she knew not to talk about money or religion, the rest should be easier.

A middle aged woman wearing a print dress and crisp white apron greeted Murdoch. “Good afternoon, sir. May I show you to a table?”

“Certainly. One away from the middle of the room would be preferred.”

“Follow me. I believe we have an alcove table for two open. I will bring your tea while you look at the menu. Earl Grey?”

Murdoch glanced toward Marie. “Acceptable?”

"Lovely." So far, so good, she thought.

Settled in with tea and sandwiches, Murdoch spoke first. "Tell me more about your family."

Marie replied, explaining Leo could be a charmer some of the time. "You know my father is a night watchman. My mother works two days a week at a bank. And your family?"

Murdoch spoke about Rose, her love of crafts and reading.

"She's quite the chatter box but don't presume she's not listening to everything adults say."

It was clear to Marie, Murdoch adored his little sister.

"And your parents?"

"My mother is very busy doing good deeds, as they say. She is a great mother and a kind person. I always counted on her support growing up." He paused and smiled. "I love my mother." He stopped talking, clearly a bit embarrassed by his admission.

Marie waited for Murdoch to mention his father. When he didn't, she opened her mouth to ask but let the moment pass.

"Your father's a night watchman. What exactly does he do?"

"He works for the city home and keeps an eye out for trouble overnight. Most of the time it's quiet but when there's trouble, it's usually big trouble." She risked the question. "And your father?"

Murdoch hesitated. "He spends most of his time at the hospital. He's a surgeon." He lowered his eyes, picked up his cup. "He's a serious man."

Marie sipped her tea. *Murdoch and his father seem to be on unfriendly terms.* "He has serious work, has to care for people who go to the hospital."

She noted Murdoch dropped the topic of his father.

"Let me ask you a question. Do your parents have a plan for your life?"

Marie let the question hang in the air. "That's rather difficult to answer." *He already knows I clash with my mother over my independent opinions.*

"They want me to be responsible, have a job, they ask about my work." She left the part about religion out.

"See, that's where my father's different. I think he believes I'm not ambitious enough." He glanced out the window. "He never asks about my work with Mr. Davis."

Marie couldn't think of an answer for that.

Murdoch sensed her reluctance to comment. "You're not saying something. What is it?"

"You said, 'I think'. Did your father ever say you're not ambitious enough?"

Murdoch sighed. "No, but he implies it quite a lot, actually." He passed Marie the dessert tray.

"Maybe you need to ask him. I imagine he has dreams for you."

"They're likely his dreams, not mine."

"So what is your dream? Have you told him your dream? By the way, I heard very little about your mother's thoughts about your future."

Murdoch glanced toward the door. "Well, get prepared to meet my mother and sister. They just entered the restaurant." He placed his napkin on the table and stood.

"Mama, how lovely to see you here. Hello Rose, Nellie. I'd like all of you to meet my friend from work, Marie LeBlanc."

Marie was terribly impressed with Murdoch's apparent ease at the sight of his mother. She wished she felt the same. But then, he had nothing to hide. She stood, smiled and shook hands with Murdoch's mother and the girls.

Murdoch took his mother's hand. "We're having a lively discussion about parents."

Marie moved back a step to place her hand on the top wrung of her chair. *Good grief, what else is he about to say?*

Rose broke the moment. “Is Marie your very special friend, Murdoch?” She smiled and turned her head toward Marie, her braids swinging across the back of her dress.

“Rose, that is not an appropriate question to ask. You have embarrassed Murdoch and Marie. Please apologize.”

“I’m sorry.”

“Nice to meet you Marie. Girls, we must find our table and leave Marie and Murdoch to their lunch.”

“Lovely to meet you as well, Mrs. Ramsay, Rose, Nellie.”

Seated, Murdoch asked, “Where were we? Ah yes, my dream. I don’t have one.”

Marie stared at him, ignoring his answer. “Are you not in the least bit anxious about what just happened?”

Murdoch frowned and dropped his head for a moment. “Why would I be anxious?” He shrugged. “We’re having lunch. My mother came to the same restaurant. Now, where were we? More tea?”

Marie nodded then continued. “But your mother saw you at lunch with me!”

“It’s 1917. We’re eating together in public, in broad daylight, not caught eloping or something else.”

Marie blushed. “I think you’re a bit naive about relationships between men and women, even if it is 1917.” She thought about shutting up but only for a moment. “I didn’t tell my parents where I was going. They’d be stunned to see me here with you.”

“Well then, you simply have to let them know before they might see us together the next time.”

“Speaking of time, what time is it?’

“Almost one-thirty.”

“Oh, goodness. Mama asked me to take Leo home from his friend’s house at two o’clock. I need to leave.”

“And we will. We’ve finished lunch. I’ll walk to the Gardens with you. You’ll have plenty of time to get Leo home.”

***

The LeBlanc family was enjoying a pleasant evening meal when Leo looked at his mother. "Marie wore a fancy dress today, Mama. It's not Sunday."

"Leo, please don't talk with your mouth full. Swallow, then tell me what you're talking about."

Leo stuck his tongue out toward Marie. "She was wearing a fancy dress when she came to Freddie's house for me."

"I'm sure your sister had a good reason to wear a pretty dress today. Tattling on someone is not nice and neither is sticking your tongue out at your sister, young man. Apologize to Marie then finish your supper."

Marie went to bed fearing the 'fancy dress' conversation was not finished.

***

Corbin changed his tie three times then picked up the first one, put it on and went downstairs.

"I will be out for the evening, Mrs. Williams."

"Enjoy the evening, sir. Daisy was relieved to hear this news. *I hope he met someone. He's 'way too young to be alone.*

***

On the train home to Halifax Jo warned Corbin that she had a dog but when he rang the doorbell, the scrabbling sound of dog's feet sounded like a pack of dogs. Surprisingly, there was no barking but he heard Jo say, "Sit. Stay."

Jo greeted Corbin wearing a striking red and white striped dress with a low-cut square neckline. Her blonde hair was loosely gathered into a bun at the nape of her neck. The mellow scent of lavender lingered in the air.

"Hello, Corbin. Come in. I see we are a matched set this evening."

Corbin looked down at his red and white striped tie, then laughed.

"This big, hairy fella is Patch." She looked down. "Patch, welcome Corbin."

The biggest dog Corbin had ever seen raised a large paw toward him. His name obviously came from the large, irregular black patch around his left eye. The rest of his body was a mix of tan and black.

"Good evening, Patch. Pleased to meet you."

With the formalities over, all three walked into a sizable sitting room with a stone fireplace. Patch sauntered across the room and curled up in front of the fire, his work for the evening done.

Corbin looked left and right then smiled. "I'm pretty sure you made some changes to this house."

"You're right. I don't like boxes so I opened it all up on this side."

To the far left, a high-ceiling orangery with several potted fruit trees opened onto a back garden. An easel draped in a cloth stood in one corner. The immediate left was clearly Jo's writing space. A substantial jumble of books sat on one end of a large writing desk, sharing the space with a tall stack of writing paper and a typewriter, all of which overlooked the side garden window. To the right of the sitting room, multiple shelves of books extended to the ceiling on both sides of a bay window. Its' stained glass sections were spectacular. Fuelled by the late evening sun, radiant reds, greens, yellows and blues spilled across the wooden floor.

"You've made amazing changes in this home. It is stunning."

"Thank you. It has taken two years. I'm more than happy to be finished."

"So you've been in Halifax for two years?"

Jo nodded. "I have. I lived in Truro for a few years after I left England." She pointed toward the fireplace area. "Choose a seat. I'll open a bottle of red. I presume you drink wine and like red?"

"I do."

Initially, Corbin felt at ease sharing a meal with this most intriguing woman. But as the evening wore on, he realized Jo was asking all the questions, particularly about his life and sharing very little about herself. When he'd asked about her childhood in England, she laughed easily and dismissed it as a typical English upbringing, a nanny, a pony and days at the seaside.

"Whatever possessed you to move to Canada?"

"My brother, Malcolm. He loved the open countryside and friendly people. I decided to escape London in early 1912 and here I am." She paused. "My parents are deceased."

"That must have been a difficult decision."

She shrugged. "Not really. I wanted a new adventure, make new friends."

"So you met Ruby in Truro?"

"Yes. She was a good friend. I loved her dearly." She picked up her wine glass.

Corbin noticed the past tense of her friendship with Ruby.

"Bill's death is such a devastating blow to her. I suggested she move in with me. Do you think that would work?" She laughed out loud. "Two independent-minded women might be a disaster though." She chuckled. "Then there would be Marmalade and Patch."

"And Patch. What's his story?"

Patch opened his eyes and looked at Corbin then his mistress.

"He's from a litter of pups on a farm outside Truro. He's a mix of shepherd and collie. Both parents are large and he was the biggest pup of the bunch. He's a dear boy, aren't you, big fella." She hesitated. "I thought his size might come in handy."

The word 'escape' and her comment about Patch coming in handy struck Corbin as a bit unusual but he chose not to question it. Time would eventually reveal the reason.

They spent the remainder of the evening discussing local politics, the war, social events and Jo's new book in progress.

***

Saturday evening in Yarmouth, Alex Wallace was welcomed into the Simmons home by the maid. She took his coat and hat, then announced his presence at the sitting room double doors.

Walter Simmons rose to shake Alex's hand then introduced his plain but pleasant looking wife Sadie, who remained seated but acknowledged his presence with a nod and "Good evening".

Alex felt Sadie's calculated gaze. He'd have to be cautious around her. He turned his attention toward a dark haired young woman who was seated in a crimson red velvet Queen Anne chair on one side of the blazing fireplace. A matching vacant chair sat on the other. He was instantly intrigued by this beauty, his new conquest.

"Have a seat, Alexander." Walter pointed toward the empty Queen Anne.

"May I introduce our daughter Lily. Lily, this fine gentleman is Alexander Ward recently arrived from...."

"Ontario. Delighted to meet you, Miss Simmons. May I call you Lily?"

"Most certainly, Alexander." She thrust her upper body forward, her dark eyes cast a sultry gaze over Alex's face.

Alex sighed. He'd just died and gone to heaven. "Call me Alex."

CHAPTER ELEVEN

SUNDAY, OCTOBER 28

After a long hunt, Walter Simmons finally captured the ideal partner for his family business venture. Alex Ward had money and was looking for a business opportunity. Walter could barely believe his good fortune. He refilled his daughter's coffee cup and posed a delicate question. "How long will you require, my dear?"

Lily struck an innocent pose. "I presume you are talking about my close friendship with Alex, yes?"

Walter nodded.

"Two weeks at most, Papa. I don't want to appear desperate." She took a quick glance at her mother and received a stern glare in return.

Walter ignored his wife's disapproval. "Will you need a larger clothing allowance?"

"No, Papa. Alex hasn't seen any of my gowns or day dresses." She smiled, then turned toward her mother. "You are quiet, Mama. Is there something troubling you?"

Sadie Simmons sat back in her chair and exhaled heavily. "You know I have, Lily. Truthfully, I find this idea unnecessary and risky, not to mention Lily's unseemly behaviour. We are not poor, Walter." Her stare toward him became more fierce. "The current ship trade provides us with more than sufficient money."

Walter reached across the table and patted Sadie's hand. She flinched. "My dear wife, one never has too much money." He withdrew his hand and picked up his coffee cup. "And beside that, life has become dull in this town. The same people, the same parties. And don't forget, Lily needs something to occupy her time until she can return to Charlottetown."

Sadie looked from her husband to her daughter and then back to Walter. "I thought we agreed to never mention that dreadful episode from last year." Then turning to Lily, "I'm of a mind to not allow you to visit Prince Edward Island, ever again."

Lily was unmoved by her mother's tone and accompanying look, knowing she and her father were of the same mind about living life to the fullest. She was sure she could charm her way out of any muddle just as she did in Charlottetown. She smiled to herself and the titillation of that very evening rushed back.

Lily and her mother were visiting Lily's grandparents in Prince Edward Island when a neighbour, Valerie Elliott struck up a friendship with Lily. The two young women soon began daily walks around the city, including the harbour area. It was a rough and tumble neighbourhood but both had a wild streak and wanted to have some 'excitement', as Valerie called it.

"Do you like liquor, Lily?"

"I do."

That was a lie. At sixteen Lily drank a juice glass of scotch while her parents were out of the house. She then spent the remainder of the evening in bed, her head hanging over a bowl.

"Well, we certainly could have some excitement at a blind pig."

Lily was intrigued. "Blind pig?"

"It's an illegal drinking hole. The rum runners use boats to get the liquor from St Pierre and Miquelon. The police are on the look out for illegal drinking."

Lily knew her grandparents went to bed early but her mother would be a problem. “Sounds like a perfect evening but my mother...”

“Tell your mother you want to stay a few days longer. You’ll have the time of your life. The liquor is pretty cheap and there’s plenty of young men for flirting.”

Two days later, while Sadie Simmons was on the train from Charlottetown to Halifax, Lily and Valerie made plans for the evening out.

“Meet me outside at ten. Stand behind the bushes so nobody can see you.”

Valerie Elliott looked and dressed much older than her eighteen years so she and twenty-year old Lily easily entered the illegal drinking establishment a block off the harbour.

By midnight, Lily felt light headed but steady enough to walk to the bar. She wanted to get away from Elmer who insisted she needed someone to walk her home. As she turned around to beckon Valerie to the bar, the door burst open.

“Everyone, stay where you are. All of you are under arrest for violating the PEI Prohibition Act of 1900.”

While three policemen rushed into the room, Lily inched along the wall toward the open door. Outside, she stepped into the arms of the fourth policeman.

“Stand still, Miss. Someone like you is exactly why we all don’t go inside.”

“Take your hands off me. Don’t you know who I am?”

Without letting her go, the officer laughed. “I most certainly do. You are a person frequenting an illegal public house and will now find yourself in jail tonight then court tomorrow. Name and address, please.”

Lilly smiled disarmingly. Not wanting the officer to smell her breath, she turned her head to the side and raised her hand to her mouth as she spoke. “My dear fellow, my name is Maddy

Ellsworth. I am the niece of your premier. I'm here visiting my family and stepped inside this building to look for my cousin. I assure you I had no idea this building was a drinking spot." She gently tapped his hand. "I doubt you want to be the one whose name is attached to my arrest, sir. Your police work might be ended."

"Maddy Ellsworth, you say. And where are you from?"

"Halifax, sir. My mother is the sister of your premier. Mama would be very upset with you should I find myself in jail." Lily then began to weep. "I beg of you, don't embarrass your premier and his family by making an error in judgment."

"Miss Ellsworth, I suggest you pack you bags and leave the city tomorrow, early."

"Thank you, sir. Thank you. I will heed your warning." She walked down the street.

Out of ear shot, Lily giggled. Then she thought about Valerie. *Oh, my God. She's probably been arrested. I better hide close by to see if she comes out in handcuffs.*

"Lily, can you hear me?"

"Yes." Lily twirled in the middle of the street, almost falling over her own feet. "Where are you?"

"Behind the lilac tree across the road. I ran out the back door before they caught me."

"Don't come out. I'll meet you at the next street crossing."

Charlottetown was a close call but so much fun. Lily's thoughts returned to the present. She didn't have time to dwell on that excitement. It was time for the new business plan and to ensure Alex steps into the trap. Her mother was speaking.

"I like my life here, Walter. Must we upset everything for the sake of money?"

"My dear, life here is tedious. Risk is exciting. We..."

"Our good name is more important than excitement. We could lose everything or go to jail."

Lily spoke up to support her father's side of the argument. "They'd have to catch us first, Mama."

Sadie Simmons kept her worries to herself while her husband and daughter planned social opportunities to pull Alex Ward into their lives. When they began to talk about the damnable scheme they were putting together, she poured a cup of coffee and went to the sitting room. Glancing at her basket of unread books, she debated between Arthur Conan Doyle and LM Montgomery. While *The Valley of Fear* was a perfect fit for the day, Sadie needed a book to lighten her mood. *Anne of the Island* it would be.

The Simmons family was far more wealthy than Alex expected and they were not in the least bit slow-witted. He would have to plan carefully, not push his idea too soon nor pressure them for a decision. When Lily's father essentially offered up his daughter, he could hardly believe his good fortune. She would be the bonus in this business deal.

Billie Stewart quickly changed out of her church dress and bounced down the stairs, heading for the door, then on to the Halifax harbour.

"See you later, Mama. I'm going for a walk with my friend."

"Not today, dear. You can't."

Billie tried to keep the anger out of her voice. "What do you mean, I can't?"

Violet Stewart's reply took a firm tone. "We've planned a small social this afternoon with a few neighbours from church. I expect you to be home to join us and meet other young people."

Billie opened her mouth to object but was interrupted.

"If this friend is Frank Murphy, we've been through this before."

"What you mean is, 'Frank is not a Protestant so I can't see him.' Am I right?"

Violet believes she has a perfectly good reason to reject Frank as a suitable suitor. Billie, christened Wilhelmina is six years younger than Frank but more importantly, he attends the wrong church.

"I've certainly never seen him in our church."

Billie crossed her arms. "That's because he doesn't go to any church."

"That's hardly a character reference, Wilhelmina."

Hoping to cool the mushrooming squabble, Cecil Stewart walked from the sitting room to the kitchen.

"What your mother is trying to say is this fellow may not have much in common with you. I've forgotten, what does he do for a living?"

"He works on the wharf near Pier 6. He has lots of factory experience, worked for a few factories since..."

Violet cut her off. "Sounds shiftless to me. Not a good omen for the future."

"He wants to be in the office one day."

Cecil carried on. "That sounds like a worthwhile goal. Is Frank expecting to see you this afternoon?"

"No, Papa. I was going to surprise him. He's usually around the wharf on Sunday afternoons and after work."

"So can we do a bit of give and take about this afternoon?"

Billie squinted at her father. "Maybe." She was used to his ways and liked how he could settle things so nobody felt cheated.

"Give us a few hours, be sociable with everyone and tomorrow, you can meet Frank after work at the wharf. Could you do that?"

Billie stared at the floor. "All right, for you Papa."

"Thank you, my dear. Lots of new people in town. You never know, there might be someone just as interesting as Frank on our street."

***

Ella and Charles sat quietly at the lunch table until Murdoch went to the wharf and Rose went upstairs to read.

The letter from Yarmouth had given her some respite from Alex and time to quiz Charles about his plan to be a politician and remind him of the unprofessional nurse. She was pretty sure Lois Fillmore was back in Halifax. She chuckled to herself and thought how having one's own money and a new-found dash of spunk changed one's perspective. She acknowledged Alex was her nemesis and she would have to deal with him. Charles, however, was someone in need of a good talking to and a correction in his cavalier attitude toward his own behaviour. Their usual companionable silence was about to end.

"I'm not a fool, Charles. This nurse business we discussed earlier must end. When exactly are you going to get rid of her?"

Charles thought this had been settled days ago. He sputtered coffee across the table.

Ella took advantage of her position. "I'm not a screamer Charles and I do not need an answer from you this minute. However, I suggest a swift dismissal of that woman so you can hold onto your family and have any hope of representing your neighbours in the government of this province."

Despite the anger Charles was harbouring, his face was calm. He waited, reading Ella's face. Retreat was her usual reaction, a bit of bluster followed by a sigh, then acceptance of her role in the marriage. Today her face looked different. She was committed, determined. He remained silent.

"I have a personal view about the possibility of your success in politics, Charles. That view is not one of optimism but I will leave my reasoning for another day. Right now, I suggest you retire to your study and devote your time to finding an answer to my earlier question. I'm going to visit Mable Cameron this afternoon. Mable always has the latest social happenings and stories to share. I find them most enlightening." She smiled knowingly, gave him a quick nod and left the room.

Gisele LeBlanc was at odds with herself about Marie and the fancy dress. Her curiosity was certainly piqued but she really disliked questioning a twenty-year old woman about where she was in the middle of the day wearing a pretty dress. She told herself to forget it and spend her time repairing the faulty relationship she had with her daughter. She felt better immediately.

Hugh Andrews avoided contact with the Halifax police, not wanting them to know he was in town. This move left him with no useful information, except that Bill's murder had occurred on Citadel Hill. To get some understanding of the murder, he spent Sunday lunch and early afternoon preparing for his visit to the Hill.

Feigning little knowledge about the Citadel over lunch, he asked the locals about the Hill. He heard about its' long history and then its' current use. Eleven years had passed since the British handed over control of Halifax's defences to the Canadian Government. The Citadel was now the command centre for the military with stores of ammunition and the army barracks.

When Hugh eased the conversation into the recent murder on the Hill, one man eyed him up.

"You a newspaper man looking for a story?"

Hugh replied 'no', rationalizing his real reason was Bill, not a story.

From that point on, the murder became the topic of interest. Hugh kept quiet. He heard a spy working on a ship did it and got away and the police had interviewed a local man who worked on the wharf. A young man who worked on the wharf thought the man's name was Fred or Frank something. A man travelling on the Truro-bound train the morning after Bill's murder said the police were looking for someone at the station. A second man spoke up.

"I saw the police that morning too. It was miserable weather, rain kept most people in the station until the last minute." He chuckled. "One young fella stayed under the eave of the storage shed right up until the end. An odd idea, if you ask me. Then he pushed himself into the middle of the boarding line. A strange fella, if 'ya ask me."

Hugh held his tongue, not wanting to sound too eager by asking a question about the pushy fella.

Truro-bound man solved Hugh's curiosity for him. "I didn't see you on the train that morning, Edgar."

"Well, of course 'ya didn't. I was on my way to Yarmouth to visit my oldest girl, Fiona."

It was a good start but not a great one. Hugh debated with himself. *What the hell, ask the question.*

"The young fella. Anything stand out about him, aside from being pushy?"

Edgar leaned back in his chair. "You sure you're not a policeman?"

"No, a writer. I'm thinking about writing a book about the Citadel."

"Fair hair, blue eyes, a wary look about him, never spoke, kept his head down. I remember him 'cause everybody else was talking about the rain, being soaked to the skin. Not him."

Armed with a bit of local knowledge, Hugh slowly walked up the hill toward the Citadel. He frequently sauntered off the path to get a feel for the place and a sense of how and where the murder might have taken place. Half an hour later he arrived at the Citadel's entrance, stood with his back to it and gazed upon the city of Halifax, its harbour filled with ships. He experienced a disappointing moment of clarity about the reality of finding Bill's killer and scolded himself out loud for such high hopes on day one. "Don't be so daft."

"Can I help you, sir?"

Hugh turned about and found himself staring at a khaki field uniform and a rifle.

The second asking took on a demanding tone. "Can I help you, sir?"

Hugh smiled. "Ahh, yes. I'm looking into the death that occurred on the Hill about a week or so ago. You didn't happen to be on duty at the time, did you?"

"Your name, sir?"

"Hugh Andrews."

"Are you with the Halifax Police, Mr. Andrews?"

"No."

"I'm afraid I cannot help you. Would you like to speak with the Officer on Duty, sir?"

"Not today but thank you."

"Very well. Have a good day, sir."

Twenty odd yards down the path he muttered, "Damn and blast."

CHAPTER TWELVE

MONDAY, OCTOBER 29

Billie Stewart got up early, ate breakfast before her parents came to the kitchen then left a note saying she would see them in time for the evening meal.

Violet Stewart stood at the kitchen table staring at the piece of paper, her lips pressed tight together.

"Look at this note, Cecil. She's run off just to avoid talking about the lovely social with the neighbours yesterday. She's become very contrary." She shook her head. "So unlike Sally."

"Now now, dear. We should be happy she enjoys her work with Angus. He likely needed her early today. Probably has a big delivery to unpack before he opens the store."

"Of course I'm happy she's happy." Violet shook her head. "It's just that darn Frank Murphy. I'm sure she'll be seeing him after work today. We should forbid her from seeing him."

Cecil Stewart felt his main job in the family at the moment was to keep some kind of peace until Billie grew tired of Frank or he of her. He had no intention of making an enemy of his daughter. He ran his hand over his paisley tie. "What do you think of my new tie?" He poured Violet a cup of tea. "We've talked about this before, dear. Forbidding her to see Frank will only make him more interesting. By the way, I'll be a bit late getting home today. The boss called a late afternoon sales meeting and wants the finance department figures. What are you doing today?"

"Sally wants a new kitchen table so I'm going to look after the baby this afternoon. I'll invite them over to eat with us. Nothing special. Chicken stew and a lemon pie. Maybe Billie'll behave with her older sister here."

***

Marie and Murdoch expected Mr. Davis would be subdued, considering he'd just attended the funeral of a good friend. But looks can be so deceiving.

Corbin's 'good morning' was followed by a smile then, "Great work while I was away, you two."

In the privacy of his office Corbin's emotions were very different. He ignored the mug of tea Marie gave him and dropped his head into his hands. Bill's death stirred up thoughts about his own future. He berated himself for being absent in his friend's life and instead, chased financial success. Bill's prediction echoed in his head. 'You'll be an old bachelor with pots of money and nothing else'. The same old worries came roaring back. He felt himself falling deeper into the darkness of loneliness. His thoughts drifted into the hinterland of his mind. It was a dark, unhappy place. He did not want to be there so stood up and paced the room. Fond memories of family and friends as a child and young boy came to mind. Then thoughts of dinner with Jo brightened his mood. They spoke of common interests, music and the theatre. Jo might be a friend but nothing more. She'd made that clear. She was perfectly happy living alone. At one point, she said, 'I'm happy not being defined by other people.' It was time to focus on work. He pushed his personal worries from his thoughts and went to Murdoch's desk.

"Let's go to the factory floor, Murdoch. I need a change of scene."

"Right you are, sir."

"Thank you for doing an excellent job while I was away."

"Thank you. I actually enjoyed learning more about how the factory operates. The men and women were very helpful."

"That is good to know."

The morning mail arrived while Corbin and Murdoch were in the factory. Marie noticed one envelope addressed to Murdoch without a return address. The post office stamp from Yarmouth was clearly visible. She presumed it was from the mystery caller and dropped it in her desk drawer with no intention of upsetting Murdoch in the middle of the morning. *God knows what it says. I'll give it to him at noon or at the end of the day.* As the office clock ticked toward noon, Marie changed her mind. She would keep the letter until the end of day unless Murdoch mentioned it.

At closing time Marie put the letter in her pocket and suggested to Murdoch they meet outside the office before going home. Murdoch had a puzzled look on his face but Marie ignored it. Instead she took hold of his hand and pulled him toward the door.

"Murdoch and I are leaving now. Have a good evening, Mr. Davis."

"You as well." Corbin walked to the window overlooking the harbour. *Lucky them. No problems.*

Marie walked toward the side of the office building then pulled the envelope from her pocket.

"Damn. It did arrive." Murdoch reached for the envelope.

"It could be a bad-tempered customer. Do you want me to stay or go?"

"Stay, of course. I have no secrets. You know them all. I drink and gamble. But not lately, thanks to you."

Marie's heart beat a little faster.

"Let's see what it says." He read aloud.

Murdoch, Your family ruined my life and now I'm going to ruin yours. You think your family is perfect but you are wrong, very wrong. Your family has a secret and I know what it is. Don't worry Murdoch, you are not the one I intend to destroy first. Don't try to find me. I'm very good at hiding. In fact, I'm excellent at the game of hide and seek. This is such fun.

Murdoch lifted his head, his eyes met Marie's. He began pacing back and forth, his breaths quick and frequent.

Marie reached out and grabbed Murdoch's hand as he paced in front of her for the third time. He stopped, exhaled slowly.

"We can't put this right, Murdoch."

"I know." He took a few slow breaths, kept holding Marie's hand. "I'm sure my father has caused this, whatever it is. He's already had one threat by the father of a young patient. I'll speak with Mama."

As Corbin prepared to get into his car, he noticed Murdoch and Marie in deep conversation. He smiled, wished he was younger, not facing a future alone.

Ella noticed everyone except Murdoch appeared to be enjoying dinner. After a few bites he would glance out the window.

"Are you expecting a visitor, Murdoch?"

"No, just thinking."

"You seem unusually quiet this evening. Is there a problem at work?"

"No, Mama."

Rose spoke up. "I bet he's thinking about Marie."

"Who's Marie?" Charles stared at Murdoch looking more annoyed than curious.

Before Ella or Murdoch could reply, Rose had the answer. "She's Murdoch's special friend. We met her at lunch, didn't we Mama?"

"Yes, we did." Then she studied Rose's face. "And what have I told you about tittle-tattle?"

"Don't tell stories about other people."

"Exactly. If you talk about others, they will talk about you."

Murdoch dropped his head, covered a grin with his hand. *She's so charming. How could anyone be annoyed with her?*

Charles was oblivious to Rose and Ella's interaction. It was nomination night and he also needed to act on Ella's demand about Lois.

"I'm sorry to rush away but this is election night for me. I will be home late. Wish me luck."

Rose jumped up from the table to hug her father. "I hope you win, Papa." She looked at her mother. "May I be excused?"

"Yes, dear."

Murdoch saluted toward his father. "Best of luck, father."

"Thank you."

With his father out of the house, Murdoch was eager to speak with his mother about the mystery letter. He'd concluded his father was the only target and he and Mama could decide on a course of action in short order. He turned toward Ella.

"May I have a few words with you later?"

"Absolutely, dear." *It's about Marie.* She hid her smile by lifting a water glass to her lips.

Later, with Rose in bed, Ella and Murdoch went into the sitting room. Murdoch closed the door and without a word, handed the envelope to his mother. He went to the liquor cabinet and poured two drinks.

"You may want brandy for this, Mama."

Ella sat in an arm chair on one side of the fireplace, Murdoch on the other. He kept his eyes on his mother's face. She was staring at the envelope. Without lifting her eyes, she said, "This letter came from Yarmouth."

Murdoch nodded but remained silent, expecting his mother to read the letter but she did not. He waited impatiently, finished his drink.

Ella frowned. "Why was this letter sent to you?"

Murdoch was baffled. She made it sound like she was actually expecting this letter. He answered her question anyway.

"Do you remember my story a few days ago about the man who called me at the office?"

She nodded. "Yes, I recall it. At the time it seemed harmless."

Again, Murdoch waited for some meaningful particulars about the envelope.

"I think you should read the letter. Then we can talk."

Ella opened the letter and continued to stare at it much longer than Murdoch expected. She appeared to be in shock, not that he knew much about shock.

"Are you feeling unwell, Mama?"

"It's a distressing letter."

Murdoch couldn't believe his ears. "Distressing?" He moved his chair to sit in front of his mother.

"Sip your brandy, Mama. This person sounds like a mad man who intends to destroy us."

Ella had no doubt about who wrote the letter but she remained silent.

"Maybe it's that man from the hospital. Remember him? His child died." Murdoch looked directly into his mother's eyes. "Papa is the most likely victim. We'll have to give him the letter when he gets home."

Ella was cornered at the edge of a precipice and in great need of a believable answer. To speak the truth would destroy her family at once. A few words close to the truth would have to suffice.

“I don’t think handing this letter to your father when he gets home is our best idea, dear. If this mad man is in Yarmouth we likely have a day or two to plan.”

Murdoch nodded his acceptance of the idea, although he longed for an explanation of the family secret.

Ella sighed with relief. *Well, the election proved to be at least somewhat helpful.*

“The letter came to you but I will deal with it.”

As Ella was talking, Ed Quinn came to mind. She was not prepared to see the police just yet, even though her own behaviour matched that of Charles’. *Infidelity is infidelity.*

Murdoch sighed. “We don’t even know who this is, so the police can’t help.”

“I know someone who might be able to help. I will talk to him tomorrow.”

“Please don’t do that. Marie’s father is a night watchman. We could hire him to follow Papa, look out for him.”

“That is a very good idea, dear. Let me talk to your father in the morning.”

Hugh accepted his swift dismissal at the Citadel as incentive to do better. After all, Sunday was his first full day of rooting out bits and bobs of information about Bill’s murder. Today was a new day and any opinion or observation by the locals was something worthy of examination. All he wanted was to get two or three names or stories to widen his circle of contacts. Then things would take off.

After breakfast, he settled down on a bench near Pier 6 with the morning paper. The pier was a busy place with no end of possible opportunities to overhear the scuttlebutt. He chuckled at his use of the word 'scuttlebutt' on the wharf. Sailors on board a ship came by the word honestly as they met at the 'watterbutt' for a drink and to share stories.

Just before noon a middle-age woman wearing a shabby print housedress and a blue wool sweater stretched out of shape dropped heavily onto the opposite end of Hugh's bench.

She wiped her rough hands on a soiled apron then, staring straight ahead said, "Hope you're havin' a good day, sir. I'm sure as hell not."

"I'm sorry to hear that, ma'am."

"When you got a bossy boss days ain't good." She crossed her arms, leaned back against the bench, her fists clenched.

"I imagine not."

"I ain't supposed ta talk ta the police about nothin'. That ain't right."

"Well, if you saw something bad happen, the police would want to know."

"There 'ya are. That's what I said ta the boss. Them police fellas gotta know things. We can't let the bad fellas get off. Mrs. Bossy keeps tellin' me to keep what I know to meself."

Hugh hesitated. Her story sounded interesting, probably nothing to do with Bill but curious never the less. He took a moment to create a casual question but the woman spoke first.

"I saw a fella right abouts here that very night. It were the same place that young woman was kilt."

"A woman was killed here?"

"Right, sir. Kilt here she was."

"Why would your boss not want you to talk to the police?"

"She runs a boardin' house. Thinks havin' the police around is bad for business."

Hugh nodded. “I understand that.”

The angry woman banged the arm of the bench and stared at Hugh. “Do ya now! It were a whole hell of a lot worse for that young woman. She’s dead! You don’t think I should talk to the police? You’re as bad as my boss. Think I’ll be leavin’ now.” She stood up.

“Please sit down. I agree with you.” Hugh waited until she stopped fussing with her apron. “My name is Hugh.”

“Pleased ta meet ‘ya, Hugh. I’m Ginny. Ginny Field.”

“Could you describe the man you saw, Ginny?”

Ginny spoke with conviction, her eyes never wavering from Hugh’s face.

“Yes, sir. Ain’t nothin’ wrong with my eyes. He were a young fella. Tall, light hair, good clothes.” She paused briefly. “I’d know the bugger’s face if I seen it again, fer sure.”

Billie rushed to the wharf after she and Angus closed the store. Spending time with Frank would banish all the unpleasantness of the previous day’s squabble with her mother, at least for an hour or so.

Barely ten minutes along the wharf, Frank stopped walking, let go of Billie’s hand, shoved both hands into his pockets and stared at the wood planking beneath his feet. “You better get home for your meal. My ma’ll be expectin’ me too.”

Billie turned toward Frank, tried to look into his eyes. “What’s the matter with you, Frank? You’ve been short-tempered for days.”

Frank lifted his head but made no attempt to look toward Billie’s face. He stared off into the distance. “Work. It’s just work... yellin’, wantin’ things done faster. You know how bosses are.”

Billie did not know. Her boss did neither of those things. She kept quiet, thinking work could very well be Frank's problem, not her.

As that hopeful thought came to Billie's mind, Frank turned toward the harbour then took a large step away from her. "Aside from them fancy boys in uniforms struttin' around like they own the place, there's too many damn ships out there, loadin' and unloadin'. A fella can't keep up." He lifted his arm and pointed toward a dark grey warship sitting low in the water. "That one's loaded with ammo. Jesus Christ, it could blow us sky high if somethin' went wrong." He raked his fingers through his dark curls, leaving them in disarray.

"You worry too much, Frank. Forget about spies, ships, men in uniform. You can't change any of that. Think about our future together. If you don't want to stay here, we could leave." She stepped toward him, took his hand.

Frank pulled his hand away, kept looking toward the ships. "You're a nice enough girl, Billie but I'm not ready to rush into things. Let's keep things the way they are." He looked at Billie. "Come see me on your lunch break tomorrow." He gave her arm a squeeze and walked away.

Billie turned for home, her heart aching. She covered her mouth with her hand and let the tears roll down her cheeks. The evening meal she was dreading would be worse than expected. At the front door she had no more excuses to delay the inevitable. She took a deep breath, practised a smile and stepped into the house.

Billie's older sister, Sally scooped baby Lula out of her bassinet and rushed toward Billie who had barely stepped into the kitchen.

"Come in, Auntie Billie. We haven't seen you for over a week. Isn't Lula growing fast?"

Billie kept her eyes down, hoping to rush to the bathroom and wash her face. "Hello, Lula. Sorry Sally, I have to use the bathroom."

Upstairs, Billie patted powder over her face, especially around her eyes before returning to the kitchen. She was relieved to see Lula was the centre of attention although she couldn't be sure her mother would not raise the topic of Frank.

During the meal Frank's words repeated in Billie's head so frequently she found it difficult to focus on the table conversation.

Billie's father tapped her arm. "Did you hear what Peter just said?"

"Sorry, Peter. Guess I was day dreaming a bit."

"A few days ago the police interviewed Frank Murphy about the murder of that policeman on the Hill. Did he mention that to you?"

Billie shrugged. "Of course he did. After all, he's the one who was there, and ran from the Hill." She hoped nobody noticed her hand fly to her chest.

Violet was quick with a warning. "See what I meant about that Frank? You better stay away from him."

Charles rushed from the house to the car, eager to arrive at the political meeting early. Tonight he would be officially nominated as his party candidate in the next provincial election. With that settled, he would confront Lois at her apartment and offer her money to leave the city and never return. He decided a years' salary sounded plenty.

To Charles' surprise the local hall was already filled with men and women when he entered the meeting room. The background noise was overwhelming with chairs being moved and people talking. He'd expected a more subdued event.

Charles soon caught site of his official opponent and a well-known suffragette. Although not legally allowed on the ballot, she was clearly garnering the room's attention. Both men and women waved placards while shouting, 'Anna, Anna'. His steps faltered. He recognized the woman from her picture and several newspaper articles on women's rights. *Anna Hopkins.*

Anna was an author and person of influence in the city. The young widow of a British military officer in 1895, she fought to remain in Halifax after her husband's death and secured funding from the British army to do so.

As the evening wore on, Charles realized his anticipated win was slipping away. People were more interested in speaking with Mrs. Hopkins and his opponent who was supportive of women voting. When his speech received polite applause, Charles knew the contest was over. Outwardly gracious toward his opponent and Anna, he felt the stinging loss sharply. He didn't like the title of loser, so quickly left the building to settle his problem with Lois.

CHAPTER THIRTEEN

Monday, October 29

After a late evening meal, Corbin took a cup of coffee to his study and picked up the phone to call Jo. When she didn't answer after a few rings, he recalled her open invitation. 'I'm home most evenings and stay up late. I like company. Come over. I'm only a few blocks away.' He decided to take Jo up on the offer. A companionable hour or two with her in front of the fireplace sounded very appealing.

"I'm going out for a walk, Mrs. Williams."

"Put on gloves. It's chilly out there."

"Thank you."

Corbin smiled to himself, put on a warm jacket and pulled a pair of wool gloves from the shelf in the hall closet and stepped out into a crisp fall evening.

At the corner, the wind had created a pile of moldering reddish-gold and brown leaves beneath the sugar maple. With childish delight, he kicked his shoe into the mound. A musky aroma of fallen leaves mingled with the scent of white pine from his neighbour's yard. For a moment, Corbin was eight again. As he stepped off the curb to cross the street, a black car sped past leaving a whiff of gasoline in its' wake. Thanks to the street light, he saw the driver. It was a parishioner from church. *Charles Ramsay. What a careless man!*

Corbin was curious about Jo's family and why she'd chosen to live in Halifax. During their earlier evening together he thought better of asking her outright. In hindsight, he realized she'd given him little opportunity to ask. She was keen on talking about her home and social events in the city. Perhaps this visit would be different. He walked the final block and rang the doorbell.

Standing outside Jo's door, he could hear Patch's expected response to the doorbell's ring.

The door opened. "Good evening, sir. How may I help you?"

The British accent coupled with a blue paisley ascot and velvet smoking jacket left Corbin speechless and to be honest, puzzled.

"I'm Corbin, a friend of Jo's. Is she home?" Hearing no quick response he asked, "And your name is?" The moment Corbin's question slipped past his lips, he regretted asking it. He sounded presumptuous and determined it was the smoking jacket that set him off.

Patch saved Corbin from embarrassment by squeezing past Jo's gatekeeper and twirled around Corbin's legs.

Mr. Paisley Ascot finally responded, "Hmm. It appears Patch is acquainted with you. You had better step inside, sir."

Jo's voice rang from an inner room. "Who is it, Malcolm?"

"His name is Corbin, my dear."

"Send him in."

Nasty surprises are well, nasty and Jo's appearance was definitely nasty. She was sitting up in bed looking as if she had come out second best in an alteration with a swinging barn door. The left side of her face was scratched, bruised and swollen. Her arm was in a sling.

Malcolm stood at the bedroom door while Corbin searched for words to open the conversation. When none came to mind, Corbin walked to the side of Jo's bed. He was met by an engaging aroma of lavender mixed with buttery whisky.

"Leave us alone, Malcolm." Followed by a hesitant, "Please."

With Malcolm gone, Jo nodded toward the comfortable looking floral print armchair next to the window. “Please, sit down.”

Before being seated, Corbin took note of Jo’s dilated pupils. “The pain must be dreadful.”

Jo offered a weak smile. “Not with all the morphine in me.” She stared at Corbin. “Don’t you want to know what happened?”

“When you’re ready.”

Jo leaned against her pillow. “I’m bloody well ready. An old admirer tracked me down. Unfortunately, Patch was in the backyard at the time.” She clenched her fists. “There are no second chances for men like him. He betrayed my trust. Betrayal is not a quality I tolerate. I get my revenge, eventually.”

Even across the room, Corbin felt intimidated and being honest with himself, frightened.

“What do you think of me now? I’m not as advertised, correct?”

To avoid the question and stop the malice spewing from Jo, Corbin asked as casually as he could muster, “Where is this man now?”

Jo shrugged, winced. “Probably languishing in the King Edward Hotel waiting for the next opportunity to return to England, if he’s smart.” Her eyes held Corbin’s gaze. Her defiance was palpable “But, he’s not smart.”

“A bit dicey on the Atlantic don’t you think, with the war on. Maybe the police could check the name at the Eddie and a couple of other decent hotels?”

“And do what?” Her snippy tone turned to full anger. “I do not want to charge him and go through the legal system. I simply want him to go back to where he came from or even better, have a fatal accident.” She offered Corbin a cold grin. “I keep my revenge to myself. This one deserves to be punished just like the other one.”

Surely, she's hallucinating. Corbin changed the subject. "And Malcolm?"

Jo's anger vanished as quickly as it appeared. "My dear brother is the doctor in the family. He's here to look after me. Thank God." She took a deep breath. "I should write an autobiography. I'm not the only tortured soul out there. I've had a few inappropriate relationships. I dare say the reader would be quite taken with my methods to rid myself of men."

Corbin took note of all the first person sentences. He winced, hopefully not noticeably.

Malcolm stepped into the room and looked directly and only at Corbin. "Scotch?"

Corbin had the distinct feeling Malcolm had been listening and intended to stop Jo's rambling revelations. He accepted the Scotch as Malcolm deftly turned the conversation to more trivial topics and there they remained.

On the walk home, Corbin's head buzzed with words to describe Jo. *Surely the morphine was totally to blame for the dark and unpleasant side of her. Did it reveal the real Jo and who was the 'other one' she mentioned?*

***

It was late. Charles knew Ella would be expecting him with the results of the nomination meeting. Her recent behaviour was much more than annoying. She had become difficult, challenging. He slammed the steering wheel then turned off the engine. *Lois better be home. I need to finish this tonight.*

Carriage Lane was free of cars but Charles parked in the alley beside Lois' apartment anyway. He pulled his collar up and hat down, just in case. The air was cool so he left his gloves on and walked the few steps to the outside door of the two-story building.

The building had been haphazardly converted from a single family home the previous year and left to weather the future unattended. The outer door squeaked and groaned but finally relented. Inside the entry, a well used broom and dustpan leaned against the scuffed wall.

Charles paused a moment to adopt a stern appearance then moved quickly down the hall to Lois' first floor apartment. He raised his gloved hand and knocked, expecting to be safely inside in moments, away from any prying eyes. A second knock brought the same response. Panicked and not wanting to call out her name, Charles tried the door knob. He felt the door give way with a creak as he stepped into the darkness. He took two cautious steps and whispered, "Lois." Thinking she simply forgot to lock the door, he walked into the kitchen and flipped on the ceiling light.

The killer had come prepared. The gaping, bloody wound on the back of Lois' head, bore witness to the heft with which she was struck.

Charles was used to seeing lots of blood but this was different. It was personal. The final trickles of blood from Lois' head had long since pooled on the two toned brown linoleum flooring. Strands of long, curly hair from her usual tidy bun were bound together by blood and strewn across her swollen cheek. Several strands had been ripped from her skull. A few remained on the floor, others were likely swept up by an attempt to clean the floor. Charles wondered, why bother? Mercifully, her eyes were closed.

The struggle had been violent. Lois had fought back. Her right arm appeared to be broken, the left fist was red, the knuckles and skin broken, probably from coming in contact with a solid object, likely the face of her assailant. A glass table lamp was shattered, the shards were strewn across the living room rug. A matching lamp stood guard on an end table. One sofa cushion was on the kitchen table. The other was on the floor, near Lois' head, the flowered pattern soaked in blood.

Despite the chaos before his eyes, the room's stillness calmed Charles. He opened the apartment door quietly, slipped out and closed it in the same fashion. Walking softly, he rushed outside and pressed himself against the side wall of the building. Hearing no voices nor cars, he inched toward the corner of the building and looked toward nearby homes and apartments, paying particular attention to those directly across the street. A few curtains were open. He pulled his hat low over his forehead, walked toward the alley and drove away, only to see a car very similar to his own parked a block away.

Ella was in no frame of mind to wait up for Charles. Tomorrow morning would certainly be a better time to hear about the nomination event, win or lose. Then there was the issue of Lois. How would he squirm out of that fine mess. She picked up a book of poetry and got ready for bed in the guest room.

Frank stood inside an old shack behind the sugar factory at the wharf. The fusty odour of decaying wood mixed with the onion like smell of body odour filled the small enclosure. He'd happened upon the shack earlier in the day then gone home to pack a few pieces of clothing, money he'd hidden in the mattress and a blanket for an overnight stay. He had nobody to talk too and feared for his life. Ivan Buckle was ready to stitch him up and that policeman, Bailey seemed pretty sure he was the man who killed the policeman, Bill Turner.

Afraid to go to work in case more policemen showed up at the wharf, he'd spent the day wandering along the railway tracks north toward parts of the city he'd never seen before, even though he lived in the north end himself. He thought about running off and starting a new life but he wasn't guilty. Having to look over his shoulder for a lifetime ended that notion pretty quick.

When the sun dropped below the horizon, he wound his way through back allies and quiet streets toward Citadel Hill. Approaching from the back, he trudged through the uneven ground until he was even with the Citadel's outer wall, facing east overlooking the city, toward the harbour. Hearing no voices and seeing no sentry, he sat on the ground and closed his eyes. He pushed away the memory of the bloody body and brought the full force of what he'd heard to the fore. The motorcycle. He heard the engine's roar much longer than he'd told Bailey. *Buckle must have come from the top of the Hill, not across the bottom.* A chill raced down his back. *Did Buckle kill the Truro policeman? Why?* He returned to the shack. Would Bailey believe him? He needed to sleep but it was a long time coming.

Before dawn Frank woke from his dream with a start. He remembered the smell of perfume on the dead policeman. He decided to stay away from the wharf for another day. He needed to think. Maybe he was losing his mind? Should he go home tonight? He'd settle that later in the day after deciding about talking to Bailey. He needed food. He slipped away from the shack before any of the factory workers might see him and headed for the North Station. There'd be food there.

***

Breakfast in the Ramsay home was rushed for Murdoch and Rose. Murdoch had a sales idea and was already heading for the front door when his father came down the stairs. Rose wanted to see Nellie before school and left moments after Murdoch. Both had forgotten about the election.

With Murdoch and Rose gone, Ella returned to the kitchen. She looked across the table. “So, are you entering politics?”

“No. My opponent had the support of Anna Hopkins.”

“Well, well.” Ella leaned forward, rested her elbow on the table, chin in hand. “I imagine that was a surprise for you.” She looked at Charles, expecting a reply. None came. “I think Mrs. Hopkins is just the sort of woman we will need in politics, just as soon as we get the vote. They already have it in Alberta.”

After Charles grunted, she finished her thought. “Your people were clearly out of touch with the majority of the membership.”

Charles reached for the tea pot, then the jam pot.

Ella matched his reticent mood and finished eating her toast. “The tea pot, please.”

“Of course.” Charles moved the pot toward her but said nothing for ever so long. Then. “It was an unexpected ending.”

Ella nodded. Was he referring to the election or the end of the affair with Lois Fillmore? She forced herself to wait him out.

The silence between them stretched, grew into minutes. The mood in the room became colder, distancing them one from the other even as they remained an arm’s length away.

Ella thoughts drifted to better times when the children left the table after an evening meal and they enjoyed time together, lingering at the table, speaking of the day just past and events to come.

Charles coughed, disturbing her reverie.

Betraying her commitment to wait him out, she spoke. “We are well beyond the time to only take notice of what is happening in our relationship. Something must be done about Lois Fillmore.”

“It’s settled. I won’t be seeing her again.”

“Thank you.” Ella gathered her own dishes and left the room.

When Charles was about to leave the house, Ella rushed to the front door. “Do you recall Murdoch mentioning the nasty telephone call he received at work?”

“Vaguely. My life has been busy lately.”

“Well, he received a letter at work threatening to expose a family secret. Murdoch and I have spoken about the letter. We decided to hire a private detective for a few days. It’s probably not needed now that you’re not a candidate for the provincial government but who knows.”

“Fine. I’ll leave that to you.”

Ella returned to the kitchen without a further comment.

CHAPTER FOURTEEN

TUESDAY, OCTOBER 30

Charles knew he was being followed the moment he left his front yard. He swore it was the same car he saw near Lois' apartment building the night before. The car followed him to the hospital and parked in the area used by staff. Ignoring an opportunity to get a better look at the driver, he grabbed his briefcase and rushed through the hospital's front door.

"Good morning, Doctor Ramsay. Nurse Fillmore failed to show up and there is no answer at her apartment."

Charles opened his mouth to respond but the efficient Nurse Dubois spoke first.

"I've requested the front desk to locate an immediate replacement to assist you. She should be here within the hour. In the meantime, I can provide any assistance you may need, Doctor."

"Thank you." Charles glanced at her name badge. "Excuse me, Nurse Dubois. I must prepare for surgery."

Janet Dubois watched Charles rush down the hallway. *What a cold fish.*

Charles threw his briefcase on the desk and paced in front of it. Eventually his curiosity quashed his fear. He inched to the side of the window and peeked out toward the parking area. The McKay Touring was nowhere to be seen. He felt relieved. But not much.

***

Marie stared at Murdoch. ”Good heavens, what are you doing here so early.”

“I could ask you the same question, Miss LeBlanc. But I won’t.” He took a deep breath. “When can I talk with your father? I’m willing to double his pay. I know he works nights. Do you think he’s at home now?”

Murdoch’s urgent tone alarmed Marie. She paused a moment then replied carefully. “Papa is usually home by eight-thirty. Then he sleeps until about noon. Your lunch break would be a better time to talk with him.”

“That sounds reasonable. I’ll need your address.” He expelled a soft snort. “I don’t even know where my girl lives.” He shook his head. “Unbelievable.”

Marie smiled but Murdoch was so distracted, he didn’t notice. She was about to warn him that her parents knew nothing about their friendship when Mr. Davis walked in the door. He looked worried.

Hugh Andrews prided himself on a lengthy and honest relationship with the Truro police but getting closer to Bill’s killer trumped everything, even his good name. What he was about to do was wrong and he knew it. Appeasing his conscience, he gave himself three days then he’d talk to the Halifax police about Ginny Field’s information. He hadn’t seen Jo since he arrived in the city. He’d visit tonight. It would be a pleasant change from chasing pointless ideas about Bill’s death.

***

Jenny Ward was her usual chatty self when she arrived at the Ramsay home shortly after Charles left for work.

"Lovely day, Mrs. Ramsay. Big news. Big city event."

"And what is this event all about, Jenny?"

"Troops. Ina at Martin's store. She heard at butcher shop."

"Ah well, it's a sure thing if Ina is spreading the word."

Jenny nodded then grabbed her cleaning bucket and went up the stairs. She leaned over the top banister.

"Mrs. Cameron is doing it."

It was only nine forty-five but Ella forced her thoughts of Murdoch and Mr. LeBlanc to the back of her mind. She needed to get the real story on the event. Mable would know what was happening. She telephoned Mable and invited herself for tea.

***

"Good morning, Mrs. Ramsay. Mrs. Cameron will join you in a few minutes. She had to attend to something in the kitchen. Please follow me to the sitting room. I will serve refreshments shortly."

"Thank you, Esther."

Ella waited impatiently to hear about this soiree for the troops. She mused about the 'something' in the kitchen. Mable would most likely be putting on a better dress and applying fresh makeup.

"Good morning, Ella. How lovely to see you. You must have some news to share. Is Murdoch getting married?"

"Good heavens, no. But he is seeing a lovely young woman." Ella stared intently at Mable. "I'm here about the big event you are planning. Apparently it's the talk of the town and I had to hear about it from Jenny."

"Yes, well I do apologize. We were at an afternoon tea with the mayor three days ago. He asked if I would organize a fall event to support the troops. Of course, I could not refuse. And now, it seems everyone thinks I'm the hostess for it." Mable smiled embarrassingly. "Of course, you know I couldn't manage all that planning. I was going to call you later today to ask your help. By the way, I was sorry to hear Charles lost the nomination."

"I believe that result is for the best, Mable. Let's move on to the big event. As the mayor has spoken with you, I expect the city will be funding the event." Ella posed a quizzical look toward Mable.

Mable's face reflected her initial confusion then caught on and replied, "Yes. Yes. Of course."

"Then we should ask the City for their plan and the amount of funds allocated before either of us commits any time to it. Agreed?"

"Absolutely." Mable hesitated. "If I may be so bold, you sound more confident than usual." Mable paused, waiting for a reason.

Ignoring Mable's insatiable curiosity, Ella replied, "Thank you, Mable." Then she quickly moved on to avoid any further discussion. "Do you have the name of the mayor's secretary?"

"No. I will call City Hall later this morning. Let's have some tea and catch up on the news."

Ella ignored Mable's rush to gossip. "I suggest we call this event, 'Support the Troops' and invite all citizens and the military who wish to attend. The price should be very reasonable, just enough to pay the people who are entertaining. A pipe band comes to mind. I believe there is also a military band. They could play. We can have a dance. Food. Buffet or sit-down? What do you think?"

"Whatever you think." Mable rang the bell for Esther.

***

Corbin and Murdoch were returning from the factory floor when Marie interrupted their conversation. “Mrs. Turner is on the telephone for you, Mr. Davis.”

“Hello, Ruby.”

“Corbin, I need your advice.”

“Advice? If I can help, yes.”

“Detective Henderson wants to talk with me about Bill speaking German and a few other things.”

“That’s curious, Ruby. Detective Henderson must know Bill spoke German. His uncle spoke German and Bill visited his cousins when he was a young boy.”

“I have to say I’m very nervous about this.”

“Don’t be alarmed. I’m sure you know all the answers about Bill they need. When are you coming to Halifax?”

“Tomorrow.”

“Tomorrow is not a problem. I’ll pick you up at the station. Bring Marmalade.”

“I could stay with Jo.”

“Staying with Jo isn’t a good idea. I’ll explain when you’re here.”

Corbin heard a heavy sigh. “Sleep well tonight.” He hung up the hand set and stared at it a moment then called another number.

“Good morning, Malcolm. Corbin here. May I speak with Jo?”

“She’s resting and asked not to be disturbed.”

“Very well. And is she feeling better?”

“Yes.”

"That is good news. Tell her I called and let her know Ruby will be in town tomorrow. She might like to see Ruby." Corbin wished he hadn't called.

Murdoch was pacing about in the front office, repeatedly checking his watch. "Can I leave yet?"

"Yes, Papa should be awake. Now remember, tell my father we work in the same office. Don't start talking about me, how we enjoy having lunch together, right?"

Murdoch nodded and headed for the door.

Less than an hour later, he was back.

"It's all settled. He starts tomorrow night, for five nights and see what happens. A friend is lending him a car. If he has something to report, he'll come here and leave a letter with you. I'm going to follow my father tonight."

"You're what?"

"He'll probably come home for dinner and stay home. The nomination is over. He really has no reason to go out."

***

Billie refused to accept that Frank had any part in the death of the Truro policeman. She concluded the police interview was the reason he told her their relationship was over. He was looking out for her good name. He didn't really mean what he said, not at all, not for one minute. She'd prove it.

Billie wanted Frank to take her away from the home she called her prison so, relying on Angus' good nature, she asked for a longer lunch break.

"I only want an extra fifteen minutes. I'll make it up tomorrow."

Angus grinned. "I bet you're shopping for someone special, maybe that new niece?"

Billie didn't want to lie so she smiled instead of nodding.

Frank's co-workers were having their noon break when Billie approached the picnic tables behind the clothing factory. She didn't have time for pleasantries.

"Anyone seen Frank today?"

Most of the men offered Billie a blank stare and shrug. One of them said he hadn't been at work yesterday either.

"Thanks."

She didn't really believe Frank would skip work. Perhaps he was ill. "Anyone know where Frank lives?"

No one was about to give away anything they knew about Frank to some love-struck girl. A few workers glanced toward each other, then resumed eating. Two sniggered, picked up their lunch buckets and walked away to another table.

Not admitting defeat, Billie walked toward a table where three older men and a lanky, red-haired younger man were talking. She stood in front of them and stared, waiting them out. Finally the younger man spoke. "Try houses near St Joseph's Catholic Church."

Billie returned to the store with a plan. But first, she needed information from Angus. "Mr. Martin, do you go to church?"

Angus hesitated. He was raised in the Anglican Church but drifted away after he left home and moved to Halifax to 'seek his fortune'. He smiled to himself. *Some fortune but I'm content and own my home.* He chuckled.

Billie studied his face. "Why are you laughing about church? My mother would collapse if she heard that!"

“I’m laughing about myself. But to truthfully answer your question. I go at Christmas and Easter. What brought on your question?”

Billie was ready with her prepared answer. “I attend the Anglican church but I’m curious about churches in the north end. Are there Anglican ones and Catholic ones?”

“Well, I’ve been to two or three funerals in that part of the city but it’s been a few years. Let me think.”

Billie forced herself to be quiet.

“The only one I really remember was when old man McGuigan died. He owned a few factories. Wealthy, bad-tempered old bugger. He didn’t leave a will. Family squabbled over the money. He came here for a special kind of cheese and his overalls. Never saw him in a suit. Lots of folks went to the funeral just to see the family act up and of course, to see inside the big Catholic church. McGuigan donated loads of money to St Joseph’s over the years.”

“Sounds like quite the church. And where is it?” She hoped she didn’t sound too eager.

“Corner of Gottingen and Russell. As they say ‘you can’t miss it’.” He paused. “You’ll never make it before dark, even if you leave now. That is, if you’re curious enough to do it right now.”

***

Lois Fillmore’s absence bothered Janet Dubois all day. Something was wrong. It was not like Lois to miss work and not answer her phone. At the end of her shift, she rushed to Lois’ apartment and knocked on the door. Hearing no reply, she tried the knob and discovered the door was unlocked. She opened the door and walked into a scene no friend should face. She checked Lois’ pulse then called the Operator and asked for ‘Ambulance, Emergency’.

***

Billie acted casually when she said 'goodbye' to Angus at closing time. Out of his sight, she raced toward Gottingen Street. She'd be late for the family's evening meal but would blame it on Angus.

Angus was nobody's fool but he couldn't fathom what Billie was up to other than it involved St Joe's Church. He locked the store quickly, pulled his cap low on his head and caught sight of Billie on Gottingen. For almost thirty minutes he kept his eye on her from half a block away.

By the time Billie stopped at Russell Street, the sun had set and the streetlights were on. Angus leaned against a print shop door on Gottingen and watched her.

When Billie entered the church, Angus crossed over Gottingen and stood on the opposite side of Russell. People walking home from work glanced at him. He considered walking around the block but Billie might leave the church before he returned. He had no choice but to enter the church.

Keeping to the side aisle with his head down, Angus sidled into a back row pew, lowered his head, pulled off his cap and began a series of furtive glances toward the front of the church.

Sure enough, Billie was at the front, leaning toward a young priest who was lighting candles for evening vespers. She appeared to be whispering to him. The priest stopped his work, turned to her and began waving his arm. Clearly, he was offering Billie directions.

Angus' stomach lurched. *This is all about Frank*. He knew it all along but didn't want to admit Billie was so deeply vested in this relationship. She was about to risk her future with a man not worthy of her.

As Billie exited the church, Angus followed, led by his heart. Billie was about to set fire to her dreams. The least he could do was pick up the ashes.

***

After the evening meal, Murdoch checked the front hall closet for a dark coat and hat then rejoined everyone in the sitting room.

Rose put down her book. “You’re acting funny, Murdoch. What are you doing?”

“I thought I left my jacket at the office.”

Murdoch had no idea how he was going to track his father. He would get in the car and drive away, leaving him blocks behind. He turned the pages of the book he was supposedly reading.

Ella glanced toward Murdoch. “I had a most interesting visit with Mable Cameron today.” She paused, causing Charles to glance over the top of his newspaper. Ella thought he looked a bit wary. “I have offered my help in planning a city event. Food, music, the lot.” Another pause, this time a message for Murdoch. “Charles, I presume you are home for the evening. You and I should go to your office, have a sherry and discuss our commitment to this event. Follow me.”

Charles rose and followed his wife. “Of course, my dear.”

***

Like any good newspaper man, Hugh had Jo’s street name and house number in his note pad. He rang the door bell, expecting to be met by Jo and Patch. He’d had a big dog growing up. Barney was his loyal companion. He missed him, even now.

The door opened. Neither Jo nor Patch were there but Malcolm was, with his usual frosty glare. He could see Patch standing several feet away. His face said, 'I've been banished from the front door'.

"Good evening, Mr. Andrews. I presume you've come to check on Jo."

"I'd hardly call it that, Malcolm. I'm in town on business and wanted to stop by for a chat."

"Very well. Come in. She's in the big room."

Entering the room, Hugh stopped dead in his tracks. "What in heaven's name happened to you?"

"Hello, Hugh darling. Take a seat. But first, a kiss."

Hugh leaned forward and kissed Jo on the top of her head. Lavender lingered in his nose.

"How's the police work going? Have you found the nasty man or are you hot on his trail?"

"I know your old tricks. Answer my question first."

"A man of course. In my own home. But let's not talk about him. He will be repaid, like the others. By the way, I'm writing again." She flashed a brilliant smile.

"That is good news. About life in England?"

"And here, of course. A drink?"

"Yes, thank you. You?"

"Absolutely. Malcolm has forbidden liquor with the lovely drugs he's giving me. I feel nothing. I'm still a teeny bit incapacitated." She points to the sling. "Be a darling and pour."

Hugh noticed lipstick on a whisky glass on the drinks cart and poured a smaller potion for Jo. For his efforts, he received a deep frown. She accepted the glass without comment and swallowed the contents in one mouthful. "Can I tell you something, Hugh?"

"Of course."

"It's about men. My book. They expect you to do what they want. I'm easily bored, according to Malcolm and that's why I need to get rid of them. The men, I mean. What do you say to that, mister newspaper man?"

Hugh put his glass on the side table and leaned forward in his chair.

"I'm a man so it's pretty hard for me to reply. And it's your story, not mine." He leaned back and sipped his drink, looking toward her, over the rim.

"You bet it is. I will be writing about my father and his unseemly ways plus all my men since then." She tilted her head and cast a smirk toward Hugh. "Of course you won't be in it, Hugh. Such a pity. I'm not bitter or worried though about the book. Not one bit. The men might be though." She smiled. "But I've settled the score with all of them, one way or another." She looked toward the stained glass window." It's not so lovely in the dark is it? I rather like the dark. Secrets happen then. You can get even and nobody knows. Do you like the dark, Hugh?" Jo didn't want an answer. She had one of her own.

"Bill liked the dark. He liked to hunt in the dark. Poor Bill." Her eyes left the window and settled on Hugh's face. "Do you think you will find Bill's killer?" She held her empty glass toward him.

Hugh ignored her request. "I certainly do want to find Bill's killer. I won't give up."

"You will have a good story to write, too." She sighed. "The lovely pills also make me tired. Thank you for the visit. And do come again, won't you?"

Hugh kissed Jo's cheek and bid her 'good night'.

The lovely pills told him much more than he wanted to hear.

Angus followed Billie as she hurried along a side street three blocks from the church, into a poorer part of the city. The only street light was on the corner, now well behind them.

Billie was being drawn into the ever deepening darkness. She ran past several small, drab-looking homes, making no effort to keep her skirt away from the dirty wooden sidewalk.

When Billie suddenly stopped, Angus darted into the weedy side yard of the nearest house. He crept toward the porch and ducked down beside the steps. The dim porch light told a tale of disregard and disrepair.

In the meantime, Billie had lifted her skirt and marched up the front steps of what Angus presumed to be the Murphy home. She gave the front door three loud knocks.

When the creaking door opened, she was greeted by a gruff male voice. "Yes."

Angus squinted. The man was back lit by the light from a narrow hallway. He didn't think it was Frank.

A female voice from somewhere inside the house yelled, "Who's there?"

"May I speak with Frank, please?"

"He ain't here and ain't been for two days. Now go away." The man shut the door in Billie's face.

Billie lifted her hand to knock again, reconsidered and walked away.

Angus waited a few minutes then followed Billie until she was on Gottingen Street. Feeling she was safe on a well-lit street, he walked home to a late meal and a large Scotch. He dreaded what tomorrow would bring.

Long after Billie and Angus were gone and his family asleep, Frank crept through the back door and fell asleep on the sagging green sofa pushed up against one wall in the kitchen. Most days, Frank's father took a quick nap there after his noon meal. Frank planned to be out of the house before anyone came downstairs.

CHAPTER FIFTEEN

WEDNESDAY, OCTOBER 31

"And just what do you think you're doin', scaring the livin' daylights outta your ma. Where 'ya been? With some woman? Maybe the one who came 'ere last night. She in the family way an' you not doin' the right thing? Wait til your Pa comes downstairs."

Frank tried to sit up but the springs and cushions were no help. He resigned himself to his fate and sank into the middle of the tired, old sofa. He gave his Ma a blurry eyed stare.

"What's all the rukus down there?" Frank's father thundered down the staircase and charged into the room. "Where the hell 'ya been? Ya had yur ma worried sick. What's goin' on?"

Frank decided to come clean. "Remember that policeman's murder?" He received two nods. "I saw him dead, on the Hill. The police think I might be the killer."

Mrs. Murphy collapsed into one of the two faded arm chairs near the window. She bowed her head, then crossed herself and began rocking back and forth. "Heaven help us."

"Take it easy, Ma." Frank's father then turned his attention to his son. "I got some questions. Why were 'ya on the Hill? Why would 'ya kill someone?"

"He spoke German. I thought he was a spy, Pa."

"Possible. Ya' can't trust them Germans right now."

Frank's mother crossed herself again and leaned forward in the chair. "But he wouldn't kill nobody." She began to cry, rocking back and forth to soothe her horrifying thoughts.

"Easy now, Ma. Why do the police think 'ya might 'a killed that policeman fella?" Without letting Frank answer, he kept talking. "Ya saw somthin' that night?"

"I saw the body, ran down the Hill and a policeman on a motorcycle saw me. That's why the police talked to me."

"And where 'ya been for the last two days?"

"I'm trying to remember everything about that night. I need the police to believe I'm not guilty, Pa. That's why I've been away alone, thinking. I don't want to be dangling on the end of a rope from that tree downtown."

Frank's mother stood over him. "Wash up. Put on your best shirt and a good pair of pants. You ain't guilty so don't look like it! Long as 'ya ain't guilty. Keep thinking. Go to the police. Don't make them come lookin' for you. Understand me?"

Frank nodded. *I'll go today and tell Bailey everything, even the perfume.*

***

Angus didn't sleep well. By six o'clock he'd eaten breakfast and had enough tea to last the whole day. He washed the breakfast dishes then paced the floor, worrying about what he would face when Billie came to work, if she did. With nothing better to do, he put on a warm coat and hat then stepped into the cool fall air. The sun had just risen. Orange and red dominated the eastern sky. The strong but pleasant smell from his old pine tree filled the air. The last of the summer annuals had seen better days. He had a little job for the weekend. *Off with their heads.* He chortled, lit his pipe.

When Angus arrived at the store Billie was sitting on the front step. She was wearing the same yellow dress as the day before, its' hem splotched with dry mud.

"Good early morning, Billie. Been waiting long?" Angus turned the key in the lock, acting as though this was an every day occurrence.

"Come in." He kept his back to Billie, walked to the counter, put on his bib apron, tied it at the front then turned to face her.

"You can stop acting normal, Mr. Martin. I stayed overnight with a friend. I washed my face and used a few pins for my hair then left the house before anyone was awake." She stared into Angus' eyes. "Just so you know, I knew you were following me last night. I knew you would. Thank you."

Risking Billie's usual wilful retort, Angus knew it was time to take charge of this conversation.

"I presume your parents haven't seen you since yesterday morning?"

Billie nodded.

"Then you must go home and explain yourself. Aside from getting on a train and never returning to Halifax, you have no other choice." He waited for an outburst about her parents.

Hearing nothing, he continued. "It is clear you are bound and determined to marry Frank Murphy but unless he is of the same mind, it will not happen. And that is the truth, Billie. Whether you like or not." He waited. Still nothing. He continued. "My guess is, getting out of your parent's house is as important as marrying Frank. You're using Frank and you don't even know it or won't acknowledge it. You don't need to explain anything to me but if what I said is true, you need to look for other solutions to solve your family war. Perhaps you could think about sharing accommodation with another young woman here in the city."

"Thank you. I would like to come back later today, if that is acceptable.

"Of course."

***

The hospital received the morning newspaper early so Lois' death was on everyone's lips. Charles muttered a few platitudes and hurried to the seclusion of his office. He picked up the receiver, his hand shaking uncontrollably and called Ella.

"Hello, Ella. I didn't do it. You have to believe me. I saw her but I didn't do it. Someone followed me to the hospital yesterday too. What will we do?"

Ella was about to put the receiver back in its' cradle but she had a change of mind. Charles was the one in trouble. It was so tempting, so easy to simply hang up, be finished with him.

"Ella. Are you still there?"

She could hear his laboured breathing.

"Ella?"

She remained quiet. Thinking.

"Are you there, Ella?"

"Yes."

"Am I on my own?"

Hang up. So easy. Then Henry's letter, Alex, the children.

"Come home early, before the children arrive. We will talk."

Ella walked to the kitchen table, glanced at the headline. **Nurse Murdered** She recalled Charles' words. *I won't see her again.* Her thoughts toward Charles hardened again. *Damn him.* She wrapped her arms around herself and rocked back and forth until her pounding heart settled and her dry mouth felt moist again.

When Jenny arrived, Ella left the house for a long walk to the wharf.

***

By nine-thirty Frank was at the police station, truly not knowing if he would leave of his own accord or have a ride in the paddy wagon to Rockhead Prison. He'd been there before for drunken behaviour and vowed not to return. *Stinkin' hole.*

"Detective Bailey in?"

"No, but I expect him soon. Wanna wait?"

God, no. "Might as well."

"I've finished the newspaper, if you want it."

Frank took the newspaper and sat in an uncomfortable wooden chair opposite the counter. The headline, Nurse Murdered was hard to miss. *A copper on the Hill, a lady of the night on the wharf and now a nurse. Did they all get stabbed?*

The outer door opened and Detective Bailey appeared. Frank was so nervous, he almost threw up then and there.

"Mr. Murphy, come into my office. Constable, bring two mugs of coffee." He glanced at Frank. "Milk? Sugar?"

"Both. Ta."

Bailey leaned over his desk, placed his left hand over the right and asked, "Do you have something to tell me?"

"I went to the top of the Hill late Monday night, to think." *God, I sound bloody daft.*

Bailey leaned back in his armchair, placed his arms on the armrests, hands dangling. "And what came to mind?"

"I remembered hearing a motorcycle engine a lot longer than I first thought." Frank swallowed, drew in a long breath and reached for his mug. Before speaking he took a sip of coffee then settled back in his chair, both hands gripping the mug.

"I believe Constable Buckle came from the top of the Hill, not across the bottom."

Bailey leaned forward and rested his right arm on the desk. "Anything else you remembered?"

Frank debated with himself long enough for Bailey to clear his throat and ask, "Anything else?"

"I slept in a shack near the wharf Monday night." Another deep breath, then hesitation.

"And?" Bailey opened his arms, raised his eyebrows.

"I dream a lot. Do you dream in colour, Detective?"

"Where is this going, Frank? I haven't got all day."

"I dreamed about that night on the Hill. The smell of perfume on the policeman's clothes woke me up." His eyes met Baileys. "A woman's perfume."

Bailey's unasked question lingered in the silence between them.

"Would you recognize it again?"

"Yes. It smelled like lavender." He didn't mention Billie smelled like lavender.

Detective Bailey and Frank stared long and hard at each other. Bailey considered Frank's new details while Frank prayed for freedom from the suspect list.

Bailey stood and shook Frank's hand. "Thanks for coming in."

***

Ella grew up in Halifax and always found the city's wharf fascinating, despite its occasional rough and tumble reputation. The people, its ships and water were a big part of her life. Over the years it restored her energy and often times cleared her head to see things in a new light. Today, her need was of a different sort. A diversion. Lord knows, she needed help from something or someone.

The sky was overcast and the cool fall air had arrived, bringing with it gusts that chilled to the bone. Ella pulled her red wool coat closer to her throat as a cold Atlantic wind tugged at her scarf. She shivered, shoved her gloved hands into her deep pockets and continued walking until she saw the two weather worn benches away from the busiest part of the wharf. She sat, preferring not to hear or see the many men and horses being loaded for the battlefields of Europe. Her heart ached for the families who were losing their daughters, sons, mothers, fathers and husbands, including her own. Her aunt in Ottawa was struggling with the loss of her husband. Her parents would stay on a few more weeks. She hoped they would return soon. She felt so alone. Her family was falling apart. Tears slipped from her eyes, blurred her vision, rolled down her cheeks. She wiped them away but others followed. Her nose ran. The hanky barely kept up. With a last shuttering breath, she stopped crying and sat back in the bench.

The sun broke through the clouds, warming Ella's face and lifting her spirits. She must keep going for her children, for herself. She wiped her face with a fresh hanky and looked toward the sparkling water, squinting at the shimmering lights, then turning her head toward the people strolling past.

Thoughts of trouble fell away as Hugh Andrews came into view. But he was new trouble. She dropped her head. *Please don't come near me.* She fiddled with her hanky, squeezed her eyes shut. She began rocking, ever so slightly.

The foot steps came closer then stopped. "Ella, is that you?"

She had no choice other than to run off and look like a half wit. Instead, she looked up and slipped into the role of a gracious, educated, society lady.

"It is. How lovely to see you, Hugh." *What are you doing in Halifax?* Instead, "I hope you are well." *He's aged well, a touch of grey at the temples, that charming, affectionate smile.*

"Very well, thank you." *It's been so many years. You look lovely. Join me for lunch. I need an explanation.* "You look well." He paused. "It's certainly not customary to see society women here alone. What brings you to the wharf?"

"I needed a long walk." *Damn. He's a newspaper man. Needed was clearly the wrong word.*

"Needed is an unusual word to describe a walk."

Typical Hugh. He wants an explanation. "I do my best thinking outdoors." *There, take that.*

"Excellent. So do I. Want to continue thinking with me?"

Touche. He's too darn quick witted.

Ella pulled her hat down as far as possible and stood up. "Thank you. However, I will decline your arm." She tucked her hands into her pockets.

An awkward silence filled their first few minutes together. Both knew something unsettling was emerging.

Ella knew Hugh well enough to know his silence was not destined to last long. She waited.

"Your eyes are red. Why were you crying?"

Ella could sense the concern in his voice but it was not the question she expected. She took her hands out of her pockets and fidgeted with her gloves, stalling for time, seeking innocuous words.

"I'm worried about my family."

"Well, that covers a lot of nothing. Are the children ill?"

"No."

"Are you going to make me guess?"

"It's personal." Ella stopped walking and turned toward the water, afraid he could tell she was skirting the truth.

Hugh moved to stand beside her. "Can I help in some way?"

"I don't believe so." She put her gloved hands back into her pockets and resumed walking. The matter was ended.

They walked in silence until Ella asked the question she'd wondered about for years. "Why were you not angry?"

He hesitated a moment. "Would anger have changed anything?"

Ella stopped walking, looked into Hugh's warm, caring eyes. "I suppose not. By then, it was too late."

Hugh was quick to speak. "Maybe." He looked out to sea. "For what it's worth Ella, I believe circumstances and other people carried you away from me." He stepped closer. "That's why I'm not angry with you. Not then, not now."

"That sounds like a safe place to end this conversation. Are you living in Halifax again?"

"I'm here until my friend's killer is found and I'm of the opinion the killer is from Truro."

"Truro?" *Alex. But surely there couldn't be any connection.*

Hugh nodded. "I think my friend tracked his killer to Halifax." He looked across the water. "Nothing else makes sense to me."

"Thank you for your company, Hugh."

"I've been walking here every day, looking for people to help in my search for Bill's killer. Perhaps we will meet again."

"Good bye, Hugh."

Ella hurried away, in the hopes she'd escape without being seen with a man on the wharf. At home with a glass of sherry in her hand, she would allow herself to think about Hugh. She'd barely closed the front door when Charles was opening it behind her. She spun around.

"Why are you here so early? It's only lunch time."

"I have no surgeries booked this afternoon."

"And you thought I would be waiting to see you in the middle of my day?"

"You said we should talk."

Ella would not allow herself to take up a discussion with Charles based on his terms. "This is so typical of your behaviour.

When you're ready to leave for church, plan a dinner party or have a conversation you have no regard for the other person. Your family is not your hospital staff, ready to do your bidding." She acknowledged her fire was fuelled by seeing Hugh. His usual probing, tempered with thoughtful interest in others continued to be one of his endearing qualities. Charles lacked even a modicum of thoughtfulness.

"Ella?"

"I have plans to meet with Mable about the city event over lunch. I suggest you eat something now and find something to do until such time that I'm available. Would two thirty suit you? Rose will be home by four thirty. Murdoch might be home by five, if he doesn't have plans with Marie."

"Who's Marie?"

CHAPTER SIXTEEN

WEDNESDAY, OCTOBER 31

The last time Corbin looked forward to meeting a visitor at a train station was when he was eleven. His father's older sister took the train from Montreal to Truro and brought Christmas gifts for everyone. Ruby would not be bringing gifts, unless you counted Marmalade. Instead, she would be bringing her worried thoughts about the police interview and grief brought on by Bill's death.

Ruby stepped down from the train shortly after noon, wearing a burgundy dress with full skirt, the hemline above her ankle, showing her button shoes. She carried a small brown suitcase in her right hand. A wicker basket hung over her left arm. Two large amber eyes peered out from under a blue plaid throw.

"Welcome, Ruby and Marmalade." With no free hand to easily grasp, he quickly squeezed her left. "How was the train ride?"

"I have to tell you, I was expecting the worst but his nibs was fascinated by the scenery flying past the window."

Corbin nodded in Marmalade's direction. "Good afternoon, Marmalade." He then took Ruby's suitcase, allowing her to ensure Marmalade would stay where he belonged. "Off we go. The car is across the street in front of the hotel. By the way, I've taken this afternoon and tomorrow off, in case you would like me to take you to the interview."

"Thank you. I would appreciate that very much."

"Mrs. Williams will have a lovely lunch ready for us, chicken I believe."

Ruby smiled. "One of Marmalade's very favourites."

As they drove away from the hotel, Corbin commented on the city. "I don't know when you were last in Halifax but right now it's a very busy city."

"I haven't been here for about three years but I've read a few stories in the Truro paper. Bill was here many times on police business. He often stayed overnight but I had little desire to entertain myself during the day in Halifax. Perhaps I should have." She stopped talking. "My friends and activities at home kept me busy. Maybe I missed out on a part of Bill's life I could have shared."

Corbin left her to her own thoughts. A few minutes later, he pointed to the Museum of Fine Arts. "Would you be interested in a visit one afternoon?"

"Absolutely."

"We could have lunch then tour the rooms."

"Lovely."

"When do you speak with Detective Henderson?"

"Tomorrow morning at eleven."

"That would work nicely."

As they made the turn into the driveway, Ruby turned to face Corbin. "This is not about you Corbin but I feel awkward being in the home of a man who is not a relative."

"I expected you would be. As I mentioned on the telephone, Jo is not able to have a house guest." He paused. "We can talk about that over lunch or later today. In the meantime, I've spoken to my close neighbours. They understand your circumstances."

"Thank you."

***

"Hello, Sir." Sergeant Bailey nodded toward Detective Henderson. "How was the meeting with the mayor about new recruits?"

"Excellent. Do you dance, Bailey?"

Bailey stared at his superior. "Badly, Sir. Just ask my wife."

Henderson continued. "So do I. Have a seat."

"I sense you have a story there, Sir. If the mayor wants to dance with you, could we save it for later today?"

"Either you don't want to hear my story, which by the way is quite funny or you have new evidence on one of the three murder cases hanging over our heads." He tipped his head toward Bailey. "Carry on."

"Thank you, Sir."

"Spill the beans."

"First, a question. Would you consider a dream sufficient information to pursue a line of inquiry, Sir?"

Henderson squinted. "Maybe. How peculiar is this dream and whose dream is it?"

"Quite peculiar and it's Frank Murphy's dream."

"Was he drunk or sober?"

"The latter. Give me your mug, Sir. I'll get coffee and tell you his story." Bailey stood up. "He also has a new recollection about the motorcycle, Sir."

"Bring a full pot."

When Bailey finished Murphy's dream story, he leaned back in his chair and stretched out his long legs in front of him.

"So what's your plan, Sergeant?"

"Well Sir, I believe Murphy's story enough to interview Buckle again." He pulled his legs back and leaned forward. "If Murphy's memory is accurate, Buckle is either a possible suspect or a potential witness. Either way, we're moving the case forward."

"And the lavender perfume?"

Bailey exhaled slowly. "I don't know, Sir. I don't want to ignore the possibility of what it might mean but it is a bit far fetched."

Henderson nodded. "Leave the perfume for later. Get Buckle in here this afternoon. Push his relationship with Murphy. If there's a link somewhere in the three cases, Buckle could be our first breakthrough."

"Will do, Sir." He stood, turned to leave.

"Wait up a minute. Two things." Henderson picked up a piece of paper. "I have an update on the Truro suspects related to Detective Turner's murder. The two assault fellas, Wallace and Young have not shown up in the Truro area. Freeman was picked-up for robbery a few days ago. He had a solid alibi for Sunday, the twenty-first. And the good news, we will have our new recruits plus the city is having a big celebration to honour our troops sometime in late November. There'll be a dance." He grinned.

"Good to know, Sir. Now I'm off to get Buckle."

Marmalade carefully inspected every inch of Ruby's bedroom while she unpacked her suitcase. Most of his time was under the bed and inside the dark, most intriguing closet. Satisfied that no other cat or mouse was about, he jumped onto the top of the bed and requested a chin rub for his hard work.

"So, as the house has passed muster, we better go downstairs for lunch."

Cats were no strangers to Mrs. Williams. Before coming to work for Corbin following her husband's death, she'd had her own home. Cats were always part of the family so by the time Marmalade showed up, she'd already prepared for the four-legged guest.

At the bottom of the stairs Marmalade was lured into the kitchen by the scent of roast chicken. Mrs. Williams closed the door behind him as he headed for the bowl of chicken pieces and gravy. The big kitchen window looked out over a backyard, a garden and trees busy with birds. She'd placed a cushioned chair in just the right spot for an afternoon nap.

In the meantime, Corbin and Ruby settled into the dining room. Their lunch conversation was casual and covered the more mundane topics people do to fill in the time before the real conversation begins.

When Mrs. Williams removed the dessert plates, Corbin suggested they move to the study.

At the study door, Ruby stood in awe. "This is not what I expected of a man's study!"

"Thank you, I think."

"Honestly, I expected a whiff of cigar smoke, a dark, cluttered desk, a couple of mismatched chairs and boring painted walls."

Corbin laughed. "Well, you're right about the desk."

"I truly like the bright wallpaper and the bookcases on either side of the fireplace. The matched chairs at the window look comfortable"

"Have a seat."

"I want to look at your art first."

"I'm a bit of a collector. Can't afford some of the best pieces though."

Ruby stared intently at a small framed picture. "Who did this piece? It really looks like you."

"A school girl. Isn't it amazing? She's about ten."

Ruby leaned in. "Nellie Quinn. That's a name to remember." She turned to face Corbin. "Where did you find it?"

"I have to admit I haven't been out and about much in the past two or three years but I did go to an art exhibit a few months ago. Nellie was there and did the portrait. Care for a small sherry?"

"Yes. I would like that. You have a favourite chair?"

"No, feel free to choose one for yourself."

Ruby settled into a gold brocade, one of two at the window then smoothed the skirt of her dress. "What's wrong with Jo?"

"You certainly get straight to the point." Corbin poured the sherry and offered Ruby her glass then sat in the opposite gold brocade.

"Well?"

He began hesitantly. "She's recovering from a pounding." Then added quietly, "By a former suitor, as Jo described him."

Ruby took a sip of sherry. "How dreadful. Any idea who he is?"

"He's an English gentleman. I use that word loosely." He swirled the sherry around. "You don't sound surprised." He took a mouthful of sherry, felt the heat burn his throat. He didn't want to go into the details of his evening with Jo but was curious about Ruby's casual comments. He hoped she would say more. He finished the sherry in one gulp.

"No, I'm not surprised. But let's talk about things other than Jo this afternoon. Could I be so bold as to ask for a visit to your business and Citadel Hill before the day loses the sun?"

"I'm at your service, madame."

Ella and Mable made great strides with the city celebration event. A venue was selected and booked for the afternoon and evening of November 24, the last Saturday in the month. They created a menu for the evening meal as well as booking the military band and a local musical group to allow for dancing. They did not know what the ticket cost would be nor how the tickets would be sold, so tomorrow Ella would visit city hall then take a sample to the printer. She felt so engaged and fulfilled she almost forgot about her troubles at home. Almost.

When Mable's longcase hall clock struck two, Ella felt the uneasiness begin. Overcoming her dependence on Charles was frightening at times. It would be easier to be agreeable but she must not do it. Her heart beat faster.

"I have something else I must do at two-thirty."

"The best of luck with the Mayor tomorrow."

In her rush to be alone in the crisp fall air, Ella almost forgot to thank Mable for lunch. "Thank you for lunch."

"If you can, come by tomorrow after visiting the Mayor and the printer."

"See you tomorrow then."

Ever punctual, Charles was sitting at the kitchen table waiting for Ella. He glanced at the wall clock which read, two thirty-five.

"I trust you had a productive meeting with Mable."

"Yes. Have you been waiting long?"

"Only five minutes."

"Tea?"

"That would be lovely."

Typical Charles. He could have made the tea. She took a deep breath and considered the discussion facing her. She made the tea then sat at the table, vowing not to speak first.

"I did not kill that woman, Ella." He rubbed his forehead back and forth. "What will we do?"

"I had nothing to do with this, Charles. You must go to the police."

"But I didn't do anything."

Ella shot him a disapproving side glance. "No?"

Charles offered her a weak smile then lifted his shoulder in a half shrug. "But I am a witness."

In turn, she offered him a shrug then a dismissive wave of her hand followed by a sip of tea.

"But what would I say?"

"The truth. That's what you say." She bit down on her tongue to fight off any further condemnations.

"But I could become a suspect."

"You probably will."

Charles crossed his arms, leaned back in his chair.

Another round of silence followed as Ella ate an oatmeal cookie, sipped her tea.

A heavy sigh broke the silence. "I'm being followed."

"By whom?"

Charles snapped, threw his hands in the air. "How the hell would I know. A man in a car like mine followed me to the hospital." He cooled quickly. "Aren't you worried? I'm your husband. For God's sake Ella, show some..."

She leaned across the table. "Show what? Embarrassment, shame, regret?" She leaned back in her chair. "Those burdens are yours to carry today." She dropped her head. *When my turn comes, those words will be mine to carry. But not today.*

When Charles moaned, she raised her head. She saw a beaten man. His once bright eyes were dull, shoulders sloped as he slouched in the chair. "I could be dismissed from the hospital."

"Yes."

"Should I go now?"

"Is there a better time?"

"No."

"You should probably call the station and ask to have an appointment with the Detective."

"Yes, of course."

Ella was about to stand up.

"We can talk about the other things when I return from the station."

"Such as?"

"Us, the children. Will you be here?"

Ella opened her mouth to reply.

Charles quickly added, "Please."

Ella nodded but remained seated as she had no intention of watching Charles drive away.

What Ella did next was baffling to herself and the policeman who later questioned her actions. Hearing the front door close, she walked down the front hall, past the vase of dried flowers, the family portraits, the pastoral paintings and into the sitting room where she stared out the front window.

After Charles waved 'good bye' and drove away, Ella continued to stand at the window. Fixated. Something she needed to know was about to happen. Moments later, a car identical to Charles' drove past the house. She ran to the kitchen and called the police. *Dear god. The children.*

***

"Good afternoon, Constable Buckle. Please have a seat. I've asked you in to discuss new information we received on the Hill murder. But first I want you to think hard about your relationship with Frank Murphy. When did you first met Frank?"

"At school. What does school have to do with a murder, Sir?"

"So you met Frank at school?"

"Yes, Sir." Ivan sat up straight in his chair.

“Tell me about school.”

“My ma made me go every day.” He lowered his head.

“So you didn’t like school?”

“Why did you say that?”

Bailey saw a fleeting flash of anger. He stretched across his desk, clasped his hands together. “You were made to go so you didn’t like school, right?

“No. I liked school, Sir.”

Bailey ignored the denial. “And what didn’t you like about school?”

Buckle forced a laugh. “Ah, you know what some people are like at school, Sir.”

Bailey leaned back into his chair. “Tell me about those people, the fun, the games.”

“I didn’t play games, Sir.”

“Or those people didn’t ask you to play? That it?”

Buckle remained silent but squeezed his hands into fists.

“I had a nickname at school. They called me Swifty. I could run fast.”

“You have a nickname, Buckle?”

“No, Sir.”

Bailey knew different. *He’s not afraid to lie.* “Let’s move on. You were on the hill at the Citadel the night Detective Turner was murdered. Is that correct?”

“Yes, Sir.”

“And you saw Frank Murphy there?”

“Yes, Sir.”

“And you saw Frank Murphy run down the hill from the Citadel?”

“Yes, Sir.”

“And you saw Frank Murphy run across the street at the bottom then disappear into city streets?”

“Yes, Sir.”

"And you roared after Frank Murphy on your motorcycle?"

"Yes, Sir."

"And you don't like Frank Murphy."

"Ye.." Buckle shut his mouth.

"I take that partial answer to mean you do not like Frank Murphy. If that is true Constable Buckle, is it also true you have spoken untruths about what you did, about what you saw and about what you heard on Citadel Hill the night of Detective Bill Turner's murder?"

Ivan Buckle whispered, "Yes, Sir." Then dropped his head and began crying.

Sergeant Bailey almost felt sorry for him.

Bailey called the front desk to request another Sergeant in the building and a stenographer come to his office.

"Sergeant Eric Hurst, you will serve as my witness for the formal statements to be made by Ivan Buckle, currently a member of the Halifax Police Force. Constable Ivan Buckle, we will now proceed to take your formal statement identifying your actions and untrue statements made in interviews in this office regarding the murder of Detective William Turner on the night of October 21, 1917. Further to that, you will be immediately dismissed from the City of Halifax Police Service. I will remove your badge from the uniform. You will return all your uniforms to this office tomorrow morning, no later than nine o'clock. Be advised, you may be further formally interviewed regarding the actions you took on the night of October 21, 1917. The date and time for such interviews will be at the discretion of the City of Halifax Police Service. We will begin." He nodded toward Connie, the stenographer.

***

Billie Stewart looked like a different person when she returned to the store in the late afternoon. She greeted Angus warmly and served waiting customers with her usual pleasant but cheeky ways. When the store was empty of customers, she approached Angus.

"Mr. Martin, I want to thank you for helping me this morning and for all you've done for me since I began working here. I hope you aren't angry with me about last night."

"I was more worried than angry."

"When I went home, everyone was there. My parents, my sister, her husband. They were so worried, they'd already called the police. And you're right, I want to be away from my parents."

"So, have you an idea or made any plans?"

"No, not yet."

"And Frank?"

"Frank would never kill anybody. He needs someone like me to believe in him. And besides, I really like him." She raised her chin in defiance, challenging Angus to change her opinion.

Angus straighten his tie.

"I've seen you do that with customers many times. You're either frustrated with me or don't know what to say. Which is it?"

"Then let me tell you a few truths. You cannot continue to argue with your parents. Either stop arguing or find another place to live, now. About Frank. I'm betting Frank is at the centre of your arguments. I won't tell you to stop liking Frank because life doesn't work like that. If Frank has told you he doesn't want to see you any more, you have to accept that, hard as it may seem. There, I've spoken my mind. You're a smart young woman. The rest is up to you. Now, let's move that shipment of art supplies onto the shelves. Nellie will likely be in this week."

CHAPTER SEVENTEEN

Wednesday, October 31

When Charles Ramsay failed to arrive for his afternoon appointment regarding the death of Lois Fillmore, Will Henderson called the Ramsay home. He knew it could be difficult but was necessary.

"This is Detective Henderson of the Halifax Police. May I speak to Mrs. Ramsay."

"Speaking."

"Hello, Mrs. Ramsay. Your husband did not appear for his meeting with me this afternoon. Is he at home?"

"No but I expect him soon."

"In that case, I would like to speak with you. May I come to your home?"

"Is that really necessary, Detective? It's quite simple. Charles obviously chose not to speak with you. But come along, you'll likely find him here when you arrive."

"Thank you."

Charles Ramsay seemingly vanished into thin air. A constable on his rounds discovered an abandoned McKay Touring a few blocks from the police station. He thought it unusual that a fancy car would be in a vacant warehouse lot for an hour in the middle of the afternoon. There was no sign of a driver and no blood in or on the vehicle. Constables began knocking on the doors of businesses and homes in a five block radius.

Detective Henderson met Charles Ramsay once. Despite the circumstances, Ramsay appeared emotionally detached from the situation, presenting himself as a confident, dominating figure to those not in his social status. He'd never met Mrs. Ramsay and prepared for the same behaviour.

Standing at the Ramsay front door, Henderson hoped there were no young children in the house. If so, perhaps they had a nanny who already had the children occupied in another part of the home. He pushed the doorbell and to his surprise, the door was opened by a tall, dark haired young man wearing glasses. The worried face told him the young man knew something terrible had happened.

"Good evening. I'm Detective Henderson. Is Mrs. Ramsay at home?"

"Yes, come inside. I'm Murdoch Ramsay."

"Thank you, Murdoch." Henderson stepped into the hallway, stopped and waited for direction to the sitting room or more likely, left in the hallway until Mrs. Ramsay arrived, to take him to a grand room. Neither happened.

"Come to the kitchen. My mother's there."

Surprised by the casual greeting, Henderson walked the elegant, long hall to meet the lady of the house.

"Mama, this is Detective Henderson. He's here to..."

"I know why he's here, dear." Ella looked at Henderson. "Please sit down. My name is Ella Ramsay. Would you care for tea or coffee?"

"Coffee, please. And sugar. Thank you." Henderson was puzzled by Ella Ramsay's composure in the face of her husband's absence, then dismissed the notion because of her status in Halifax society. She was expected to maintain her composure at all times. Apart from her visible pallor, she looked every inch the wife of a successful doctor sitting in her large modern kitchen. Her hair was in an up-sweep and her dress a deep green checked cotton day dress with tiered skirt. Pockets, collar, cuffs and bib were trimmed in white lace.

Murdoch placed the coffee in front of Henderson and left the room.

Ella continued. “Have you found him? Is that why you’re here?”

Henderson reached for the sugar bowl. “No. But this can be a good sign.” He added sugar and stirred the coffee. “Can you tell me a bit of your husband’s background. It might assist us in our search.” He removed his notebook and a pen from his pocket.

“Charles’ father is deceased and his mother resides in England. He has two older brothers who live in Ottawa. Their communication is limited to an annual Christmas card. I doubt they had anything to do with the disappearance.” She paused. “Before you proceed any further Detective Henderson, you need to know why and how my husband disappeared. I can give you the answers.”

Henderson ignored Ella’s last remarks. “And your husband’s work, please.”

“He is a surgeon but you already know that.”

“Please proceed with your information about why and how your husband disappeared.”

When Ella finished her story of Charles infidelity and his discovery of Lois Fillmore’s body, she looked Henderson straight in the eye. “My husband did not run away, he was taken by a man I saw outside this house. That man drove a car very similar to that of my husband’s.”

Henderson remained silent.

“Are you shocked, Detective?”

“I’m curious.”

“About what?” She spread her arms open, shrugged.

Henderson leaned back into his chair. “Well, aside from your composure while your husband is missing, I cannot recall interviewing anyone whose information both explains, then complicates the case." He leaned forward and finished his coffee. "Your directness is also rather unusual."

"In what way?"

Henderson regretted this last statement the moment it was uttered. He'd presumed Mrs. Ramsay would be a society lady who avoided such delicate issues as infidelity.

"My apologies Mrs. Ramsay, my comment about your directness was not deserved."

Ella nodded. "Accepted. I've known about my husband's infidelity for some time, Detective. Make no mistake, he is a cheater but he is not a murderer." She stood. "More coffee?"

"Yes, please." Henderson paused a moment. "So, you're telling me you believe your husband has disappeared simply because a man with the same kind of car followed him? Your reasoning appears a bit hasty, don't you agree?"

Ella placed two cups on the table, then sat down. "No." She wagged her finger in the air. "That car is very relevant, Detective. The man driving that car is your murderer and he took Charles."

"You appear firm in your belief." He paused. "Take me back to the discussion you mentioned earlier. The one when you and Doctor Ramsay talked, then he decided to go to the police."

"What do you mean?" Ella stared at Henderson.

"Was Doctor Ramsay eager to tell his side of the story or..."

Ella's back stiffened. "Are you suggesting we had an argument about what he should do? If so, we did not. We were very civilized. I pointed out he was responsible for the situation and he should go to the police and explain himself. He agreed."

"Hmm. It sounds like everything was settled at the table." Henderson sipped his coffee. "Why did you go to the front window?" Henderson's pen hovered over his notebook, ready for the answer. He expected Ella's response would be most revealing.

Ella shrugged. "I felt drawn to it."

"Hmm. And when did you find out your husband was being followed?"

"Well, he told me at the table."

"And that made you go to the window when he left."

Ella looked away. "I suppose so." Then back to Henderson "I had to go to the window. I can't explain it any other way."

"You seem very sure he was being followed."

Ella nodded.

"Are you certain you have not met or seen this man who drove a car similar to your husband's?"

Ella furrowed her brow and leaned away from the table. "What are you implying? That I know that man?" She opened her hands in disbelief. "Why would I?" Then she leaned forward. "You think I hired that man to kill my husband, I did no such thing!" She leaned back into her chair, crossed her arms. "I think you should leave now." She stood up.

Henderson remained seated. "One more question, if you don't mind. Did you tell the constable who answered the telephone that the car you saw was similar to your husband's?"

Ella's reply was cold. "I believe so but I was distracted and needed to call the home where my young daughter was visiting her friend. It is time for you to leave, Detective."

Henderson finished the last of his coffee and stood. "That's all for the time being but we will talk again." A few steps away from the door, he turned around. "By the way, did you know the victim, Lois Fillmore?"

"Absolutely not. Good-bye, Detective."

***

When Henderson returned to the station, Bailey was debriefing Sergeant Surrette who supervised the door canvass. Henderson stepped into the room.

Surrette looked up. “The canvass is finished, Sir. Doctor Ramsay was not seen by anyone in the five block radius of his car.”

“Has the car been taken to the police building lock up?”

“Yes, Sir. We had a second look at it, but we found nothing. It would appear Ramsay walked away with the keys and anything else he had with him. If there was a scuffle surely someone would have heard or seen something. Maybe he went with someone he knew, Sir?”

“Or with someone who had the barrel of a gun pointed at him.”

“Or a knife.” Said Bailey.

***

Corbin and Ruby’s late afternoon began pleasantly. The weather cooperated for their visit to the Davis Footwear factory. Ruby was keenly interested in the process of making footwear.

When they left the building, she offered some advice. “I understand your bread and butter is men’s shoes, particularly the work wear kind but why are you not paying more attention to women’s footwear?”

Corbin looked at Ruby’s shoes. “Hmm. Maybe you are onto something there. Interesting heel and buttons.” He bent down for a closer look. “Those buttons have no use at all!”

“Precisely. They are decoration. I love decoration on my footwear. Many women do.” She tilted her head. “Maybe you need to think about that.”

Their visit to the harbour to view the war and supply ships was cut short by a sudden, brief rain shower which sent them running to the car. There, they plotted their next stop.

“Could we stop at Citadel Hill?” Ruby quickly added, “Just a stop. I’m not sure I want to get out of the car. I’ll decide when we are there.”

Corbin had avoided passing by the Hill since the murder, even if it meant a longer drive to a meeting within the city. For Ruby, he would endure the painful reminder. “Of course, we can stop.”

At the Hill, Ruby sat inside the car for several minutes. “I’m getting out, just to look from here.”

Corbin opened her door, helped her out and waited, leaning on the front of his Ford motorcar.

After a few minutes, Ruby left the car and stopped at the bottom of the well worn footpath. She looked around at the dying foliage and lifted her head toward the imposing Citadel on the top of the hill. Some part of her mind urged her forward. A few feet along the path, her heart could no longer endure the pain. It knew Bill left her forever at this very place. She dropped to her knees and wept. Raw grief wracked her body, more overpowering than when she first heard of his death.

Corbin walked to her while fighting back his own tears. He stood by Ruby until she was able to stand with help and accept his hanky.

“Thank you for being such a good friend, Corbin. I know this was not easy for you either.”

“Shall we carry on and visit Point Pleasant Park for a bit of exercise before dinner?”

Ruby nodded, patted Corbin’s hand and waited for him to open her door.

***

Angus Martin was fired up. Frank Murphy was unfit to be a partner for Billie Stewart. As Billie was unable to see Frank for what he truly was, he was prepared to get her the proof. He worked later than usual, ate a sizable chunk of cheddar cheese and went to the hidden bar close to his store. He knew Frank frequented that particular watering hole and hoped he would show up and behave badly.

To Martin's great pleasure, Frank was already in the room and in a lively mood. He figured Frank was close to the noose and letting off steam.

Glancing around, Angus spotted Ivan Buckle alone in a back corner table. Ivan's mother shopped regularly in his store and Ivan accompanied her on occasion. As an adult, Ivan retained his childish petulance. Tonight, he looked mightily unhappy.

A pint in hand, Angus nodded to the fellas he knew and sat at an empty table to wait for Frank to cause trouble. The truth often came to light when trouble erupted. He settled in to watch the fireworks.

If nothing else, Hugh Andrews was persistent. He'd heard on the q.t. there was a secret bar near a general store, several blocks north of the harbour. A change of scene and a change of people might offer useful information in his pursuit of Bill's killer.

When Hugh arrived, the place was alive with laughter. Not one to insert himself into a group of folks already enjoying each others' company, he walked toward a table where a middle aged man was sitting alone. He smiled toward the fella with sandy hair, wearing glasses. "Waiting for someone?"

Angus had no real excuse to deny the man's request to sit. He looked decent enough, well-groomed, good clothes. "No, have a seat."

Hugh thrust his hand forward. "Thank you. I'm Hugh Andrews in town to write a story about the city and its' people during the war. And you, sir?"

"Angus Martin, grocer." He shook Hugh's hand heartily. "My store is not far from this spot."

"Been in town for quite a while then, I bet."

"Going on twenty years. I've seen a lot of changes."

"And hear a lot of opinions, I bet." Hugh paused just a moment. "You're probably following the murder on the Hill. I'll be using it in the story. Have any thoughts?"

Angus was keeping an eye on Ivan Buckle who was keeping an eye on Frank Murphy and downing beer at a rapid pace. "Customers talk a lot but I don't get involved too much. I need their business. I keep quiet a good part of the time."

Hugh got the message and drank his beer. A few minutes later, he spoke. "Who's the fella in the overalls and rolled up shirt sleeves? He seems to have the gift of the gab. He'd be a good fella to talk to about life in Halifax."

Angus stopped himself from saying what he was really thinking. Instead he offered Hugh a name and a piece of advice. "That's Frank Murphy. Likes his drink, as you can see. This might not be the time or place for a conversation with him, if that's what you were planning."

Hugh laughed. "Your right. Want a second beer, Angus?"

"Thank you."

With Hugh gone to the bar, Angus took a long, steady look in Ivan's direction.

Ivan was standing up but doing a poor job of it. His legs were shaky, his upper body weaving about like a flag in a stiff breeze. When his table mate urged him to sit down, Ivan was having none of it. "I'm goin' for him. Lost my job 'cause of him. Irish bugger."

Ivan stumbled then propelled himself forward off a nearby table. Gaining momentum, he glanced off people and tables until he crashed into Frank, his arms flailing about.

A couple of patrons grabbed Ivan and marched him out the door.

Hugh had a front row seat to the evening's excitement. He handed Angus a beer then laughed. "That was entertaining. Who's the fella they sent packing? What was meant by 'lost my job'?"

Angus thought hard about how to answer these direct questions. He settled on an economy of truth. No details. No opinions. "Ivan Buckle was shown the door. Sounds like he lost his job as a policeman. Frank has been interviewed by the police regarding the murder of that policeman from Truro. And that is all I will say, Hugh."

"I have no problem with that. So, do you have any interest in politics?"

"I do. I gather you might as well."

"I sure do."

***

Point Pleasant Park was the perfect place to shed the unpleasant experience at Citadel Hill. The newly fallen leaves crunched underfoot and the crisp, sharp smell of fall soon brought back casual conversation. When Corbin and Ruby played an impromptu game of 'name that tree', their hearts became lighter.

The companionable, quiet drive home was quickly ended inside the house. When Marmalade saw his mistress from the front window, he rushed to meet her and spun around her ankles until Ruby picked him up. His purring brought Mrs. Williams from the kitchen.

"My goodness Marmalade, you sound like Mr. Davis' motorcar." Everyone laughed. "The evening meal will be ready shortly. The days are so short now. I've put on the dining room lights. And a pot of tea is there. Come along Marmalade, it's your dinner time, too."

The stop at the Citadel left Ruby and Corbin emotionally exhausted but Corbin's favourite meal, beef stew with fresh biscuits and apple pie was just what they needed.

"Mrs. Williams is a marvelous cook. Her pastry is worthy of a medal."

"Well then, you'll just have to visit more often."

Ruby smiled but made no commitment.

Corbin sensed she was distracted, had something on her mind.

"Let's go to the sitting room. The seats are far more comfortable there. A sherry?"

"Yes. Sorry, my dinner conversation was less than stellar but I do have something you must know. Jo has been a friend for years. We've spent many hours together, walking, reading, visiting neighbours. She can be kind and caring." She sipped the sherry, looked out the window. The glass resting on her lap.

Corbin knew there was more. He didn't interrupt her thoughts.

Ruby remained silent, her eyes looked beyond the trees, beyond the dark sky to a place only she could see. She began to weep, the tears glistened then rolled down her cheeks.

Corbin pulled a handkerchief from his pocket, gave it to her and took away the glass. Her face was flushed from crying and the sherry. He waited for Ruby's deeper understanding of Jo to be revealed.

Ruby was about to say something she had never allowed to pass her lips, never offered to anyone. She despised having to utter them. She was certain the words would change everything Corbin thought he knew about Jo. Her fragile voice began so quietly, Corbin could barely hear her. He moved to kneel beside her chair.

"Jo relied on Bill to get out of her liaisons. There were a few. Perhaps one of those men killed Bill. Jo knows something."

When Ella tucked Rose into bed, she explained away her father's absence by using his work at the hospital. Tomorrow she would tell her a kinder version of the truth.

With Rose settled, she and Murdoch went to the sitting room. Ella told him about Henderson's interview, including the inference about her involvement.

Murdoch shook his head. "He's just poking around. Don't trouble yourself about it."

Ella took a deep breath. "You realize Papa's disappearance will be in the newspaper tomorrow."

"I do and I will be going to work anyway. Mr. Davis will be away from the office." He finished his tea. "Mr. LeBlanc was supposed to have five nights' work. He took time off his regular job to help us. Unless you think otherwise, I'm going to pay him anyway."

"That's fine, dear." Ella sat for several minutes. "In all of this, we must not forget about Alex Wallace. Where do you suppose he is?"

Murdoch shook his head.

They sat quietly for a short while, then each picked up a book. Neither one could concentrate so they exchanged the books for magazines they had already read. Going to bed seemed a more reasonable idea. There, worry trumped sleep until exhaustion took them to dreamland. Even there they were unsettled.

CHAPTER EIGHTEEN

THURSDAY, NOVEMBER 01

Early Thursday morning a howling wind roared across the Atlantic, bringing with it a rain storm that assaulted Halifax. The water drummed on the city's roofs and lashed windows from the harbour to Citadel Hill. Inside the Ramsay kitchen, Ella pulled her sweater tighter despite the warmth from the cast-iron stove. The morning newspaper remained unopened, face down in front of Ella. She did not want Rose to see the headline. **Local Doctor Missing Feared Dead.**

Even if the rain stopped, the day would not get any better for Ella. She wondered about Charles. Perhaps he was already dead, thrown into some field outside the city. He didn't deserve to be murdered.

Murdoch leaned across the table. "I will call for a taxi to drop Rose off at school then take me to the office. Would you rather I stay home?"

"No, I'll be fine alone." She continued to stare at the window as a curtain of water rolled down the pane. "I'm supposed to meet with the Mayor later today about the city event on the twenty-fourth."

"You could put it off for another day, Mama."

"What day would be better? Your father could be missing for days. The city event must go on." She poured a second cup of tea. "It'll be a distraction." She looked up at Murdoch. "It's not as though I'm shopping." She looked down at the cup. "He doesn't deserve this."

Rose skipped into the kitchen to eat her breakfast. "Hooray, it's raining! I can wear my rain boots."

Murdoch served Rose her porridge and milk. "You and I will also have a taxi car ride."

"That will be fun. Is Papa gone to the hospital already?"

Ella hesitated. "I hope you will see him this evening. He could be away for a few days."

"I miss him."

Murdoch shot a look of disapproval at his mother.

Ella intentionally took no notice of him. "If the rain is terrible at home time, Murdoch will come in a taxi car to get you."

"Can Nellie come too?"

"Yes, my darling. Nellie can have a taxi car ride home too."

"This will be so much fun."

Murdoch pulled Rose's pigtails. "Finish your breakfast, Rosy. It's almost time to go."

"My name is not Rosy, Murdochy." Then she ran out of the room, hoping Murdoch would chase her. "Bye, Mama."

Murdoch stood behind his mother's chair and gave her a hug. "Call me if you want me to come home."

***

Murdoch ran from the taxi then lingered under the Davis Footwear awning to catch his breath and wipe his glasses. He debated about telling Marie the truth about why his father was missing. His old self would say 'keep things close to your vest'. He turned the door knob.

Marie looked up. "You look awful."

"Thank you. It's always good to start the day off on a positive note." Murdoch shook the rain off his Mackintosh and hung it up. "Have you seen the morning paper?"

Marie opened the folded paper. "Oh, Murdoch." Her eyes misted over. "Is this your father?" She stood and embraced him then quickly stepped back. "What happened?"

"Someone took him. I'll make a quick visit to the factory and be back shortly."

Marie took the mail and newspaper into Corbin's office then waited for Murdoch to return. Her mind was so fully focused on Murdoch and his family, she had ignored the details on one of the envelopes.

When Murdoch returned, he brought his chair to Marie's desk. They sat together and talked about the whole sordid ordeal with the nurse, his father being taken away on the way to the police station and the man in the car outside the house. "It has to be someone with money. Cars are not inexpensive."

"How's your mother?"

"Trying to be hopeful. Rose thinks he's away for a few days." He shook his head. "We'll have to tell her tonight because the children or teachers might say something to her tomorrow." Murdoch dropped his head into is hands. "What a bloody awful muddle."

Marie took Murdoch's hands in hers. "I'm so, so sorry and frightened for your father, your whole family."

"Thank you. The worst part is waiting." Murdoch looked around the office then exhaled heavily. "On a brighter note, I've a new business idea. Women's shoes with fancy decorations. I've noticed my mother's shoes." He looked down at Marie's plain black shoes. "You could wear our new ideas, increase the sales."

"I like shoes. I'd volunteer to wear them."

"Good. I'll include you in my sales idea to Mr. Davis." His smile soon faded, thoughts of his father, the uncertainty, the worry. He took an envelope out of his pocket and passed it to Marie. “Here’s the money for your father’s work. Thank you for caring about my family.” He leaned forward, took Marie’s hand in his and kissed her on the cheek.

***

Angus Martin always kept his promises, including the ones he made to himself. But when Ivan Buckle attacked Frank in the bar, he gave up on his secret promise to Billie for the time being. There would always be another day to prove Frank an unworthy partner for her.

“Good morning, Mr. Martin.”

“And to you Billie but you should have skipped the ‘good’ part. That rain is a devil of storm.”

“How was your evening?”

“Met a new fella called Hugh Andrews. He’s writing a story about the city and people who live here. You’ll likely meet him soon.”

“Why would I meet him?”

“He knows about the store and all the talk and gossip that goes on in here. The store’s a perfect place for him to meet people, don’t you think?”

Billie shrugged. ”Guess so.”

***

Jenny Ward, Ella’s half-day maid arrived late and very wet all thanks to waiting for a trolley and walking the last two streets to the Ramsay home.

“Good grief, Jenny. You can’t possibly stay in those shoes and that dress. Both are soaked. Come upstairs. I’ll find a day dress for you to wear. I'll dry your clothing in the kitchen while you work. What size shoes do you wear?"

"Seven. Thank you." Jenny looked away briefly, "Is Doctor Ramsay missin', ma'am?"

Ella nodded.

Jenny covered her mouth with her hand, her eyes filled with tears. "Sorry. People was talking." She picked up her cleaning bucket and walked toward the staircase, her wet dress leaving a trail of water on the hardwood floor.

"Thank you, Jenny."

By noon Jenny was gone, the rain had dwindled to the odd shower, the sun appeared.

***

The morning drive to the police station was quiet. Ruby appeared hypnotized by the windshield wipers as she fiddled with the handle of her purse. At the same time, Corbin was deep in thought about Bill's association with Jo.

As the police station came into view, Ruby was the first to speak. "I'm really nervous, Corbin."

"Remember two things. You know why someone heard Bill speak German and the police are working hard to find Bill's killer." He got out of the car, opened his umbrella and assisted Ruby from her seat and into the police station.

Sergeant Bailey stuck his head around Henderson's door. "You sure you don't want me to interview Detective Turner's wife, Sir? He was your friend. This will be hard on both of you."

Will shook his head. "Thanks but I have to talk to Ruby myself. She deserves that respect, hard as it may be for me."

Inside Henderson's office, Ruby willed herself to sit still, even though her insides were jelly.

"Thank you for coming, Ruby. I know this will be difficult for both of us but I need your thoughts and recollections. Coffee or tea?"

Ruby declined both.

"Let's begin."

Will asked all the questions she and Corbin talked about, including Bill speaking German. Just when she thought the questions were finished and she had inched forward to stand up, Will began speaking again.

"I have a few more questions. Maybe you can help me. As you know, Bill came to Halifax once a month for a regular meeting. Do you know anything about these visits? Did he ever mention names, talk about being followed or fear for his safety? Would he take risks?"

Ruby's mouth fell open. Momentarily unable to speak, she shook her head, her eyes locked on Will's face. "How dare you imply I would know such details about Bill's work? I'm annoyed that you would suggest such a thing, Will. Police business was not my business. You two were friends. You should know he would not take unnecessary risks nor tell me he was being followed."

Will took Ruby's hand to help her stand. "Thank you for coming. I'm sorry I upset you. We will be in touch again."

While Ruby sat in the station lobby waiting for Corbin, she came to the conclusion Will knew more about her husband than she did.

When Corbin arrived, Ruby seemed incapable of finding her way along the sidewalk, let alone getting into a car parked across the street. Corbin took her arm and helped her into the passenger seat.

"What happened in there?"

She looked up at Corbin. "Detective Henderson seems to think I know more about Bill's work in Halifax than I'm telling him. How would I know what he was doing here?"

Corbin got into the car then learned across the seat and took her hand. “We will talk over lunch.”

Lunch was quiet, especially at the beginning. Ruby was struggling with the implication she would know about Bill’s work in Halifax, that he was somehow responsible for his own death. She couldn’t make enough sense of it to form a question, let alone talk about it. They each had a cup of tea and half a sandwich before words were exchanged.

“Why would Will expect me to know what Bill was doing in Halifax? I didn’t know or wanted to know the details of Bill’s cases.”

“I have very limited understanding of police methods so what I’m going to say is a guess. Will may understand you have no detailed information about any of Bill’s cases but he’s created the possibility of a second opportunity to speak with you. In the meantime, that possibility will prompt you to think about what he asked.”

“Now you have me really wondering.”

Corbin offered a reassuring smile. “Save the wondering for the train ride home. First, let’s finish lunch and go to the art museum before we pick up Marmalade and I take you to the train. English trifle or chocolate truffle cake?”

“You’re a good friend, Corbin. I truly appreciate everything you are doing for me.”

“Here’s to friendship.” Corbin lifted his cup, as did Ruby.

Accepting Charles was probably gone, Ella hoped he had not suffered. After lunch, she dressed for the meeting with the Mayor. Closing the front door, she breathed deeply and readied herself for what was to come today. Tomorrow and the days after would have to take care of themselves. The taxi car showed up on time and she was soon at City Hall, where she met the mayor.

"Mrs. Ramsay, I truly did not expect to see you today. It is not necessary for you to carry on with the event planning, given your circumstances." The mayor faltered a moment then regained his composure. "I'm very sorry to hear about your husband."

"Thank you, Your Worship. I really need to keep busy but do not want to be seen socially. I'm sure you understand my point."

"Yes, yes, of course. We will help you with anything you need. I'll arrange a private room and one of my office staff will work with you this afternoon. I believe this meeting is about the ticket design plus a visit to the printer. Correct?"

"Yes. Mrs. Cameron and I have booked the military band and a musical group which will provide dance music. We also have a dinner menu proposal."

"My, oh my, you ladies have done a wonderful job. Thank you. The City will create a free afternoon outdoor event for anyone who wishes to attend. There will be a focus on family and children at that event. We are considering a treasure hunt, definitely a clown or two."

"That is a wonderful idea for those not able or not interested in an evening event."

"Miss Parsons will assist you this afternoon. She's a friend of Anna Hopkins. Do you know Anna?"

"No, I've not met her but I do recognize the name."

"Miss Parsons is quite talented at this sort of thing. She also knows our budget limitations. She will take the material to the printer for you." He walked to the door then turned around. "Thank you, Mrs. Ramsay. We are very appreciative of your work for the City, especially today. On a personal note, I have spoken with the police department and advised them to work around the clock to find your husband."

"Thank you."

"I'll be right back with Miss Parsons."

Ella prepared herself for the talented Miss Parsons.

***

"Hello, Mable. I'm inviting myself over for a quick visit before Rose gets home. It's about the November event. Hope you don't mind terribly." *Mable's attitude regarding my socializing will be a good indication of what I can expect from my society friends.*

"That would be lovely. Any news about Charles?"

"Unfortunately, no. I am very worried." She paused for a moment. "The November event has good news. There will be an art show. I'll be there in about fifteen minutes."

"We are very concerned about Charles, Ella. We can speak further about this when you are here. I will have strong tea ready or would your prefer a sherry?"

"Tea will be fine, Mable."

She managed to get home before Rose arrived and prepared herself to tell Rose about her father. In the midst of her thoughts during the preparation of Rose's after school apple and cheese, the front door slammed shut and Rose ran down the hall.

"Mama, Mama. Do you know Papa is missing. Nellie told me today when I was leaving school to walk home."

Ella pulled Rose close to her and hugged her tightly. "Yes, I do." Then she let go. "Eat your apple and cheese then I'll read you a story. The police are looking for him because someone took him away from his car."

"But why would someone take him away?"

"We don't know. Likely someone who is angry. You can sleep with me tonight."

"We can read in bed together."

"That sounds lovely and cozy."

"Murdoch should be home soon. Do you want to help me set the table?"

"Yes. Do Murdoch and Marie know about Papa?"

"I'm sure they do, dear." *Marie is already part of the family!*

Marmalade slept most of the train ride home, leaving Ruby plenty of time to consider the implication posed by Detective Henderson. His questioning suggested she knew something about Bill's cases and his murder. It was a personal affront. The leap to defend Bill and herself had been quick. At the time, she had been very angry with Detective Henderson.

As the train made its' way toward Truro, Ruby became immune to the whistles and rail squeaks as she came to a different point of view about the meeting. Will was so earnest in his questioning, she examined the real possibility that she might indeed know something.

Arriving home, she went to the sitting room and carried two boxes of her journals into the bedroom. Marmalade gave each box and lid a thorough inspection. Finding nothing to threaten his comfortable life, he went to the food dish for his evening meal as Ruby warmed up a bowl of vegetable stew and a biscuit. She sat at the kitchen table and stared at the back garden. It held many happy and sad times.

After supper, Ruby got into bed, positioned her pillows for support and began reading her journals starting with January 1911, the year she met Bill Turner. She skimmed over her walks and notes about the weather. Instead, she focused on social activities and the people in their lives. In March of 1912, Jo Robinson arrived from England to live with her brother, Malcolm. June 22 of the same year was their wedding day. They went to Halifax for their honeymoon. She fell asleep reading August 1912.

CHAPTER NINETEEN

Friday, November 02

Following a fitful sleep, an early breakfast and sipping her second cup of tea, Ruby was still mithering about Will's inferences and her role in helping to solve Bill's murder. His tone was out of place and hurtful. *Perhaps I'm being overly sensitive.* As she finished the tea, a niggling notion roiled around in the far reaches of her mind. It didn't manifest itself into a face or a location, but a heightened sensitivity to something or somebody. It was there but out of reach. Perhaps she did know more than she thought.

Prolonged fussing over something never worked for Ruby. What did work was a diversion. Walking. Baking. Painting. One of those would surely clear her fuddled mind, allowing the sensation to reveal itself. She put on a warm coat and comfortable walking shoes then left the house. An hour later, she returned home with a clearer idea of what she had to do. Reading her journals would be the best way to stimulate memories which would be helpful. When she opened the front door, Marmalade was sitting in front of his empty bowl.

"Did that long nap make you hungry?"

Large green eyes blinked, twice.

"I suppose sleeping could make you feel peckish." She dropped a few chunks of fish in his bowl then turned to the kitchen counter. A sandwich and a pot of tea sounded like an excellent idea. With the sandwich and pot of tea on the side table, she settled in to begin reading 1912 again. She would make notes.

1912

February

Jo Robinson arrives from England. She's living with her brother Malcolm, who is a doctor. She must have money. She's not interested in finding work.

September

Mary comes for a visit. She thinks Jo is manipulative. Bill has a new constable, Adam Taylor. He likes Jo and she openly flirts with him.

December

Jo, Adam and Hugh Andrews are here for Christmas dinner.

1913

May

Hugh, Adam and Jo help us fix-up the little house we bought. Jo is unhappy with Adam. She is very open about this. It's embarrassing

June

Adam is transferred to Halifax. Bill denies he arranged it. Later Jo thanks him in front of me.

She wants to skip the rest of the year but pushes herself through.

July

We lost our baby girl before we got to know her. Bill is shattered. I'm broken. We struggle. Jo is here most days.

She writes while I cry. She's writing a book. She and Bill look after the vegetable garden.

August
Bill and I try to cheer each other up. Most days it's a struggle. Jo gives up on the book saying she is bored with it. She spends time here most days.

September
I feel a little better. Jo and I walk every day.

October
My father dies in a farm accident. Mary comes to stay for a week. She cautions me again about Jo, her behaviour and motives. Still walking with Jo. She's here every day but is gone by supper time. Bill has two murders to solve.. He 's away from home many evenings, went to Halifax one day.

December
Bill's new constable, Phil Campbell likes Jo. She's interested in him. Jo visits occasionally. Bill says she is writing again and spending more time with Malcolm. Bill is still away many evenings but talking more. He was in Halifax one day. Hugh and Phil come for Christmas dinner. Phil says he's enjoying the job. Malcolm telephones to say Jo is ill and she will stay home with him. Jo appears tired of Phil.

1914
January
Jo still visits occasionally but doesn't stay long. Bill goes to Halifax for one day.

Ruby stops reading, circles the last sentence and a few previous ones. There is no striking memory yet, just some things to consider later.

February
The murders are solved. Bill is back to his old self, laughing more. Hugh is here for dinner a few times. They have long into-the-night discussions. Jo comes once for dinner while Hugh is here. She looks troubled, leaves early. Bill goes to Halifax late in the month for one day. Phil is transferred to Dartmouth.

Ruby circles the note and reads on.

March
I join the book club. We meet once a week in the church basement. Jo visits occasionally. Bill is in Halifax for one day.

Ruby circles the note and reads on quickly, through the remainder of the year. Bill went to Halifax one day every month. This is the meeting with detectives from Halifax, Dartmouth, Truro and Amherst.

1915
July
Jo moves to Halifax on July 12.

Bill was in Halifax 1 day for each of the months in 1915. He stayed overnight in late July and mid August. Jo visits Malcolm in September. She helped with our garden. Hugh came for Christmas dinner. Jo stayed home with Malcolm.

1916
April
Jo visits Malcolm and us. She's happy, excited about the book.

June
Jo visits Malcolm. She's stopped writing and joyless. Bill avoids her.

August
Jo visits Malcolm and us. She's happy one day, upset the next.

Ruby finds the three day visits in October, November and early December. She remembers asking Bill about them. He had a reasonable answer. He was an additional detective with Dartmouth investigations. Was he?

December
Jo visits Malcolm for Christmas. She visits us. She was very thoughtful, quiet and strangely affectionate when she left. I asked Bill if he was still helping her. He said he was because she has big problems, with men.

1917

Ruby studied the year closely. Early October was the only month with any remarkable entry. Jo was in Truro and came to the house late one evening. She was openly angry with Bill, calling him a liar. She remembered Jo yelling. “You lied to me. I won’t forget that.” After she left, Bill shook his head saying, ‘She was drunk and still having problems with men’.

Ruby closed the 1917 journal and put all of them away. Frequency and duration of Bill's visits to Halifax would not answer Will's questions. It was more personal than that.

***

A sharp-eyed Halifax police constable walking to work on Duke Street early Friday morning spotted a car similar to Charles Ramsay's travelling north on Barrington Street. He rushed to the police station to speak with the duty constable. "Albert, who's on duty?"

"Sergeant Surrette's here." He raised his voice." Sergeant, we need you here tout de suite."

"Tell me what you saw, Constable."

"It was a car like the one in the lock-up. It was going north on Barrington. The male driver was in a hurry."

"Good work, Constable. I'll get a motorcycle on the chase."

***

Murdoch was the first one in the office Friday morning. He was making coffee when Corbin arrived. Murdoch nodded. "Good morning, Mr. Davis."

"And to you. How are you feeling, Murdoch?"

"I'm worried and can't understand why it happened." He shook his head. "Who would kidnap a doctor? Where is he? We just want an answer."

"Let's hope it's soon and good news."

A few minutes later, Marie came through the door. She looked around the office and passed the morning mail from the front door mailbox to Corbin. "Was there an early meeting?"

"No, Miss LeBlanc. Just two fellas who didn't sleep well last night." He looked in Murdoch's direction. "Give me a few minutes."

Marie waited until Corbin went into his office. "Any news?"

Murdoch shook his head and walked to his desk.

Corbin soon returned and passed an envelope toward Murdoch before returning to his office.

Murdoch nodded then went to Marie's desk with the letter. "How did I miss that letter?"

He read the note. *I'll be in Halifax soon. Alex Wallace*

He shoved the note inside the envelope and turned toward his desk. "We better get to work. I need something other than Papa to think about."

***

"Good morning, Sergeant Bailey. We have a man in a holding cell. He told Sergeant Surrette his name is Clifford Fillmore. Traffic picked him up earlier for speeding. His car is like the one we're looking for."

"Excellent news. Good work. Are we expecting Detective Henderson at the usual time?"

The desk constable glanced at the appointment book. "Yes, Sir. No outside appointments in his book this morning."

"Is Sergeant Surrette still here?"

"Yes, Sir. He figured you'd want to speak with him. He's in the lunch room."

Bailey poured a cup of coffee and sat down across from Surrette, note book at the ready. "Great work this morning, Sergeant."

"Thanks, Bailey. Being in a new role takes some time."

"So what happened with this Fillmore fella?"

"We caught Fillmore speeding in a car like the one the doctor drove. A telephone call to the town of Dartmouth, confirmed Clifford Fillmore owns a house in the town. He says he was away at the time of his wife's death. When Lois Fillmore's body was found in Halifax there was no evidence of a man living in the apartment with her."

By ten o'clock Henderson was ready to interview Clifford Fillmore. Henderson walked into the interview room and was met with a surly stare by a man pacing in front of his desk. Henderson acted casually and sat behind his desk. "Good morning, Mr. Fillmore. I'm Detective Will Henderson."

Clifford Fillmore was well dressed, mid forty and obviously used to getting his own way as he continued to strut in front of Will's desk. Between sentences, he stroked his bushy black moustache. "It's certainly not a good morning. Why am I in a cell? Speeding warrants a ticket not the lock-up. Take me to a telephone and I will have my lawyer here in short order."

"Sit down, Mr. Fillmore and I will explain what is going on here."

Fillmore sat down but not before demanding, "Where the hell is my car?"

"Your car is locked up in the police garage."

Fillmore jumped up. "Why? I demand you release it to me. I'm prepared to pay the speeding ticket and be on my way."

Henderson leaned back in his chair. "This is getting us nowhere, Mr. Fillmore. If you prefer to stand, do so. I am investigating the death of your wife and the disappearance of Doctor Charles Ramsay."

Fillmore dropped into his chair, his mouth fell open but nothing came out.

"Mr. Fillmore, your black 1914 McKay Touring motor car is a match for Doctor Ramsay's. Your motor car was following Doctor Ramsay when he disappeared."

Fillmore was still sitting on the edge of his chair, his wide-eyed stare locked on Will's face. "Lois is dead? Who the hell is Charles Ramsay? I've been in Montreal for the past two weeks and I have the train tickets to prove it."

"Why were you in Montreal?"

Fillmore fell back into his chair, his bluster gone. "Lois is dead?"

Henderson pressed on. "Montreal?"

Fillmore looked at Henderson, his eyes roamed the room, unfocused. "A meeting with a company to buy my machine parts, sign the contracts." He leaned forward. "She's really dead?"

"Yes, I'm sorry to tell you that Mrs. Fillmore is deceased." He waited a few moments. "Are you able to prove that Montreal meeting?"

"Yes. Give me a piece of paper and you can have the name and phone number."

"We'll do that before you leave. I have more questions. When did you last see Mrs. Fillmore?"

Fillmore fell back into his chair, looked up at the wall behind Henderson, then down at the desk, his head shaking. "I'd say about three months ago. We didn't get along. She left me about that time, moved over to Halifax."

"And how do you know she moved to Halifax?"

"She called, wanting money. Told me where she was living."

"So you went to see her with the money?"

Fillmore paused briefly, closed his eyes. "I told her no, about the money." He opened his eyes. "I never heard from her again."

"Hmm." Henderson continued. "You live in Dartmouth. And your business?"

"I own two machine shops, both on the Halifax side."

"Your car and Doctor Ramsay's car are unique, both made in Amherst. The company stopped making those cars after 1914.

How do you explain your car following Doctor Ramsay's vehicle on the afternoon of October thirty-first?"

"I can't. I wasn't here. Has to be someone else."

"You mean there is a third black 1914 McKay Touring in the city?"

"No. I don't mean that." Will noticed Fillmore's blunt, gruff manner had vanished. "I've only seen one other. Guess that one belongs to this Ramsay fella." He paused. "Someone else drove my car."

Henderson lifted his eyebrows, his face reflecting a puzzled look. "And so, where was your car during your time in Montreal?"

"In my garage. On my property in Dartmouth."

"Are you telling me someone took your car from your garage to kill your wife and follow Doctor Ramsay?"

Fillmore's eyes locked onto Will's face. "I am."

The fight had been knocked out of Fillmore with the death of his wife but Henderson needed to secure the information he needed. "Left the key in the car, did you?"

"Hanging on a hook above the shelf."

"Any names come to mind?"

"Not at the present time."

Henderson noticed Fillmore's expression change, ever so slightly. He had an idea about the 'who' was driving his car. "Mr. Fillmore, I want you to stay within the confines of Dartmouth and Halifax until I say otherwise. An officer will take you home on the ferry to retrieve the travel documents that prove you were in Montreal during the period of time you reported to me. And finally, if your documents are accurate, we will release your car to you later today. Have I made myself clear?"

"Very."

"Come with me and meet Sergeant Surrette. He will take you home and bring you back. Before you leave, give me that Montreal company and phone number."

With Clifford Fillmore out of the building, Henderson went to Bailey's office.

Bailey lifted his head. "Guilty for murder, kidnapping?"

"He says he has an ironclad alibi for the past two weeks. He's cunning and I suspect, can be aggressive when confronted or needs to be. He's also quick with the answers. What he told me may not stand up so well under scrutiny. Surrette is taking him home for his travel documents."

"Is he likely to run, Sir?"

Henderson shook his head. "With his precious car locked up, I doubt it." He smiled. "In case he was planning something, I sent Constable Barlow along. It's his first day on the job."

***

Sergeant Surrette was in luck. The car ferry to Dartmouth was about to leave. The usual topics about the weather and the war passed the time on the ferry.

Fillmore lived near the ferry landing in an older, well kept single story house set close to the street. The small front yard was orderly. The garage was placed at the back of the property, well hidden from the street. A high wooden fence and mature trees separated Fillmore from his neighbours.

When Fillmore entered the house with Surrette to get the travel papers, Barlow went directly to the outbuilding. The doors were unlocked. He pushed each door aside on its track and stepped inside, onto a dirt floor. Sun from the south-facing window lit up the interior. A warm, musty smell of hay lingered in the air.

On the side walls a variety of old hand tools, a horse collar, leather straps and fittings were reminiscent of its former use. It had been a barn for a horse and carriage. Along the back wall a wide shelf held several new tools and various small car parts.

Among them Barlow noticed a car door handle, steering wheel and a large stack of clean rags. Everything was spotless and laid out with great care.

Barlow casually walked the length of the shelf, his hand trailing along its smooth front edge. He guessed the tools were part of the man's business or maybe something to do with the maintenance of his own car. He hoped to own a car one day. As he was about to leave, he noticed a dirty rag in the corner of the shelf, partially hidden by a paint can. The rag was in sharp contrast to the other items on the shelf.

Curious, Barlow leaned forward. The rag was dry and had large, dark grey stains. They were definitely not paint. A few strands of long curly, light brown hair clung to one corner. At first he didn't know what to do. Leave it or take it? He decided on the latter then carefully folded it to protect the hair and put it in his coat pocket.

Clifford Fillmore found himself in the interview room after returning from Dartmouth. He was not at all pleased. When Henderson entered, he jumped up. "What the hell is the problem now?"

Henderson held up a towel with the end of his pen. "Sit down, Mr. Fillmore. Do you recognize this bloody towel?"

"No, why would I?"

"It came from your garage." Henderson returned the towel to a paper bag. "Sit down. We believe it was used to clean up blood at the scene of your wife's death. How did it get into your garage, Mr. Fillmore? Don't bother making up an answer. You may collect your car and leave the police premises but do not leave the Dartmouth, Halifax area. Sergeant Bailey will show you out."

Minutes later, Henderson and Bailey were staring at the paper bag. "What do you think, Sir?"

"I believe Mr. Fillmore is thinking hard about who swiped his car for a few days and I'm thinking about the morgue. I hope

Doctor Ashton kept hair samples from Lois Fillmore's body. We need to compare the colour and curl of the two."

"It's my turn to go to the morgue, Sir. By the way, do you have any mints in your desk?"

Will smiled and opened his desk drawer.

At the end of the day, Corbin stepped out of his office, a broad smile on his face. "Congratulations, you two. You have doubled the sales from October 1916. I know neither of you are in the mood for a celebration but I want to acknowledge your work in a tangible way. Here is an envelope with some money inside to do what you wish. When things look brighter, and they will, the three of us will go out for dinner together. Murdoch, you mentioned a sales idea. Come into my office and we'll talk about it."

A few minutes later Marie heard a bit of laughter from the office, then both Murdoch and Corbin came out and walked to her desk.

"I hear you want to wear Davis Footwear fancy shoes around the city, Miss LeBlanc."

"I do, Mr. Davis. And maybe winter boots? I like Murdoch's idea and I love shoes."

"Yes, his idea is a good one. A lady friend recently said the same thing." He patted Murdoch's back. "I hope your father is found unharmed. See you both Monday."

Ella was sitting at the kitchen table, her heart heavy. "You're home earlier than I expected, dear."

"Mr. Davis had good news on the annual sales, ending October thirty-first so we left a bit early. He sent his regards to you."

"He sounds like a lovely man."

"There's more good news. We will be making fancy women's shoes. It was my idea." He paused. "That's the good news. Here's the bad news." He handed the envelope to his mother.

"I was hoping Alex was dead." She sighed. "This." She tapped the note. "And your father." She began to cry.

Murdoch sat beside her, took her hand in his. He glanced toward the stove. "I smell chicken. I'll peel the potatoes and turnip then put them in separate pots of water. Rose can set the table."

"And the gravy?"

"You better make the gravy or we won't be able to eat it!"

"You're a fine son, Murdoch. I'm proud of you."

"Thank you, Mama. We'll be okay."

Clifford Fillmore was blistering mad. After getting his car into the garage, he began talking to himself. "Who the hell left that damn rag in the garage? Which one of you took my car to follow that doctor? Tomorrow, I'll be makin' a couple of very personal visits to get answers."

CHAPTER TWENTY

Saturday, November 03

Clifford Fillmore slept a few hours immediately after going to bed simply because he was exhausted by the ordeal with the police. Now wide awake and angry, he wanted answers. Lois' death was real but he didn't believe for one minute that she deserved to be murdered, even if she was free with her charms. *Who the hell killed her? Well, that was Henderson's problem.* Then there was his car. That was his problem. The muscles in his neck and jaw tightened.

While his eggs boiled, Clifford made a pot of tea and buttered two thick slices of brown bread. The names of several shady buggers and light-fingered fellas came to mind. He'd look stupid if he accused all of them so what he needed was a real serious short list. While eating breakfast, he picked up a pencil and whittled a long list to three names. He figured all three would have a reason to 'borrow' a car. Two were thieves, the kind of men who carried guns and took on guards and bank tellers. They hit and ran. A new town, a new heist. The third fella was a liar and a braggard with a nasty streak. He was a suspected rum runner, muscular, mouthy and used his fists to settle things. He'd start with the liar.

Clifford parked his McKay in the visitor area and walked to the backside of the hospital where a large building had a separate entrance for janitorial and maintenance employees. He pulled on the heavy door. The hinges creaked and squealed. He whinged. If the target saw him and ran, his plan would be scuttled.

Inside the large, open room the usual chatter and occasional shout of workers competed with the gurgling and humming sounds from laundry equipment. Floor cleaning equipment was on the opposite wall, where Clifford spotted Oliver White filling his water tub. Clifford walked in White's direction then stood beside him. "I need a simple answer from you, White."

Oliver swung around and faced Clifford, a forced smile plastered on his bearded face.

"Mornin', Cliff."

"What the hell happened to your eye?"

Oliver gingerly touched around the swollen eye. "A little dust up with a fella that disagreed with me a few days ago. It's nothin.'"

"Looks a lot more than nothing."

"Nah, just colourful, is all."

"When did that happen?"

"Monday night."

"And where was that?"

"Outside a drinkin' hole. You're full of questions, Cliffy." Oliver grinned.

Clifford nodded. "Been out of town for a while. What have you been up to the past week or so, other than getting a black eye?"

"Nothin' much." Oliver clenched his fists, shifted his posture, inched closer to Clifford. "You suggestin' I did somethin'?"

"I'm thinking this 'nothin' much' included driving my car around Halifax. That true?"

"Had it out for a spin once, that's all." Oliver shrugged, his eyes cold and empty.

"Not good enough. I want to know why and I want details, like where did 'ya go."

Oliver looked toward the door. "Let's step outside. We can talk without these other fellas hearin'."

Not on your life. "We're just fine in here. Start talkin'."

"I had a little job that needed doin.'"

Clifford's eyes widened. "You stole my car for a little job?"

Oliver screwed up his face. "Well, it was a personal thing, Cliff. 'Ya know. Involvin' a lady friend." Then he offered a shameless grin. "I did put gas in it after."

Clifford had heard enough. He had his answer.

"Never again. You got that?"

"Sure thing, Cliff." Oliver moved to pat Clifford on the arm but Clifford had already taken a step toward the door, his jaw clenched. He gripped the steering wheel all the way to the police station.

***

Bailey knocked on Henderson's door and stuck his head into the room.

"I'm off to the morgue. Wish me luck."

"For a good result on the towel or keeping your breakfast in your stomach?"

Bailey rolled his eyes. "Thank you, Sir. I appreciate the support."

"When you're back, let's review the Mollie Brown file with Sergeant Surrette. The family of that unfortunate lass needs answers."

"Yes, Sir. Surrette has his men on the wharf making inquiries."

"Enjoy Doctor Ashton's company at the morgue."

***

Ruby concluded Bill's murder had to be revenge. Wrestling with that decision kept her awake late into the night. When morning finally arrived, she sat at the kitchen table, ready to put her overnight thoughts to work. Dates and numbers meant nothing to her. It was all about people and therefore, more painful than looking at dates on a calendar.

Who wanted Bill dead? Perhaps someone he'd put in jail? He didn't talk about those people but that was Will's bailiwick anyway. That settled, she turned her full attention to people she knew.

Malcolm Robinson. Jo had difficulties with Malcolm so she looked to Bill for help. *Did Malcolm resent Bill's relationship with her?* Maybe he thought we'd uncover the family secrets Jo so often alluded to? Physicians could be murderers, especially ones with a healthy dose of self-importance and a lot to lose.

Jo Robinson. Her sister Mary thought Jo was a bit strange, secretive but then Yvette thought everyone but herself was off kilter, as she would say. Jo relied on Bill to get her out of trouble. Why would she want to get rid of him? If Bill refused to help her, his life might have been at risk. Jo seemed to know a lot of people. People who could get rid of Bill.

Adam Taylor and Phil Campbell. They were two of Jo's suitors. What did those two policemen think of Bill when he transferred them out of Truro to please Jo? Where are they now?

Who are the other suitors Bill chased off when he was in Halifax? *I'm sure she would have had one or two.* Only Jo knows the answer to that question.

Ruby sat back in her chair and placed her pen on top of the notes she'd completed. It was time for reflection.

Jo's dependency on Bill subtly increased over time. She recalled the many times Jo and Bill were in the garden or in the kitchen together, especially during her own grief. Jo's visits were less frequent and shorter prior to her move to Halifax in mid July 1915. She often missed the usual dinner gatherings and when present, seemed troubled and annoyed with those present, especially Bill. Her drinking increased. Her contact was a telephone call once or twice a month. She would ask how 'my dear Bill' was before mentioning a party in Halifax and a name or two. In late June she called, demanding to speak with Bill. She recalled Jo's comment. "I think Bill doesn't like me anymore but I need his help." She sounded drunk. In September Bill acknowledged Jo was having trouble with men again. *Does Will have a suspect list? If not, I'll offer him mine.*

To her own surprise, Ruby began to cry great sobs. Her hand went to her heart. Marmalade jumped on the table and wiggled his face into a space between her neck and her arm. He turned on the motor and purred until Ruby lifted her head.

"Thank you, Marmalade. You are a fine gentleman. I need more coffee. I'm sure you would like a saucer of warm milk."

***

Oliver White figured Fillmore would go straight to the police so he left work and hurried home. The house was empty. He grabbed the money from a tin can behind the tea pot and two apples from the cupboard, then put on his winter coat and walked away. Getting out of town in a hurry was his biggest worry. While walking, he created a new version of himself. Fred Black was unmarried and looking for work in the next town.

Duncan MacDonald was going to visit his mother in Truro. He was pleased to see someone walking on the side of the road. The fella would be company. He stopped and picked up Fred Black. Amazingly, Fred Black was going to Truro for work and also going to visit his mother.

When Duncan asked Fred why he didn't take the train, Fred said he wanted to see more of the country at a slower pace. *Better than being found by the police in a train car.* The drive from Halifax took considerable time with stops for gasoline on the way.

Arriving in Truro, Oliver could hardly believe his good fortune. He was a free man and in a busy town. He stepped out of the motor car onto Queen Street then turned his head to thank Duncan. "Thank you for the ride, Duncan. You're a life saver."

"Enjoy the visit with your mother, Fred."

"Thank you, Duncan. You are most kind."

When the car was out of sight, Oliver rushed along Queen Street in search of a general store. To save his own life, he'd taken the money his wife kept for food and the savings for their son's winter coat.

Oliver figured he was the one who earned it, so it was his. He shrugged. Halifax would take care of Virginia and the child somehow.

The general store had everything Oliver needed. He bought shaving soap, a brush and straight razor then walked to the train station where he used the men's restroom to shave off his beard. Seeing a man in a train uniform standing behind a counter, Oliver stepped forward. "I need a ticket to Montreal."

"Very well, sir."

Oliver had trouble counting and reading so he opened his hand and let the station agent take the amount he needed. "I forgot my glasses and can't read the sign over there. When can I leave?"

"You have a few hours to wait, sir."

Oliver nodded and sat down. Unable to read the discarded newspapers, Oliver soon started to pace the empty waiting room. He felt the station man's eyes on him. It annoyed him. He stuffed his hands into his pockets and made tight fists. He wanted to hit the station man, stop him from staring, judging him. He couldn't wait in the building any longer. He couldn't wait to go to Montreal either. He'd start walking again tomorrow. He marched to the counter. "I'm not going to Montreal. I want my money back."

"Absolutely, sir."

Oliver bought a cheese sandwich at the store, and walked around town until the sun went down. After dark, he creapt into a church and fell asleep on a pew.

***

Detective Henderson was pleased to see Bailey enter the office with a satisfied look. Surrette appeared far less positive.

"Before you two begin, we have new information related to Doctor Ramsay's disappearance and an update from Truro. Clifford Fillmore was here earlier. According to him, Oliver White used his car to 'do a little job' while he was in Montreal. I recall White's name from a discussion with Doctor Ramsay about a threat at the hospital. I have constables looking for White. He's missing from his work at the hospital and his wife doesn't know where he is. Questions?"

With silence as the answer, Henderson continued. "Now about Truro. Freeman will be watched when he's out of jail for robbery. The other two, Joseph Young and Alexander Wallace are more elusive. So, we need to get in touch with the Amherst and Yarmouth police. Either would be a good place to hide." He looked at Bailey. "What do we know about the towel?"

"Sir, the bloody towel hair is like Lois Fillmore's hair. Now that we have a potential car thief, we may also have a suspect in the murder of Lois Fillmore."

Surrette shook his head and leaned toward Henderson's desk. "Sir, that Oliver White fellow stole Fillmore's car to kill Fillmore's wife?"

"According to Mr. Fillmore, White did just that. It's also possible White was hired by Fillmore to kill his wife. You're going to learn a lot about what drives people to kill. Revenge is one and it can fester for years. Old wounds don't always heal. Fillmore's lead remains valid and our job is to follow leads. Now, tell me about Mollie Brown."

"Well Sir, I wish we had a lead like Mr. Fillmore gave you. Honestly, we are not making progress. I'd like to put up a poster in the businesses around the wharf. Do you approve?"

"I do. Let me have a look at one before you take it to the printer."

"Thank you, Sir."

"Anything else?"

Bailey spoke up. "I'd like to have a word, Sir."

Surrette nodded and left the room.

Bailey remained seated. "Sir, Surette did a fine job as a constable. He is observant, works well in the team, can lead. I know he will be good as a sergeant."

Henderson laughed. "Of course he will. Give him a few months and nothing will surprise him."

***

Hugh Andrews had a couple of things weighing heavy on his mind. The first was Jo. He was trying to figure out what to do about her rambling conversation about men and Bill in particular. Maybe the answer was to do nothing at the present. After all, she was taking pills and drinking alcohol. If she knew something about Bill's death, surely she would've gone to the police. Corbin knows her. He'd call Corbin today.

The second thing was about himself. He'd never had trouble keeping his word to others but relying on himself occasionally brought angst to his own door. He'd committed himself to come clean with the police today and he would but what he knew about Bills' murder was likely not worth a detective's time. That bothered him a great deal. He'd been in the city a week and had little to show for that time. What he knew about the young woman on the wharf could be helpful. He'd keep his word but first he'd have lunch at his favourite place near the harbour, where he would mentally prepare for the meeting. He looked forward to the tasty food, hearty helpings and staff who remembered him with a nod or 'hello'.

Hugh really didn't want to sit with anyone so he hurried toward a table for two in the corner near a window. He put his coat on the back of the empty chair, hoping everyone would assume he was waiting for a lunch partner to join him. The plan was working until a young man who carried himself like an off-duty soldier made eye contact. It was too late to be a grumpy bugger and shake his head in the direction of the fella but he'd eat quickly and do his mulling on a bench outside.

"Good afternoon, sir. Thanks for offering the extra chair. I'm Doug Todd."

"I'm Hugh Andrews." Hugh nodded, smiled weakly and dipped his spoon into the fish stew. *As if I offered him the bloody chair.*

"That stew looks good. It's hard to decide here. Me, I like the fish sandwich. That brown bread is good with anything. I see you have it with your stew." He stared at Hugh. "Have we met?"

Hugh shrugged. "No. I've only been here a week." Hugh dropped his head, hoping Doug Todd would keep quiet.

A low, steady hum drifted across the table toward Hugh. "I'm not usually off on these things. That's it. I knew it. I saw you on the Hill. I was on patrol duty. You were looking around. So you are with the city police. You can't trick me."

"You're partly right. I want to know who killed Bill Turner on the Hill but I'm not a police officer." Hugh felt a tickle of excitement course through his body. "I guess you're the soldier I spoke to alright." Something was about to happen. Hugh knew it. He felt it. The tickle became a full-body tremor. "You're just the man I want to talk to. Did you see anything the night of the murder?"

"I am required to keep quiet about that incident. Only Officers can speak about that evening and only with the police and they have already." He stopped talking for a moment. "What I can say is, I did not see anything."

Hugh noted the emphasis on 'see'. He leaned across the table. "But you heard something, didn't you?" He grinned. "I'm going to the police station this afternoon. What you didn't say could be helpful. There will be no mention of your name or position."

Doug Todd nodded. "Thank you. Think motor. Now, I'd like to hear why you're so interested in the murder of a Truro policeman."

For the time being, Ella accepted she had no control over what would happen with either Charles or Alex. However, she was steadfast in her belief that keeping busy was the best way to stave off her worries about both men. She picked up the telephone and called Mable, ready to discuss the details regarding the art show as part of the celebration dinner evening. She intended to have Nellie Quinn's art on display and if Ed and Clara agreed, Nellie would attend the event. It would be well past her bedtime but good opportunities sometimes only come around once. Ella's unspoken intention was to anonymously pay all Nellie's expenses to attend the Victoria School of Art and Design when she was old enough to do so.

The day was agreeable so she left the house to walk the few blocks to Mable's home. Hearing a motor car pull out from a side street, she looked over her shoulder, held her breath. When Robert Fraser waved, she exhaled and waved back.

Mable was quite excited about the art idea. "What a clever idea, Ella. How on earth did you come up with this one?"

"Rose and Nellie are friends." She did not mention that Nellie's father, Ed was a friend. Mable would love to know that story then spread it far and wide. "I'll speak with the efficient Miss Parsons at City Hall and suggest she contact Nellie's school for the art work and invite other local artists to attend. I believe we have authors and photographers who would be pleased to be included."

"And how are you holding up, my dear?"

Ella was blunt. "I'm keeping busy. The end of the day is the worst. The unknown is a close second. The police cannot seem to unearth any leads. Murdoch is a wonderful support. Rose is upset, as any child would be. She misses her father." She took a deep breath. "I must be going. Thank you for your support, Mable."

With some time before Rose would be home, Ella dropped her Support the Troops event papers on the kitchen table and called for a taxi car. She would walk around the harbour and get a taxi car home.

It was mid afternoon when Hugh arrived at the police station. When he entered, there was an air of urgency about the place.

"Good afternoon. My name is Hugh Andrews. I'd like to speak with someone about the murders of Bill Turner and the young woman found on the wharf."

"One moment, sir." Constable Rogers left the desk to knock on Henderson's door.

Hugh soon found himself in a room with three police officers. The air was electric. He felt his pulse race. He was in on the cusp of something urgently important.

"Good afternoon, Mr. Andrews. Constable Rogers tells me you have information for us. I'm Detective Henderson and these gentlemen are Sergeants Bailey and Surrette. Begin when you're ready."

Hugh took a deep breath, introduced himself as a journalist from Truro and friend of Bill Turner, then recounted the information Ginny Field offered about the death of the young woman on the wharf. He described the man on the wharf and that Ginny Field could identify him.

Bailey's eyes never left his note book as he recorded every word Hugh spoke.

Henderson looked in Surrette's direction and nodded then watched as relief washed over Surrette's face and his shoulders fell back onto the chair.

Without naming his source, Hugh went on to share the motor noise on the top of the Hill the night his friend was murdered.

Henderson was curious, raised his hand. "Is this unnamed source a former policeman?" He was thinking Ivan Buckle.

"No, Detective. It is not."

Henderson's mind wandered. *But did Buckle murder Bill? Why?* When he returned to the present, Hugh's description of the tussle between Buckle and Frank Murphy was ending. He casually asked a question.

"And where was this tussle?

Hugh had no intention of revealing the exact location of the illegal pub. "On a street far from the wharf."

Henderson smiled to himself then rose to thank Hugh and shake his hand. "We may need to see you again. Where are you staying, Mr. Andrews?" Hugh named the Bird's Nest Inn then Henderson walked him to the front door of the station. "Thank you, again Mr. Andrews."

Hugh felt an immense sense of relief. He needed to walk. What better place than the harbour, only a few blocks away.

Minutes later, he saw Ella standing on the wharf and darted behind the shed close to the Sailors Hotel. This shabby and shadier part of the harbour would not appeal to Ella so why was she here? He expected her to turn around quickly and return the way she came. He longed to speak with her but this was not the time nor place.

Ella lingered, not far from the Sailors Hotel. Despite the gusty wind, the water and people were soothing. She stared at the people busily loading and unloading barrels and boxes. Small boats hurried between the wooden wharves of Halifax and Dartmouth. In the middle distance, cars drove on and off the ferry. People came and went. She glanced at her watch and wandered back toward the quieter part of the harbour.

Jimmy Sheppard and his wife, Ruthie, lived on a farm a few miles outside the city limits of Halifax. On Saturday afternoon, Jimmy was checking his farm fences along the country road when he spotted a soaking wet, tattered plaid blanket in the ditch near his driveway. Thinking it should be put in the rubbish bin, he pulled it out of the muddy water. One open eye of a man's grey face stared up at him. *Lord love us, he's dead.* Bile rose in Jimmy's throat. He gagged, dropped the blanket, ran to the house, rang for the police and requested Ruthie pour him a Scotch.

"A dead man in the ditch?"

"Don't go look. You'll never forget what you see."

***

Will Henderson was familiar with the route to the Ramsay home. He took no pleasure in knowing this as he turned the key in the police car about ten o'clock that evening. He wanted to lessen the shock for Ella. Ringing the doorbell seemed an intrusion so he knocked. He hoped Murdoch would open the door and he did. Henderson nodded. They walked toward the kitchen together.

"Good evening, Mrs. Ramsay. I have news about your husband."

"Please sit, Detective." Ella clenched her hands together, knowing already what she was about to hear. She rocked ever so slightly and gently back and forth in her chair.

"We found Doctor Ramsay a few hours ago. I'm sorry to bring you sad news. He died of a stab wound. I believe it was quick." He chose not to share the condition of the body nor how it might have gotten to a quiet country road outside the city. That was still a mystery he had to solve.

CHAPTER TWENTY-ONE

Sunday, November 04

On Sunday morning Will Henderson and his fellow citizens of Halifax woke to a foggy, drizzly day with a cold wind coming off the water. Will looked out the kitchen window and shivered. With Charles Ramsay's body found, he had four unsolved murders on his desk. While he was thankful the city was prepared to hire more police officers, they would arrive weeks from now. He said 'good-bye' to his mother and opened the door to the large enclosed porch with windows over looking the front yard and street. It was a restful retreat in summer with indoor plants and comfortable chairs but not today. He shivered again, thankful he'd brought both his winter coat and boots into the kitchen after visiting the Ramsay home. He started the car and headed toward the station.

When the church organist boomed her stirring rendition of *Holy, Holy, Holy! Lord God Almighty* from the choir loft, Oliver sprang bolt upright in the pew. Not a church goer, he didn't recognize the hymn but knew he had to make a run for it. He pushed the heavy oak door wide open and rushed headlong into the chilly morning air. It was Sunday. The stores were closed and few people were on the streets. He retrieved half a mashed cheese sandwich from his coat pocket, walked to the train station, used the toilet then headed for the next town, Amherst.

The location and condition of Charles Ramsay's body was on Henderson's mind. The accumulated blood had discoloured his body to a deep purple and putrefaction had bloated the body significantly. Restraint marks on his wrists and ankles were noticeable. A gag had also been used. He estimated the death occurred at least three days earlier. The single stab wound, deep and near the heart was likely the main cause of death. He couldn't see any other damage from a human or animal. He guessed the creatures hadn't been keen to get wet. He'd go to the morgue himself for this one.

Will slowed the car and stopped for a couple of soldiers who marched out of the fog to cross the road. *God, they look so young.* He continued his train of thought. The Ramsay and Fillmore cars were clear of blood so Ramsay had to have been killed where he was found or moved there by another vehicle. No motor car tire tracks were found on the Sheppard property, including around the shed which was near the road. What other method of conveyance was used? Fillmore implied that White killed his wife. Was White a double murderer and why? Thanks to Hugh Andrews they had fresh leads on the Turner and Brown cases.

At the station, Will shifted his focus to the search teams. He settled on three teams for the four murders. An early morning call to the Dartmouth station's detective okayed his secondment of Sergeant Adam Taylor. He would be at the station by ten o'clock, in time for the morning meeting.

Will recalled when Bill transferred Constable Taylor from Truro to Halifax in '13. He was promoted to sergeant in '14 and in mid July the following year, he requested a transfer to Dartmouth. Although it was an uncommon move, the Dartmouth detective indicated there was no questionable reason provided on Taylor's file. What the file did note was Sergeant Taylor's impressive work. According to the detective, Taylor was easy to like. With the Dartmouth connection, Will wanted Taylor to work the Ramsay and Fillmore cases. He'd save his additional ideas for the meeting.

Ella was up before five o'clock to face a new kind of life. She was fortunate to have her own funds, unlike many war widows who would struggle every single day for the rest of their lives. She would not isolate herself from society and wear black for months. She was and would be part of her community and contribute to it. Murdoch and Rose deserved nothing less.

The city's damp cold and dense fog isolated Ella in her own home. Rose would be home for the day. No visiting Nellie, even if it was Sunday. She would fill their hours with indoor activities. Baking, reading and perhaps painting would pass the time. But first, the heart-crushing talk. Telling Rose her Papa was not coming home again would break her heart. She knew nothing of the cruelty grown-ups could do to each other but she was about to find out. Her life would be changed forever. Ella's heart ached for her.

Ella's parents were still in Ottawa. She'd send a telegram, freeing her from an emotional conversation until they returned home. Detective Henderson indicated the body would likely be released in a few days. The casket would be closed for the service. After lunch, she would call the church office. Then a call to Mable, who could be counted on to ensure the neighbourhood and church members would be informed.

Murdoch wanted to speak with Marie before a special Sunday edition of the newspaper became available. Undoubtedly, his father's death would be the headline. After breakfast, he would sit with his mother as she spoke with Rose then call for a taxi and go to the LeBlanc home. It would likely be a short but awkward few minutes. Sometime in the afternoon he would call Mr. Davis.

***

With introductions and social conversation over, Will asked the three sergeants to take a seat.

"Murder does not pay attention to the days of the week so thank you for being here, gentlemen. Egos don't count for anything in this station and it sounds like all of you know each other well so we should be able to get these three teams up and running quickly. Questions? Comments?"

Three head shakes.

"Fine. We have four cases. Mollie Brown is in your hands, Surrette. Hugh Andrews gave us a grand boost about the identity of a suspect yesterday. You'll need to speak with Hugh's witness then connect with the Yarmouth and Amherst stations and determine if our wider search with suspect descriptions turns up anything." Will paused and chuckled, "In your spare time, dig into the list of months and dates of detective meetings for 1915, 1916 and 1917 then identify Bill Turner's known presence for these meetings. Also, identify assaults and deaths for two days on either side of Bills' presence in Halifax. Constables working the front desk can give you a hand with the search."

Will noticed a puzzled look from Sergeant Taylor. "A question, Sergeant Taylor?"

"No, Sir. Maybe later."

"Next up, Detective Turner's case. Sergeant Bailey, you've been on this. Carry on. My gut tells me you might want to know what Surrette finds out from Yarmouth and Amherst. Those two murders were close together in time. Just a feeling but maybe it's time for the lavender dream?"

Surrette and Taylor stared at Bailey but said nothing.

Will knew those two would be onto Bailey the minute they left the room. And so did Bailey. He ignored the side glances from his fellow sergeants. "Probably, Sir. Also, that train departure a few days ago is still bothering me."

"Sergeant Taylor, you have the Fillmore/Ramsay cases. You have Dartmouth connections. Same cars. A fella on the run. Did he do both? Where is he? Have family somewhere? The bloody towel in Fillmore's shed. Can you connect that to Oliver White? What does his wife know? Where was Ramsay killed?" He looked across the room. "Comments? Questions?"

Three 'No, Sirs' echoed in return.

***

Hugh still wanted to meet Frank Murphy. Aside from the killer, Frank was likely the last person to see Bill alive. He felt so anxious to find Frank, he took a chance Angus would be in the store on a Sunday. It would not be open for business but maybe Angus was inside. They could talk. He knocked on the door and it opened.

"Good morning, Hugh. You run out of shaving soap and hoped I'd be here?"

Hugh laughed. "Good morning. No, to the soap but I do have a favour to ask."

"Go ahead."

"How can I find Frank Murphy without going to his home?"

Angus opened his mouth but Billie was quicker to answer. She moved toward Hugh and stood with her arms crossed.

"So you're Hugh Andrews. That question is a big question." Her tone was chippy.

Angus jumped into the discussion. "Hugh. This is Billie Stewart, my shop assistant. She offered to help this morning, even though it is Sunday. According to Billie, Frank's at work but not talking much."

Billie stepped closer to Hugh. "That's right. I've been there three times this week."

"Where's work?"

Billie stepped back, leaned on the counter. "On the wharf. I'm a close friend. If he won't talk to me, he won't talk to you."

Angus wanted to move the conversation forward with Hugh. "Thank you, Billie. Can you start pricing the box of kitchen towels in the store room, please."

Billie nodded. "Nice meeting you, Mr. Andrews."

"Likewise." Hugh raised his eyebrows, a smirk on his face. "Well, she's challenging."

"Some days, very."

"What's the story about those two?"

"Billie wants to be free of her parents. She sees Frank as her way out. He's not buying what's on offer."

"Sound like it's time to give up."

"Tell that to her. On second thought, maybe not. Now about Frank. I suggest you wander around the businesses on the wharf tomorrow. I don't know where he works but lunch time would help. Mind you, it's becoming a bit nippy on the wharf these days. He might eat inside the factory. I'm not much help to you."

"Thanks." Hugh turned to leave.

"You got any plans for lunch?"

"It's a little early for that."

"You can stay here and talk for a couple of hours then come to the house for a big bowl of clam chowder."

"You've got a deal. Can I help with anything?"

Angus pointed toward two big boxes of kitchen utensils and one of rubber boots.

"These need to be priced and put out for display."

***

Jimmy Sheppard leaned against the back of the black Captains chair in his cozy enclosed front porch, his winter jacket on and a well-worn tweed cap on his head. The door into the kitchen was wide open. He spoke to his wife, knowing full-well she'd have something to say about where he was going, but he told her anyway.

"It's looking better out there, Ruthie. The sun's now shining. I'm going to the shed."

"Don't trip over that step again. The last time you did that, you were laid up for near a week." Ruthie Sheppard turned back to the kitchen counter and continued punching out cookies from the cookie dough. The grandchildren loved to eat the star, animal and heart shapes. The family was coming over for Sunday supper. They lived across the road.

Jimmy finished pulling on his rubber boots and stepped outside. The front yard was soggy in a few spots from the downpour three days before. He picked out the dry areas on his way toward the shed which was close to the road. He'd figured most of the things in the shed were for fencing and ditch clean-up so why have it right up close to the house. Today, he needed the wheelbarrow. He wanted to pull the weeds along the road and in the ditch where he found the dead fella. He shivered and pushed the memory out of his mind. Nasty business.

At the shed, Jimmy unlatched the door and swung it open. The wheelbarrow was not in its usual place, against the back wall. Instead, it was directly in front of him. Jimmy's jaw went slack, his eyes widened then slammed shut to protect him from the bloodied wheelbarrow before his eyes. He stood frozen on the spot then, following a few deep breaths, he opened his eyes. The bloody wheelbarrow was still there. Without regard for the few soggy spots, Jimmy rushed to the house and collapsed into the Captains chair. "Ruthie, call for the police. Tell them we need that detective fella Henderson here, right quick. After that bring me the bottle of Scotch and a glass."

***

It was not the norm for Detective Henderson to attend follow-up site investigations but Ruthie Sheppard sounded pretty determined he should be there so he rode along with Sergeant Taylor and the driver, Constable Rogers.

"This could be our break. What do you think, Sir?"

"Well Sergeant, it certainly explains why Ramsay's car was clean but where was Ramsay between his disappearance on Thursday afternoon until yesterday?"

"First question to Mr. Sheppard is, when was the last time he was in the shed? We should park on the road, Sir. Some tire tracks in the yard might help us."

"Good idea, Taylor."

Ruthie and Jimmy were waiting in the porch as Henderson took a wide birth around the front yard to reach the house. They beckoned him inside. "Have a seat, Detective."

"Thank you. You doing alright, Mr. Sheppard?"

"A stiff shot of Scotch and I'm just fine. Want one?"

Ruthie stared at Jimmy. "Hot tea would have been just fine."

Henderson declined the offer and both let Ruthie's comment pass.

Ruthie tapped lightly on the window. "What are those two doing?"

"Sergeant Taylor and Constable Rogers are examining the ground between the front gate and the shed. They're looking for tire tracks, Mrs. Sheppard."

"That might be hard, Detective. The wind and a bit of sun dried everything out from Thursday afternoon on but we had drizzle this morning."

Henderson turned to Jimmy. "When were you last in the shed, Mr. Sheppard?"

"Let me think."

Ruthie waited a few moments then spoke up. "It was Wednesday morning. I asked you to take the empty geranium pots to the shed."

Jimmy nodded.

"You ever see the need to close that front gate?"

"Nah, who would want in here to take anything we have."

"You may be right there, Mr. Sheppard but it sure looks like someone killed Doctor Ramsay and left him in your shed."

Ruthie covered her mouth, her eyes wide, tearful. "Oh no. Surely it isn't our Doctor Ramsay."

"You know Doctor Charles Ramsay?"

"He operated on one of our grandchildren. Such a lovely man. Who would do such a thing?"

Jimmy made no comment as he was thinking. "You know, our son-in-law works at that hospital. He told us a fella from the hospital was very angry with our Doctor Ramsay." Jimmy looked at Ruthie. "Do you remember the name Norman told us?"

"W something. Walsh? Warren? White? That's it, White. I don't know what his first name is though."

***

Ruby saw no reason to delay her interview with Detective Henderson. “Marmalade, pack your bag. You’re going to see Mrs. Williams again. We’re going to Halifax tomorrow. On second thought, I better call Corbin first. After all, tomorrow is Monday. He may not have time for me. If he doesn’t, we’ll take a room at the King Eddie. I wonder if they allow cats?”

Marmalade listened attentively. When there was silence, he strolled toward the food dish and sat down in front of it.

“Good idea, Marmalade. I’ll have an egg salad sandwich with tea. It will settle my thoughts. Fish for you.”

CHAPTER TWENTY-TWO

SUNDAY, NOVEMBER 04

Sunday morning traffic toward Amherst was light but Oliver kept walking. Every minute not in handcuffs was a minute of freedom. Finally, an old Ford car pulled up behind him. When the driver blew the horn, Oliver bolted into the ditch. *Shit, they're onto me.*

"Hey, there fella. You wanna lift?"

"Yup. Goin' to Amherst?"

"Jump in. I need some company. I hope you like to listen."

"I sure do. The name's Fred Black. No wife, and lookin' for work."

After lunch with Angus, Hugh was at loose ends. With no particular place to go and nothing specific to do for the late afternoon, he returned to the inn and spent some time reviewing his notes. He skimmed over the sketchy sentences and random words he'd taken when the locals were talking about train rides to Truro and Yarmouth the day following Bill's murder. To date, they meant nothing to him and still didn't.

During his interview with Detective Henderson, he considered mentioning Jo Robinson. As a friend of Bill's, she might have useful information. Now, he was thankful he'd let his random thought remain just that. Her drug induced ramblings on Tuesday evening ruled out her reliability, at least for now. Having enough of his own company, he went to the telephone at the inn's front desk.

"Hello, Corbin, Hugh here. I'm wondering if you are free to discuss a few thoughts I have about Bill's death?"

"Sure am. Stay for dinner."

"Thanks. Dinner sounds like a good offer. What's the address?"

Corbin was eager to discuss Bill's death. He also wanted to talk about his visit with Jo on Monday evening. Perhaps Hugh would have some insights. He went to Mrs. William's private rooms and knocked on her door. "I apologize for the short notice but could you prepare for a dinner guest? His name is Hugh Andrews."

"I'm cooking a chicken, Mr. Davis. I'll put an extra potato in the pot." She offered him a grin then went on. "Don't you worry, sir."

In a matter of minutes, Corbin heard the front door bell. "I'll answer the door, Mrs. Williams."

"Come in Hugh. Can I take your coat?"

Hugh looked around as Corbin hung up his coat. "Big house for one fella, Corbin."

"Well, it is. I bought it for the quiet back yard. Some old trees out there, including a couple of apple ones and two big maples. They were the selling feature. Come in." Corbin led the way to the sitting room.

"Have a drink? Scotch suit you?"

"Can't turn that down. I see you're an art collector." Hugh was standing in front of the several pieces on the long outside wall.

Corbin laughed. "Hardly, but I have a couple of pretty decent ones. You?"

"No, but I know what I like. Fall scenes and water."

"Can't go wrong there, in my opinion. Have a seat."

Settled across from each other on either side of the window looking out on the backyard, Hugh decided to satisfy his curiosity quickly. “Are you related to the Davis family who farm west of Truro?”

“I am but left home early to seek my fortune in the big city.” He chuckled and was about to add a self-deprecating joke when Hugh voiced a response.

“It worked.”

Corbin nodded. “The money part, yes.” He looked out the window then returned his gaze toward Hugh. “Not long ago, Bill reminded me I have pots of money and nothing else.”

Hugh took a deep breath. “He mentioned that to me too but mine was not about money. It was about chasing stories.”

Both briefly withdrew into their memories of Bill and their own regrets.

“Excuse me, Mr. Davis. There’s a telephone call for you.”

“Thank you, Mrs. Williams. This is Hugh Andrews, a newspaper man from Truro.”

“Pleased to meet you, sir.”

“Just Hugh, Mrs. Williams.”

“Excuse me for a moment, Hugh.”

Hugh sipped his Scotch then stood up. A painting of red, gold and bronze maple trees by Helen Johnson had caught his eye and he wanted to look at it again. In moments, he was surrounded by the maples, taking in the forest floor’s earthy aromas of decaying leaves, mushrooms and compost.

Corbin returned and stood beside Hugh. “I see you like that one. It’s just outside Wolfville.”

“Yes, yes. I know the area. Acadia University is there. A lovely setting.”

”I met Helen a few years ago at an art show at the University.”

Hugh turned away from the wall. “Guess it’s time we return to why I’m here.”

"That call was from Murdoch Ramsay. His father's body has been found. A terrible time for the family."

"How do you know Murdoch?"

"He's my salesman. Smart young fella. Very likeable. I imagine you don't know the family."

Hugh hesitated then decided if Corbin was going to be a friend he better be honest. "I knew his mother Ella quite well many years ago."

Corbin nodded. "A story for another day, I imagine?"

"Indeed. So back to thoughts about Bill. My first thoughts are actually about Jo. I've known her for a few years. I can understand you may be reluctant to speak openly about her but I'd like your thoughts on what I witnessed Tuesday evening. But first, when did you last see her?"

"Monday evening. The medication was affecting her thinking. I telephoned today. Malcolm answered. I would say she's still taking medication. She did mention Malcolm was planning a trip to England soon."

Hugh nodded. "Medication and alcohol." Then he paused. "On Tuesday, she was in a vindictive mood, told me she's writing a book about her men, including her father. She said she'd settle the score with all of them." He shrugged, sipped the Scotch. "Then she talked about poor Bill hunting in the dark. And what the hell would that mean?"

"Are you saying she may know something about Bill's death?"

"Well, Bill helped her get rid of some men. But I don't know what that really means. I know Bill transferred a couple of young Truro constables to Halifax for her." He sighed heavily. "She may not be in any condition to talk to the police right now. I don't know what to do next about her. What are your thoughts?"

"Malcolm was there on Monday and she was in the same frame of mind you described. She wanted revenge on the man who assaulted her. She talked about writing an autobiography, including how to get rid of men."

"How to get rid of men? That's unbelievable. Well, she doesn't have any close friends so I can't get help there."

Corbin winced. He didn't have close friends either.

"Excuse me, gentlemen. Dinner is ready."

The dinner conversation moved on to business, the war and speculation about post-war Halifax.

When Mrs. Williams brought a sticky pudding to the table, Hugh asked, "Can I move in, Corbin?"

As the meal was ending, Corbin received a second telephone call.

"Hello, Ruby. How are you this evening?"

"I'm ready to see Will again."

Corbin nodded to himself. "That sounds good. Sorting things out is helpful."

"Marmalade and I will be in Halifax tomorrow. We don't want to bother you though."

"That is not a problem. I'll meet you at the train station and bring you here then return to the office. You can speak with Detective Henderson from here and set a date and time to meet."

"You are a true friend, Corbin."

"See you tomorrow. Bye."

While Corbin was gone, Hugh was in the kitchen speaking with Mrs. Williams. Back at the table, he had a story for Corbin. "Mr. Williams worked with my father on the railway. Both were conductors. Mr. Williams was about fifteen years older and taught my father the ropes. I love this kind of story. Mrs. Williams is a great cook. How did you find her?"

"Through Cookie Gilmore and Robert Fraser."

"You lost me there. You know Robert Fraser because..."

"Company business at the bank and Cookie was the Fraser's housekeeper for years. Robert suggested I talk to her about finding a housekeeper."

"Is Margaret Fraser related to him?"

"Margaret's his wife. Why do you ask?"

"I know a Halifax story from about twenty years ago. It was fascinating. Margaret Bell married Thomas Bishop a con-artist, big-time crook, connected to hit men in Montreal. I was told she later married a banker by the name of Robert Fraser."

Corbin nodded. "It's a small world."

"So, do you know a fella called Frank Murphy?"

"No. Who is he?"

"According to Angus Martin, he was a suspect in Bill's murder and is now a witness. I want to talk to him."

"Do you know everyone, Hugh?"

"I'm working on it." He grinned.

Corbin shook his head then became serious. "We need to get Jo off the medication then get her to the police. If she's off the medication, she should be able to remember the names of men Bill followed for her. Someone lured him to the Hill."

"How do we convince her?"

"Getting rid of Malcolm would be a good start."

Hugh nodded. "That trip to England would be helpful. Do you think we could convince Jo to go to the police about the recent assault?"

"If she stops taking the medication, she might. For you, not me."

"But, how do we get her off the medication?"

"You know, I wonder if Malcolm's keeping her on the medication because he knows something about her we don't? Maybe I should talk to Ruby about Malcolm. He has a medical practice in Truro.

"Why is he spending so much time with Jo?"

"Good questions. Talk to Ruby. Hear what she has to say." Hugh stood up. "You know, I think Frank Murphy is my best option right now. I'll have to give up walking the wharf and find a secret bar every evening until he shows up."

"That sounds like hard work." Then Corbin started to laugh.

"I'm willing to try it. Meet me at the corner of Hollis and Lower Water tomorrow evening at seven. I'll bring Angus along."

***

It was late afternoon when Oliver White arrived in Amherst. His ride in the old Ford was bumpy. Sterling, the driver was a bachelor farmer, a man of many words going to town to see a friend. That suited Oliver just fine. He needed to keep moving and didn't care much about talking.

Not long after Oliver was dropped off in Amherst, he realized the town was home to German-speaking men walking around town, accompanied by guards. In the middle of town he saw a large building fenced off on all sides with a guard posted at the front gate. Annoyed, he took several long strides toward the guard.

"What's this place?"

"It's an old foundry, sir."

"Who's in there?"

"German prisoners of war, mostly sailors caught out in the Atlantic. They're sent here by train from Halifax."

"How many you got in there?"

"Several hundred."

Oliver felt his body temperature rise. He waved his arm around in the air. "They're Germans. Why are they free, out on the streets to do God's knows what?" He clenched his fists.

"They're working for us, sir. Right now they're building new homes, other buildings and repairing some."

Oliver clenched his teeth, his shoulders tightened. "They should all be locked up, all the time." He wanted to hit someone. At the hospital, he'd leave work and pace in circles around the parking lot. On the very bad days, he went into the wooded area behind the hospital and yelled. He stuffed his hands into his coat pockets. *That bitch nurse and killer doctor deserved what they got. Thought they were better. I showed them.* His fingers caressed the money. His shoulders unwound. His head felt lighter. He breathing slowed. He kept walking until all the voices in his head faded away but his two bad deeds were still there. Terrified of swinging from a tree in Halifax, he went to the railway station to think.

***

While Hugh and Corbin were discussing Jo, Detective Henderson's constables and sergeants were at work both in and out of the police station.

Sergeant Pierre Surrette was en route to the boarding house to speak with Ginny Field and bring her in for an interview regarding Mollie Brown's death. He had descriptions of Alexander Wallace and Joseph Young for comparison.

Two constables were deep into the records of detective meetings in Halifax during 1915, 1916 and 1917. They were looking for Bill Turner's name on the rosters and if any assaults or deaths occurred two days on either side of his presence in Halifax.

Sergeant Adam Taylor was quickly getting re-acquainted with his old station and sergeant duties. He liked being in the Halifax station up until 1915 when Jo Robinson moved to the city from

Truro and Bill Turner was in the station too frequently for his liking. He planned to keep his head down and avoid the subject of his transfer.

Nothing in the file notes specifically spelled out a connection between the Ramsay and Fillmore files but in Taylor's mind there seemed to be a connection. He'd have to ask Detective Henderson about that point then get out of the office to do the work. He went to Henderson's door.

Will was confident in Sergeant Taylor's ability to handle the two murders but he was still curious about why Taylor transferred to a smaller station two years ago.

"Come in, Sergeant. Have a seat. I imagine you have a few questions about the murders. Fire away."

"Thank you, Sir. In the group briefing, there were a few words about a double murder. What are the facts?"

"The close timing of both murders is most likely driving the speculation. The facts, as we know them at the moment, don't fit a double murder." Will raised his index finger. "Having said that, never discount any possibility, Sergeant. Clifford Fillmore's estranged wife was killed prior to Doctor Ramsay. So far, we have no witnesses for either one. Fillmore's car was involved in the Ramsay murder and Fillmore was out of town during the time of both murders."

"Understood, Sir."

"Any other thoughts, questions?"

"No, Sir."

"If you need an additional constable for the door to door canvassing on the Fillmore murder, Dartmouth station has offered support. We have a description of White from Fillmore. As you know, it's in the file. I doubt the White family has pictures, so ask his wife for details. He has a beard."

"Thank you, Sir."

"Now, I have a couple of questions. You looked puzzled during the information about Detective Turner's death. Do you have a question?"

"Not really a question, Sir but I was wondering why the monthly detective meeting dates would help solve Detective Turner's murder."

"That is a reasonable question, Sergeant. The dates may correlate with other criminal activity." Will had an opening and he took it. "I noted your transfer to Dartmouth in mid July two years ago didn't show a reason. Was there one?"

"Nothing in particular, Sir. I worked with a Dartmouth Sergeant on a big case. We struck up a friendship so I transferred."

Will nodded. "I won't keep you any longer, Sergeant. Have a good afternoon."

"You too, Sir."

***

Sergeant Bailey sat quietly in one interview room, alone. He'd closed the door. Beside him sat a pot of coffee and a mug. There was nothing to run around about, no files to review. His work was focused on remembering the feeling he had at the train station. The day was miserable. Rain saturated his coat, dripped from his hat onto his face then rolled into his collar. He shivered, recalling the recollection. People shuffled, heads bowed. He was frustrated, not being able to see clearly through the drizzle, not being able to search the trains for one of those three men, described by the Truro station. The more he focused on his thoughts, the more they eluded his grasp. Maybe it didn't really matter anyway. Thwarted, he moved on to Frank and his lavender dream. He knew where Frank lived. He'd go there and hope he was at home. He glanced at his watch. Three-thirty. Sunset was less than two hours away. He left the office to follow a hunch.

***

At four o'clock, Sergeant Surrette knocked on Henderson's door.

"Come in."

"We have an identification in the Mollie Brown case, Sir."

"Good work, Sergeant. Which one?"

"Alexander Wallace, Sir. The blue eyes and light hair did it."

"Well, well. Now we have to find him. At this point, I'd guess he's not in Truro." Will smiled. "What do you want to do, Sergeant?"

"Have a look in Yarmouth, Sir. Call Truro, get more details about him. Family, work, friends."

"You're in charge. Good work, Sergeant."

"Thank you, Sir."

***

Sergeant Bailey and Frank Murphy returned to the police station after making a stop at a little shop near Angus Martin's Grocery.

"I'm hungry, Frank. If you want a bite to eat, help yourself to the other sandwich. There's a fresh pot of tea on the way."

Frank nodded and picked up the other brown bread sandwich with sliced beef. "Thanks."

"So tell me your current thoughts about the lavender dream."

"I've had it again, Sergeant. I smelled lavender."

"And...?"

The desk constable knocked on the door and came in. “Your tea, Sir.”

“Thank you, Constable.”

Frank was enjoying the sandwich. He looked at ease, as though he’d solved a personal problem.

“Go on, Frank.”

“At first, I thought the person in the dream might be Billie Stewart. She works in Angus Martin’s Grocery store. You know her?”

Bailey shook his head. “No. And you’re sure about the dream?”

Frank nodded. “I smelled lavender but it wasn’t Billie.” He finished the sandwich.

“Why do you say it wasn’t Billie, even though she wears lavender powder?”

“I don’t mind tellin’ ‘ya but I’m a bit worked up about what I’m goin’ to say. This time the dream had a person in it. I smelled lavender and hair fluttered past me. It was light coloured, blonde I’d say. Then I woke up. I didn’t see a face though. Billie’s got dark hair.” He exhaled. “How can that be? I never saw anyone that night. I was terrified then and I’m terrified again. What if someone knows somethin’ about me? Maybe the killer saw me.” Then he remembered Billie’s warning about the killer coming to get him. He stared directly into Bailey’s eyes.

“Your name and your information is kept in the station. Only the police have access to it.”

Frank let out a big sigh. “I sure hope you’re right.”

Bailey could not believe he was about to launch a search for a blonde killer, wearing lavender powder.

CHAPTER TWENTY-THREE

Monday, November 05

Ella stood in front of the mirror, her reflection proffering an unfamiliar mix of grief and accompanying calmness. The grief cast back the sadness her children were experiencing with Charles' death. A child can be orphaned at any age. Its' accompanying sorrow is not an easy road to travel, even if that very road is fraught with unhappy twists and turns. The calmness personified herself. She pondered the word. Yes, she was free from the disquieting emotions of the horrific event and no, she did not find consolation in Charles' death. An unfaithful man does not deserve a murderous exit. She put an extra pin in her bun and turned toward the hallway.

At the top of the stairway, her mother's words upon the death of her sister Adele, came rushing back. 'Stiff upper lip and carry on.' Damn that, she wanted her children to feel grief and move through it in their own time. God knows, she hadn't come to terms with Adele's death, all these years on. She cried for Adele. One never does stop grieving for those dear ones now gone.

Rose stood at the bottom of the stairs. "Mama, come for breakfast. Murdoch's made lopsided pancakes."

"I'll be down right away, my dear."

Murdoch was busy at the stove but stepped away to kiss his mother's cheek. "Good morning, Mama. I hope you slept well."

"At times." Ella poured herself a cup of coffee and sat at the table. Rose immediately sat on her knee.

"Thank you for preparing breakfast. I imagine you are not going to work this week."

"Mr. Davis suggested I return to work after the funeral or when I'm ready."

"I have to meet this kind man."

Rose looked up toward her mother's face. "Am I staying home, too?"

Ella nodded.

"Mama, when is Papa going to sleep in the ground?" Her eyes filled to overflowing as she clung to Ella's neck.

"On Friday we will be in church for a service then we will take Papa to the cemetery. Do you remember when Nellie's Auntie Katherine went to the cemetery last year?"

"Yes. Nellie goes there sometimes."

"Perhaps you can go to the cemetery together. Now take your seat to eat."

It was difficult for Murdoch to accept the loss of his father, despite his dislike of the stern lectures he'd received since childhood. He'd hoped for more time to settle things between the two of them but it wasn't meant to be. He kept his back to the cemetery conversation, delayed turning about and being seated at the table.

Ella sensed his hesitancy. "Come, sit, Murdoch. Your pancakes are getting cold. We can clean everything later."

"They look funny but taste good, Murdoch."

Rose was talking and chewing at the same time but Ella pretended not to notice.

"I will be making funeral arrangements at the church this morning. Jenny will be here to clean. She doesn't need any direction. She's a bit talkative so it's best you both stay in the sitting room and allow her to complete her routine. Reading while she's here would be a good idea."

"I brought the morning paper in, Mama. It's in the sitting room."

Rose swallowed quickly, "Why is it there? It's always here on the counter for Papa."

"I imagine Murdoch wanted to keep the paper away from the flying pancake batter."

Rose straightened up in her chair. "It's time I learned how to make pancakes."

Murdoch waved his arm in the air. "I'll be the teacher."

"No thank you, Murdoch. I want to make round ones with Mama." She began to cry, climbed onto Ella's lap and threw her arms around her mother's neck. "Papa will never eat my pancakes."

***

Sergeant Bailey was in the station shortly after sunrise. What would he say to the team about Frank Murphy's latest interview? Five times he practised and five times it sounded laughable. He needed help but was reluctant to ask for it. When he heard Detective Henderson's voice in the hallway, he knocked on Henderson's open door.

"Sir, I need an opinion."

"You've come to the right place, Sergeant. I have plenty of them. What is your subject?"

"Lavender and hair, Sir."

"Ahh, I thought you might seek my advice about Frank's dreams. Coffee?"

"Thank you, Sir."

"I've given this some thought." Henderson paused for a mouthful of coffee. "You might want to think about a second opinion on the lavender. Perhaps former constable Buckle will have something to say about lavender. After all, he did see the body."

"Thank you, Sir. I now have a new line of questioning."

"Bring Buckle into the station. It might prompt a better result. So, what did Frank actually say?"

"After the first dream, he thought he was smelling a friend's lavender powder so didn't want to mention her by name."

"But he's still convinced the aroma of lavender was on Detective Turner's clothing?"

"Absolutely. At the end of the second dream, he again smelled lavender plus a flutter of light coloured hair."

"What thought comes to mind?"

Bailey's eyes locked onto Henderson's face. "The lavender tells me it's likely a woman, Sir. The hair could be a woman or man."

"Mention it. We need to consider all options."

Bailey wasted no time in going to Ivan Buckle's home. "Good morning, Mrs. Buckle. I'm Sergeant Bailey. Is Ivan at home?"

Alice Buckle continued to wipe her hands on her apron. "No need to introduce yourself. I can tell a policeman a mile off. I'll get him." She curled up her lip and stared at Bailey before shutting the door in his face, leaving him outside in the brisk morning air.

Buckle came to the door wearing a warm but worn black jacket and flat cap. His usual short brown hair looked like it needed a good trim. His surly attitude was on full display. "What did I do this time?"

"It's not what you did but smelled. Get in the car, Ivan. We can talk at the station."

The short drive to the station was steeped in silence as Buckle stared out the side window as though he was about to see some startling event occur on the wooden sidewalk flashing past. Bailey couldn't be bothered striking up a meaningless conversation.

Bailey intended to get Buckle in and out of the station before the teams would meet for the late morning meeting. He brought a pot of tea and two mugs into the interview room where Buckle had made himself at home by reading the morning newspaper. "Bit of news there about that doctor fella." He tossed the paper on the table. "And no, I know nothing about the Ramsay murder."

Bailey ignored the bravado. "Does your nose work well, Ivan?"

"My nose works just fine. What's this about?"

"Helping find Detective Turner's killer would go a long way to improve people's opinion of you."

Ivan stared at the opposite wall, creating several facial contortions he intended to serve as deep thinking. "What is it you want?"

"I want you to close your eyes and keep them closed until I tell you to open them."

Buckle looked doubtful. "Is this a joke?"

"No."

Bailey waited until Buckle complied. "You're on the Hill the night Detective Turner was killed. You're close to the body. Staring at it. Keep your eyes closed. Ignore what you are seeing around you. Ignore what you are hearing around you. Now take a deep breath and breathe out slowly. What are you smelling?"

"Blood. I smell blood."

"Keep your eyes closed. Do you smell anything else?"

Ivan shook his head. "No."

"Keep your eyes closed. Try another deep breath."

"Just blood." There was an angry edge to his words.

"Open your eyes. Thanks for coming in. I'll drive you home."

"That's it? I'm supposed to smell something else? What's this nonsense about anyway?"

"I thought you might recall something else from the murder site. You didn't."

At home, Buckle didn't trouble himself about the smell nonsense. He walked into his tumbledown shed behind the house and began washing his reliable old Model T.

***

A great deal of chatter preceded Henderson's arrival in the meeting room. He could hear their voices from the front desk. He stepped into the room and closed the door. "Good morning, gentlemen. Let's begin with Sergeant Surrette."

"Thank you, Sir. I have been in contact with the Yarmouth and Amherst stations. Truro gave me more details about Wallace's background. A loner, raised by an aunt after his mother, Dora was placed in an institution in Dartmouth. His father, Henry Wallace is deceased. He's smart, violent and as we already know, fair-haired with blue eyes. No results from the posters, Sir." He paused. "The review of detective meetings for 1915 through 1917 and the identification of reported assaults and deaths for two days on either side of Bill Turner's presence in Halifax will be ready this afternoon."

"Thank you, Sergeant Surrette. Sergeant Taylor, you're next."

"Sir, before we move on to Sergeant Taylor, I would like to take the train to Yarmouth today. I think Wallace could be there, Sir. He's smart. He'd leave town in the opposite direction of Truro."

All eyes were on Will Henderson. Would he agree with the new Sergeant?

"Sometimes hunches pay off. Pack your bag, Surrette. Be careful, this fella is no fool." He tapped his index finger on the table. "Telephone the Yarmouth station now and make their station your first stop. They have a couple of constables. Use them."

"Yes, Sir. Thank you, Sir."

"Carry on, Taylor."

"I spoke with Virginia White, Sir. She's a frail young woman who I believe is afraid for her life. She says her husband is away overnight sometimes and away from home some evenings during the week. She couldn't recall anything unusual about the end of October or the beginning of this month. She's alone with a young son and not aware of any family White might have in the area. She accepted my offer to contact City services on her behalf." He breathed a heavy sigh. "White is about six feet, muscular, bearded, dark brown hair, brown eyes, scar near left brow, walks aggressively." Taylor paused a moment. "I took her a few groceries, Sir."

"Fine work. You did the right thing about the groceries. Where is Mrs. White's family?"

"PEI, Sir. I've been thinking, would Surrette's poster idea work for me with White?"

Henderson leaned across the table "Where do you think he might be?"

"Well, Truro is closest but he could have made it to Amherst by now. I doubt he'd use the train. It would cost money and he'd probably feel locked up, turn on somebody."

"Call Truro and Amherst. They can look for him and put up a few posters. Now, let's talk about nurse Fillmore and Doctor Ramsay. Clifford Fillmore's convinced White killed his wife and left the bloody towel in his garage. If White did kill Ramsay, where was Ramsay kept before ending up in the ditch? How did White move Ramsay to the ditch when Fillmore's car was in the garage before Friday morning? It was clean so it wasn't out in the rain storm or after on Thursday. He must have used a second car. Did he steal one?"

"I'll talk to Mrs. White again about cars then to Jim and Ruthie Sheppard. Constables on the street should keep an eye out for abandoned cars. I'll hand that information over to the constables."

Henderson nodded then turned to Bailey. "Sergeant Bailey has new evidence. You're on deck, Sergeant."

"Thank you, Sir." Bailey looked intently at his sheet of paper. "My case has taken on a pleasant smell." Keeping his head down, he glanced sideways at Henderson who had also developed a keen interest in the floor.

Sergeant Taylor looked from Henderson to Bailey and back to Henderson. "Sir, are you two up to something? I don't understand the joke."

"I have a witness who saw Detective Turner's body on the Hill the night he was murdered. Recently, he's been interviewed twice regarding his dreams. His dreams involve the smell of lavender and somebody with fair hair. The killer could be a woman."

Taylor looked toward Bailey. "Any female victims in our files wanting revenge against the police? Personally, I wouldn't waste too much time on that woman angle. They're rarely killers."

Henderson sighed. "But they do kill. If there are no additional comments, it's time to get to work, gentlemen."

Sergeant Taylor went directly from the meeting to the telephone with two tasks in mind.

"It's Sergeant Taylor from Halifax calling. We need help."

"Go ahead."

"Thanks, Constable. We think you may have a murder suspect in Truro. We'd like a few posters put up in busy places on your main street describing a man by the name of Oliver White. How soon can this happen?"

"A couple of hours."

"Excellent. Here's the description but I suspect the beard is gone by now. Make sure one is in the train station."

Then he had the same conversation all over again with a constable in Amherst.

***

Ruby and Marmalade arrived in Halifax to a warm welcome from Corbin.

"Hello again. I hope both of you are feeling well."

Hearing Corbin's voice, Marmalade pushed his head over the rim of the basket and looked up. Seemingly giving Corbin the 'all clear', he blinked then ducked under the plaid blanket.

"Thank you, Corbin. This seems to be a habit." She smiled.

"I didn't realize Detective Henderson wanted to see you so soon."

"He doesn't but I want to see him. I have a few thoughts he may wish to consider."

"That sounds intriguing. I'm sorry I cannot take the afternoon away from the office. My salesman is out of the office. There was a death in the family so I expect he will be away for the remainder of the week."

"Anything to do with the doctor who was found?"

"His father."

"Oh, good heavens."

There was a pause as Ruby bolstered her resolve with a heavy sigh. Her eyes had a far-away look. The end of Bill's investigation was becoming very clear to her but she wondered how soon Will was going to get there. "Take me to the house so you can return to work and I can call Detective Henderson."

Corbin saluted, "Yes, ma'am. Right away, ma'am."

"Sorry, Corbin. It's just that I don't want to be a bother or interfere with your business." Then an afterthought. "How's Jo?"

"Not fit to entertain friends."

Ruby nodded. "Back to old habits then."

"And I have something else to tell you. I'm out for a beer with friends this evening."

"Don't worry about me. Marmalade and I will have a lovely evening with Mrs. Williams." She smiled. "So, you and your friends have a secret liquor hide-out. Well, well, quite the anti-prohibition fella, aren't you." She laughed. "I suppose you also acquire your lovely whiskey by prescription from the pharmacy?"

"You've found me out. It's medicinal, of course."

***

Taylor's third task following the meeting was considerably more difficult. Although he could not get Virginia White and her little boy out of his head, he needed Mrs. White's help to find Oliver. With groceries from Angus Martin's store, he revisited the White's meager lodgings.

"Thank you, Sergeant. You are so kind. Please have a seat. I'll make tea."

"Thank you, Mrs. White but I just had a big cup. However, I would like to ask you a few more questions about your husband."

Virginia nodded and sat on the other kitchen chair.

"Have you heard from your husband since we last spoke?"

"No. He's never been away more than one night. I hope he hasn't been hurt by someone and can't get home."

Taylor sidestepped her subtle plea for help and changed the direction of the conversation altogether.

"Your husband must be a busy man with his work at the hospital."

Virginia was quick to support her husband. "Oh, he's a hard worker, Sergeant. And he even finds time for evening work."

Taylor leaned forward in his chair, his hands clasped together on the table. “Evening work?”

Virginia’s look became serious. “Yes. I told you before he’s away many evenings. Every week he brings home extra money from the evening work.”

Illegal gambling raced across Taylor’s mind. He drew his eyes together, wrinkles appeared on his brow. He’d start with the obvious and see what turned up.

“So, this evening work is extra hours at the hospital?”

Virginia shook her head. “He runs errands.”

“Errands.” Taylor nodded, accepting the answer as valid. To his surprise, Virginia continued talking.

“You know, picking up and dropping off parcels for people.”

Taylor nodded again. “Ah, parcels.” Then a puzzled look crossed his face. “Does he have a bicycle for these errands?”

Virginia smiled and shook her head. “No, no. He uses a car.”

“So your husband has a car?”

Virginia sat back in her chair. “Heavens, no. We’re too poor for that.”

“Then whose car would it be?” He expected her response would be ‘Clifford Fillmore’.

Virginia visibly straightened her upper body. She spoke proudly. “His friend, Ivan.”

“By any chance, do you know Ivan’s last name?”

“Buckle. Ivan Buckle. Oliver told me he’s a policeman. You must know him.”

Taylor could barely believe what he’d heard. He muttered a quick thanks, excused himself and stood on the sidewalk. He needed time to take in the tangled web Virginia White innocently unveiled. He made hurried notes. Buckle has a car! What are these errands? Who else is running errands? He drove slowly toward the Sheppard home, muttering over and over again. “Who’s spinning the web?”

CHAPTER TWENTY-FOUR

Monday, November 05

Ruthie and Jimmy Sheppard were unable to add anything new to Taylor's knowledge of the bloody wheelbarrow. On Wednesday morning the wheelbarrow was in its usual place. Jimmy found the body in the ditch Saturday and the bloody wheelbarrow on Sunday. No wheelbarrow tracks were found on the Sheppard property. However, Taylor was curious about the Sheppard's daughter and son-in-law who lived across the road. "You have family across the road, is that correct?"

Ruthie nodded. "Our daughter Roberta and son-in-law, Norman MacKenzie."

"I'd like to talk to them. They might have heard or seen something."

Taylor looked at the small building at the end of the MacKenzie's dirt driveway. He walked across the road and checked for wheelbarrow tracks. Seeing none, he then had a look inside the shed. Empty. No blood or potential evidence was present. Then he walked the short, rutted lane to the clapboard house. Roberta MacKenzie met him at the door of an enclosed porch wearing men's work pants and a plaid shirt closely resembling one owned by his father. Her light brown hair was gathered on the top of her head, held in place by a dark green ribbon and a tortoise shell hair comb.

"Come in. I was expecting you."

"Thank you. I'm Sergeant Taylor." He looked about quickly, noticing a pair of work gloves hanging over the rim of a well used basket and four pairs of rubber boots all neatly lined up beside a long wood bench.

Roberta's hazel eyes evaluated Taylor in great detail. "I'm Roberta. Come into the kitchen, Sergeant."

Taylor removed his cap. Blonde curls fell over his forehead.

The room was spotless, the furniture meager but well kept. Yellow print curtains framed the front window.

"Can I offer you tea, Sergeant?"

During his time as a police officer, Adam Taylor's curiosity was always piqued by the offer of tea despite the circumstances people found themselves in, good or bad. Tea for celebration, tea for misery. He'd determined people needed time to savour the euphoria of impending happiness or steel themselves for grim news in the offing. Tea was a perfect but oft too brief diversion. "Thank you. No milk. No sugar."

Delaying the inevitable was of no use, even for those who were innocent bystanders. He surmised Roberta MacKenzie could be one of them. After all, her husband worked with Oliver White. He avoided lengthy pleasantries and went to the heart of the case. "Doctor Charles Ramsay was found dead in the ditch across the road from your home. Did you see or hear anything unusual between the afternoon of Wednesday, October thirty-first and Saturday, November third?" He held her gaze, sipped his tea.

"No, Sergeant." She held Taylor's brown eyes with her own while he asked a second question.

"Were you out of the house during that time, perhaps into Halifax. You are only minutes away by car."

Roberta looked away then returned her gaze to the center of the table where a glass jar held a splendid, ruby red dahlia.

"We don't have a car, Sergeant." She lifted her head, looked the Sergeant in the eye. "We usually walk or take a horse and wagon. Now and then Norman borrows a car from a fellow worker for a special event."

"That must be handy. What friend would that be?"

"Oliver White." Roberta hesitated. "And he's not a friend. We pay him." She delayed, her mouth open. "I'm not sure Oliver really has his own car."

Taylor ignored the last comment and pursued his intended line of inquiry. "I assume your husband is at work in the hospital today?"

Roberta breathed deeply, leaned back in her chair, straightened her upper body, looked Taylor in the eye. "Yes. He walked to the city then took the city's transportation to the hospital. That's his usual routine. I doubt Norman knows any more than I do, Sergeant."

"That is very possible. However, I would like to speak with him. Please give me a brief description."

Having received what he needed, Taylor thanked Roberta. When he reached the door, he turned around.

"What is that shed near the road used for?"

"I sell garden vegetables there."

Taylor nodded. "Thank you."

Roberta lingered inside the open door as Sergeant Taylor walked down the lane. *He certainly is an intent young man.*

In the car, Taylor glanced at his watch and headed for the hospital. He was familiar with the hospital buildings from a previous case and parked close to the building housing the cleaning staff and equipment. Ready to produce his badge, he opened the door and looked for a stocky man with a receding hairline, wearing wire-rim glasses. A man of that description walked toward him.

"Norman MacKenzie?"

"Yes."

"I'm Sergeant Adam Taylor with the Halifax police."

Norman's shoulders sagged. "Thank God, you're here."

"You're very pale, Mr. Mackenzie. Are you feeling alright?"

"Yes. I must talk to you."

"I understand, sir. I've just spoken with your wife. Is there somewhere we can talk or would you rather come to the station?"

"No, let's get this over. I want to tell you everything I know and think about Oliver White. We have a small room in the corner for coats and boots. There's a table and chairs. Follow me."

Taylor looked around the room. It was certainly small and with the door closed, just short of being claustrophobic. He caught a whiff of soiled socks mingled with fish and sweet pickles. He offered MacKenzie a mint then popped one into his mouth and began the interview. "What do you want to tell me, Mr. MacKenzie?"

"Oliver White works with me but he's not here today. He frightens me. He has a terrible temper. He doesn't own a car but borrows one from a friend by the name of Ivan Buckle." Norman stopped to catch his breath. "He brags at work about his night-time business."

"What do you recall about the bragging, Mr. MacKenzie?"

"He mentions getting people liquor. Here's what I think. When the Temperance Act was passed seven years ago, all of the province, except Halifax was under prohibition. People here were free to drink alcohol. Last year when the City also came under the Act, Ivan and a couple of other fellas saw a chance to make money. They got into cahoots with workers at the port or off trucks from Montreal and started delivering liquor to secret drinking places in Halifax. Likely homes, too."

Taylor nodded. "Know anything else about White?"

"No. He never talks about family, mostly brags about himself and women."

"Women?"

"Nasty words about them, especially about the women working in the hospital."

"Anyone in particular?"

"Never any names but he's said a few things about the nurses."

Taylor made a mental note to share MacKenzie's nurse comments with Detective Henderson.

"Any idea how Oliver got to know Ivan Buckle?"

Norman shook his head. "Can't help you there, Sergeant."

"Thank you, Mr. MacKenzie. This has been a great help."

Norman stood up then hesitated.

"Anything else on your mind, Mr. MacKenzie?"

"My in-laws, Sergeant. Finding that body and the bloody wheelbarrow. It's taking a real toll on them. And it's all my fault."

Taylor was more than curious. He was a bit sharpish with the question. "How's that?"

"White knows I live outside the city. Not far mind you, but far enough. He also knows Roberta's folks live across the street, live a quiet life, in bed early. I'm carryin' a lot of guilt."

"I understand your point." Taylor extended his hand. "Thank you for your assistance today."

Taylor returned to the station and tapped on Henderson's door. He was waved into the room just as the telephone rang.

"Detective Henderson speaking."

"Will, it's Ruby. I have information for you."

"When will you be in Halifax?"

"I'm here now."

"Oh, you're here! Would four o'clock this afternoon be suitable?"

Taylor guessed it was Ruby Turner in Halifax again. He kept his thoughts to himself.

"I'll see you then. Good-bye."

Henderson looked toward Sergeant Taylor. "Do you have news?"

"Yes, Sir. The Sheppard's son-in-law was very helpful about White's evening business and his comments about women at work, specifically nurses. We have a witness."

"Excellent, Sergeant. I expect everyone is waiting for us. Tell us the details at the meeting."

Henderson stepped into the sergeant's afternoon meeting, both anxious and curious. Bill and Ruby were on his mind.

Within minutes, the file search team produced evidence of four instances of assault arrests with Bill Turner's name associated with the files.

Why the hell was Bill involved in Halifax police business? He asked for the files, wanted to look for other names, try to make some order out of the search team's findings. He listened to the case updates with one ear, his mind captured by Ruby's impending visit. *Was she about to remove the shroud hanging over his friend's murder and unmask the guilty individual?*

***

Since Bill's death, Ruby wore navy, dark red or dark green dresses and suits, refusing to bow to the old rule for widows. She had never looked good in black and was not about to start now. She stepped into the police station wearing a deep crimson tunic-style suit, black shoes with buttons and a small black fedora with a crimson band. Feathers were not her favourite decoration on anything so she'd removed the offending feather from the hat and gave it to Marmalade. It soon became a popular plaything before a nap.

Ruby waited impatiently in a chair near the front desk. She was certain her conclusion regarding Bill's death was correct. However, she was uncertain about herself. Speaking aloud most certainly would be her undoing. She fiddled with the handle of her purse all the way to Will's office.

Detective Henderson turned around after closing his office door and faced a woman he liked but whose future he was about to change forever. "Would you like to begin, Ruby?"

"Thank you." She passed an envelope to Will. "I've written everything down in the event I could not speak and I'm afraid that is the case. I've been a fool, Will. The contents of the envelope will confirm I am."

"I can't imagine you being a fool, Ruby."

Ruby straighten her body. "You know something I don't?" Her brow was raised.

"We're still piecing things together. I haven't had an opportunity to confirm anything."

Ruby stood. "I need to go."

"Go where?"

"I don't know. Somewhere."

"Let me take you for a walk in Point Pleasant. The trees are past their best but it's peaceful."

"It is. I've been there with Corbin. I look forward to being there again."

Ella was weary at the end of another difficult day. Rose was finally in bed, following three tearful outbursts and Murdoch was supposedly reading. She had just looked in on him. He was staring out the window, the book unopened on his lap.

The telephone rang as she finished putting the evening meal's clean dishes in the cupboard. People meant well and her upbringing demanded she acknowledge their sympathy.

"Hello."

"Ella, it's Hugh."

Her heart stopped or at least it felt so. "Hello."

"I will not dwell on the obvious but simply say I am sorry about your loss."

Ah, ever 'to the point' writer. "Thank you."

"Please call me if I can be of help."

"Thank you."

"Good night, Ella. Sleep well."

Any connection with Hugh always brought back the old 'what if' questions. This evening's call was no exception. She joined Murdoch, picked up her novel and stared at the page not seeing, not reading. Thinking.

Ruby smiled toward Will then stepped into the car. Their sparing moments in Will's office were long gone. "I enjoyed that walk very much. Walks always put things right in my mind. Thank you."

"Don't forget about the Troop Celebration on the evening of the twenty-fourth. I think you would enjoy the opportunity to meet a few new people. One of my sergeants told me the tickets will sell out quickly. To be on the safe side, may I buy a ticket for you tomorrow, along with mine?"

"And one for your mother, I hope." She smiled. "Thank you, Will. I know this is also most difficult for you."

When they reached Corbin's driveway, Will waited until Ruby was inside then he went to Dartmouth. It was time to be a detective.

Inside the Dartmouth station, Will introduced himself and asked to speak with Detective Williams.

"Thank you, Sir. I'll call his office."

A short, balding chap with a rosy face and cheery looking nature rushed down the hallway and put out his hand to greet Will.

"Welcome, Will. It's been a long time since we spoke in person. What brings you to my patch?"

"Good evening, Fred. Do you have a few minutes to satisfy my curiosity?"

"Absolutely." Fred looked in the direction of the front desk. "Constable, bring us each a mug of coffee, please." He nodded toward the hallway. "Come to my office."

With their casual conversation about Will's mother and Fred's wife and children over, coffees on the desk and the door closed, Fred opened the conversation. "What's on your mind, my friend?'

"Tell me about your Sergeant Adam Taylor. He started out in Truro, transferred to us then moved to Dartmouth, a smaller station. Did he ever give you a reason for that quick move?"

Fred smiled. "He's an interesting fella. Keeps to himself more than I'd like. Likes to work alone. Doesn't appear to have any friends in the station or out of it. He's thorough, digs for the details but not detective material yet. To answer your question, I can only guess it was personal because his work is first rate."

Henderson nodded. "That helps."

"Is he a problem for you?"

Will shook is head. "Not at all. He's good at his work, does all the things you mentioned but I have a niggle about him in the back of my mind."

The two old friends continued their conversation until Fred's wife called him to come home before his dinner was stone cold.

Will laughed. "My mother can't find me or she'd be saying the same thing."

***

Both Angus and Billie were busy all day but Angus was not oblivious to Billie's skittish behaviour. She was distracted while serving customers and completely abandoned her usual conversations with people she knew well. He'd wait until the store closed before getting to the source of the problem. Frank appeared to be out of her life so it was probably another row with her parents.

By six o'clock, the accounts were complete and it was time to go home.

"Mr. Martin, I want to tell you something."

"I noticed you were preoccupied today. Go ahead, then we can talk about how to deal with the problem."

"There is no problem, Mr. Martin. I'm leaving Halifax on the train tomorrow."

"Where are you going?"

"I bought a ticket to Montreal so I guess that's where I'm going. Thank you for everything you've done for me." Then she ran out the door and didn't look back.

Angus stared at the door long after it swung closed. *I've failed her.* He let the tears flow before locking the door and going home. Meeting Hugh and Corbin at a private pub was just what he needed.

CHAPTER TWENTY-FIVE

Monday, November 05

Returning home, Corbin found Ruby reading. A glass of sherry sat on the side table. Crumbs on a small plate were evidence of a shortbread cookie, or two. Marmalade was asleep on her lap. He opened one eye, then closed it lazily.

Ruby offered a tired smile. "As you can see, both of us are quite at home."

Corbin sat in the chair opposite her. "That pleases me. And the meeting with Detective Henderson, it went well?"

"I think so. I left him my ramblings. I'm sure he will do with them as he sees fit. We took a walk in the park after the brief meeting."

Corbin was about to respond when Ruby dropped her head and began to stroke Marmalade. Keeping her head down, she unfolded her story.

"In Will's office I was so angry and ashamed of myself I could not fully explain what I'd discovered from my journals. But I gave him a letter outlining what I believe happened." She looked up. "I lived in a world with liars and cheats. What a fool I've been."

Corbin chose not to challenge Ruby's view of herself, just yet. "And the park?"

Ruby lifted her head. "Will." Then she stopped a moment. "Will suggested it might help me feel better."

"And did it?"

"While I was there."

"And now?"

"Reading my journals was very revealing. My life with Bill was a made-up world. A staged play. People playing roles to suit their fancy. I feel like I was the only real person, an honest person. Those early years must have meant nothing to him." She looked out the window. "I can't come to terms with it all right now."

Marmalade jumped off her lap and walked toward the kitchen.

"I think Marmalade just gave us a hint. Are you hungry?"

"I am."

"Well, let's see what Mrs. Williams has prepared for the evening meal." Corbin stood up. "We can talk about your next steps over our meal."

Ruby rose from her chair. "I've already decided to move to Halifax. The Truro house holds too many traitorous memories."

"Sounds reasonable to me."

Marmalade was already nose deep in his fancy dish. Corbin noticed it was one of his late mother's 'good' dishes, a Limoges tea cup saucer.

"Ah, I see Marmalade is served first. And what are we having, Mrs. Williams?"

"Fish, Mr. Davis. Same as Marmalade, Sir."

Corbin grinned. "Thank you, Mrs. Williams. Then we'll see you in the dining room shortly."

At the table, Corbin opened the topic of Jo's brother, Malcolm.

"Malcolm Robinson's name came up in conversation earlier this evening. He seems to be in Halifax a great deal of the time. Doesn't he have patients in Truro?"

"Indeed he does; however, Jo is Malcolm's first priority. It is a strange relationship."

"How so?"

"Malcolm was a well-established physician when Jo arrived from England in 1912. I could tell her arrival was a surprise. Malcolm isn't a social person. In fact, he's off-putting and he went everywhere Jo went. I don't know if he was protecting her from all of us or keeping her out of trouble. Maybe it was a bit of both. I found it very annoying, especially at gatherings." She shrugged. "Some people were openly skeptical about her sudden move from England. I dismissed most of it as gossip." She breathed a heavy sigh. "Over time Jo and Malcolm dropped a few bits about life in England. I understood the family was wealthy." She took a deep breath. "So this is my understanding of all the pilather. Jo's parents died in a house fire. The fire was started by candles on the Christmas tree and Jo escaped. Jo and her parents were at odds with each other. The story was, there was suspicion surrounding her involvement with the fire." She shrugged. "Guilty or not, I don't know but she came to Canada."

"A serious way to rid yourself of a problem."

"Murderous intent comes to mind. Anyway, Jo and I spent a considerable amount of time together, in the garden, walking. She was writing a book but she didn't seem to make much progress with it. She rarely spoke about her adult life in England. The childhood parts were important though. They lived outside London. She had a nanny, a pony. One evening after a few glasses of wine and Malcolm not around, she told me she left England to escape a brutal man. My impression is she's a deeply troubled woman."

"Why do you think she moved to Halifax?"

There was no hesitation. "To get away from Malcolm and continue an old relationship."

"With?"

"I think you know the answer, Corbin."

***

Angus Martin considered himself a law-abiding citizen despite the recent shuttering of Halifax's legal drinking establishments. He refused to use terms such as blind pig to describe the once thriving, legal bars. He'd given Hugh and Corbin the location of the secret bar and reminded them to arrive discreetly and separately after five-thirty. He was counting on Frank Murphy being there, hopefully sober.

By six o'clock, the three men were well into the discussion about the city's murders and specifically that of Detective Bill Turner. Angus was over-whelmed by the information and determination Hugh and Corbin shared in order to solve their friend's murder.

By six-thirty Angus was certain Frank would not appear or if he did, he would be too drunk to provide any sensible answers. While he was suggesting they try again later in the week, Frank walked through the door accompanied by his brother, Joe. Nervous but knowing Hugh was eager to speak with Frank, Angus walked toward their table.

"Good evening, Frank, Joe."

They both nodded, "Angus."

"A fella by the name of Hugh Andrews is here with me." He pointed to the table where Hugh and Corbin were seated. Hugh nodded. "He's a friend of Bill Turner, the..."

Frank held up his hand. "What's he want?"

Angus did not detect any reluctance in Frank's response. "Would you answer a few questions about that night on the Hill?"

"He a police or newspaper fella?"

"He's a newspaper man but this is very personal for Mr. Andrews. Hear him out, then you make up your own mind. That alright?"

Frank nodded. "Send 'im over."

Joe stood up. "I'll get you a beer and find another place to sit."

Angus returned to his table. "He's sober and willing to talk."

Twenty minutes later, Hugh returned to Angus and Corbin. "He told me everything about that night." He took a deep breath. "You two will not believe this part. The man's had dreams about the murder scene twice and he smelled lavender and saw light coloured hair."

Angus leaned across the table. "Do you believe him?"

"Yes, I do. He's already spoken to the police about it."

Corbin was quiet.

Hugh looked at Corbin. "Is it possible?"

Corbin nodded. "It's possible."

Angus looked from one to the other. "Did I miss something?"

More than a week had passed since Alex Wallace arrived in Yarmouth. He'd read a couple of recent Halifax newspapers, both leaving him confident about his future. The Halifax police were far away and in his estimation not too clever, giving him time to insinuate himself into the Simmons family. He had already inferred he was wealthy and looking for a new business prospect. After meeting the family, he escorted Lily to lunch once and accompanied her to the park twice. The damn woman was playing the prude. He might have to teach her a lesson.

Alex stood before the mirror in his hotel room fussing with his cravat all the while making adjustments to his story for the evening with the Simmons family. He had two lies to tell. The first, intended to panic the Simmons family then a second, a coup de grace lie to force them to bow to his will. Wooing Lily into an intimate relationship remained an integral part of his big plan to scoop up the Simmons money and disappear.

***

Walter Simmons crossed the threshold from the hidden room into the family sitting room then tuned the key in the lock. With Lily's help, he moved the unwieldy tall potted plants to hide the ornate double doors. The family secret and survival was in the elaborately decorated room, accessible from inside the house and only by the family. At night a different access was available to invited guests. That access was by climbing a decorative exterior staircase.

Luring Alex as a source of money to expand Walter's existing business was a stroke of luck. His illegal gambling premises was tailored to wealthy citizens from Boston who could arrive and depart by boat.

The Simmons family gathered in the sitting room to review their scheme to separate Alex from his money. They were prepared to disclose their secret business and feign a deep interest in an expansion, thus garnering Alex's money. Sadie and Lily would provide details for the expansion of the secret room.

Alex was expected within the hour. Walter smiled, adjusted his tie and sat down to wait for Alex to walk into his trap. The maid was soon at the door to the sitting room.

"Mr. Ward is here, sir."

"Come in, come in, Alex." Walter shook Alex's hand warmly. "Good to see you again."

"Thank you, Walter. Good evening, Mrs. Simmons. Lily. All of you will have to pardon my excitement. Earlier today, I had a most enticing business offer from the train company to consider a new proposal." He nodded and smiled broadly, his blue eyes twinkled with excitement. "This is a great town. I'm delighted to remain here for a considerable amount of time." He smiled toward Lily.

"Sounds interesting, Alex. Have a seat."

Alex walked to Lily and clasped her hand in his. "I intended to call on you today but the past two days have been full of activity, arranging for money, reading documents. I apologize sincerely. My business should be concluded by Thursday. Perhaps I could call on you Thursday afternoon?"

"That sounds delightful, Alex. I believe there will be a concert in the park that day."

Alex took the red chair near Lily. "Wonderful. I do love a good concert. Will there be a choir?"

"Absolutely."

"A sherry or something stronger, Alex?"

"Stronger, please."

"Ladies, a sherry before dinner?"

Lily took advantage of the captive audience and described a recent shopping adventure she had in Halifax with friends. "I adore Halifax. So many shops and charming men in uniform."

Alex knew Lily was doing this to annoy her mother. He feigned interest while waiting for Walter to approve the train idea. Otherwise, he was about to lose access to the Simmons money. Eventually, there was a lull from Lily's drivel.

"The train expansion sounds good to me but you've been quiet Walter. What do you think?"

Walter's suspicion regarding the railway expansion was strong. As a resident of Yarmouth, he hadn't heard of any such idea. He concluded Ward was slippery about the truth but proceeded with his original plan, separate Ward from his money.

"I have a better offer than the train company, Alex. Here's my proposal. Forget them and join my family in an expansion of our business. We'll show you the books and you can be part of a business that will have your name on it."

"Oh, Papa that sounds so wonderful. Having Alex with us every day is a dream come true. He's such a delightful conversationalist during our strolls through the park and such a gentleman."

Walter shot her a look that said 'don't over do it, missy.'

Sadie clenched her fists. *Greed will be our undoing.*

Alex put on his best grateful look. "This is such a tempting offer, Walter. Having my name on a business is something I've prayed for. So far I've only been an investor." He nodded at Walter and smiled toward Lily. He knew Sadie was going to mean trouble. He'd work on her later.

"I believe you would fit right in. You're a sharp fellow." Walter could already see the new money in his bank account.

"I'm also considering a rum running business for us. The wharf is right there."

Walter had no intention of considering rum running at the wharf, the very wharf he wanted for his gambling clientele. "Well now, that would cause a problem for us. We have a gambling business, Alex. People come in and leave by ship. Rum running is a sure way to attract police attention to the wharf." He feigned a deep, puzzled look. "Just a thought, you could add your money to ours and we could expand the gambling business. We'd have a bigger space for gambling. Just one very big business. How's that sound, Alex?"

"If you put my name on the business, my money is yours."

"Agreed. Let's have a look at our gambling room before the evening meal."

CHAPTER TWENTY-SIX

Monday, November 05

When Pierre Surrette stepped into the dim light of the Yarmouth station platform everyone on board quickly disappeared into the shadows. Left to fend for himself in a strange place, he felt vulnerable. He flinched when the crunch of fallen leaves was accompanied by an unfamiliar voice.

"You look lost, sir. How may I help?"

Surrette turned around. The man looked vaguely familiar but the hat pulled low over his brow prevented a clear look at the face. "Main Street."

"Follow the street lights."

Surrette watched the stranger fade into the shadowy darkness of what appeared to be a lane between several large homes. Following the lights was good advice. There it was, Main Street. The police station half way down the street, its' light a beacon for those in need of help.

Yarmouth's town constable extended his meaty hand across the desk toward Pierre.

"Good evening, Sir. I'm Constable Emile Ferguson. You the policeman I'm expecting from Halifax?"

Surrette grasped and shook the big hand of the man with ruddy complexion and impossibly curly brown hair. Grey strands had already conquered his sideburns. Ferguson looked fit. Surrette was relieved. Wallace was a runner. Surrette nodded.

"Good evening, Constable Ferguson. I'm Sergeant Pierre Surrette from Halifax, looking for Alexander Wallace. I brought a description."

"Welcome to Yarmouth, Sir. Call me Fergus. Everybody else does." He glanced at the description with accompanying sketch.

Surrette wasted no time in getting into the details. "Have you seen this fella?"

"Can't say I have, Sir. He could be gone by now unless he's taken an interest in work here. The town is mighty busy with the wharf and new businesses."

"I think Mr. Wallace might be lying low here. He could be known by another name. We're pretty sure he killed someone in Halifax."

"Well, first thing tomorrow we better start huntin' for him. In case you're wonderin', I've a young second-in-command constable joining us. He'll be here in the morning. What time do you want to start huntin'?

"Sun's up about seven. Eight-thirty work?"

"Sounds fine for me, Sir. Now about your lodging. I've got a place for you to stay just off Main Street. Maggie Matthews has a spare room, now that her daughter's married off. Turn right when you step out the door and then turn right again onto the street with the white church on the corner. Maggie's house is the third on the left. It's a yellow two-story with a big veranda. You can't miss it."

Surrette smiled to himself and set off to find Mrs. Maggie Matthews. Thanks to the street lights and the white church, he didn't miss it. He knocked lightly, not wanting to draw the attention of neighbours. When the door opened, so did Surrette's mouth.

"Sergeant Surrette?"

Surrette nodded. A woman close to his own age wearing a red evening gown, her hair a crown of curls with glittering pendant earrings beckoned him to come inside. “I don’t usually greet guests so well dressed, Sergeant. I just returned from the playhouse and yes, I was in the play not in the audience. Can I make coffee or tea while you take your bag up to the room?”

Surrette swallowed hard. “Either would be lovely, Mrs. Matthews.”

“Call me Maggie. The room is upstairs, the second door on the right. The water closet is at the end of the hall. You can’t miss it.”

When Surrette returned, a pot of tea, ham sandwiches and cookies were on the kitchen table. “Thank you. The train ride was tiring.”

“I’m always a bit hungry after a performance so I will join you. Fergus mentioned you are here for a serious reason.”

“I am and hope it doesn’t take long.” He wasn’t about to explain further.

“It’s none of my business. I have enough to do without sticking my nose anywhere it shouldn’t be.”

“From what I’ve seen in the dark, Yarmouth is a pleasant, quiet place to live.”

“It is. I’ve been here almost five years. We moved from Boston to join family.”

Surrette was curious about this interesting woman and used to questioning people but he forced himself to be silent. Her life was none of his business.

“My husband, daughter and I were encouraged to come so we did. It was a bit strange at first, moving to a much smaller place. My husband was already in the boat-building business.” Maggie dropped her head. “I still miss him. I’m sorry. The accident happened three years ago. At the wharf.”

“I’m sorry to hear this.”

"That's why I take house guests. I like the company. Now that my daughter's married, it is very quiet here." She offered a shy smile. "And you Sergeant, been a policeman a long time?"

Her disarming smile also made Surrette smile. "Eighteen years, all in Halifax. First a night watchman then I joined the police. I like figuring things out, why people do terrible things to other people."

"Ah. Come to the dining room."

Maggie switched on the light. A large picture puzzle covered one end of the sizable table.

"I'm afraid you will be forced to share your meals with this monster, Sergeant. You came on short notice and I am not putting it back in the box." She laughed from her heart.

"And neither should you." Surrette grinned then picked up a puzzle piece, studied the picture in progress and placed the piece to complete a small red rose in full bloom.

"You're a puzzle man!"

Surrette was smitten.

All day Monday, Oliver White made sure he didn't linger too long in any part of town. When evening arrived, he thought about sleeping in a church again but was frightened he'd be discovered this time. He begrudged giving the old woman any money for the little room on the main floor of her Amherst boarding house but he needed somewhere to hide and rest. He paid the money and flopped on the bed for a late day rest. When he woke, the room was in darkness. He liked the dark. Felt free in it. Free from people who told him what to do. Free to do what he wanted. He was hungry so wandered into the kitchen.

The old woman stared at him from her rocking chair in the corner. "Going out?"

"Lookin' for supper, since you don't feed people."

"Alice's All Day Breakfast is just down the street. Turn right."

Having successfully escaped the police, Oliver felt he earned something better than eggs and went in the opposite direction, toward the railway station. Finding nothing on the way, he stepped inside the station intending to ask the fella at the desk where to eat.

When Oliver saw his face on a big poster just inside the door, he bolted back outside and hid in a thicket of dense shrubs. It was dark and he had no idea where the next town was or how to get there. He rushed to the safety of Mrs. Fanning's boarding house and decided to leave Amherst at daybreak. He stripped to his underwear and went to sleep. Not long after, he woke with a start and jumped out of bed. It was still black outside and someone was knocking on his bedroom door.

"Who's there?"

"Amherst police. Come out or we'll go in."

Oliver pushed up the bedroom window, put his right leg out, touched the ground, then the left.

"Oliver White, you're under arrest for murder and indecent exposure. Get your clothes. You'll have a cozy cot in the police station then a car ride to Halifax in the morning."

***

It was four o'clock Tuesday morning and Alex Wallace was staring at the ornate tin ceiling from his bed in the Grand Hotel. The man at the train station crossed Alex's mind but he ignored it. Today, the Simmons family offer would take precedence. The gambling room was beyond his wildest imagination. Electricity and elegant cloth covered tables offered roulette and poker. A bar providing sandwiches and drinks was off to one side, near the water closets. He could understand why the Simmons were eager to expand but he had to get answers before offering up his cash in order to steal theirs. He replayed the previous evening's questions and answers with the Simmons family.

"Who works in here?"

"We do. We collect the money, pay the winnings and look after the food and liquor sales. By the way, the liquor is a very tidy income."

"But who works at the gambling tables?"

"Now that is a hush-hush subject, Alex. Let's just say, the fellas working my boats have many jobs."

Alex caught sight of a door that looked like it opened to the outside. He nodded in that direction. "Do guests both enter and exit through that door?"

As usual, Walter answered. Lily stood next to Alex, her arm discreetly brushing his. "Yes. They never see our living quarters. They're escorted from and back to the wharf and enter the house up the stairs from the back alley."

"Excellent. And is the door locked at all times?"

"Yes. You'll get a key as soon as you deposit the agreed upon amount of money in my bank account and meet with me to show the bank receipt."

Alex rolled off his bed and opened his travel bag to check the amount of money he had set aside for a business adventure, in this case a deposit into the Simmons' bank account by two o'clock. He reasoned his banking activities would leave about a half hour to board the ship and slip away from Nova Scotia. The amount fell a little short of what he agreed to with Walter. After breakfast he'd make up for the short fall at the pawn shop near the wharf. He'd keep the prostitute's cheap earring. It had a long, sharp hook that might come in handy but he would sell her gold broach. His father's whisky bottle with crystal glasses would get a considerable price. All for a good cause. Me.

Knowing he was not returning to the hotel, Alex packed his diaries and extra clothing into the travel bag and placed the items for the pawn shop into a carpet bag he'd stolen from a store before leaving Halifax. He ate a big breakfast, put it on his account and slipped out a side door, thus avoiding his final room and board bill.

***

Surrette woke early to the smell of coffee and bacon. Carrying his shaving gear and fresh clothing to the water closet, he thought about the day ahead. Wallace was violent and policemen don't always come home at the end of the day. He shook off the dark thoughts and put on a smile for Maggie and himself.

"Good morning, Maggie." He looked across the table. "This looks and smells lovely."

"Thank you, Sergeant."

"Call me Pierre."

As Maggie turned to leave the dining room, Surrette looked up from the table.

"Aren't you joining me?"

"That is not normally done."

"This is not a normal day for me. Sit down, please. We can talk."

Half an hour later, they were well acquainted, having shared childhood stories and life in Halifax and Boston.

"Should I prepare lunch and an evening meal for you?"

"No. I don't expect to have a routine day. If I show up, we will work something out."

Surrette walked to the door.

Maggie held it open for him. "In case you can't recall the way back to the station, walk up the street and turn left at the church on the corner. That'll get you on Main Street. The station is on your left. You can't miss it. Bye for now. Have a safe day."

***

Ever the careful planner, Alex walked to the wharf after breakfast and booked passage under the name of Alexander Ward on an American vessel bound for Boston at four-thirty. Leaving his travel bag in the ship's storage, he negotiated with the pawnbroker then placed the tightly rolled carpet bag under his arm, ready for the bank deposit. As he stepped onto Main Street, he saw three policemen outside the station. After a few minutes, the three policemen went their separate ways. With or without the Simmons' money, he decided to flee Nova Scotia today. Keeping his head down, he went to the rail station to read newspapers until he went to the bank after noon.

***

When Surrette and Ferguson met Constable Miller they planned the search route. Surrette and Ferguson would take the residential areas, knocking on doors in search of a male matching Alex Wallace's description. Miller would cover the downtown businesses, describing Alex to business owners. By noon they would compare notes.

Surrette was alert to the possibility of Wallace escaping by sea either on a passenger ship or by private means. Before meeting up with Ferguson and Miller he'd taken a quick walk along the wharf, identifying Wallace's potential opportunities.

The afternoon would be a three-man deep search at the wharf, unless Wallace was already in custody.

As cuffed Oliver White was marched into the Halifax police station by the Amherst officers, he stuck out his chin, dark eyes riveted on Detective Henderson.

Henderson ignored White while shaking hands with his Amherst comrades. “Thank you, fellas. We appreciate your support. Stay around. Help yourself to whatever’s on the lunch room table. We’ll have a meal out together as soon as Mr. White is locked up.”

White shuffled sideways to lean on the front counter, only to be pulled back into place by Henderson.

When Sergeant Taylor greeted the Amherst men, White snorted and pulled on his cuffs, still playing the bully.

Taylor promptly marched him into the interview room and pointed to the lone seat on the side of the table opposite the door and waited for Henderson to join them. “That’s your seat.”

Henderson entered the room and motioned to White. “You were told to sit, Mr. White. Now, sit.” He waited until White complied then seated himself.

“I’m Detective Henderson. I recall you being a guest in our city prison not that long ago. Seems to me that was about your altercation with Doctor Ramsay. But I digress. I understand you’ve been sightseeing the past few days.” He pointed to the other person White was holding in his glare. “This is Sergeant Taylor. He’s been looking for you. Now, I have a few questions before you join the lads in Rockhead Prison. By the way, some of them have less patience with bullies than we have. You might want to consider your behaviour there and keep your mouth shut and your fists in your pockets."

White leaned across the table toward Henderson. "I ain't saying nothin' to ya."

"Sit back, Mr. White. You're in my place now. Why were you running, Mr. White?"

"None of your damn business."

"Don't kid yourself, Mr. White. It certainly is my business. You know Lois Fillmore?"

"Never heard of her."

"You work in the same place and never met her? Her husband has a different opinion. We also have information that proves otherwise. How about Charles Ramsay, know him?"

White's eyes darkened. His nostrils flared. He stared at the ceiling.

Henderson stood up, leaned against the far corner of the room. He wanted to see White's hands under the table. They were clenched. "I hear Doctor Ramsay was a fine man. A good doctor."

White banged his hands on the table, stood up. "How would you know that?"

"Sit down, White." Henderson smiled at him as Taylor pushed him down into his chair. "People tell me he was a great man in the operating room."

White jumped out of his chair, his face scarlet. He spat the words out with spittle. "He was a friggin' butcher. Killed my little girl."

Henderson delivered a matter of fact response. "That's what revenge does to you, Mr. White. You wanted him dead, lost control of yourself and you killed him."

Henderson's smooth confident manner enraged White.

"Like hell I did and you can't prove it."

"Sit down. Mr. White."

"You got nothin.'"

Taylor placed his hand on White's shoulder and pushed, hard. "Don't you worry, we have lots of evidence to present."

Oliver sat, more from exhaustion that compliance but he continued to display all the tell-tale signs of anger; red face, dark eyes, clenched fists and heavy breathing.

Henderson continued, his delivery casual. "I hear you don't like Germans, Mr. White."

"What lyin' bastard told you that?"

Ignoring the question, Henderson sat back in his chair, crossed his arms. "Well, I'm waiting."

"They're killing us."

"Try again and this time tell the truth."

"Sister's married to one. Never liked him. Never will." Spent, he leaned back into his chair.

"Don't get too comfortable, Mr. White." Henderson offered a slight smile. "Oliver White, I'm charging you with the deaths of Lois Fillmore and Charles Ramsay. You will be transported to Rockhead Prison tonight and have a special guard. In case you're wondering, tomorrow we'll start rounding-up your liquor-running friends, like Ivan Buckle. I'm thinking some of them might exchange lighter sentences for information on your activities."

Two hours before the passenger ship was scheduled to depart for Boston, Alex deposited his money at the bank and asked for a receipt which Walter had demanded. Then, following Walter's request he went to the wharf area. While looking for Walter, he noticed a man stepping onboard the passenger ship. Alex thought this most unusual as the captain denied him boarding until one hour prior to sailing. When a second man stepped onboard a sailing yacht, his breathing became faster. *They're here. Looking.* He lowered his head and pulled his hat over his forehead.

When Surrette began walking in Alex's direction, Alex calculated the risk in running as too high. Rather than casually walking away, he turned his body toward a jumbled stack of discarded buoys and impossibly tangled fishing nets, then pulled the bank receipt out of his pocket, feigning intense interest in it.

Oblivious to Alex's precarious circumstances, Walter walked toward him. "You get it done?"

"It's all in the bank. Here's the receipt."

Walter glanced down. "Here's your key to the gambling room. Come to the house this evening, We'll toast the business."

Alex nodded and Walter rushed away just as rowdy crews of fishing boats headed toward the wharf. Alex grasped the key and joined them, despite the risk of getting closer to his captors. On the wharf he veered away from the group and walked toward the beach, distancing himself from immediate danger.

Alone on the deserted beach, Alex understood the full, fearful situation he was in. He struggled to climb to the top of the sandbank while avoiding the sharp, spiky dune grass. His feet slid and sank into the shifting sand. He grasped for breath while continuing to turn the key over and over in his hand. At the top, he rushed away from the dunes to briefly catch his breath behind a shed, then bolted toward the Simmons house. Reaching the alley, he bent over from fear and exhaustion. He must make a plan. *Having a plan means being in control. Without a plan, bad things happen.* He walked up the outside stairs of the Simmons home, unlocked the door and went inside. He sat on the floor under a gambling table, rocking his fear away.

***

While Surrette was speaking with the ship's captain, Ferguson and Miller walked the length of the wharf, seeking information from everyone. A few men thought they'd seen the man described. One in particular had something to say. "He's not a sailor, constable. A land lover, for sure. He talks to a fella called Simmons. A business owner. Let me think now." A few seconds passed. "Walter Simmons, that's it."

Ferguson and Miller waited for Surrette to step off the ship. Constable Ferguson spoke up. "Sir, Wallace is connected to a fella by the name of Walter Simmons. I've had some suspicions about him recently."

Surrette added, "Wallace is travelling under the name of Ward. He has a berth on this ship sailing at four thirty."

Constable Miller smiled, looked at Surrette. "So we wait here and arrest him when he shows up to board, Sir."

"He's a smart fellow, Miller. I don't think it'll be that easy. We need a plan 'cause he's sure to have one."

While the police made their plan, Alex had his own to complete. He returned to the bank. "Good afternoon. I'm Alex Ward. I have an account under this number and would like to withdraw the funds." He glanced at his watch. Departure time was drawing close. He'd need time to avoid the police and still get onboard. He exhaled anxiously.

"I'm sorry, Mr. Ward. There is no money in the account number you provided."

"Please check again. Perhaps I gave you an incorrect number. Here is the number again.'

"I'm sorry, sir. That account is empty. It was all withdrawn a while ago."

Alex nodded and stepped outside the bank. Time was running out. The sun was dropping in the western sky, its rays spread across the harbour in brilliant yellow, orange then red. He had a choice. Get on the ship or stay in Yarmouth. The hanging tree flashed through his mind.

***

Surrette had a three person plan. Patrol the street parallel to the wharf, patrol the sand dunes and the beach end of the wharf and hide onboard the passenger ship.

A block from the wharf, Alex spotted one man from the wharf coming out of the side street. *Policeman, sure as hell.* With great restraint Alex walked slowly toward the house on his side of the street. It had a fenced front yard with a closed gate and a row of bushes behind a low rock wall. He jumped the rock wall and laid low. He was breathing fast. Peering over the wall, he saw the policeman walking toward the end of the street. He jumped over the wall, back onto the street and moved down toward the wharf. There, he looked left then right. He could feel his heart pounding No policemen were in sight. He saw the ship. He saw freedom waiting. His saw his new life waiting. He threw the useless receipt and key into the darkness, raced toward the ship and stepped aboard, into the waiting arms of Sergeant Pierre Surrette.

CHAPTER TWENTY-SEVEN

TUESDAY, NOVEMBER 06

Sergeant Surrette and the ship's captain had prepared to subdue Alex Wallace. Two husky seamen were standing on either side of the entrance and the captain strapped on his pistol.

When Wallace collapsed in a heap onto the ship's floor, Surrette was certain it was a ploy. He expected Wallace to jump up, lunge forward and knife someone or take the closest person as a hostage. Neither happened. Wallace burst into uncontrollable sobs, curled into a ball and wet himself.

Surrette snapped the cuffs on Alex and asked Constable Miller to retrieve Wallace's belongings from the ship's storage room. He checked for weapons and found a paltry sum of money and diaries.

Before leaving the ship, Surrette arranged for Walter Simmons and his family be denied travel out of the port of Yarmouth. He authorized Constable Miller to organize a search for the Simmons family and to contact the Halifax Police of their whereabouts.

***

From a distance, Walter Simmons watched the commotion around the ship then saw Alex taken away in hand cuffs. He rushed home to empty the safe.

“Sadie, we’re leaving for Digby. Pack a loaf of bread and some cheese. Take clothing for a few days.”

Lily wandered into the office. “What’s happened, Papa?”

“Alex is going to jail and we could be next. Start packing. No fancy dresses.” Then he called out to Sadie. “Only two dresses for each of you. Wear a warm coat, hat and boots. And hurry.”

***

At the police station, Surrette charged Wallace with the murder of Mollie Brown and locked him in the station’s only cell.

“Well done, Constables. I’ll stay in the station until morning. Ferguson, could you bring a couple of sandwiches and a big pot of tea to the station. Mrs. Matthews might be willing to provide what I need. Also, bring my travel bag along as well. Now, which one of you wants to take a long train ride to Halifax tomorrow?”

Ferguson responded, “I’ll go, Sergeant.” Then nodded toward Constable Miller. “Miller has young children.”

Surrette nodded. ”Thanks again to you both. Excellent work.”

Alone in the station, Surrette telephoned Halifax and asked for Henderson. “Wallace is locked up, Sir. He has diaries. He isn’t talking but the Walter Simmons family here is likely connected to him. We are looking for them. By the way, we didn’t see Young anywhere in town but Yarmouth is a good spot to skip the country by ship to Boston.”

“Be careful coming back. Don’t do this alone.”

“Yes, Sir. I’m taking Constable Ferguson with me and Wallace will be cuffed all the way. We’ll be in our own train car.”

When the sandwiches arrived, Surrette kept his distance from the cell. “Stand against the back wall and I’ll place a sandwich and tea inside the cell.”

Surrette felt as though Wallace was staring right through him, planning his next move. He shivered involuntarily.

***

As the sun rose on Wednesday morning, Constable Ferguson arrived at the station with his travel bag. “Take a break, Sergeant. I’ll not go near the cell.”

Surrette stepped into the first blush of the day and felt a chill run down his back. He pulled up his collar, turned right then right again onto the street with the white church on the corner. He walked toward the yellow house with the big veranda. Standing on the veranda, about to knock, he had second thoughts about his intention.

Being a careful, somewhat restrained man got Pierre where he was today. He shoved his hands back into his pockets and returned to the sidewalk where he began mumbling to himself. “She seems happy enough living here. What if she turns me away?”

Maggie Matthews opened her front door and stepped onto the veranda. “Sergeant Surrette, what are you doing out here? Come in, warm up, have an egg on toast.”

“Thank you.” He stepped inside. “I have to get back to the jail soon.” He swallowed hard. “Would you like to visit Halifax sometime? I could show you the city. You could stay with my sister or in a hotel or a boarding house.”

“That would be lovely. Now, Fergus is quite capable of minding the station so sit down and I’ll prepare your egg and toast.”

“Yes, ma’am.” They smiled at each other.

***

The hours-long ride to Halifax in a train car with Alex Wallace was an endurance test for both Surrette and Ferguson. Wallace was cuffed, hands front, his breathing steady. He'd reverted to a feral state, eyes dark, wound up like a tight spring, body poised to lash out, take advantage at any time.

As the train slowed to a crawl on the approach to the station, the conductor opened their car door, bringing with him a great swirl of thick fog.

Wallace stuck out his foot as Surrette was shouting to the conductor. "Get out, get out."

Surrette tripped over the falling conductor and came down hard, hitting his shoulder against a passenger seat. Ferguson leapt over both of them and scurried out the open door as Wallace melted into the dense fog. Surrette was not too far behind, although his pace was remarkably hindered by his wounded shoulder.

Alex darted between two train cars parked on a siding, across a dock overflowing with workers and soldiers. Ferguson gained on him, but only momentarily. Alex dodged through the mass of people, then jumped off the wharf into the fog and onto the ferry just departing for Dartmouth.

It was all over for Ferguson when Alex leapt into the fog. The water gap was now too large to risk.

Surrette arrived within moments. "You did your best, Constable."

"Thanks, Sergeant. Surely some men onboard will overpower him when they see the cuffs."

***

Ella completed Charles' funeral plan at the church in the afternoon and returned home in time to receive a telephone call from Anna Hopkins.

"Hello, Mrs. Ramsay. Anna Hopkins speaking."

"Hello, Mrs. Hopkins." *What could she want from me?*

"Please call me Anna. We haven't met but I'm calling to express my condolences regarding your husband's untimely death. It must be a trying time and I do hope you and your children are doing well."

The English accent reminded her of Nana MacPherson, crisp, concise and meaningful. "Thank you, Anna. We are carrying on with life. Rose, who is nine, is having the most difficulty. Her friend, Nellie and family are a great support."

"Is your Nellie my Nellie Quinn? I saw her name on the list of local artists for the upcoming event."

Anna sounded lovely, a bit intense but lovely. "Yes, she is."

"Can we talk about the Celebration or would you rather decline considering the circumstances?"

"Life goes on Anna, and I intend to have one."

"Splendid. Can I call on you tomorrow afternoon, say two o'clock?"

Contrary to the old rules, Ella did not want her children, or herself for that matter to be hidden from the public and wear black for months. As Murdoch and Marie were eating their evening meal in the King Edward Hotel and Rose was with the Quinn family, she took the opportunity to have a late afternoon walk on the wharf and see the sun set. It was quite foggy but a stiff breeze at the wharf could change all that.

Fog intrigued Ella. At times it was frightening, pulling her away from her comfortable, safe sense of self into its roiling underbelly of the unknown. At other times it was comforting, enveloping her in a shroud of secrecy. After all, she was a keeper of secrets herself. *Everyone kept secrets, at least once in a while.*

Today, the swirling dense fog was comforting. Charles' funeral would be in two days and she trusted Detective Henderson to solve his murder. She stepped into the shroud and moved closer to the wharf. Although some distance from the ship loading and unloading areas, she could hear the high pitched whinnies of the war horses. They were distressed and frightened. And no wonder. They had been taken from their farms and families across the country and carried in box cars to the port of Halifax.

Inside the rolling shroud, she could not fully trust what she was hearing. A male voice was yelling 'stop, stop' about something. When the voice became louder, closer, there was no mistaking what she heard. "Alex Wallace, stop. This is Constable Emile Ferguson of the Yarmouth police. Stop."

Ella caught a glimpse of the running man. *It's him.* Her thoughts were on fire with anger. The bugger's lose. She ran toward the street and hailed a taxi.

Alex had no intention of surrendering. He was onboard the steamer, hidden behind a supply of boxes, rope and barrels. Handcuffed and feeling sore after hitting his shoulder and chest while jumping onboard, he grappled with the lining of his coat pocket for several minutes. Eventually he pulled the prostitute's earring free. Despite the cool, foggy air blowing over the open deck, he was sweating. Fearing he would drop the earring, he leaned against the hull and closed his eyes for a few minutes. When the ferry's engine began to slow down, his heart raced. He brought his wrists together. Then using his left thumb and forefinger to grasp the earring, he guided the earring's hook into the lock. His wrists bled from the twisting cuffs. He hated blood. It smelled bad. His stomach roiled. He gagged. Nothing happened when he turned the hook right. Sweat trickled down both sides of his face. He turned the hook left and his hands fell from the open cuffs. For a moment he was immobilized by his own success then he heard footfalls pass his hide out. He stood up and joined the others leaving the ferry, inching into the middle of the group and stepping off the ferry a free man.

***

Dora Wallace was finally free. For too many years, she'd been locked away from society, deemed a risk to herself, fed pills and slop for food. Thanks to new ideas and treatment, she was being released from the asylum in Dartmouth.

"You'll see a busy city, Dora. Lots of ships in the harbour and the military everywhere. More women are working, taking jobs men normally held as they go off to war. I'm confident you'll be successful and expect to see you two weeks from today."

"Thank you, Doctor Hopps."

"Now, do you recall our discussion about Alex's recent letter?"

"Yes, when he tried to see me a few weeks ago."

Hopps nodded. When he asked Alex how he found his mother, the answer was chilling. 'I'm not stupid and I'll be back again. Here's a letter for her.'

"That's correct. We've talked about Alex before. He was very agitated and belligerent with me that day. Seeing him would not be in your best interest. I highly recommend you not initiate contact with him nor accept his approach to you. If at any time you feel threatened by Alex, I want you to contact me right away. You have my telephone number?"

"Yes, Doctor."

"As you want to go to Halifax, a hospital attendant will walk with you to the ferry."

Dora was excited to start her life anew. She recalled being taken from Halifax to Dartmouth on a ferry so she wasn't too concerned about the ride. Her money from Henry's estate would allow her to get settled in a decent rooming house, buy two new dresses and save the rest. In a day or two she'd look for a lady's shop needing help. Her coat was dated but buying a new one seemed extravagant as she was rarely outside, except for walks on the grounds with an attendant. The new coat would have to wait. Unconsciously, she ran her hand over the old scar on her neck and tucked errant curls under her hat. *Alex could be quite nasty at times.*

"Here we are, Dora. Best of luck and don't forget to contact Doctor Hopps if you need support."

Dora needed a coin for the ferry ride. She could no longer avoid looking into her purse. The familiar clench in her stomach returned, always connected to Alex from the time he was a child. She removed a coin and the envelope then opened the letter.

Dearest Mother, I hope you are feeling better. In case you don't know, Father died. I inherited some money, sold the house and everything in it. I was told your share of the money was sent to the asylum for you. Father and his sister should never have had you locked up. I took care of them for you. It has been difficult for me since you left. You should have fought harder to stay with me. If you are gone the next time I try to see you, I will track you down. You better have a good reason for leaving me. Alex

She returned the envelope to her purse and waited for the ferry to arrive. As the ferry docked, she saw Alex walk off, his collar up, head down, clinging to the edge of a small group of fellow travellers. As they dispersed, he dashed into a back ally. She boarded the ferry grieving for what was and what might have been. She was living through her problems and Alex was too, just in a different way. *Perhaps Doctor Hopps could help him.*

***

The desk constable at the police station watched as a distraught women rushed to the counter. “Good afternoon, Madam. How may I help you?”

“I must speak with Detective Henderson.”

“Your name, Madam.”

“Mrs. Ramsay. Ella Ramsay.”

“Thank you, Mrs. Ramsay.”

Ella was barely seated when Henderson arrived at the front desk.

Ella stood. “It’s about Alex Wallace. He’s in Dartmouth, running from the Yarmouth police. I was at the wharf when it happened about twenty minutes ago.”

“Wait here, please.” There was a pause. “How do you know Alex Wallace?”

“I knew his father years ago.”

CHAPTER TWENTY-EIGHT

WEDNESDAY, NOVEMBER 07

Too late, Ella realized Detective Henderson had a new person of interest, herself. Her indiscretion should be none of his business. Alex would soon be in custody for murder and her connection to him would end.

"Come to my office, Mrs Ramsay. We can talk there."

Not about Alex Wallace, we're not. "I see no need for that."

"Please bring us tea and biscuits, Constable."

"I have a family at home, Detective. This is unnecessary."

Entering his office, Henderson pointed to a chair in front of his desk and took the other beside her. A heavy sigh was followed by a look of relief settling across his face.

Ella sat upright, ready to offer an excuse and leave the room, tea or no tea. She stared at Henderson, trying to read his face. *He's very good at this game.*

Will smiled. "Thank you, Mrs. Ramsay. Any assistance in capturing a suspect is most helpful. Your effort today is very much appreciated. Ah, here comes the tea. Sugar?"

"No, thank you."

"You had quite the ordeal. I trust you are feeling better."

Good. He's forgotten his original question.

"Alex Wallace, tell me again how you know him?" He looked at her with total innocence.

He's very, very good at this. "I knew his father years ago." *I know this game.* Ella brought the cup to her lips, let it linger there before taking a slow sip.

Henderson offered her a biscuit. She shook her head and continued to sip the tea.

"How are the children?" Then he paused. "I'm sorry. Murdoch's not a child. Rose, isn't it? How is she? I expect it has been difficult."

"Thank you for asking, Detective." Ella had a feeling Henderson was trying to get chummy. She was having none of it. "We are managing. Speaking of Rose, I must be going."

"It's cold and getting dark. I'll drive you home."

Ella hesitated. Without a reasonable excuse, she was forced to accept. "Thank you."

As they stood to leave, Henderson was called to the front desk. "Excuse me for a moment."

Henderson took the receiver, listened then responded. "Good work, Surrette. Hiding in a shed! Have one of ours guard his Rockhead cell overnight. No physical contact. No conversation. I just received Wallace's property from the train. The diaries will be crucial to the case. Bring him here tomorrow morning at nine, cuffed and under guard. Both he and White will be transferred to the Dorchester Penitentiary in New Brunswick tomorrow afternoon." He returned to his office. "We can be off now, Mrs. Ramsay."

***

The evening meal at the King Edward dining room began with Marie's unsuccessful attempt to remain unmoved by the grandeur of the gracious room. White tablecloths and attentive waiters.

"Oh, my goodness. Do you come here often, Murdoch?"

"Not often. Usually when Papa is, sorry, was eager to go."

"How is Rose?"

"She cries often. The Quinn family has been so, so helpful in keeping her active with them, Nellie in particular."

"Angus Martin told me Nellie is an amazing young artist. Have you seen her work?"

"No but Rose tells us about it."

"Will you be returning to work next week?"

"I think so. There is no reason to stay home."

Marie was having doubts about dinner. *He's grieving. Perhaps we should not have come.*

By the time dessert was served, their conversation had reached its natural end and Marie's old self-doubt had surfaced. *Is he truly interested in me or just fascinated by someone so socially different from himself?*

Across the table, Murdoch sighed but made no effort to speak. He offered a weak smile.

Marie put herself in Murdoch's shoes. *Maybe he's worried about being head of the family, even with a mother who is a most capable woman.* She lifted the Limoges tea cup and finished the tea.

"Another cup?" Murdoch's voice sounded far away, a little unclear.

"I'm fine, thank you."

Murdoch forced another weak smile and turned his attention to his napkin. *Will she be comfortable in my family? One hasty conversation with his mother and Rose in a restaurant didn't account for much. He had to know.*

"Will you come to Papa's funeral?"

Religion had been in the back of Marie's mind. "I plan to." *Unless my mother or father makes a fuss.*

Murdoch opened his mouth to talk about religion but was interrupted.

"Good evening Marie, Murdoch."

Marie lifted her head and Murdoch turned around. "Good evening, Mr. Davis."

"May I introduce, Ruby Turner. She's visiting from Truro." He looked at Marie. "She also likes fancy shoes. As she is moving here, maybe you two should work together on our new shoe line."

After a lively but brief conversation about shoes, Corbin and Ruby moved on and Marie whispered, "Is she connected to the Truro detective who was murdered?"

"I believe she's the widow."

"My goodness, how interesting that she's moving here."

Murdoch checked his watch. "If you're ready to leave, I'll call for a taxi."

Marie nodded.

When the taxi reached Marie's home, Murdoch walked her to the door and kissed her hand. "I hope to see you Friday morning at St. George's."

Inside the LeBlanc home, Marie's mother was knitting a pair of mitts for Leo and her father reading the newspaper. He lifted his head. "That Doctor Ramsay's funeral is Friday. I expect you're going since you work with his son, Murdoch." He returned to the newspaper with one eye on his wife.

"Dinner with a friend this evening was Murdoch Ramsay, wasn't it?"

"Yes, Mama. We are good friends. I like him."

Gisele LeBlanc continued knitting. "Be careful. He may not turn out to be such a good friend after all."

***

Overnight Henderson continued to think about the interview with Alex Wallace. *Why had Alex come to Halifax in the first place? He had no apparent connection to Mollie Brown. There had to be more to his story. He didn't kill Charles but there's a connection with Ella. Does it even matter now?*

***

The following morning Henderson and Surrette waited in the interview room for Alexander Wallace. "Yarmouth was quite the hunt, Sergeant."

"Absolutely, Sir. Ferguson and Miller are very skilled. I'd like to have them recognized in some way."

"I agree. Let's work on that after we have White and Wallace locked up in Dorchester."

"Thank you, Sir." Surrette took a very deep breath. "Wallace's escape from the train was the most frightening. So many innocent people were vulnerable. I have to admit I was frightened he'd take a hostage."

"After we settle this interview, feel comfortable talking about the whole thing with me. It's good to get this type of experience off your mind. Oh, here they come. Don't stand. That'll give him a sense of importance. He's smart, cunning, unpredictable. We'll keep him double-cuffed, one wrist to each arm of the chair.

When Alex entered the room, Henderson pointed to the single chair placed on the side of the room opposite the door. "Sit in that chair, Wallace." He glanced at the badge of the closest constable then pointed to the handcuffs on the table. "Constable McInnes, double cuff the prisoner to the arms of the chair."

Alex watched as his arms were pulled apart, then lifted his head toward the ceiling.

Surrette scanned Wallace's face and body. He found no resemblance to the whimpering man on the ship nor the devious man on the train ride from Yarmouth. *Who is he now?*

"My name is Detective Henderson, Mr. Wallace. You are here regarding the murder of Miss Mollie Brown on the night of October twenty-second, this year. We have a witness but I'd like to hear what you have to say."

Wallace continued to stare at a location on the opposite wall, not far from the ceiling.

He's in his own head. Henderson shifted his gaze to the same place on thc wall and waited, and waited.

Surrette glanced at this watch, noting the time.

The silence prevailed.

Surrette cleared his throat and simultaneously looked at his watch. Five minutes had passed.

"It was her fault. I only defended myself." Alex was murmuring to himself.

Henderson remained silent, kept staring at the wall. "So she deserved what she got?"

Alex frowned. "She was prettier than Lily."

"Who is Lily?"

"She's gone away now but the other one was prettier."

Henderson kept his eyes on the wall. *Did he just admit to killing another woman? Mollie was prettier?*

"Her dress was blue. I like blue. I kept the earring."

"Mollie's earring?"

Alex nodded. "Women don't like me."

"Why is that, Alex?" No answer. "Anything else about that evening with Mollie, Mr. Wallace?"

"No." He said.

"Why were you in Halifax, Mr Wallace?"

Surrette turned his head toward Henderson, a puzzled look on his face.

Wallace remained silent. Henderson pushed. “Maybe looking for work?”

Wallace shook his head. “I had money.”

“Or somebody? Mr. Wallace, I think you were in the city for another reason, became frustrated and Mollie Brown lost her life.” He paused. “Do you know Ella Ramsay?”

Alex yelled, “Bitch”, dropped his head, rocked back and forth in his chair then lifted it from the floor as he lunged across the table toward Henderson, his eyes cold, lips tightened and nostrils flared.

Surrette and a guard bolted from their chairs, slammed Wallace’s chair to the floor and held it there.

Henderson continued to sit calmly. “I have my answer, Mr. Wallace. I also understand you were acquainted with a Walter Simmons in Yarmouth. Care to comment on that?”

“He’s a crook. I was more interested in Lily.” He curled his lip and snickered.

“Thank you, Mr. Wallace. You’ll have another opportunity to talk about the Simmons family. In the meantime, Alexander Wallace, I’m charging you with the murder of Mollie Brown and escaping lawful custody. Take him away, officers.”

As Wallace was being escorted from the room, Henderson remained in his chair. “By the way, Mr. Wallace, did you know Detective Bill Turner?”

The answer was instant. “That rough copper deserved what he got but it wasn’t me.”

***

Ella's parents returned from Ottawa Wednesday. Her mother insisted on being with Ella when the dressmaker arrived shortly after lunch on Thursday.

Ella was more than pleased with the new shorter dress lengths and relaxed silhouettes but footwear was her failing, especially decorative buttons on boots and shoes.

When Ella stepped out of her dressing room wearing an ankle-length black crepe dress, her mother's mouth dropped. She appeared uninterested in the silk collar, long cuffed sleeves and tucked waistline.

"Ella, whatever have you done? And the boots, blue buttons up the side!" She dropped onto the bed where she covered her mouth with her hand and whimpered, "Oh, my."

"Now, now, Mother. Don't upset yourself. Times change."

"Where is your hat? Do you actually have one?"

When Ella put on the small black hat with a modest brim and short veil, her mother said nothing but her eyes popped larger than Ella could ever remember. "Thank heavens, you're at least wearing one!"

"It will be fine, Mother. Now, I'll put on my day dress and we can have a pot of tea. It seems to help solve all the world's troubles, except the war, of course." She sighed. "I heard the horses at the wharf earlier this week."

"Poor things. I don't imagine they'll return home, even if they survive."

Not long after Ella's mother left, Anna Hopkins arrived.

"Thank you for seeing me, Ella. I understand your situation but we must get a few things done."

"May I ask you a few questions first?"

"Absolutely."

"Tea?"

"Yes. I'm a Brit."

As Ella was getting the tea she continued with her questions. “How did you become so independent almost twenty years ago?”

“I didn’t have a close relationship with my family in England so returning there after my husband died was not a good idea. The suffragette ladies were working to achieve what I wanted, women to be equal in society. So, I joined them. Right now, we are pushing for the women’s vote in the next provincial election.”

“And writing. Have you always been a writer?”

“It started in England when a friend of the family suggested I write for the local paper. Interviewing people, telling their story. That sort of thing. When I came to Halifax, I had to push my way into the paper by interviewing interesting people. Do you know Margaret Fraser?”

“Not well. We’ve spoken after church. She lives a few streets from here.”

“Margaret knew the prominent people I wanted to interview so that’s really how the column started.”

“Thank you. I guess we better get to work on the ticket sales and the people assigned to their duties.”

“But first, how are you really feeling?”

Ella began to cry. “Sorry. I feel overwhelmed, vulnerable, frightened about the future, worried about Rose growing up without a father.”

Anna looked into Ella’s eyes. “You’re normal then.” She smiled, her own eyes glistening with tears.

Ella chuckled. “Thank you.”

“It takes time to work through all of those things you mentioned. Be kind to yourself.” She paused. “I’ve been wondering if we should start a widows group at the church. Just to talk, support each other. It could be for anyone, not only St. Georges. Maybe widowers, too? What do you think?”

“I would attend.”

"Excellent, Now about the tickets. They are going quickly. I expect we will sell out."

"That's a relief."

"And we have everyone for the children's outdoor and indoor afternoon activities assigned. We need two more for the evening, a greeter at the door to welcome everyone and someone to monitor the food table, the coffee and tea urns. By the way, I don't expect you to work, Ella."

"Murdoch and his friend, Marie are going to take Rose to the children's afternoon events." She hesitated. "I would like to work a couple of hours as a greeter."

"That would be wonderful. You will be with someone else." She looked at her notes. "Would five to seven be possible?"

"Perfect."

"So, let's work on the speakers. All the politicians want time! I say the fewer the better."

"Speakers or politicians?"

"Both!"

"Can I be the one with the hook to pull them off the stage?"

They both laughed, their fingers threaded together.

As Anna was leaving, Murdoch came through the front door.

"Perfect timing, Murdoch. This is Anna Hopkins. We are working together on the Celebration event."

"Hello, Mrs. Hopkins. I overheard your name mentioned at the Eddie last evening."

"Good heavens. I hope it wasn't an outburst against women in politics."

"Well, it was about politics and about you being a good candidate for the next provincial election."

"Well, I would not be opposed to running but women need to get the vote before that can happen."

"I understand it's very close to happening." He lifted an eyebrow toward Anna.

"It is, indeed but I must leave this discussion for another time." She turned her attention to Ella. "The mayor is expecting me to provide an update on the event before the day is over. Bye, bye for now."

As Ella closed the door she tilted her head toward Murdoch. "Politics?"

"Just an article I read in the newspaper at the bank today. Don't worry, I've no aspirations to be a politician."

"I'm relieved. And how is Marie?" Murdoch's hesitation answered her question.

"She's probably coming to Papa's funeral. Her parents might not approve."

"Oh dear."

"By the way, I saw a fellow in the bank today from my Dalhousie days. Do you remember Tom Adams?"

"In fact, I do. He was the talkative one in your little gang a few years ago."

Murdoch grimaced at the word 'gang'. "He's with the bank and looks very serious wearing the requisite white shirt and dark tie. We're getting together one day next week. He sent his condolences to you."

"How kind." She looked at her watch. "I have time to take a walk. Can you bring Rose home from the Quinn home?"

"Yes, if she'll leave!"

She hugged Murdoch and went to the closet for her coat. "Take gloves for Rose."

When Ella stepped around the corner of a building to face the waterfront she was peppered with wind-driven water. As a Haligonian, she was used to the Atlantic and its ways. She moved closer to the wharf. The waves were dangerously high, relentlessly pounding the dock, spray flew in all directions.

In the short distance Ella could see the ferry from Dartmouth plowing toward the dock. Several passengers were clinging to anything bolted down. Ella knew exactly how they felt, floating without an anchor. Threats and murder had visited her and so had their companion, fear. Like the ferry passengers, she too was holding on, waiting for the fear to end.

The morning newspaper identified Alex as having been charged with the murder of Mollie Brown but it offered Ella no relief. Destroying her family while behind bars might still be within Alex's grasp.

She felt a presence beside her.

The presence spoke. "What on earth are you doing here?"

She looked steadily into Hugh's eyes. "I could ask you the same question, Mr. Andrews."

Hugh ignored the response. Today was not the sort of day to spar with her. "I am sorry about what happened to Charles. How is everyone getting on?"

Ella didn't want him to read her face. He'd always been good at that. She turned to face the water. "I think we are still in disbelief but Rose has a great friend and Murdoch is helping me with those things that have to be done: papers, the funeral, the bank." Her voice drifted away.

"If you need help, I can offer my assistance."

"Thank you." She took a deep breath and turned to face him. "Why are you here, really?"

"If you mean Halifax, Detective Turner's murderer has not been found. I believe there's an intriguing story behind the murder but I'll leave it there for the time being."

"Always a bit of mystery from the writer, hmm? And today?"

Hugh offered a polite lie. "I needed a walk." He quickly changed the conversation's direction. "I suppose you will be side-lined from the social scene for a while."

"Actually, I'm helping with the Troop event but yes, I won't be front and center at anything."

Hugh response was sharp. "Your mother will see to that."

A smirk flashed across Ella's face. "Do I sense a wee touch of anger in your tone?"

"Well, she had her motives then and probably still does. I still have the old wounds."

Ella side-stepped the 'then' and 'wounds' part of his answer. "I am offering more modern options for her to consider."

"Good for you."

"Isn't there an expression 'better late than never?' I believe it's from Canterbury Tales."

"Could that expression cover renewing a friendship with you?"

"In time." She turned toward the roiling sea.

Hugh remained silent. Waited for her new thoughts.

"Lately, I've been reflecting on what you said about circumstances, people and anger. I'm no longer the naive young woman I was nor do I agree with every word my parents utter." She glanced at her watch. "I must go. I look forward to seeing you again, that is, if you remain in Halifax."

Hugh smiled. "I have just found another reason to do so."

Late in the evening, Detective Henderson finished his reports relating to Alexander Wallace's interview then lifted the boxes containing the man's property from the floor to his desk. He searched for the diaries.

The disturbing ramblings of a manipulative man without a conscience jumped off the pages in Wallace's diaries. His detailed admissions of torture and murder were difficult to read, even for a hardened policeman. *Mollie's death saved Ella.*

CHAPTER TWENTY-NINE

Friday, November 09

Detective Will Henderson barely knew Charles Ramsay but he wanted to attend the man's funeral. But before that, he needed to visit Alexander Wallace. The man's diaries were filled with venom and intended vengeance against Ella Ramsay. Why?

Wallace appeared barely coherent when Henderson approached his cell. He kept his distance, clapped his hands. "Look lively, Wallace. I have a couple of questions."

Wallace remained on his cot, staring straight at Henderson, his eyes dead cold, piercing. "I'm already in jail. Get out."

"I read your diaries last night, Mr. Wallace. You have quite the legacy of mayhem and death in your history."

Wallace pursed his mouth into a self-satisfying smirk.

"You mentioned Ella Ramsay."

Alex rushed from his cot and shook the door. "I didn't touch her." He kept one hand on the door. "Get outta here."

"Well, that's a very poor answer, Mr. Wallace. But let's move on. How about the rest of the family, touch them?"

"No." He turned his back on Henderson. "You woke me up. Get out."

"Why do you hate Ella Ramsay?"

Wallace swung around, grabbed the bars, eyes locked on Henderson, his face flushed. "That bitch ruined my life. Look at her daughter, then look at me."

Henderson wished he hadn't asked the question.

***

Marie intended to leave early for Doctor Ramsay's funeral service in order to secure a seat in the back row of St. George's Church. As she sat down for breakfast alone, her mother walked into the kitchen in her dressing gown.

"Are you going to the Ramsay funeral this morning?"

"Yes. It is the right thing to do."

"It is but your father and I want to know what this Ramsay fellow's intentions are. We'll have a family conversation this evening."

Marie was shaking inside but she had to face the truth, speak of it out loud, calmly. "There is no need for any such meeting, Mama. This is about religion, not Murdoch and you know it. Do not disguise it with 'intentions', whatever that means. Religion should not dictate who our friends are. Murdoch and I are good friends. Do you understand what I am saying?"

"I am not willing for you to carry on with this friendship, as you call it and keep Murdoch away from us. We need to see this young man, talk to him."

"Not now. He..."

"Yes, I know. This is the wrong time for visits. In a few weeks, it will be possible."

"Thank you, Mama. Now I really must get ready."

Marie had never been inside St. George's or any other church but her family's church. After securing an aisle seat in the third row from the back, she had plenty of time to admire the rounded walls, balcony, pipe organ and stained glass windows. She took notice of the similarities with her own church. The pews, kneeling cushions, bibles, and hymn books looked familiar. The peaceful silence was comforting. She considered the earlier conversation with her mother until hushed voices brought her back from her inattention. She watched as the pews filled.

The Ramsay family entered last. Marie's heart lurched. Mrs. Ramsay wore a veiled hat which hid her face. She held Rose's hand. Murdoch walked alone, slightly behind his mother. Both Rose and Murdoch had been crying. Their faces were flushed and eyes focused on the floor, deep in their own thoughts as they passed the many pews before being seated in the front row, nearest the coffin. She remembered walking behind her grandfather's coffin last year. It was the hardest walk she had ever taken in her life. She smothered a sob in her handkerchief.

Marie did not attend the interment. Instead she walked to the office during which time she thought about religion and her relationship with Murdoch. In her opinion, they were not connected. But maybe her mother's point of view had to be considered. She too wanted to know what Murdoch was intending but that conversation would not take place with her parents. Near the office, she bought a sandwich from a small restaurant. She needed the comforting personal space of her familiar desk and chair at Davis Footwear.

By the time Henderson arrived at St. George's Church, the pews were filled and people huddled together outside in the chilly mid-morning air, made somewhat bearable by the pale sunshine. Faced with no choice but to offer his respects by waiting outside, he did so.

When the procession of clergy, casket and family made its way toward the cemetery, Henderson took note of any mourners who might be of interest to him. In that category he included Frank

Murphy and Angus Martin both of whom appeared very friendly with Hugh Andrews and a well-dressed, slender fellow with salt and pepper hair. The four silently made their way toward the grave while he hung back. As the mourners gathered around the grave site he was thinking he'd just happened upon something meaningful but was at a loss to understand what it meant.

Through an opening in the group, he saw Ella and her children, her parents and two older men. Each portrayed a slight likeness to Charles. He took several steps backward, returned to his car and drove to the station.

While Detective Henderson continued to wrestle with his own thoughts about the foursome at the Ramsay funeral, Frank, Hugh and Corbin were already eating lunch with Angus in the store owner's home. Days earlier they decided Jo needed to meet with Detective Henderson. She knew Bill and could offer insight into his death. Today, they were tasked with how to make that happen.

"Without a doubt, Malcolm needs to be out of town. He'll never let Jo go to the police station, even with him." Corbin then scanned the table. "Anyone have an idea?"

Frank put his spoon back in the bowl of clam chowder. "Have Henderson go to her house?" He expected the objections and held up his hands. "Let me finish. Or we arrange for Malcolm to return to Truro."

Hugh stared at Frank. "How in heaven's name would we do that?"

Frank was quick to answer. "I don't know but there aren't many ways to come at this thing."

Corbin was stroking his moustache. "Why has Henderson not made a connection between Jo and Bill already?"

Hugh answered. "Why would he?"

Corbin continued. "Well, they both lived in Truro. Ruby says she was part of the social group, was her friend."

Angus said, “What if Henderson knows there’s a connection already and is looking for something more substantial to warrant an interview?” His question went unanswered.

Frank thought about the blond hair in his dreams then looked at the other three men. “Is she a blonde? Does she wear lavender powder?”

The three men stopped eating.

Frank looked at their faces. “I’ve had a few dreams about that night on the Hill. I believe someone with blonde hair was there. I also smelled lavender.” He paused. ”Sergeant Bailey knows.”

Frank’s revelation was met with silence.

In the end, it was Hugh who nodded. “Yes to both. She’s a bit strange at times but a murderer? No.” He looked at Corbin who waffled long enough to force Hugh to continue. “Corbin, you and I have to get her away from Malcolm. That’s our only option.”

Corbin was wide-eyed. “You and I?”

“I see no other way. Get her out of the house. Have dinner with us at your house. Sell it as a way to have a social life again.”

“How do we manage that? Ruby’s staying with me while shopping for a house.”

“When is that taking place?”

“Let me think. She went home on Tuesday and said, ‘I’ll see you Monday’.”

“Perfect. Call Jo this evening. No, visit her this evening and plan for Sunday dinner.”

Corbin was anxious. “If you fellas think I’m nervous, you’re right. There’s a lot depending on this meal.”

“I understand, Corbin. But for Bill’s sake, we need to try.”

Angus brought out the Scotch. “Before I open the store, a wee dram to your success, Corbin.” He did not want to mention Billie’s name in Frank’s presence but he needed a new assistant. “Anyone know someone who could work with me in the store?”

There were no responses.

***

Dora Wallace read about the fate of her only child in the Halifax newspaper. Nothing could have prepared her for Alex's murder charge, not even seeing him run from the police. At the time, she guessed he'd committed a robbery. Even that conclusion baffled her thinking. Following Henry's death, Doctor Hopps received a letter from Henry's solicitor telling her both she and Alexander would receive an inheritance. *What had Alex done with his money? Why did he kill someone? He needed help because I failed him.* A sweeping rush of sadness passed through her body. She ate breakfast quickly, hoping her landlady would not guess she was connected to a murderer. One day, she would go to the police station and ask about her son. But not today.

Dora dressed warmly with her old coat and a new plaid scarf. Today she'd continue her search for work. She'd been honest, telling people the truth about her time in the asylum. Business owners were quick to give her short shrift. It was time to be more selective in talking about her past.

Dora had never worked in a general store but the sign was tempting. She walked in and asked the only person there about the job.

Angus described the work, asked her a few questions, including when she could begin.

Dora's reply was swift. "Would now be acceptable?"

***

Marie took her time walking home from work despite the cold dampness in the air and an available trolley ride. She needed time to reflect on what she experienced in St. George's Church. It felt very familiar to her own church: the priest, the prayers, the singing. Attending Doctor Ramsay's funeral had been difficult. Her heart ached seeing Murdoch and his family grieving. She dreaded opening the front door, afraid the day would end with a family quarrel after Leo was in bed. She took a deep breath and stepped inside.

"You're late."

She nodded toward her mother. "I walked home. I needed to clear my head, as Mr. Davis would say when he takes a walk around the block sometimes."

"Was that church like ours?"

"Yes, Leo it was. Very much like ours."

"Papa ate early and went to a meeting. Something about the big disturbance at the City Home last night. He told me there should be more night watchmen on overnight but the city thinks otherwise."

"Let's eat, Mama. Leo likely has homework."

Leo rolled his eyes. "Mrs. Hastings is very strict."

Gisele looked at her son, barely maintaining a straight face. "Is she now! And I'm thinking you might not be the quietest student in her class, Leo LeBlanc." She looked at Marie. "When the homework is done, you and I should talk about St. George's Church. I'm interested in what you have to say."

Corbin dawdled over his dessert so long Mrs. Williams came into the dining room. "Is there something wrong with the walnut cake, Mr. Davis?"

"No, it's very good. I'm delaying something I have to do."

"Well, it certainly won't get finished if you don't start. I'm sure someone is waiting for you to do something."

“Right you are, Mrs. Williams. I’ll be out for an hour or two.”

“I see rain on the window. Put on your warm coat and gloves. I bet we’ll have wet snow before next week.”

Corbin smiled. *What would I do without her?* He decided to take the car to Jo’s, even if it was only a few blocks away. A few minutes later, Corbin rang the doorbell and waited for Patch to meet him at the door, hopefully without Malcolm.

Jo opened the door, looking very puzzled. “Corbin, come in.”

Patch was patiently waiting for his handshake.

“Good evening, Patch.” The formalities over, he walked into the sitting room and sat beside Jo’s chair.

“Let me take your coat. What brings you here?”

“It’s been almost two weeks since the assault and I wanted to make sure you were improving.” He looked around, saw no sign of Malcolm. “Are you on your own?”

“Yes, why wouldn’t I be?” She led the way to the sitting room.

“You were badly beaten. Sometimes recovery takes a long time.”

“I’m sure you imagined it was far worse than it really was. Please sit down.”

I’m not the one who’s imagining. “Malcolm gone home?”

“Earlier this week. He mentioned something about a trip to England next week. A drink?”

“A small Scotch would be fine.” *England?*

“You still have family in England?”

She shook her head. “No, not really. A few cousins but they’re much older than either of us. I think he wanted to get away.” She turned her back and moved toward the drinks cart.

A curious choice of words. “He actually said that?”

“As a matter of fact, he actually did. Sometimes he worries me.”

“How so?”

"He fusses over me, which I don't want or need." She gave Corbin a small drink then sat down. He noted her glass was definitely not a small drink.

"So, what really brings you here?"

"Sunday dinner at my place. Hugh is coming so I thought it would be a good idea."

"A good idea for what?"

"To talk." *Damn, it's off the rails already.*

"You look serious. Talk about what?"

"Do I look serious? I was at a funeral today. That's probably it." *Why did I say that?*

"Someone I know?"

"Doctor Charles Ramsay." *Don't you read the paper?*

"Malcolm reads the paper and keeps me in touch with events. I am too busy writing my book."

"And how is that coming along?"

"Better since Malcolm left." She laughed. "He can be such a pain."

"Maybe, but he did look after you."

"Maybe it wasn't his conscience but the Hippocratic Oath." She refilled her glass. "More Scotch?"

"No, thanks. That sounds a bit unkind."

"He was obsessed with Bill's murder, looking for articles about it in the newspaper, talking about it."

"Why?"

"Who knows." She lifted her glass to drink then looked over the rim instead. "Besides, neither of us should be connected to Bill's murder inquiry, especially not Malcolm."

Corbin wanted to ask another 'why' but he'd wait until tomorrow, after Jo had a couple of glasses of Scotch and Hugh could also hear the answer. "So, what would you like Mrs. Williams to prepare for dinner tomorrow? Then you can update me on the book."

CHAPTER THIRTY

SATURDAY, NOVEMBER 10

Murdoch was uninterested in food, isolating himself and finding reasons to avoid reading to Rose. Ella accepted he would be grieving the loss of his father, despite their differences of opinion on many subjects but this was not about grief. Deep down, inside her heart, Ella knew it was about someone or something else in his life. As his mother, she wanted to help and do so soon. She went to the bottom of the stairs.

"Murdoch, Rose. Breakfast is ready."

"Thank you, Mama." Rose's voice drifted down the stairwell but no response came from Murdoch.

She started up the steps.

"I'm on my way."

Over breakfast, Murdoch's apathy was clear to Ella. She steeled herself, dreading what might come next. Drinking? Away all night?

In the early afternoon when Rose left to play with Nellie, she asked Murdoch to come to the kitchen.

"Is there a problem, Mama?"

"Yes and most likely it involves both of us." She hesitated. "You look tired. Your eyes have dark shadows under them. What is bothering you?"

Murdoch shrugged. "I'm just lost without something meaningful to do. Don't worry about me."

"But I do worry and I don't believe what you said is the whole truth. Am I right?"

Murdoch's response was silence.

Ella remembered those days. Silence was Murdoch's reply to everything he did not want to discuss. "I will offer some options. Something at work is worrying you. You are trying to solve the problem alone. You feel more responsibility for the family and don't know what to say to me about it. You and Marie are at odds about something."

"That one."

"Thank you. I don't want to be a nosy mother but talking with Marie is your best solution."

Murdoch open his eyes wide. "I think it's about religion."

"That's a prickly one."

"Or social position."

Ella furrowed her brow. "Good heavens, I hope not."

Murdoch was about to leave the room when Ella asked him to stay.

"You look worried, Mama."

"I am. Please sit down. As you know, Alex Wallace is in jail for murder."

Murdoch nodded. "We're rid of him. Isn't that good news?"

"Alex had diaries and now Detective Henderson has them. There are things in them that include me."

Murdoch sat back in his chair. "So that's why he was threatening us?" He shook his head. "Honestly, I don't want to know what he wrote. It's the past. What difference does it make today? None to us."

"Well, Detective Henderson may want to discuss those diary entries about me."

"But I don't need to hear them. Tell him to go away. Rose and I aren't involved."

Ella had been fretting over telling Murdoch about Rose. *It seems untimely, so soon after Charles' death.*

Murdoch interrupted her thoughts. "Did Papa know about the diaries or what happened that made Alex so unbalanced?"

"I don't believe so."

"Then let's not talk about this again. Agreed?"

Ella nodded but she knew it was not over.

***

Following the evening meal, Rose and Murdoch joined Ella in the sitting room.

"Mama, I'd like Murdoch to read out loud to me. Do you mind?"

"No. I'd like to listen too."

And so Murdoch began. "Anne of Green Gables by L.M. Montgomery."

Rose piped up. "Her name is Lucy Maud, Mama. Did you know that?"

Ella nodded and asked Murdoch to continue.

Well into Chapter One, the telephone rang.

"You two carry on with Anne." Ella left them and walked toward the kitchen. "Hello."

A soft female voice responded. "Mrs. Ramsay?"

"Yes, speaking."

"My name is Dora Wallace. Do you remember me?"

But you're dead. Ella hung onto the telephone receiver with one hand and steadied herself against the wall with the other.

"Ella?"

"I do, Dora. I do remember you."

"I'm feeling much better and living in Halifax."

"That is good to hear, Dora." *Does she know about Alex?*

A difficult silence followed.

"I was sorry to read of your husband's death, Mrs. Ramsay."

"Thank you."

"Do you have children? None were mentioned in the newspaper but I recall you had a young boy."

Rose's strong likeness to Alex hurtled through Ella's brain. "Yes, two children. Dora, I..."

"I'm feeling much better now. I wonder if you would be interested in a visit? I thought perhaps we could recall happier times."

Ella's heart was racing. She had to get off the telephone. As she was about to say 'goodbye' and hang up, Dora continued.

"I'm a bit lost in the shadows of my old life this evening. Thinking about Alexander. Would tomorrow afternoon be appropriate?"

"I have a visitor tomorrow, Dora. Call me on Wednesday and we can set a day at that time. I hope to be feeling stronger then. Thank you for calling." She walked toward the sitting room, her mother's voice ringing in her ears. 'Honesty is the best policy'. *Not today it isn't.*

"Murdoch kept reading, Mama. Do you want me to tell you what happened to Anne?"

Ella smiled. "No, Murdoch can continue." Within minutes, the door bell rang. The sudden sound startled Ella.

Seeing Detective Henderson waiting on the other side of the door was the final straw for Ella. "Why are you standing on my doorstep and what do you want? Don't you have a home to go to?"

Henderson's face changed colour to a deep shade of red as he sputtered an apology. "Sorry."

"I buried my husband yesterday. Are you totally devoid of all empathy?" She turned her back on him. "Come inside so we can get this over with."

Will was cowed, trailed behind Ella into the kitchen and waited to be told where to sit.

"Do you want coffee or are you able to talk without a cup in front of you?"

Will felt the frost in the room. He tried to think of something to raise the temperature but offered a weak, "I'm fine."

Ella took a very deep breath. "If you say so. Now, please tell me why you're here. And it had better be good." She sat on the side of the table opposite Will.

"I'm here to apologize, Mrs. Ramsay. First, for my unannounced visit just now and secondly, for questioning you in my office. I've spent considerable time reading Alexander Wallace's diaries. You were the intended target."

"Thank you. Alex is pure evil, Detective. I knew I was the target from the moment he rang the doorbell weeks ago." Her tone softened. "I'm truly sorry Miss Brown had to die."

"Wallace had a long list of victims. Miss Brown is not the only one. We have more work to do."

"You have one more complication, Detective. Alex's mother is now in Halifax."

"Oh, dear."

"I'm having a coffee. I recall you have milk, no sugar."

***

Murdoch took his mother's words to heart and knocked on the LeBlanc family's front door mid-afternoon on Sunday.

Marie's father opened the door. "Murdoch! Come in. Come in. We were sorry to hear about your father. How are you doin' lad?"

"Some days are easier than others. Thank you for asking." He rushed to explain his visit. "My sister Rose and I are here to take Marie for a drive to the park. I hope she's at home."

"Come with me. I think she's reading in the front room."

Murdoch followed Benoit along the short hallway toward the small front room. He noticed the coolness of the room the moment he crossed its' threshold. He suspected the door was usually shut. The room itself felt crowded with a flowered carpet, flowered sofa and two matching chairs plus four hardwood ones. It seemed to him the LeBlanc family had lots of visitors. The papered walls displayed a few dower faces.

"Murdoch! What are you doing here?" Marie's mouth remained open as she jumped out of the chair.

As Benoit tilted his head toward Murdoch, he spoke to Marie. "He's here to take you for a ride in his fancy car."

Any further conversation was halted when Gisele LeBlanc entered the room. The mood became much less friendly.

"Marie is going to take a ride with Murdoch." Benoit quickly followed with, "Young Rose will be with them."

Gisele tucked her hands into her skirt pockets and remained silent, although her eyes sent a strong warning to Marie.

"Thank you Murdoch but I think it would appear inappropriate for you to be seen driving around in your father's car so soon after his death." She offered a weak smile. "Perhaps later would be better."

Murdoch cast his eyes toward Gisele and Benoit then settled them on Marie. "You are probably correct, Marie. Excuse me." He turned and left the room.

Benoit followed him to the front door. "I apologize, Murdoch."

Murdoch muttered, "thank you," and rushed to the car.

"Where's Marie?"

"She can't come for a drive today but you and I can. Point Pleasant?"

Rose put her hand on Murdoch's arm. "Did Marie say no?"

Murdoch stared out the windscreen. His answer reflected what had really happened in the front room. "No, she didn't but someone else did for her."

"Is she sick and can't talk?"

Murdoch laughed. "You are so clever. No, she's not sick and I think she will be able to talk much better tomorrow."

"Good. Will you teach me to drive?"

"Yes, someday when you're older."

During his time as a newspaper man, Hugh had unabashedly challenged people about their reasons and ethics when making decisions and acting on them. He reasoned the reader needed to know the whole story and he dug deep and wide to give them exactly that.

Tonight the stakes were high and he was uneasy about what would be unearthed. If Frank's memory about blonde hair and lavender was accurate, two questions needed to be asked. *Was Jo a witness in Bill's death or did she kill him herself? Either way she must be interviewed by Detective Henderson.*

Hugh arrived at Corbin's only to discover Jo was already there, drinking Scotch.

"Good evening, Hugh. Corbin and I were just talking about work."

"Work? That sounds very unexciting." He bent down to offer Jo a hug. *Lavender.*

"Actually it isn't. Corbin asked the question, what do I like most about my work?"

"And the answer was?"

"I work on my own time."

Hugh accepted a Scotch from Corbin and asked, "What's your answer?"

"The people I work with."

"And you?"

"The people I meet."

"Excuse me, Mr. Davis. Dinner will be served in ten minutes."

At the table, the conversation moved to what they wanted to be doing five years from now.

Jo had a quick answer. "Being world famous because of my book." She laughed so heartily, she had to place her wine glass on the table. "Sorry, I'm being a bit silly."

Hugh took a chance and began to dig deep, "Malcolm on his way to England?"

"No, the ship sails Wednesday, I believe."

"How's your relationship with him these days?"

Corbin was taken back by Hugh's pointed question, then he remembered their relationship was years old. He'd stay out of whatever was to transpire between the two of them.

Jo finished her wine then offered up her empty glass to Corbin. He filled it.

"Malcolm, Malcolm. Ever the meddling brother." A heavy sigh followed. "He sees it as protecting me."

"Good heavens, who would you need protection from in Halifax?"

She dismissed the seriousness of his question with a wave of her hand. "You know Malcolm from our Truro days."

"But it was different in Truro. You moved away from all of that." He guessed. "And things ended."

"It doesn't end when one person won't accept the end."

"Pardon me, Mr. Davis. Dessert?"

Corbin pulled his thoughts away from Jo's words. "Absolutely." He smiled at Mrs. Williams despite her inconvenient timing.

Hugh dug deeper, "That's unfortunate. Desperate people sometimes do desperate things."

"Sadly, that is true."

Hugh dug wider, opened a new line of questions. "I've met a few desperate people in my work. You?"

"Oh, yes. Two recently." She looked directly at Hugh. "If you're thinking Malcolm is a desperate person, he isn't. But, he's possessive." She went silent. Drank more wine.

Hugh waited until dessert was served and Mrs. Williams was out of the room before he opened his mouth to continue. Jo interrupted him.

"Dreadful things can happen when possessive people collide." Jo picked up her dessert fork then returned it to the table.

"What are you saying, Jo? Did someone you know do something dreadful?"

Jo covered her eyes. "I've said too much. You both think I know something." She opened her eyes and stared toward them, moving from one to the other.

When Hugh and Corbin remained silent, she became impatient. "Well?" She smiled a little. "You can't possibly think I did something, do you?" Her face showed overt signs of anger then a quick outburst. "I did not murder Bill."

Hugh took a deep breath. "But, do you know something?"

Jo returned to her dessert, clearly signalling her refusal to answer his question.

Hugh was unabashed by the reaction he had caused. He returned to deep digging. "Jo, I think you do know something. Something you are afraid to share because it's personal." Then he stepped into the deep end. "When you're vulnerable you need protection, someone to fight your battles no matter what it takes. What happened, Jo?"

It began as a whisper. "I don't know. Not for sure." With effort, she lifted her head and spoke in a shaky voice. "Malcolm might have murdered Bill."

Silence commanded the room.

Hugh knew from experience, remaining silent never solved a problem. He needed Jo to break her silence and solve this problem. He leaned across the table.

"Staying silent will not solve Bill's murder, Jo. If you agree to tell Detective Henderson what you suspect, Corbin and I will be with you. Can you do that?"

She shook her head. "He's my brother. I'm not sure of anything. It's just a feeling."

"Alright. You're not ready. All we ask is you think about this. Our offer to accompany you still stands."

"I need to go home. Call a taxi for me, Corbin."

After Jo's departure, Corbin had an uneasy feeling in the pit of his stomach. Something she said triggered a memory.

Hugh looked at Corbin. "You're quiet."

"Jo said something, something about being possessive. It feels important but it won't come back to me." He hesitated. "Carry on."

"Think she'll change her mind?"

"Maybe. At least Malcolm isn't in the house."

"We don't have much time. He's leaving in a few days."

"That's it. It's a number. She mentioned two desperate people. Who do you think they are?"

Hugh considered the question. "I think Jo described herself. She had a risky relationship with Bill while she lived in Truro and I believe she moved to Halifax to end the relationship." He went on. "Despite her protest, Malcolm is desperate. Hell, even Ruby could be desperate enough. Both of them had personal reasons to want Bill dead."

Corbin couldn't imagine Ruby murdering Bill. He kept quiet while Hugh mulled over their situation.

"Truly our only role here is to get Jo into Henderson's office. What happens next is up to her."

"Well then, we wait and see. Does she want to hang her brother or not."

Jo Robinson went home confident she had confused both Hugh and Corbin about Bill's death and avoided attention on herself. Malcolm was incapable of murdering anyone himself but he was most certainly capable of arranging a murder. Should she take on Detective Henderson or not? It would be fun to spar with him. She would sleep on the idea and decide in the morning.

CHAPTER THIRTY-ONE

SUNDAY, NOVEMBER 11

Murdoch Ramsay went to bed on Sunday night, his mind brimming with new thoughts about his future. Rose filled his afternoon at the park with her cheerful love of life. She wants to be a teacher like Miss Rogers, who is the best teacher in the whole world. In her spare time, she wants to write children's books. His mother filled the late evening with conversation. She encouraged him to consider his relationship with Marie from her point of view then talk with her. She asked about his work and what did he want to do in the future. Tomorrow he would return to work with new thoughts to share with Marie and Mr. Davis.

Marie LeBlanc had endured the worst afternoon and evening of her life on Saturday. Leo was visiting a friend and her mother took the opportunity to discuss Murdoch Ramsay's intentions, at length. She sat through her mother's protracted stream of sentences. Neither she nor her father made any effort to comment. It would have been pointless. Marie was terribly sad and terribly angry. Overnight Sunday she cobbled together a plan to put an end to the miserable life she saw as her future without Murdoch and bound to her family. She would be a spinster, alone, bitter and sad. Tomorrow morning, she'd speak with Mr. Davis about leaving Halifax and ask if he had any recommendations about work elsewhere.

Jo Robinson woke Monday morning to the sound of her telephone ringing. Patches bounded off his big cushion in the corner of the bedroom and raced Jo to the candlestick telephone sitting on her writing desk.

"Hello?"

"Good morning, Jo."

"Malcolm, what do you want this time of the morning?"

"I plan to be in Halifax tomorrow. Are you alone?"

"Of course I am. You've made sure of that." Then she added, "Try not to be so bossy this time." She hung up and looked at Patches. "You're so lucky not having an older brother."

Patches quizzically tilted his head to one side followed by a dash to the food dish.

As Patches devoured breakfast, Jo sat with a big mug of tea and a slice of toast. She considered the fun she could have with Will Henderson while dumping her bossy brother into the middle of a murder investigation. Even better, as he's preparing for a voyage to England. Today she would do it. She'd take on Detective Henderson.

***

Monday morning was grey. The constant drip, drip of small drops of rain was a perfect match for Marie's sad outlook on her life. Her wool hat managed to keep her hair dry but it would be smelly by the time she reached the office. *Another bit of unpleasantness for the day.*

This was the one day Marie wanted Murdoch to be later for work than Mr. Davis. She crossed her fingers for good luck. *Be late, be late.* Then she picked up the newspaper. The headlines were big and bold. **Mollie Brown Killer Caught and Yarmouth Family Arrested for Operating Illegal Gambling Business**

When Corbin walked through the door, Marie couldn't believe her good luck. They exchanged pleasantries and she followed him into his office, carrying his morning coffee.

"Do you have a few minutes, Mr. Davis?"

"Most certainly."

When Marie finished speaking, Corbin was unable to find the words to express his surprise at her shocking decision. Her relationship with Murdoch looked promising at the King Eddie restaurant but it was not his place to pry into her personal affairs.

"Mr. Davis?"

Corbin put his hand on Marie's shoulder. "What can I do to change your mind, Marie?"

Marie fought back tears. "There's nothing you can do, sir. I need to get away from Halifax."

As Corbin opened his mouth to say more, Murdoch stepped into the room. Oblivious to the nature of the conversation, he smiled and spoke. "I come bearing new ideas." A large smile lit up his face until he looked closely at theirs.

Corbin looked in Murdoch's direction. "Perhaps you two would like to speak privately. I will make my way to the factory floor."

Marie followed Corbin as far as her desk then sat down.

Murdoch waited until Corbin closed the front door. "What happened?"

Marie kept her head down. "Papa and I sat through a lecture about you Saturday. There is no way to save this friendship." She turned her face toward Murdoch. "And don't argue with me, please. I'm leaving work and the city. Don't try to stop me."

Before Murdoch was able to respond, Corbin rushed into the room. "I'm so sorry to interrupt. There's a problem in the factory. We need another hand on deck. Murdoch, go to the factory. You'll need to stay there. I'm calling the fire department."

Marie wrote a note to Murdoch and left it on his desk.

***

"Good morning. Halifax Police. How may I help you?"

"Is Detective Henderson available?"

"Yes, he is. May I have your name and your message, Madam?"

"No. I will be there within fifteen minutes."

"Thank you, Madam."

Constable Roach left the desk to advise Henderson of a mystery female visitor.

"Thank you, Constable."

Henderson reached into his desk drawer for a large envelope labelled 'Ruby Turner'. He quickly reviewed Ruby's detailed notes and left the envelope on his desk, carefully covering 'Ruby' with a single sheet of paper. He was working on his second mug of coffee when Jo was escorted into his office. He'd guessed correctly. He stood and extended his hand to her.

"Sir, Miss Jo Robinson to see you."

"Thank you, Constable" *Blonde. Lavender.*

Will offered his best smile. "Good morning, Miss Robinson. Please have a seat. How may I help you?" He in turn sat, then placed his hand on the envelope long enough for Jo to take note of the gesture and the name.

Jo arranged her skirt carefully then lifted her head and smiled broadly. "Actually, I can help you."

Will maintained a cordial response. "This sounds intriguing. Please continue."

Thinking Henderson was hooked, Jo grinned and said, "You should interview my brother, Malcolm."

Henderson nodded and raised an eyebrow.

Hearing no reply, Jo offered a stunned appearance for a moment but continued. "He knows a considerable amount of detail about Bill Turner. Therefore, he could advise you where to look for clues to unearth the culprit." She sat back in her chair, expecting the detective to quiz her.

With a few well-placed comments, Will easily made the transition from friendly Will to Detective Henderson. "That is a curious suggestion, Miss Robinson. I expect you might be correct in your assessment about your brother's knowledge of the victim but I highly doubt your brother and his details would be useful to me."

Taken aback by the detective's sharp dismissal of her help, Jo paused but eventually spoke, her tone unchanged. "You're not interested in assistance with Detective Turner's murder?"

"I'm most interested in assistance. However, I prefer the 'first person' approach." He leaned forward. "Are you personally able to provide first person details?" Hearing no quick reply, he leaned back into the chair and waited.

"I knew Bill quite well as I do his wife, Ruby. Truro is a small town." Jo shifted in her chair, looking slightly uneasy. She smiled.

Henderson did not respond in kind. Instead, he provoked her. "Do you have any actual details?"

Jo was cornered, annoyed with herself. She offered trifling details of life in Truro, all the while planning a quick exit from the room. She ended with, "Bill could be most annoying, demanding."

Henderson thought he might be making headway toward something important, maybe even a confession. He called the front desk.

"Constable, can you find Sergeant Bailey and send him to my office."

"Why did you do that?"

Jo's ill-tempered question brought an immediate answer. "Miss Robinson, I sense you have important personal insight into Bill Turner's life. I would like to hear those details. Sergeant Bailey will take notes."

Jo sat stiffly in her chair as Henderson stood inside the open office door waiting for Bailey.

"Good morning, Sir. I just returned from Rockhead. You wanted me?"

"Come in. I want you to take notes. Sergeant Bailey, this is Jo Robinson. She has personal information to share regarding Bill Turner's life and possibly, his murder."

"Good morning, Miss Robinson."

Jo nodded in Bailey's direction. She had no intention of legitimizing this casual conversation.

Henderson looked intently toward Jo. "Now, where were we?"

"We weren't anywhere, Detective." Jo re-arranged her skirt.

"Back to Malcolm for a moment." Henderson glanced toward Bailey. "Malcolm is Miss Robinson's brother. Miss Robinson initially suggested I ask Malcolm for help in finding the culprit in Detective Turner's murder."

"Duly noted, Sir."

"Miss Robinson, can you tell us your relationship with Detective Turner?"

Jo knew that was coming. "Both Bill and Ruby were my friends in Truro."

"Thank you. And in Halifax?"

"Long distance friendships are hard to maintain."

Henderson let her offhand response slide but noted it mentally for use another time.

"What was Detective Turner like as a friend?"

"He was kind, funny. He and Ruby entertained many people. Malcolm and I were always invited."

"And when he was working on a case, did his behaviour change?"

Jo shrugged. "Not with friends."

"Mrs. Turner would beg to differ with you on that, especially when he was in Halifax. What is your relationship with Ruby Turner now?"

"It's non-existent."

"And why is that, Miss Robinson?"

For the first time Jo's suppressed annoyance gave way to visible uneasiness. She straightened her skirt then spun her sapphire finger ring around several times. "He toyed with me for months then went back to Ruby." She hunched up her shoulders. "Relationships change."

"And then you killed him." The finality in Henderson's voice was unmistakable.

Bailey was caught off-guard by the accusation but he kept his eyes on Miss Robinson's face, looking for a weakness in her resolve. Seeing none, he returned to the note book.

Jo felt her head buzz. "It wasn't me."

"So you say. How do you account for the smell of lavender on Bill's clothing the night he died?"

Jo kept her head down. "He came to see me in the late afternoon. We..."

"There is no need to provide those intimate details, Miss Robinson."

Before Henderson could say anything more, Jo leaned forward in her chair. "You need to talk to Malcolm."

Henderson offered a subtle sneer. "So, he's your alibi for that evening?"

"He was in Halifax that day."

"I do intend to speak with him. As for you, Miss Robinson, don't leave the city. Where is your brother right now?"

"In Truro, packing for a trip to England. He leaves Wednesday. He arrives on the train tomorrow."

Following Jo's departure, Henderson and Bailey returned to Henderson's office. Bailey spoke first. "She came here with a story but why now?"

"She's clever. Probably came to find out what we know."

"Think she planned to implicate Malcolm?"

"Yes, if she needed to. I'm not convinced she's the killer."

"And Malcolm?"

"A strong possible because of Jo's statement about Bill treating her badly. He's the older brother, the protector. Meet him at the station tomorrow, bring him in for an interview. We'll wind him up, see what happens."

Not long after Marie left Davis Footwear, she realized she had made a terrible mistake. It was the middle of the morning. She had not planned anything, including packing her suitcase. For a person intent on leaving town quietly, she bungled the entire thing in spectacular fashion. She could think of no other thing to do but walk to the train station, check the train departures and ticket prices then go home in the late afternoon. On the way, she'd go to the bank and withdraw her savings.

At the train station Ruby glanced at her watch and greeted Corbin with a hurried 'good afternoon'.

"And you, as well. You look very business-like today, Ruby."

"I am indeed. I intend to buy a house today or tomorrow. How did you find the one you bought?"

"A fella at the bank told me. The city has a few men who are home sellers."

"How does it work?"

"They know who is selling a home and arrange for you to see it. You pay the owner and the owner pays the home seller for doing his job."

"That sounds pretty straight forward. Where do I find a home seller?"

"Would mine do?"

"Yes. Can I meet him today?"

Corbin picked up Ruby's luggage. "Let's go to my office and call him. Did you sell your home in Truro?"

"I did. A neighbour has a relative who wants it."

"Wonderful news."

As they were about to exit the station, Corbin put his hand on Ruby's arm. "I see someone I must speak with. The car is parked left of the door. I shouldn't be long."

"Hello, Marie. Are you waiting for someone?"

"Mr. Davis! I..."

"May I sit down?"

"Yes."

Corbin noticed she'd been crying. "Marie, I'm quite fond of you and Murdoch. Is something troubling you that I can help solve?"

"No, Mr. Davis. Even Murdoch and I can't solve this."

"So you two share a problem?"

"Yes."

"So, it sounds like someone else is causing the problem."

Marie nodded.

"I know you don't run away from a challenge at work."

"Thank you, Mr. Davis."

"So, is this problem worth leaving town?"

After a long sigh, "Maybe not."

"Do you think Murdoch would want to solve the problem with you?"

"Yes." Marie let her eyes linger on Corbin's face.

"Would you like a drive home or to the office?"

"Home, please. If that's alright with you, Mr. Davis."

"You will have to share the back seat with Marmalade."

"Who?"

"Come with me. You'll meet him and see Mrs. Turner again."

"She's the lady who visited the office and I met at the King Edward restaurant, correct?"

Corbin nodded. "I think you'll like her."

In the car, Marmalade popped his head out of the basket and studied Marie's face very carefully then turned his full attention to the scenery swishing by.

Corbin nodded in Marmalade's direction. "Have you told him he's moving?"

"I have. That's why he's now having a serious look about."

"Ahh. Makes purrfect sense."

Marie laughed loudly which then warranted another intense look from Marmalade.

Davis Footwear suffered minimal damage thanks to the quick response of the firemen. Murdoch and Corbin remained in the office until the end of the work day. Corbin did not mention Marie's name but guessed she was using her considerable creativity on someone at home.

Murdoch telephoned his mother to say he would be home late. "Don't wait up for me."

Murdoch intended to walk the harbour and think of ways to get Marie back into his life. But his good intentions started to unwind when he caught sight of one of his favourite watering holes. His past reached out and pulled him into his old black hole.

He picked a table in the corner and downed his first double Scotch in one gulp. It burned but felt good. He thought about Marie, his embarrassing visit to her house. He liked Marie's father, Benoit. He would talk to him, maybe tomorrow. The second drink was not as helpful. He simply felt sorry for himself.

When Murdoch went to the bar for a third drink, Paddy Kelly feared for his livelihood. Prohibition was in place. He'd quietly moved his legal, bustling downtown pub to a run-down building near the rail yards. Its' existence was by word of mouth and any attention was bad attention.

Murdoch had been a good patron in the past but his behaviour could mean big trouble for Paddy.

"Murdoch, ease off. Sit for a while. I can't afford to have you stumble outta here and meet a copper." He took a closer look at Murdoch. "What the hell's the matter with ya, lad? Your pa's death hit you hard? Somethin' else?"

Murdoch leaned across the bar, steadied himself. He was in no mood or condition to reply. Instead he threw money on the table, waved at Paddy and staggered out the door. A blast of crisp fall air hit his face. "Can't a fella have a drink before dinner?" Then he tripped over a lose sidewalk board and fell against the side of a brick building.

Ed Quinn was off work and heading toward the hardware store when he spotted Murdoch lying in the ally. "Murdoch, that you?" Ed moved closer. "Good heavens, man. What have you done? You chin's bleeding. At least your glasses are in one piece."

Murdoch wiped the back of his hand across his face, missing the blood completely. "Guess I had a little too much to drink."

"I'd say more than a little. Let me help you up. Are you going home?"

"I am."

"Good but you can't wander around the streets looking like this. You'll get picked up by one of the constables and find yourself in Rockhead. Bella's Bakery is still open. Come on, let's have something to eat. You need a damp cloth for your face."

"Two raisin scones, a large pot of tea and a damp cloth, Bella. Thanks."

Seated at the corner table, Ed got right to the issue. "What brought this drinking bout on? Your father's death?"

Murdoch rubbed his forehead. "No. A good friend's planning to leave town."

"Must be a very good friend."

Bella arrived at the table. "The tea will help whatever's ailing 'ya."

When Bella left the table, Ed continued. "How's work?"

"It's very good. Mr. Davis is a fair man, likes new ideas."

"So this is about something else."

Murdoch nodded. "It is. A friend that is very important to me."

Ed patted Murdoch on the shoulder. "I bet your mother will listen and help you with this. In the meantime, let's talk about your work."

With the scones and tea finished, Murdoch stood up. "Guess I better walk home and sober up."

"Excellent idea. I'm sure your mother will want to see you."

CHAPTER THIRTY-TWO

MONDAY, NOVEMBER 12

"Good grief. Where have you been?" Ella covered her nose. "You smell awful." Then she stared more intently at his face. "And what happened to your chin?"

"I spent an hour with Ed Quinn then I walked home. Before that, I had too much to drink and fell down in an alley. Before that..."

Ella held up her hands. "Stop, please. I understand you have a story to tell but have a bath first. And don't go into Rose's room smelling like you fell into a vat of Scotch. In the meantime, I'll make you a chicken sandwich."

"Thank you, Mama. It's been a terrible day."

Ella waved her hands in the direction of the stairway. "Off you go."

As Ella began making the sandwich, she wondered what the second 'before' was all about. She concluded Marie would likely be at the centre of the muddle. It would be a big teapot conversation with Murdoch. While waiting for him, she read The Canadian Home Journal magazine her mother brought from the visit in Ottawa.

"I'm here, smelling better but still have a problem."

"That's not a surprise but I am disappointed you thought drinking would solve it."

"That's what Mr. Quinn said." He took a bite of the sandwich.

"And this problem is?"

"Mrs. LeBlanc."

"Go on."

"Rose and I went to Marie's home yesterday. With the car."

"Uninvited?"

Murdoch shrugged. "I thought Marie might like a surprise ride to the park." He finished the sandwich.

"Well not all surprises are good ones. Continue."

"Mr. LeBlanc invited me in."

"Of course he would. He knows you and would be hospitable."

"Marie refused to take a ride in the car." He waited for a response. Hearing none, he said, "Maybe I should have asked her first, at work?"

Ella ignored the question. It was too late to discuss the merits of something already uttered. "Why is Mrs. LeBlanc the problem?"

Ignoring his mother's question, Murdoch pressed on. "There's more to my story. Today, Marie told Mr. Davis she's leaving Halifax." Murdoch finished his second cup of tea and continued. "Mrs. LeBlanc doesn't like me because I don't go to their church."

Ella raised her eyebrows. "And how do you know that?"

"Well, I don't know for sure. She hasn't said that to me." He shrugged but his brow remained deeply furrowed.

"So, Marie's going away because her mother doesn't approve of you. Did I get that part correct?"

"And her mother doesn't even know me."

Murdoch's frustration was plain to see but Ella continued. "Leaving Halifax seems a hasty decision on Marie's part." She looked at Murdoch to offer a reason.

"She didn't talk about leaving with me."

"And you and Marie have been meeting without her parents knowing, yes?"

Murdoch nodded. "We arrange to be together after work."

"What do you want to do about this muddle?"

"Convince Marie to stay here."

"Well then, you better think about how to speak with her and quick. She could already be gone."

Murdoch shook his head in frustration. "That's my problem, Mama. How do I do that?"

Ella opened her mouth to respond as the telephone rang. "Hello."

"Mrs. Ramsay?"

"Speaking."

"This is Marie LeBlanc. We met at the restaurant. I was with Murdoch."

"How nice to hear from you, Marie."

"If Murdoch is there I would like to speak with him."

"He is. Just a moment."

Ella beckoned toward Murdoch, passed him the receiver and went upstairs to see Rose, who was colouring a very large picture of fall trees.

"Hello. Are you calling from the train station?"

"No. I'm at Susan's house down the street from home."

"Susan's house?" He paused. "Can I see you before you leave?"

"I'm not leaving."

"You're not!" A big sigh followed. "What happened?"

"Mr. Davis was at the train station. I'll tell you everything tomorrow. I'm going home now."

"Don't worry, things will work out somehow."

"See you at the office tomorrow."

Murdoch was the first one at work the next morning. He started the coffee pot and made tea but still no sign of Marie nor Mr. Davis. He imagined all sorts of dreadful events, none of which left Marie nor Mr. Davis alive. He went to the factory to confirm all was in good order. The smell of fresh paint reminded him of the factory fire.

"Murdoch, do you know anything about the new ladies shoes we are working on?"

"I do, Teddy. How can I help you?"

Murdoch whirled around. Marie was standing behind him.

"Is it three big buttons or four small ones?"

"It's four small red ones and a pair with blue buttons, too."

"Thank you, Miss LeBlanc."

"You're here! I thought you might change your mind overnight."

Marie smiled. "Mr. Davis wants to see us, in his office. We have a new contract for winter boots."

"What's happening at home or dare I ask?"

"It's quite cold at the moment." Marie shook her head. "My mother is one determined woman."

"And your father?"

"He likes you but he never puts up a fuss about anything. Mama has always been the decision maker." She snorted. "So much for saying women are weak." She winked. "I think Papa quietly does what he wants, just never argues or lets her know about some things he does."

"Huh. So your father is a silent ally. We could talk to him."

"I think so too. Let's talk after work."

Just before noon, Sergeant Bailey set off for the railway station, armed with a physical description of Malcolm Robinson, as provided by his sister Jo.

Shortly after the train arrived, Doctor Robinson was in Henderson's office. "Good afternoon, Doctor Robinson."

Ignoring common courtesy, Malcolm launched into an objection regarding his forced presence. "I'm not about to lose my passage on the ship to England over some implausible story my sister dreamed up." He rolled his eyes. "After all, she is an author. So, why am I here and be sharpish about it."

"Doctor Robinson, I do not pursue invented leads in murder inquiries. I strongly advise you to sit back in your chair and respond to my queries about your knowledge of and connection to Bill Turner."

Malcolm opened his mouth to speak but was cut off by Henderson. "And I, only I will be the one asking the questions. Tell me about the social life that included Bill and others in Truro."

"The whole social activity in Truro was rather boring, Detective. My role was and still is the overseer of my sister, who at times gets in over her head with men. A quiet word from me sent them running."

"Did that include Bill Turner, Doctor Robinson?"

"Yes." Malcolm opened his mouth to expand on his short answer but was waved off by a gesture from Henderson.

"And her move to Halifax was prompted by one of these men, Doctor?"

Robinson's hesitant reply was noted by Henderson. "I suggest you ask my sister that question, Detective. She should speak for herself...with you."

At the end of a half hour, Henderson was satisfied Malcolm Robinson knew little about Bill and his life, other than what he observed at social events. He concluded Malcolm was a man solely absorbed by himself and he had a strong alibi for the night of Bill's murder. However, Henderson did not miss the inference that Jo be interviewed again.

"Thank you for your time, Doctor Robinson. Have a pleasant trip."

Henderson escorted Malcolm to the front door and returned to speak with Bailey, who was quick with an observation.

"The man eliminated himself, Sir."

"Exactly, but not before he pointed the finger at his sister. He wanted to give her a jab as a farewell word."

"Miss Robinson is firmly connected to this murder. In what capacity, I'm not too sure at the moment. We'll have another interview in a few days."

Marie and Murdoch's conversation after work was filled to overflowing with uncertainty. They sat opposite each other with a large pot of tea in the middle of a table in a restaurant a few streets from the wharf. At least, the room was alive with the chatter of several people who were sharing the events of the day with friends. They would have no eavesdroppers.

"We need your father's help. Do you think he will agree to arrange a conversation with your mother?"

"I think so. He likes you. But what questions would we ask Mama?"

Murdoch lifted his shoulders in a half shrug. "Do we have questions other than why she doesn't like me?"

"Probably not." She stared into his eyes. "Really, I think it's more religion than you."

"So, how do we talk about that? I go to church, just a different one."

"Honestly, I don't know."

Murdoch reached across the table for her hand. "We are not children and we are not seeking approval of our relationship. We are adults making a decision about someone we like. I do hope your mother will accept the decisions we make in the future. For example, Mr. Davis might open another factory and we might leave Halifax."

Marie shook her head. "This will not be easy, Murdoch."

"I understand but we need to make decisions for ourselves." He took Marie's hands in his. "I expect my mother would not be happy if I moved away. I think that's what parents do. They worry about their children, want them to be safe, nearby."

"I agree. It's just that I really dislike quarrels, with anyone."

"This isn't a quarrel, Marie. This will be about your mother getting to know me and accepting we have a strong friendship."

"I like those words. I'll use them with Papa and suggest he use them with Mama."

Marie tugged one hand free from his and grinned, shrugging one shoulder.

Murdoch asked, "Is something troubling you?"

Marie hesitated then muttered, "What if this doesn't work?"

"Do you remember the first day you arrived for work on your bicycle, wearing a split skirt?"

Marie nodded. "I was so angry with my mother." She shook her head. "She did not want me to wear that skirt."

Murdoch grinned. "I was infatuated with you then and there. The way you spoke, your confidence captured me."

Marie reached for Murdoch's hand and squeezed it. Then she looked up, caught his eyes with hers and smiled as tears rolled down her cheeks.

Murdoch offered his handkerchief. "I needed you then and I do now."

Marie looked at the handkerchief. "I'll wash this and give it back the day we speak with my mother."

"You have a deal, Miss LeBlanc."

When Marie stood to leave, Murdoch walked toward her and clasped her tightly in his arms.

"People are watching, Murdoch!"

"Let them. I don't care. You're my girl." He smiled. "Now go home and speak with your father."

As he walked Marie toward the door, a few folks clapped their hands and one man shouted, "Well done, young man."

The early evening walk home for Marie was fraught with worry. *How will I approach Papa? When will I approach him? Would Papa and Mama notice my awkwardness at the evening meal? Should I ignore him and confront Mama? Oh, that's right, this isn't an argument. I'm a grown woman who can defend herself.*

Marie dreaded turning the knob on the front door and facing an almost impossible task.

"Hello, Marie. You are a bit late."

"Yes. I had an after work conversation with Murdoch."

"Well, well. And how is the young man?" Marie's father smiled in her direction then toward Gisele.

"He's well."

She heard her mother respond. "That is good to hear."

Marie got the sense she was in a play with other actors who were familiar with a script she was not.

She cautiously asked, "Where is Leo, Mama?"

"He's with a friend for the evening."

"Why?"

Benoit answered. "Your mother and I want to talk with you over our evening meal."

Marie nodded as her mother went to the kitchen. *They've teamed up against us. I've lost before I can begin.* She began to cry.

"What is the matter?" Benoit patted his daughter's hand.

"It's nothing, Papa."

"I doubt that very much. Dry your eyes and tell me what happened today."

"Murdoch and I talked. I want to talk to Mama."

"Well then, you will have your chance when she returns to the table."

Marie nodded, kept her head down, recalling what she agreed to do when with Murdoch.

"That stew smells delicious, Gisele." Benoit turned toward Marie. "Mama wants to ask you a few questions."

Marie lifted her head, determined to defend her independence and her relationship with Murdoch.

"That's true, but first let's fill our bowls with beef stew. Benoit would you pass the biscuits, please."

Marie took a spoonful of stew and waited for what would come next.

"Marie, do you think Murdoch would have a meal with us? I would like to understand the character of this young man myself."

"Yes, Mama. I know he would be very happy to eat with us."

"Then you two decide the day."

***

"Good morning, Ella. Anna speaking. How are you on this unkind day?"

"It certainly is unkind at the moment. I'm not keen on grey skies and nippy breezes. I just sent Rose off to school in a winter hat and mittens today."

"Well, I'll be happy as long as the sun shines on the twenty-fourth."

"Agreed. Do we have an alternate plan if we have unkind weather for the children's outdoor events?"

Ella heard a little giggle.

"Yes, we do. I'll give you the details at the meeting."

"And are we meeting at your house today?"

"Yes. Can you bring Mable with you? That smart Miss Parsons from the City will be attending as well."

"Mable and I will share a taxi car."

There was a pause from Anna then, "I recall your husband had an automobile. Do you still have it?"

"Yes. Murdoch drives it."

"I want to learn to drive. Shall we learn together?"

Ella laughed. "Do you really think people will feel safe with one of us behind the steering wheel?"

"Likely not but after a while they'll stop running for cover along Gottingen Street." She laughed. "Think about it. Perhaps Murdoch could teach us."

"I'll ask him. No promises though. See you soon."

Ella hung up the receiver. *She reminds me of Adele. Unstoppable.*

By late morning, Ella was alone with her thoughts. It was time to make an account of her life in the wake of Charles' death. On the positive side of the ledger, her children were returning to their daily routines with the occasional emotional upset, the troop event was well in hand and she felt safe and more confident following the arrest of Alex Wallace.

On the other side of the ledger, Dora Wallace's presence in Halifax was awkward, to say the least, especially as she thought the woman was dead. Then there was Hugh. She wanted to pepper him with questions but she was afraid of the answers plus she could not bring herself to make a telephone call to him.

Ella did her best thinking at the harbour and so she stepped into the nippy, grey morning to sort out the two awkward situations. Finding Hugh would be a gift and perhaps a new beginning. She caught sight of him, hands in his coat pockets gazing at the brooding charcoal fog hanging over the harbour. It stretched out to sea as far as the human eye could see. The muffled sounds and faded shapes of ships created a cheerless seascape. Hugh was not alone.

Ella held back until Hugh was by himself then stepped forward to stand silently at his side. She was determined to wait him out.

Eventually, Hugh began speaking of Bill's murder and his work with friends Corbin, Angus and Frank. His eyes remained fixed on the dark sky. "It doesn't bode well for an arrest anytime soon."

Ella sensed his deep disappointment. "Don't punish yourself." She gently grasped his arm. "You've done your best."

"My best, our best is not good enough, Ella."

"And that blonde woman just now?"

"Jo Robinson. A close friend of both Bill and Ruby in Truro." There was a slight delay as Hugh considered his next statement. "She was walking on the wharf." Then in the same tone of voice, "She may be the murderer. At the very least, she knows more than she is admitting."

Ella's eyes popped open, her head shot forward. "Pardon me? The police must have spoken with her!"

"Oh, yes. Earlier this week, so she tells me." He breathed out heavily and turned to look at her. "I left you in the lurch again, didn't I?" Without waiting for her response, he berated himself in a tone Ella had not heard from him before. "I ran off to play policeman when you needed me." He took her hands in his. "Am I too late, again?"

Ella dismissed the question and squeezed his hands. “Your here now. That’s all that matters.”

***

In the early afternoon, Detective Henderson sent Sergeant Bailey to Jo Robinson’s home for the purpose of interviewing her in the police station.

Upon her arrival, Jo laughed heartily then addressed a comment toward Henderson. “He did it, didn’t he?”

“What do you mean, Miss Robinson?”

“Malcolm. He thinks I know who killed Bill.” She laughed. “So here I am and he’s on his way to Jolly Old England.”

“Ah, well. The latter is true, yes. But it is my job to determine if you can help me with the former.”

“Well said, sir.”

Henderson winked at Bailey then looked toward Jo. “I understand you are an author. I understand they have quite the vivid imagination.” He waited.

“Yes, well. This is the latest version of my life. I quite like it. Being the author, writing about myself and others. Now, do you have a serious reason for this interview or have you taken a liking to me?” She sat without waiting for Henderson’s direction.

Henderson did not crack a smile but he wanted to. Instead a deep frown formed as he leaned toward Jo. “Miss Robinson, you are connected to this murder in some fashion and I am done, finished and ended with the game that you are playing. You will tell me what you know or you will spend a few hours in Rockhead to consider your next move.” After noting Bailey’s wide-eyed stare, he sat down.

Jo straighten her shoulders and gave him a haughty look.

"That sounds like you have eliminated me from the suspect list so I am free to implicate others."

"No, you are are not off the suspect list and no, you are not free to offer up a willy nilly list of names."

Jo covered her mouth to silence herself but her eyes were smiling.

"Let me help you with the list, Miss Robinson. You, Alex Wallace, Joseph Young and Malcolm Robinson had good reason to dislike Bill. Are there more names for my list?"

"Not that I know. Who are Alex Wallace and Joseph Young?"

Henderson ignored the question. "Now tell me why you are innocent?"

Jo opened her mouth to object her presumed guilt.

"I already know you and Bill spent time together the afternoon of his murder. That does not preclude you from following him to the Citadel and stabbing him. You have blonde hair and wear lavender perfume."

"That is your hypothesis, Detective? Look at your list, again sir. There are others not on that list who had opportunities and reason." She narrowed her eyes and zeroed in on Henderson's face. "I suggest to you that I would not be any juror's first choice as a murderer. Unless you intend to detain me, I expect Sergeant Bailey to drive me home."

CHAPTER THIRTY-THREE

Friday, November 16

Ella sat in her quiet kitchen enjoying the lovely morning sun beaming through her window. The usual morning rushing about was over. Now Alex Wallace and Hugh Andrews were on her mind.

From the day Alex Wallace arrived in Halifax, Ella lived in fear that Rose's background would be exposed. She now knew she was the only target and Alex's threat about Rose was a way to torture her until he could kill her. He wanted retribution for an old wound, one he mistakenly believed put his mother in the insane asylum. She suspected Charles knew Rose was his daughter in name only, but he loved her and that was all that truly mattered. She would tell Rose her story, when time and her maturity offered the opportunity.

Away from the emotional conversation with Hugh at the harbour, Ella was having second thoughts about inviting Hugh for dinner Sunday evening. The old Ella would have called Hugh and made an excuse for the cancellation. Not now. Tonight, she would talk to Murdoch and Rose individually and explain she was having a friend for dinner. She wanted to but would not ask Murdoch or Rose to keep Hugh's visit a secret from her mother. For a moment, she felt like eighteen again, timid and indecisive. Then it passed.

***

The early part of Will Henderson's morning was spent sitting alone in his office. It was clear to him that nothing but a chancy option would move Bill Turner's murder forward. The door was closed, a signal he was not to be disturbed. This knowledge included Constable Rogers at the front desk. But at ten o'clock, Rogers knocked on Henderson's door, placed a tray with coffee, milk and oatmeal cookies at the door and spoke the word 'coffee'. When Rogers returned unscathed, Surrette patted his back before leaving to investigate a reported robbery at a drug store off Gottingen Street.

With the suspects in the Brown, Fillmore and Ramsay murders behind bars, Will had considerable time to focus on the suspects in Bill's death. He had already spent untold hours since that grim discovery on the Hill four weeks prior. With Ruby's suspect list and the memory of Jo Robinson's impassioned outburst about potential suspects, Will felt as though he'd come up against a brick wall. Perhaps the lavender scent and Frank Murphy's blonde hair dream did not come from the same person. Perhaps he'd been thinking about people too close to Bill or those with very obvious reasons for revenge. A new idea came to mind. He leapt out of his chair to find Sergeant Bailey. He found him writing a report. "You busy with something important, Sergeant?"

"Is preparation for a jury important, Sir?"

"It is, but not right now. I need you to listen to me."

"I always listen to you, Sir."

"Yes well, we can discuss that at your next performance review." Will removed the exaggerated scowl from his face. "I have a new thought about Bill's murder. Come with me."

***

Marie and Murdoch would be having a Saturday evening meal with her parents and the Sunday meal at the Ramsay home. While eating Friday lunch together both of them admitted they were nervously excited about both family meals.

In the meantime, Benoit was offering Gisele some advice about staying calm. “Prepare something we like to eat and please stop fussing about Murdoch. He’s probably nervous himself. Everything will be fine. We all want the same thing. Get to know each other, eat a good meal.”

“That’s easy for you to say. All you have to do is talk. What if I ruin the meal?”

“My dear, this is not about food. And when have you ever ruined a meal?”

“Eleven years ago. I under-cooked a turkey.”

“Are you cooking a turkey tomorrow?”

“No, but...”

Benoit put his arms around Gisele. “Cook what you want to but make sure we have an apple pie for dessert.”

“Benoit, you are incorrigible!”

“I am not, whatever that word means.”

Gisele sighed, “You do know what it means. I heard you saying it to Leo a few days ago. So there.”

Benoit put on his coat and cap. “Don’t forget the apple pie. I’m off to the barber before going to work.”

Corbin had just returned from a lunch meeting when Marie forwarded a call to his office. ”Hello, Corbin speaking.”

“I’m so excited. I’ve bought a small house a few blocks from you.”

“The important question is, did Marmalade approve it?”

"He will. It has a lovely room looking over a backyard with lots of trees. That means there are lots of birds. It feels like a cozy cottage, perfect for me."

"When can you move?"

"The lady who owns it is moving in with her son and daughter-in-law in a week."

"Ideal. And your furniture in Truro? Can someone move everything?"

"I'm leaving all the big pieces Bill and I bought together. I want this house to be mine."

"You and the master of the house can stay with me until everything is settled."

"Thank you." There was a long silence.

"Ruby?"

"It feels a wee bit scary to be on my own but I'll be alright."

"Of course you will. I don't doubt it for a minute. I will be home about five-thirty and you can give me all the details on the cozy cottage."

"Bye, bye for now, Corbin."

Ella was quietly settled in the sitting room planning for the Sunday evening meal when the telephone rang. She picked up the receiver and heard Dora's voice respond to her 'hello'.

"Ella, I hope you are feeling better. I'm still having trouble sleeping. It's very hard to know my dear Alex is in prison. I am working in Mr. Martin's store but have not made any friends at the boardinghouse. I think it might be a good idea to go to church and maybe make friends there. It's so lonely not having anyone to talk to."

"It does take time to make friends, Dora. Church is a good idea."

"Will you have lunch with me tomorrow?"

"I'm sorry, I cannot. I have a meeting." Ella paused to consider her next words. "Dora, have you talked with your doctor? He might be able to help you with your concerns. You've had a big shock since leaving the hospital. Promise me, you will talk to him."

"Thank you, Ella. Good-bye."

Bailey and Henderson had a closed-door discussion early Friday afternoon. The topic was serious, so serious each dropped the detective and sergeant ranks and questioned the other on the rationale and way they would present the questions. Henderson would take the lead and Bailey was free to jump in if he failed to mention something relevant.

"If we're wrong, our employment could be over. At the very least, our reputations ruined."

Bailey nodded. "He's at the front desk. I'll ask him to join us."

Detective Henderson was very good at detecting darkness in others. He levelled his gaze at the man sitting across the desk and began unearthing the man's shadowy side. "Thank you for joining us. Sergeant Bailey and I are working on a line of inquiry regarding Bill Turner's death. We would like your involvement. Are you interested?"

"Absolutely, Sir." Adam Taylor's confidence was on full display.

"Good. Good. Can I presume you are comfortable working in this station?"

"No problems, Sir." Taylor relaxed, leaned back into his chair.

“That’s good to hear, Sergeant.” Then, with a few well-placed words, Will moved from the comfortable welcome to a series of probing questions. He leaned forward. “Sergeant, before your transfer to the Dartmouth station, did you notice any unusual behaviour in Detective Turner? I’m referring to the Bill you knew in Truro versus the Bill when he was in Halifax.”

Taylor shook his head. “No, but in Halifax, I had very little contact with Detective Turner, Sir. I would have no way to measure what you asked.”

Henderson nodded. “Yes, yes. I can see that.” He rested his chin on his hand. “Now, that transfer from Truro to Halifax would have been arranged by Detective Turner, correct?”

Taylor nodded. “Of course, Sir.”

Henderson furrowed his brow. “Did you request that transfer, Sergeant?”

Taylor straightened up in his chair. “No, but I appreciated Detective Turner’s trust in my skills to work in a larger station.”

Henderson felt it was time to strip Taylor of his rank in the questioning. “I understand you enjoyed the work and social life in Truro. A small town, close friends, social events, that sort of thing. Were you ever a little angry with Detective Turner when he forced you to give up all that?”

“Why would I be angry? It was a good opportunity for me, Sir.” Taylor smiled then took on a more rigid tone. “Nobody forces me to do anything.”

Henderson took note that his own rank was also gone. “You had very close friends there.” He paused. “I remain puzzled by that decision. Too bad I didn’t ask Bill about it. But, let’s move on.” Henderson sat back in his chair. “You moved to the smaller station in Dartmouth in 1915, two years after the transfer to Halifax. Why did you request that move?”

Taylor was clearly agitated. "As I mentioned a few weeks ago, I struck up a friendship with an officer in Dartmouth. We worked well together on a case and I asked for a transfer."

"Sounds reasonable. Oh, I forgot to mention something about your close friendship with Jo Robinson in Truro. Would she be able to assist with our inquiry?"

"Who told you about that?" Taylor failed to keep his latent anger out of his voice. "Who?"

Henderson ignored the answer which resulted in Taylor's face becoming even redder. "I want to return to your desire to transfer to Dartmouth. Detective Brown in Dartmouth speaks highly of your work but has concerns regarding your preference to work alone. Do you care to comment?"

"Detective Brown has never mentioned that to me." Taylor leaned back, tightened his lips, clenched his jaws. "So, what does all this have to do with Detective Turner's death?"

"You worked closely with Detective Turner and I imagine you have some thoughts on why he died. Now's the time for you to offer names of people who might have a reason to kill him. They could be persons unknown to Sergeant Bailey and myself. You're here to help expose the killer. Would an interview with Jo Robinson be helpful?"

Taylor nodded. "Yes."

"I've talked to her. I believe she mentioned your name. Quite an interesting person, don't you agree?"

"Yes, she is." Taylor began to fidget.

"Do you still consider Jo Robinson a very close friend?"

"Not after I left Truro."

"Is she a possible suspect?"

Taylor considered his options. Eventually, he replied. "Possibly."

Henderson noted Taylor's shoulders relax. "Any others?"

"No." Taylor looked at ease.

Henderson raised the stakes. "In my policing experience I've noticed that people will do almost anything for something they really want. What did you really want when you transferred to Dartmouth?"

Taylor leaned forward, signalling he was not about to step onto the slippery slope toward a confession. "I didn't want anything. A smaller station is easier to work in. Fewer people getting above themselves."

Henderson ignored Taylor's attempt to change the direction of the conversation. Instead, he brought the discussion to real cases and real people, ones Taylor knew about. "Alex Wallace wanted revenge for old wounds from his childhood. When he couldn't kill the intended target, he took his anger out on Mollie Brown." He noted Taylor's eyes darken, his back arch. His hostility was building again.

"Consider your man, Oliver White. More than anything else in the world, Oliver White wanted Charles Ramsay and Lois Fillmore dead. He wanted revenge for the death of his child and the personal rejection from Mrs. Fillmore. White was angry, not likely to forgive or forget those who wounded him. What did you really want when you transferred to Dartmouth?"

Taylor gripped the arms of his chair, forcing himself to shut out Henderson's words but Henderson continued. "I think you have wounds too. I believe Bill Turner transferred you to Halifax so he could end your relationship with Jo Robinson and have her himself. When Jo Robinson moved to Halifax, you saw an opportunity to renew that relationship. Bill's frequent presence in Halifax was then a direct threat to you. You moved to Dartmouth but never forgot nor forgave Bill Turner for the hurt and loss of Jo you endured. Those wounds festered all these years, then you killed him."

Taylor looked ready to explode, his face red, nostrils flared.

Bailey readied himself to grab him.

Henderson carried on with his final words. “You tallied up the score against Bill and took your revenge out on him at the Hill.”

Taylor jumped up, towered over Henderson’s desk. Bailey pulled him back into his chair and held him there. “That son of a bitch ruined my life, so I ruined his.”

***

Policeman Murders Policeman The Saturday morning edition of the newspaper was shocking news for the residents of Halifax but Hugh, Angus, Corbin and Frank were more shocked than anyone. Frank got in touch with the others and invited them for an afternoon beer on him, at their favourite drinking place.

Corbin telephoned Ruby.

“I’m relieved it’s over but I have to say Jo had a role in this. She used both Bill and Adam for her own selfish reasons. One man is dead and the other will be. It’s sad, terribly sad.”

***

November twenty-fourth was a week away. Ella, Anna Hopkins and other committee members were completing their plans for the day-long event. Ella was distracted and Anna noticed.

“Are you connected to either of those two policeman in the morning paper?”

“No, why do you ask?”

“You seem preoccupied.”

"It's Murdoch. This evening he has a meal with the parents of the young woman in his life. It seems the mother doesn't care for him."

"I do hope it goes well."

"There's more. Murdoch's friend, Marie will be at our home tomorrow and I've invited an old friend."

"Woman? Man?"

"Man."

"Ahh. I now understand. Well, look at it this way. All will be revealed within forty-eight hours."

***

When Monday morning arrived, the world was still spinning on its' axis and the Ramsay and LeBlanc households were faring well.

"Mama, Mr. Andrews is funny."

Ella smiled. "Why do you say that, dear?"

"He made all sorts of farm animal noises when you were in the kitchen. He invited me to his friend's farm outside Truro. Can we go?"

"One day, yes." She went to the stairwell. "Murdoch, you're going to be late."

"Yes, yes, I know. Two family dinners over a weekend is tiring."

"You're only twenty-one!"

At the breakfast table, Ella recalled Anna's reminder. She looked at Murdoch. "I want to drive the car. Will you teach me?"

"I will teach you provided you only drive during the day. Agreed?"

"If I do, you promise me you will take me where I want to go after dark."

Murdoch nodded.

“Oh, Anna Hopkins wants lessons, too.”

Rose wasn't planning to be left out. “I want to sit in the back seat for the lessons. Someday I’ll need to drive, too.”

Murdoch rolled his eyes. “What have I gotten myself into! Marie also wants to drive.”

***

Marie was in a rush to get out the door Monday morning but Leo was still asking questions about Murdoch. “What does he do at the office?”

“He sells shoes and boots to companies that sell them to their customers. He also helps manage the factory where the shoes and boots are made.”

“Does he have lots of fancy suits like the one he wore Saturday?”

“Yes, he does.” She put her hand on the door knob.

“And does he always wear a tie?”

“Yes, Leo. Good-bye.”

“Mama, I want to be like Murdoch.”

“Well then, you better learn more about arithmetic and go to school for many more years. Think you could do that?”

“Yes, I do. Murdoch wears glasses. Do you think I need glasses?”

RESOURCES

A History of Hangings in Nova Scotia (Deanna Foster)

Booze (J Clinton Morrison Saltwire E-Edition, publish date unknown)

Citadel Hill National Historic Site (Nova Scotia Tourism)

Civilization.ca - *A Chronology of Canadian Postal History*

Fishermen (www.fivefishermen.com)

Halifax and South Western Railway 1901-1918 (Wikipedia)

Halifax Citadel National Historic Site Government of Canada/Parks Canada site

Halifax Explosion personal stories https://archives.novascotia.ca/explosion/personal/ History of 5

Memories of Taking the Train on PEI, 50Years Later (Sara Fraser CBC News Nov. 10, 2019)

Memory Nova Scotia – Halifax NS Insane Asylum (Halifax Municipal Archives)

Nova Scotia Carriage and Motor Car Company (Wikipedia)

Nova Scotia Hospital for the Insane Leung, C. (2015, March 11)

Postal Delivery (Civilization.ca - Chronology of Canadian Postal History)

Prohibition in Canada (The Canadian Encyclopedia)

Psychiatry in Canada a Century Ago (V.E. Appleton - Canadian Psychiatric Association Journal Vol.12 No. 4)

The Coast Railways and its Successors https://yarmouthhistory.ca

The Hidden History of the German POW camp in the Heart of Amherst, Nova Scotia (Emma Smith/ CBC News Nov. 2018) www.warmuseum.ca

The Prohibition Era and Rum Running by Devonna Edwards (Fairview Historical Society Articles Archives) Undated

The Wars (Timothy Findley, 1977)

Try a Little Temperance (Jacob Boon, The Coast Halifax, N.S. March 14, 2013)

Women and the Vote (The Canadian Encyclopedia)

Thank you for reading *Old Wounds.*

We would love if you could help by posting a review at your book retailer and on the PageMaster Publishing site. It only takes a minute and it would really help others by giving them an idea of your experience.

Thanks

pagemasterpublishing.ca/by/dianne-palovcik/

To order more copies of this book, find books by other Canadian authors, or make inquiries about publishing your own book, contact PageMaster at:

PageMaster Publication Services Inc.
11340-120 Street, Edmonton, AB T5G 0W5
books@pagemaster.ca
780-425-9303

catalogue and e-commerce store
PageMasterPublishing.ca/Shop

About the Author

Dianne (Taylor) Palovcik began her writing career after retirement when she challenged herself to write a novel. Her work focuses on Canadian history, bringing it to life with relatable characters, strong storylines and detailed settings.

Dianne's successful debut novel, *In Trouble* is disturbing and illuminating fiction, a story of unwed mothers and forced adoption in Canada during the 1960's.

Old Wounds is her third novel. *In Trouble* was recognized by the Writers Guild of Alberta in 2020 with an in-depth interview of the author and her work. *Not All Widows Wear Black* weaves an engaging Victorian tale complete with lies, revenge, murder and a touch of romance.

Dianne lives in Alberta, Canada. She is a graduate of Acadia University and completed studies at the University of Alberta, University of San Francisco and Lakeland College. When not writing, she enjoys time with family and friends, plays golf badly and travels with her husband.

Follow Dianne on Facebook: DiannePalovcikAuthor